The Inheritor

The Inheritor

MARION ZIMMER BRADLEY

TOR®

A TOM DOHERTY ASSOCIATES BOOK

New York

THE INHERITOR

This book is printed on acid-free paper.

A Tor Book
Published by Tom Doherty Associates, Inc.
175 Fifth Avenue
New York, NY 10010

Tor Books on the World Wide Web:
http://www.tor.com

Design by Judith Stagnitto Abbate

Library of Congress Cataloging-in-Publication Data

Bradley, Marion Zimmer.
The inheritor   /   Marion Zimmer Bradley. — 1st trade pbk. ed.
p.   cm.
"A Tom Doherty Associates book".
ISBN 0-312-86293-8 (pb)
ISBN 0-312-85996-1 (hc)
I. Title.
PS3552.R228I53   1997
813'.54—dc20   96–33983
                                                        CIP

First Tor Edition: May 1984
First Trade Paperback Edition: March 1997

Printed in the United States of America

0 9 8 7 6 5 4

To Gavin Arthur
in loving memory

Prologue

THIN WISPS OF GREY fog played in the street; clouds seemed to sit atop Twin Peaks, and the great striding giant of the TV tower, emerging like Orion knee-deep in mist, stood above the hills of San Francisco. Stray tendrils stole into the garden, the tiny square of lawn edged with the spiky green and grey leaves of herbs. A lemon tree, its white sharp-scented flowers and yellow fruit nestled side by side in the dark gloss of leaves, sprawled against a wall, and the mingled sweet and medicinal smells of flowers and herbs drifted through the window open to the fog.

Even inside, thin fog wisps drifted against the panelled walls of the room called the studio. The woman kneeling at the potter's wheel by the fireplace raised her eyes to the creeping fog and clenched her teeth against panic. The last weeks had frayed her nerves, but she was not a coward and was not ready to give in. She loved the house; she loved the garden and the panelled studio.

It was like an old Basil Rathbone movie; gaslamps shining through the London pea-soup fog, Sherlock Holmes standing by the open fire. Fog was simply a part of living in San Francisco, sweeping in through the Golden Gate every evening, out to sea again in midmorning.

She turned her attention again to the pot taking shape on the wheel; a flat dish, shaped like a Greek *kylix.* Blue glaze, she thought, Wedgwood blue; or dark glaze, cobalt, and an overlay of dark red, flowed on to give a shot-silk effect.

The wheel turned, a soft hypnotic sound.

The fire began to die. It sank lower, hissing, as if struggling with the fog. The woman at the wheel let it come to a stop, rising to mend the fire. Resinous kindling-sticks; a crackle of the dried juniper branches she had gathered in the Berkeley hills, which slowly took flame and shot up with a cheery roar, driving back the dank mist. She stood with her hands stretched to the kindly warmth; but outside, the windows were so white she could not see the garden. She felt the chill from the open window and went to close it. Fog was beautiful.

When it stayed outside where it belonged.

She went back to the wheel, her fingers caressing the moist clay. Tenderly she shaped the delicate flare of the rim.

The fire was sinking again.

Something must have been wrong with that last load of firewood. Why should she have this sense of the fog as a hostile entity, lurking in corners to watch her work?

She hates me. She doesn't want me here.

But that was idiotic. Before she knew it, she would be like her sister, seeing ghosts in every corner, bringing messages from the departed. She had heard the rumors and, after all, the families before her had been unlucky. A sudden death; a suicide. The stuff of which hauntings were made.

But everyone who had known the woman who had lived here in peace to the ripe age of eighty-four, and died at her piano, told the same story. She had been the gentlest, kindest soul alive. If her presence should cling here—not that the woman at the wheel believed such rubbish—why should that remaining presence be anything but benevolent, especially to a fellow artist?

She mended the fire again, for some reason reluctant to turn her back on the flickering shadows. If there should be a ghostly presence, would it not linger in the elegant music room, where the woman had died? It was not even a story of violence; the police had carefully checked it out. A kindly old lady, who had collapsed and died peacefully at her own piano, among her collection of antique harpsichords. Such a ghost, if indeed there were ghosts, could leave only the peaceful whisper of a more kindly age.

It was dark outside. Four in the afternoon; tea-time. No doubt the British, in that fog-haunted country, had invented their ritual of afternoon tea to chase away the blue devils of sea-fog and lowering darkness. She snapped on the studio lights, banishing the darkness, and went across the mist-shrouded yard along the little brick walk to the kitchen door. The white cat sat on the back wall, washing its face. She had tried to coax it with fish and liver, but it remained stubbornly aloof.

The cheery lights reflecting from copper pots, the homey smells of plants in hanging baskets, soothed her as she put on the kettle. She would not allow nerves, fog and her own morbid imagination to drive her out of the studio and ruin the best day's work she had done in weeks. The clay had reached that perfectly moist, malleable stage, and the emerging lovely shape was still a kinesthetic memory, almost an itch in her fingers. If she left it now she would never get it back again.

She carried the steaming cup into the studio and set it down near the wheel. Her hands went out to seek the unfinished shape, and recoiled. Under her fingers the graceful *kylix* was a formless and slimy blob, unpleasantly gelatinous, like dead flesh.

The last time this had happened she had believed, against the evidence of her own senses, that the white cat had gotten in here and crushed the work on the wheel. But window and doors were shut, and where in the bare walls of this studio could a cat be hiding?

Then she saw it, lying across the wheel, blood mingled with the clay, four limp paws still twitching. She drew a shocked breath; how had it come here, and who had mauled the animal? Was he still hiding somewhere in the garden, violence still unspent, to be completed against *her?* She knelt to examine the body, and as she stretched a reluctant hand, it was gone; only the slime and the ruined clay. No invader, no violence, but the evil, the *thing* in this house, destroying the finest work she had done this year. Tears of rage stood in her eyes.

The fire was dying again and this time she had no heart to rebuild it. This time she was beaten. She stood up, and the boiling tea overturned, scalding her ankle, flooding the potter's wheel and the ruined *kylix*. She screamed with frustration and pain.

"All right! All right! You've won! I'll go! But why? Why? Why?" With a sob of inarticulate rage and defeat she ran out, banging the studio door shut behind her. She would never enter it again.

CHAPTER

One

"IT'S A BEAUTIFUL HOUSE." Leslie Barnes turned regretfully from the panorama before her. The early lights of winter dusk twinkled below her, and on a clear day, she knew, the entire bay would spread out here, where now the lights of the Golden Gate made a ribbon of jewels above the fog.

Perhaps for this view she could make minor adjustments, remodel the small room off the foyer—no, there was no time or energy to spare for that. Her work must come first.

"It's truly a lovely place, the nicest I've seen. But, as I told the agent when I first called, I must have a separate room or two to see my clients."

"Clients? You're a lawyer, Miss?"

"A psychotherapist."

"The rooms on the ground floor—"

"I'm sorry," Leslie repeated. Why was she apologizing? This was her business. "My sister is a student at the Conservatory, and we need room for a grand piano and a harp."

The agent shrugged and sighed. "This place will go fast, you know. I have three people waiting to see it, and I couldn't even guarantee I could hold it till Monday."

"It simply isn't large enough," Leslie repeated. But she looked again with regret at the view she would have loved to live with.

The agent saw her regretful look and pressed on. "Look, one of the people considering this house is a family with three teenage kids; that little room we showed you, they're going to put two girls in there and let the boy have the attic room. You take the little downstairs room off the garage for your patients, and the piano can go in the living room—" He was sounding like a reasonable man beset by a silly woman who didn't know what she wanted, and when Leslie shook her head he said, "Well, lady, I think you're making a big mistake, I really don't have anything else to show you. That place on Geary, maybe—"

"No parking; besides, I can't live in a place where neither Emily nor I will dare step outside after dark."

He shrugged. "Well, if we get anything, I'll call you. But you're not going to find anything bigger than this, unless you're talking about half a million dollars."

The unspoken part of that, *you're too fussy,* stayed with her as she went to her car and watched the agent drive off in his. But she had a right to be fussy; it was the house she would live in, perhaps forever. She could not afford to move again within ten years. And she was not sure marriage was for her, in spite of Joel—

Her thoughts ran a familiar track. If he could get it through his head that her work was important to her, as important as his law career, not just a stopgap until Mister Right came along. She stopped herself.

She was always telling her clients not to enter any serious relationship with the idea of changing the other party. She could accept Joel as he was, marry him and live with him that way, or she could refuse him. But he wasn't going to change, or if he did it would be for his own reasons which had nothing to do with her.

In any case she must build her home with the assumption that she would live in it for years. San Francisco was necessary; she could no longer live in the East Bay, with Emily at the Conservatory. The long commute every day by public transit was expensive and took up precious time as well as draining energy Emily needed for practice.

Maybe, she thought, as she turned onto the skyway approach to the Bay Bridge, she *was* too fussy; the piano could have gone in the living room—she would, after all, have been down with her clients half the day or more. The little room downstairs off the garage would have made an office, with some remodeling; at worst she could have found office space somewhere outside. In any case it would have been no worse than the rented apartment, cramped even for one, and since Emily had joined her, bulging at the seams with her office and Emily's piano. The harp was still in storage.

And how could she, with the small amount of family money coming from her grandmother, who had for a short time been a concert harpist and recording artist, afford anything more spacious than that little jewel on Russian Hill? Emily's share was earmarked for the Conservatory, and even so Leslie would probably have to help her before she was through. But at whatever cost they must have a place with space for them both; Emily was already chafing at the necessary rule that she could not practice until the last client had left for the day.

She had a good counseling practice, though not as good as it could have been; she still set her fees on a sliding scale based on ability to pay, instead of doing as her colleagues insisted she should do: charging what the traffic would bear. Counseling, they said truthfully, was a luxury service, and the higher fees were set, the higher the therapist's reputation. How much good had she really done with the school counseling, which was just part of the system, which she had doled out in Sacramento—

Leslie felt she had a singular rapport with disturbed teenagers. She had been cheated out of her own adolescent rebellion; when the whole world, it seemed, had been rebelling, everything from protest marches to pot, she had been working hard to survive, put herself through graduate school, and was already fighting Emily's battle for freedom. Their mother had successfully forced Leslie into taking a position as a school counselor instead of opening her own office as a therapist; and now their mother was determined that Emily's talent could be best served by earning a certificate to teach music. The idea of Emily teaching in the chaos of the public schools was rather like imagining Secretariat hauling a coal cart. Or more accurately, Leslie thought, visualizing her high-strung and highly gifted sister giving music lessons, Maria Callas as a high school basketball coach.

She had resolved that Emily should have her chance, even if it meant she herself must spend her life teaching. The inheritance had come too late for a normal adolescence or carefree college days for Leslie; but it meant freedom for Emily. And the scandal which had driven Leslie out of the public school system had at least freed them both. Her mother, Leslie reflected bitterly, had been glad to see her go. But she would never forgive her for taking Emily away.

Leslie cursed as a huge double-trailered semi truck cut into her lane of traffic, remembering the headlines splashed across the *National Enquirer.*

PSYCHIC TEACHER LOCATES BODY OF MISSING SCHOOL-GIRL!

PIGTAIL KILLER TRAPPED BY PSYCHIC!

A fluke, Leslie reminded herself. Everybody had a psychic flash now and then. She clenched her teeth, gripping the wheel . . . the traffic was heavy; she had hoped to be back before rush hour traffic built up on the Bay Bridge; there must be an accident on the Bridge. She concentrated fiercely on the crawling car ahead, trying not to see again before her eyes the flash of Juanita García's body in the drainage ditch, covered with blood, long hair tightly braided by the killer who had raped and mutilated four young girls.

No, she would not remember that. She had a different life now, and a different world. Joachím Mendoza, dubbed "the Pigtail Killer" for his habit of braiding the long hair of his victims, was still on Death Row. Leslie did not approve of capital punishment, but would not have lifted a hand to save his life; she had seen Juanita García's body, had led the police there.

What if the newspapers had made a Roman holiday of the lucky hunch or psychic flash which had led to the killer? The local headlines had lasted only a day or two; *Schoolteacher finds pigtail killer victim.* And who ever remembered what was printed in tabloids like the *Enquirer?*

She had left the notoriety in Sacramento. When she relocated in San Francisco, it would be entirely behind her. If she ever found a place in San Francisco. This was the fifth house she had turned down.

She knew herself well enough to wonder why she kept finding reasons to reject every new house. The perfect house, she told herself firmly, just didn't exist. One way or another, she would have to make up her mind to some compromises. She tried hard to dismiss her own indecision as she took the freeway exit and drove through the Berkeley streets to the tiny house she had rented when she came to Berkeley.

She pulled up and parked in the driveway. The lease here was up on May first: she didn't want to be stuck with a lease for another year.

But she could think about that later. She was seeing a new client for the first time tonight.

Mentally she riffled through the file. Eileen Grantson. Fourteen. Disruptive behavior, temper tantrums, breaking china, lying about it, constant fights in school. Broken home; father has custody, mother remarried and living in Texas, no siblings. The girl probably had a right to be angry at the conditions of her life. It would be easier to deal with a girl already able to express her anger than one who claimed she felt none. The human mind, Leslie told herself, was a fearful and wonderful thing, and that was why she had become a therapist; because she had never lost her sense of wonder about all the things the mind could do.

Eileen Grantson was not a prepossessing teenager. Her hair was mousy and lank, eyes a pale washy blue, hidden behind thick plastic-rimmed glasses. She slumped in a chair as if her spine was made of poor-quality cardboard.

In nearly an hour she had said almost nothing; Leslie had had to extract a few admissions from her by painstaking questions. Most teenagers were all too ready to pour out all their grievances against the world.

"You get very angry with your father sometimes, don't you, Eileen?"

"He's crazy," said Eileen sullenly. "I think he throws those old dishes around himself so he can pick a fight and say I did it."

Leslie maintained her reassuring smile, and asked, in the neutral tone she had been trained to keep, "Why do you think he would do that?"

"Because he hates me. He's my daddy and I love him, but he doesn't want anybody to love him. He didn't love my—" Eileen gave a small stifled gulp and snuffle. "That guy my mom was running around with, he was just the excuse. If my daddy had loved her she wouldn't of gone away." The words came out in a single long stream, but then Eileen, as if what she had said had frightened her, relapsed into a limp puddle of silence and self-pity.

Leslie, listening, thought over what she had heard. Was she on the fringes of discovering a case of father-daughter incest? (Freud had called it a common fantasy; what a shame he had not lived to discover how far it was from a fantasy, even in that sick Victorian age where stiff Victorian fathers had wielded almost life-and-death power over their powerless, traumatized daughters.) Maybe Grantson, unable to acknowledge his own guilt, had made a healthy gesture; put his daughter into a therapeutic situation where, sooner or later, she would be sure to tell their guilty secret and free them both.

But now she did not think so. Grantson himself had sent the girl, and sounded as if he had a very real grievance against his daughter. And Eileen's account of the divorce sounded circumstantial.

Leslie asked gently, "Why are you living with your father instead of your mother, Eileen?"

"I don't like that guy my mother married," Eileen said sullenly, "and who wants to live in Texas? All my friends are here. Not that I've got that many friends. They lie about me all the time."

Something inside Leslie suddenly bristled. "What do they lie about, Eileen? What do they say about you?"

"The same lies my father does." Eileen did not lift her eyes from the floor. "Nobody likes me. They tell lies. They say I break their things. And I didn't. Maybe I would if I could, they hate me, and I hate all of them, so there! Who wants to hang around with that dumb crowd anyhow! And how could I break their damn violin strings anyhow when I'm across the room? All right, so I wanted to play first violin and that damn rotten teacher stuck me in second violin, he's got tin ears, he's at least a quarter tone flat all the whole time, what the hell does he know about it? I want to quit Orchestra and violin lessons anyhow and my father says I'm too young to know what I want to do with my life, by the time I could make up my mind I wanted to play the violin I'd be too old to learn, so he makes me practice all the time. I think he's afraid if I do anything except practice the goddam fiddle and go to Sunday school I'll screw around and get pregnant or something!"

A familiar complaint and a familiar problem. For the first time, Eileen sounded like any of the other teenagers she had counseled. "You think your father is afraid that you're involved with sex?"

She shrugged, staring again at the floor, and Leslie knew she had asked that question too soon. She glanced briefly at the cuckoo clock on the wall, elaborately carved, Austrian, tacky; but it was easier on the teenagers to hear the impersonal striking of the clock than to end the session herself. It would strike in, perhaps, six minutes. She had accomplished as much as she was likely to accomplish in a first session. She had almost ruled out the idea of an incest victim, which was something. She was probably dealing with an uncomplicated case of an awkward teenager, at the most trying time of adolescence, resenting and half blaming herself for a broken family.

A teenage girl, motherless, without an acceptable mother substitute, a father absorbed in his work, with little energy for his solitary daughter. And Eileen was the pawn in this struggle. Perhaps she could help the girl to see that she was not the target of this hostility, that her father's problems were her father's problems and not her fault, that her mother's flight was her mother's problem and not Eileen's inadequacy as a daughter.

"Tell me about those dishes your father says you broke," she said calmly, knowing it would bring them to the end of the hour in a state of tension which would keep the girl thinking about her problem until the next session.

"I don't know anything about them. They were just there on the floor. He threw one right at me and then he said I did it," Eileen said, raising her voice for the first time. "I didn't do it! It wasn't any accident either! He *threw* it at me!"

"Why would he do that, Eileen? You think he threw it? At you?"

"Because he hates me," Eileen cried. "He wants me to get in trouble so I'll have to go live with my mother in Texas. He hates me! He hates me! *He hates me!*"

The box of Kleenex unobtrusively placed on the table behind Eileen's chair—but she had not cried and Leslie had never had to tell her it was there—rose abruptly from the table and came flying at Leslie across the desk. Dazed, Leslie ducked. She would not have thought that the girl had had her hands anywhere near the box. And Eileen seemed such a quiet, unaggressive girl! "Eileen—"

"Now I guess you're going to say I'm doing it too," Eileen shrieked, getting up out of the chair precipitately. The ashtray on Leslie's desk suddenly rose, hovered a moment in the air, and went flying in a great rush at Eileen. It struck her above the eyebrow, the sharp corner drawing blood, and the girl fell down into the chair, screaming, covering her face with her hands.

"Now you're doing it," Eileen screamed. "You're doing it too! Look at the blood! Why does everybody hate me? Why does everybody lie about me?" She cowered in the chair, smearing the blood on her face, staring in horror at her fingers.

Into the silence the cuckoo clock struck smartly five times.

• • •

"NO, I DON'T ACCUSE you of doing it, Eileen, and no, I don't know how it happened," Leslie reassured the girl again. "Drink that up, now, and don't worry. We'll talk about it next time. And if anything more happens, you can call me—all right?" She took the paper cup from Eileen's hand. "There's your father to pick you up."

Eileen was still sniffling.

"He's not going to believe this. He hates me. He'll blame me no matter what."

"So don't tell him," Leslie said briskly, and put a wad of clean folded Kleenex into Eileen's hand. She blinked, touching the Band-Aid on her forehead with scared fingers.

"What'll I say if he asks me what happened?" She was clinging now, demanding attention, help, more reassurance. Leslie didn't blame her, but she couldn't encourage it either.

"Tell him the truth, if you want to. It's your choice."

"He won't believe me."

"Then don't. Say you cut your forehead on the corner of the desk." Already Leslie was wondering if that had been what really happened. Had they shared some weird hallucination? But she had also doubted the moment of intuition—psychism—which had shown her the body of Juanita García in a drainage ditch. She patted Eileen's shoulder gently again and shoved her into the hall. Her father's car was at the foot of the steps. Eileen thrust her arms awkwardly into her down jacket, struggled into her backpack and ran clumsily down. The car door slammed behind her.

It was a relief to step inside and close the door.

She might have believed that Eileen had somehow, unseen, reached the box of tissues and flung them across the desk. But neither of them had been within reach of the ashtray.

She knew she hadn't thrown it. And Eileen couldn't have reached it without getting up out of the chair, and then she could hardly have thrown it at herself, hard, and been back in the chair in time for the ashtray to hit her hard enough to draw blood.

Leslie went back in the office and picked up the ashtray. There was a smear of blood on the sharp corner; it felt warm and tingled in her hand, and she had to force herself to put it carefully down. Her impulse was to drop it, draw her hand back in horror.

It's starting again, the kind of thing I thought I'd left behind in Sacramento. She remembered something she had read about the parapsychology studies at Duke University; a famous psychologist had said, "On any other subject, one tenth of the evidence would already have convinced me; on this subject, ten times the evidence would not convince me, because I know it to be impossible."

Now she was faced with evidence and did not know what to believe. She sat down at her desk and forced herself to write up the session, adding her own observations and what she had seen—*or what I thought I saw,* she added to herself grimly—and filed the account away before she could challenge the reality of it in her own mind.

She seemed to remember that there had been a study of poltergeist phenomena by a reputable psychologist; tomorrow she would go to the Berkeley campus library and dig it out. If she had a poltergeist for a patient, she ought, at least, to know what was known about them, if anything. After that session she wanted nothing more than to make herself a cup of tea, draw herself a bath with millions of scented bubbles, soak in it for an hour with a frivolous book, and think about nothing till the next morning.

However, the light glowed red on the answering machine, and she forced herself to rewind and play back the tape. There might be a message from a new client, Emily might have called to say she would be late, the real estate agent might have called back to tell her about another house, or Judy Attenbury might be forcing herself to vomit her dinner again.

But there was only one message.

"Joel here, Leslie. I was out of the office all afternoon taking Bobby to a ball game, so I have to stay overtime to make up for it. Give me a call and we'll get a bite together when I finish, okay? Love ya. 'Bye now."

She smiled; how like Joel that was. Bobby was a black ghetto child Joel had adopted in the "Big Brother" program, and he spent a considerable amount of time with the kid, taking a real interest in him. She wondered what he would have had to say about Eileen and her poltergeist, and wished she could tell him. But what happened in a counseling session was only a little less inviolate than what went on behind the screens of the confessional. And what could a lawyer do to help? You couldn't drag a poltergeist into court and have it bound over with an injunction to keep the peace, or to cease and desist!

She waited while his office phone rang twice; at last his voice, curt and preoccupied.

"Manchester, Ames, Carmody and Beckenham."

"Joel? It's Leslie."

"Les!" The voice changed, became warm and welcoming. "I hoped you'd call. All ready to go? Pick you up in ten minutes?"

She laughed. "Where are we going?"

"Put on your fanciest outfit and I'll take you dancing at the Claremont. I'm due for a celebration; the judge threw the Hanrahan case out of court. Insufficient evidence for a true bill."

"How wonderful, darling!" She knew he had worked long and hard over the Hanrahan case, for relatively little in the way of fees, and this was a very real victory for him. "But could we have a raincheck on the celebration? I had a rough day and another lined up for tomorrow; I'd really rather have a quiet bite somewhere, and an early night." Besides, she remembered, the Claremont food, though splendid, was expensive.

"All right, honey; we'll go to that little Greek place you like, the one on College Avenue," he agreed. "Or if you're really too tired, I could pick something up and bring it over?"

That was what she loved about him; he was always concerned about her, always ready to change a cherished plan, even at a moment's notice.

"No, Greek food sounds wonderful. And we'll celebrate some other time, I promise."

"I'll pick you up in twenty minutes, then?"

"Fine."

In high spirits she ran up the stairs, pulling off her jacket and blouse, choosing a fresh silk print in a raspberry red that made her dark eyes glow, and ran a quick brush through her short dark curls.

If she had believed in destiny, she might have thought that she had left Sacramento to meet Joel Beckenham. Such a difference from Nick—

She had never really been serious about Nick Beckenham. They had dated a dozen times, shared a liking for Italian foods, for the revival of Big Bands from the forties when neither of them had been born; he was halfway engaged to a former classmate of Leslie's, finishing up a Master's degree in Chicago, and while Margot was away, Nick went out with Leslie. She had kissed him two or three times on the cheek, no more; they celebrated together when he was promoted from patrolman to detective. And it was not true that he had come to question her about the missing schoolgirls, though two of them had been pupils at the high school where Leslie was on the counseling staff. She might even have been the last to see Juanita

García alive; the girl had been in her office only the day before her parents had reported her missing, and no one had seen Juanita after the girl had left the counseling center.

"Except the murderer," she had said dryly to Nick, "or are you indicating that I'm a suspect?"

"Don't be silly, Les." The young policeman laughed, but his face was still troubled. "There's a nut out there; we've got three girls dead already. Same age. They all have long black hair. . . ."

That was when she had seen it clearly; like her own face reflected in a mirror, or under running water. She had heard the high, rising note of horror in her own voice.

"She's in a ditch . . . a drainage ditch," she heard herself say, "with her hair braided. He liked to braid their hair. . . ."

"How did you know that? Leslie, that's what we kept back, so we could weed out the crazies who called in with fake confessions. Down at the station we're calling him the pigtail killer because he braids their hair after they're dead—"

"I saw her," Leslie whispered, "lying in the ditch. A drainage ditch by a windmill. Wearing her black leather jacket—"

Nick had piled her into the black and white police cruiser then, siren screaming. She had never gone to look at Juanita's actual body. She had seen it, in that terrifying underwater flash, clearly enough. A real girl, a girl who had been in her office the day before, Juanita García, sixteen years old, and black hair falling to her waist. Black hair, braided into intricate strands. She had heard herself babbling; she had seen the killer's hands, the killer's face. Joachím Mendoza's face, with the crescent-shaped scar and the mended harelip with a moustache split along the scar, and the broken eyebrows. She had seen it later when they picked him up and found braided locks of hair and the girls' bloodstained panties in his room, and she was still seeing him, from time to time, in nightmares. Nick's squad car partner had sat there staring with his mouth open while she was babbling out her description. He had never believed, she supposed, that she had seen Mendoza's face only in her mind. He never stopped wondering if somehow she had been involved, even an eyewitness.

Nick had been nice. He had stood by her, reassured her about her own sanity. But the *Enquirer* had kept calling, had wanted to fly her to Chicago to try and get psychic impressions about a new sex murder. And there had been crank calls and crazies, until she had cut it all off. And of course there had been Juanita García's mother, who had burst into a tirade of abuse at the funeral.

"Why didn't you get your psychic flash when she was in your office, why didn't you warn her before she went out to meet that crazy killer? You wanted her to die so you could get your name in the papers?"

Leslie said what was true; that she would have given a year of her life if she had known beforehand, if she had foreseen that Juanita was to walk from her office into the hands of an insane killer. She would have warned the girl, would have begged Juanita to be careful. But no fateful flash had crossed her mind when Juanita stood sullen in her office, habitual truant, delinquent, stoned out of her mind on pot and contempt. What made the García woman think Juanita would have listened to a warning about murder? She hadn't listened to anything else her teachers and counselors had ever said.

She became aware that she was staring into the mirror, seeing Juanita García's long dark hair, her drowned face under water, instead of her own face. The telephone was ringing; she made a dash for the extension in the hall. Over the noise she heard the sound of a Bach prelude; Emily was home and had begun practicing.

"Hello?"

The voice was thick, curdled and strange; she had a hard time making out words in it. But disturbed persons sometimes found it hard to get what they were saying out; their thoughts frightened them too much.

"I'm sorry," Leslie repeated patiently, "I can't understand you."

"Is—is—is Alison there?"

"I'm sorry; I think you must have a wrong number."

The voice mumbled, protested indistinctly, finally clicked away into a dial tone. Leslie hung up. Crank call, or innocent wrong number? They had taught her when she was putting in her time on a suicide prevention hotline that there were no wrong numbers; they dial your number for a purpose, even if they have to hide it from themselves. She wasn't quite sure she believed it—surely it wasn't as cut-and-dried, as Freudian, as that, surely fingers sometimes slipped or eyes read the wrong digit in a telephone book. She heard footsteps on the stairs and recognized them as her sister Emily's; she was putting pearl studs in her ears when Emily looked into her room. Tall, coltish and seventeen, dark auburn hair drawn back into a formal bun, Emily's adolescent rebellion took the form of overprecision rather than grubbiness. She had studied ballet for four years before she had finally chosen the piano, and it still showed in the long delicate neck on which her head was a long-stemmed lily, the posture which gave her the illusion of more height than her modest five foot seven.

"What was the phone, Les? Was that Mommy?"

Leslie shook her head. "Wrong number."

"Did you get the house?" Emily asked eagerly.

Les shook her head. "Not quite big enough—no good place for an office *and* a piano."

Emily sighed. "It sounded so good when you told me about it. Are you going out?"

"Joel and I are getting a bite of dinner somewhere. There's hamburger in the freezer."

Emily made a face, and Leslie remembered she was going through a vegetarian phase again. "I had some salad on the way home; all I want is a carton of yogurt. Did the piano tuner come?"

"I didn't have a chance to call him. Is there something wrong with it, Em?" She came down the stairs, catching up her camel-hair coat, and glanced into the big old square living room; Emily ran her hands over the keys and grimaced. "Can't you *hear?*" Her look of contempt was promptly concealed; she said with careful kindness, "Call him tomorrow—*early,* won't you, Les?"

"You call him," Leslie said with cheerful brutality, "you're the one who can't live with it the way it is. I have an early appointment, and I'm seriously thinking of calling another agency; this one doesn't seem to have anything more to show me." Emily wandered to the piano, sat down on the bench and ran off a few scales, tilting her head and grimacing. "Les, do you have any real honest-to-God crazies among your patients? I know, you can't tell me anything about your clients," she mimicked impatiently. "It's just that when the phone rang I got a little scared. There was a real crazy call earlier today. The—the person didn't really talk at all. Just kind of—" she hesitated. "—kind of buzzed. And *breathed.*"

"Nothing wrong with breathing," Leslie said. "Everybody does it twenty-four hours a day."

"Only this wasn't just breathing. Whoever it was, was doing it on purpose—oh, damn it, that's not what I mean either. I didn't get the idea this was the kind of call you'd call a heavy breather. Not a sex call. I wasn't even sure it was a man. It felt—" again Emily hesitated, choosing her words. "It sounded sinister. Kind of, well, *menacing*. I got really bad vibrations."

"It sounds as if it might have been the same person," said Leslie, thinking over the texture of the call. It was someone more seriously disturbed than any of her clients. She was a therapist, not a medical doctor or a psychiatrist; her clients suffered from commonplace neurotic problems, from the pressures and stresses of society or jobs, marriage troubles, inability to adjust to school or parental expectations.

And even a psychiatrist could do little, Leslie thought, against the more grievous wounds to the human mind and spirit. One of her clients, Susan Hamilton, was the single parent of a brain-damaged child; at seven, Christina could not or would not speak, and was just beginning toilet training. There were a handful of labels for her: brain-damaged, autistic, learning-disabled, emotionally neglected, retarded. Labels, but no help. Speech therapists and special education programs could do little more for Chrissy than to train her as they would train a dog, make her somewhat less offensive to social sensibilities. Leslie could do nothing for Christina, and little for her mother except to allow her to vent her enormous rage at a blind and uncaring universe which dropped this enormous burden on her, which had destroyed her marriage and now would probably destroy her.

"No, none of my clients is seriously disturbed," she agreed, then thinking of Eileen Grantson, was not so sure. "Did they ask for me by name?"

"No, no name, no words at all. It was awful, Les, it didn't even sound human. Like a lost soul crying from purgatory."

Yes. That was exactly what it sounded like. But tonight Leslie didn't want to think about lost souls. Not with Juanita García's face still before her eyes, haunting her, not after the sight of that ashtray flying across the room, Eileen's forehead bleeding, she wanted to be nice and rational. Man, she remembered one of her professors saying, is not a rational animal, but a rationalizing animal.

Emily frowned, bending her head close to the keyboard.

"I ought to have been a violinist, so I could tune my own instrument. Listen, Les, maybe I ought to study piano tuning. I *do* have perfect pitch, and it's awfully well paid. The Conservatory is so *damned* expensive. If I could earn some money it would be easier on you, too—"

"We'll manage, honey. Just be patient. Believe me, I know what it's like, when I was in college I had five dollars a week and my bus fare, and I couldn't tell you how many times I walked home four miles to save the bus fare! It just about kept me in toothpaste and Tampax. And speaking of toothpaste and Tampax, I wish sometimes you'd get your own instead of cadging mine all the time!" Behind her words, she realized what she was doing; ordinary sisterly squabbles to lighten the memory of that ashtray flying across the room. She heard steps on the porch.

"There's Joel now. Have a good supper, Em; I'll be home before midnight, I suppose—"

"Unless Prince Charming carries you off for the night," Emily suggested, and Leslie shook her head.

"Early appointment tomorrow."

"Take your keys," Emily said. "I'm going to be out late; I'm babysitting the Simmons' brat, and I do mean brat. That's why I think piano tuning would be easier. Even on the ears."

Leslie checked her purse for keys. "Be sure to lock the deadbolt, then," she admonished, and went to let Joel in.

Two

THE FOOD WAS GOOD, crisp salad rich with feta cheese, minced chicken spiced with cinnamon and cardamom, stuffed with raisins and wrapped in delicate layers of pastry. Joel, handsome and exuberant, ordered a bottle of good wine, and prepared to tell her all about the Hanrahan case. Leslie, who was always on the alert and eager for clues about a patient's mental state in her own work, loved hearing Joel talk about his work.

"Hanrahan—that was indecent exposure, wasn't it?" she asked. "Was it a frameup?" Men who exposed themselves rarely went on to serious crimes—they were at the opposite end of the spectrum from a Joachím Mendoza—but they were, invariably, deeply disturbed.

"Hell, no, this one was really stupid," Joel said, stuffing a morsel of fragrant chicken into his mouth, trying to speak; then laughed and finished chewing. At last he said, "Remember the rock concert last year? No, you were still in Sacramento, weren't you? Okay, well, you know what goes on at those things; kids necking, making out, petting, all the way up to screwing under those blankets they carry. You've seen it."

Leslie had. She thought it tasteless, but then she had always lived where she had abundant privacy.

"So—?"

"So Hanrahan's gay. And he and the man he's lived with for nine years—they're partners in a little bookstore up on Castro—were watching all the kids, and it made them feel romantic. So they were holding hands. Hands, for Godsake, and some old lady complained and some redneck cop arrested them for L-and-L—lewd and lascivious behavior." He grabbed his wine, swallowed and half choked in his indignation.

"Joel, they *must* have been doing something more than just holding hands, to get arrested!"

"That's what I thought. But the old lady who brought the complaint had actually taken a Polaroid snapshot of the 'disgusting' behavior," Joel said. "I *saw* the picture, Les. Ron was holding Joe's hand, and Joe had his head on Ron's shoulder. Real dirty stuff! For Godsake, Les, I'm not queer and I haven't got a lot of sympathy for the kind of guys who hang out in the bars, not to mention that I can't imagine why a guy would want to make it with a guy when there are all these gorgeous women in the world—" He put down his fork and smiled at her tenderly. "But arrested, for that, with all that was going on around them?"

"I don't understand it either. What could possibly—?"

"Supposedly, according to the old lady and the redneck cop, they were scandalizing the young people around them—who were all so busy screwing that they wouldn't have noticed it if the President had been getting it off with a donkey on the bandshell! Anyhow, we finally got it thrown out of court. But I felt sorry for Ron. It got into the papers, and Joe's parents didn't know he was gay."

"Well, I'm glad he didn't have to go to prison, on top of everything else."

"Would have been the county jail; L-and-L is a misdemeanor, not a felony. But it's a crime it was ever brought up. Talk about *ridiculous!*"

"Well, it's not the only idiotic case of that kind," Leslie said. "A friend of my mother's almost got run in by a policeman for breast feeding her baby in a supermarket. The kid was hungry and yelling. Of course, that was a long time ago, but Mom told me about it when I was twelve."

"Well, I can think of better places to breast feed a kid," Joel said. "I hope when you start in on *ours* you stick to the home grounds, honey." Leslie blushed and smiled at him as he forked salad into his mouth. "Or you could try hiding out in our car. There was a case last year—guy drove through the tollgate on the Bay Bridge stark naked. Judge threw the case out, saying a man's car was like his home—he was entitled to dress, or not dress, any way he wanted to, in his own car. That's the law."

"*Lex dura; lex est,*" Leslie quoted with a chuckle, and he said, "I like the other old saying better: *the law is an ass.*"

"What a saying for an up-and-coming lawyer, darling!" she teased.

"And who's in a better position to know?" he countered.

"The old ladies who complain," Leslie said, "are really worse off than the people they try and persecute. And we *are* making progress. At least, your friend Hanrahan didn't go to jail. Suppose he'd had a judge who felt his own sexuality threatened by two men holding hands?"

"I don't like to think about it," said Joel soberly; then, by an effort of will, brightened. "Just the same, it all has its funny side. Nick told me a crazy one when we were on the phone. Seems he got called out on a complaint where one of those same old ladies said a man on their block was running around naked inside his apartment. So Nick went to check out this would-be Hottentot tot—"

Leslie leaned back and listened, remembering Nick Beckenham. He had, after all, introduced them; when the scandal had fully broken, and Leslie had moved to the Bay Area, he had driven her down in a rented truck, called Joel to help unload it, and suggested that Joel take Leslie out to dinner. He had probably expected the same brotherly relation that he himself had with Leslie, not a conflagration.

Maybe she had been ready for a new man to match her new life. Old enough to be settling down, her mother had said; Leslie was twenty-seven, by her mother's standards almost an old maid. Mother would have approved of the rising young lawyer even more than of his policeman brother. Though, no doubt, she would have disapproved of his defense of a "scandalous" cause like Ronald Hanrahan's arrest.

". . . so the man said, 'Madam, will you please show me where you observed me naked in this apartment?' and of course the old biddy couldn't have seen anything at all unless she had her nose pressed right up to his window! So he turned around and pressed charges against her for window peeping!"

Leslie laughed heartily, but through the laughter she saw that Joel was looking at her seriously.

"You do look tired, Les. Rough day?"

"Very." And wouldn't he stare in amazement if she told him about the poltergeist? Was it going to cause trouble between them, someday, that he could share these stories of his work, while she could say nothing about her own? Someday they must talk about that. When they were together, they were having too good a time to discuss shared feelings; yet someday, certainly if he was thinking about marriage and children, they must.

"But I'm back to square one on the house hunting, Joel. It was too small for an office on the premises, *and* Emily's piano. So I have to start all over again."

"You know how I feel about that," he said forthrightly. "I've never made any secret of it. If you were hunting for a house for the two of us, instead of one for yourself, it would be different."

Her heart sank. So it was going to be a confrontation. It was her own fault; she shouldn't have mentioned the house hunting, not tonight. But they couldn't go on avoiding the subject.

"The two of us, as you put it, aren't ready for a house. Am I supposed to stick it out in that little rented place until you're ready to get married?"

He fussed with the wine, pouring another glass. "You really ought to have some more," he said. "I don't want to drink this all by myself." A smile strayed around the laugh lines at his long jaw. "You really want to be responsible for my being hauled in on drunk-and-disorderly?"

She watched, loving him. "I'll take responsibility for drunk," she retorted lightly, "but disorderly—that'll be on your own head, love." He was not nearly as tall as Nick, who topped six feet. When she hugged Joel, their bodies fit perfectly, cheek to cheek.

Our bodies fit too perfectly. That's why we never get to talk about serious things.

He said, sipping from the glass, "Leslie, listen to me. I'll marry you now, if you're really using this house thing to put the pressure on. I still think we ought to wait, but if it would make you happy—"

She blinked, not following what he was saying. "I don't want to get married, not yet. We both agreed we'd wait till Emily was finished at the Conservatory, and you were moved up to a senior partnership. By that time, my practice—"

"Oh, your practice! Come on, Les. On the level. Isn't this why you're pushing this house hunting bit—to push me into grabbing while the grabbing is good, before you get your life all laid out on your own? You're ready to build a nest, and if we can't do it together, you'll do it on your own?"

He sounded so reasonable that for a moment she actually wondered: could her motives possibly be that devious? Then outrage took over.

"You can't possibly believe that, Joel!"

"Well, I've been thinking it over. Maybe you're right. Maybe we ought to get married, start building together, not separately. We love each other, why not settle down, start building a rational life together?"

Man is not a rational, but a rationalizing animal. She said quietly, not wanting to escalate this into an argument, "No, Joel. I think we should stick to our original plans; you want to establish your career without the demands of a wife just yet, and I want to establish mine and see my sister educated."

"But you're still set on having a house all your own?"

"Is there a reason I shouldn't, Joel?"

"Yes," he blurted, "I don't want you to set yourself up in a life so full you won't need me!"

"Darling, I don't think you need to worry about that," she said, reached across the table for his hand and held it. "But just as you want to establish your career, so I want to get settled in mine—"

"Now you sound like one of those damned women's libbers. Your own property. Your own career. All this about what you want. Not what *we* want, or what *I* want. Me, me, me, that's all you're thinking about!"

She gasped at the monstrous unfairness of this. "It's what you said you wanted, not to get married yet—"

"I've changed my mind."

"And I haven't," she retorted. "If that is what you think, Joel, we are simply not communicating, and I think we'd better not talk about it. Let's just agree to disagree on that subject. I am not what you so contemptuously call a *women's libber,* but if there is one expression I hate, that's it, and I am absolutely appalled that you would say that about me." She pushed back her chair.

"Maybe you'd better take me home."

"No, damn it!" He did not raise, but lowered his voice. "I'm getting tired of this, Leslie. Whenever things don't go your way, you refuse to talk about it. We can't run away again."

"I'm not trying to run away," she said, knowing there was some truth in what he said, she did avoid this kind of confrontation, "but you seem to enjoy a good fight. I don't."

"I'm a lawyer," he said, "and you don't get to be a good one by backing down every time you have a little difference of opinion."

"And I don't like to be put on the witness stand every time we have what you call *a little difference of opinion.*" She imitated his tone, angry now. "It isn't. It's basic. I can't reason you out of it—I tried. What you mean is that you want me to sit here while you bully me into changing my mind, since you're not going to change yours. And because I don't want to sit here and be bullied—"

"Love, I'm not trying to bully you. But let's look at this thing rationally. What will you do with a house of your own after we get married?"

"Rent it. Sell it. Let Emily live in it till she finishes at the Conservatory. Live in it ourselves till we find one we like better. Real estate is always a good investment—you told me that yourself! Why does it bother you that I should have a good investment?" She tried to make a joke of it. "Helen Gurley Brown says that a small portfolio of good investments is very sexy."

He didn't laugh. He pushed the wineglass away, staring at his plate. His hands were long and handsome, the fingers muscular and efficient. Sensuous, too, she thought, then hardened herself against the memory which could weaken her to the very core of her being.

"So all right," he said at last. "Maybe at bottom I'm more old-fashioned than I ever thought. I'm liberal when it comes to human rights and personal freedom, but I guess when you scratch a country boy, and Nick and I are both country boys, you find a conservative. Nick's a cop; and he's a chump; he thinks law and order is something you do in the streets, where people can get carved up with knives. I want to do it the easy way; in the courts, establishing a rule of law. What was it they said, a society of laws and not of men. And that goes along with a traditional value system, a traditional profession, and a traditional marriage and home. With a traditional wife in it, I guess. And I hoped you would want to be part of that whole structure. To be—" he hesitated, searching for words, "to be half of a marriage; not a loose partnership of two independent people jogging along side by side until they find somebody they like better. I don't mind if you try out a career first—what's that phrase all you independent women are so crazy about? I don't mind if you *try to find yourself.*" But the searing contempt in the words made Leslie wince, as he went on. "I never figured you were lost anyhow. I'm ready to give you commitment for a lifetime, and that's what I want from you in return, and I was hoping you were grown up enough to make that commitment."

It was the longest speech she had ever heard him make, and she admired him for his willingness to take a stand on something important to him. But it was not her view of life, nor her view of marriage, and they should have explored it together before he had ever gone so far.

"I'm glad you have been honest enough to tell me what you want," she said slowly, thinking that she sounded like a therapist, not a lover. "But I have to be honest with you. That isn't what I want out of life. I want to be an independent person, to have a life of my own apart from marriage. Just as your career will be outside of our marriage partnership, I want mine to stand on its own. I intend to keep my own name, not become Mrs. Joel Beckenham. Do you seriously think that I can make a life managing the money you make?"

"I had hoped it would be enough for you; I will need a wife who will be an ornament to the firm, a conservative wife in a conservative marriage—"

"And I can't see marriage as based on politics, and the politics *yours,* Joel," she said. "Would you expect me even to vote a conservative line?"

"I'd hoped you would have the sense to realize it's the only rational way to go," he said. "I see marriage as pulling together, not in different directions."

"Pulling *your* way," she pointed out. "And my work—"

"You can't expect me to be happy, having you spend your life with losers and crazies," he retorted. "I'd hoped it would show you what a sick, grubby world it is out there, and realize life would be better for you as my wife. I think it's time to reassess the whole thing; get married—oh, this summer, maybe in August?—and find a house together. Maybe build one. You could keep working for a year or two, maybe," he offered, "until Emily is on her own—"

"That's very generous of you," she said waspishly, "only I am going to need time to take all this in. I am beginning to think we have both made a big mistake. I could never be happy in that kind of marriage." She pushed her chair back. "If you won't take me home now, Joel, I am going to call a taxi."

He pushed a credit card at the waiter, hurried after her. "Leslie, I'm not going to let you go like this. Please come back and sit down. Can't we discuss this rationally?"

She let him coax her back to the table, though her throat ached and she wanted to cry. "You keep beating me over the head with that word *rational*, Joel. Did you ever stop to think there is more to life than logic?"

"I thought you had had enough of the irrational in Sacramento. I thought that was one of the reasons you got out of there," he said, and pushed the wineglass across the table. "Drink it, Les. You're upset; I won't let you walk out on me like this because of a little difference of opinion."

"But it's more than that," she said, reluctantly sipping the wine and pushing the glass away, wishing it could steady her nerves. "We're miles apart, Joel. We should have talked like this before. Maybe it's my fault that we haven't. But now we should accept that what you want and what I want are different—"

"But what I want is *you*," he said, leaning over the table to grip her hand, his eyes warm in the candlelight. "We've been together long enough to know that's the important thing—that we want each other."

Treacherously she felt the warmth spreading inside her. The memory of all the good times, the sex, the togetherness, the *fun*. Something in her still wanted him. Even the logic, the severe rationality, had been welcome after the exploding hysteria of Sacramento, her face in the *National Enquirer*, the craziness. But she said, "That's only one part of life, Joel. The other things—"

"There's one thing I know," he said, "and that's this: if the sex is right, everything else can be worked out."

She said in a rage of frustration, "Joel, you haven't been listening to a word I've said! Can't you see, even if I wanted to get married now, and I don't, it would never work. Now that I know your view of marriage—"

"It's the idea every sensible man has, and every woman too, really. *Just try it—you'll like it.* Let's get married now, and I'm betting—I'm betting my whole life, Leslie—that when you see what a marriage to me would be like, you'll never want out!"

"You're betting *your* life," she said, "but I'm not gambling mine. And now I really *am* leaving, Joel, so unless you want that scene, you'd better let me go."

The waiter brought the check; he scribbled his name, not looking.

"No, Les. We have to talk this out. We can't run away from it—"

She said coldly, "Now you're repeating yourself."

"And I'll keep on doing it. I'm a stubborn man, and I know what I want, and sooner or later, you'll give in to it." He leaned to refill her glass with the last of the wine.

"I don't want it, Joel." She pushed at his hand, holding the neck of the bottle, but he laughed and tipped it into her glass.

"Did it ever occur to you that perhaps I know what you want better than you do yourself?" His fingers moved suggestively on hers, a private memory. "We only get into trouble when we talk, Les. Come home with me and let's work it out the only way a man and a woman can ever really work things out—in bed." His hand squeezed hers, his breath was warm on her face, tender and beloved even through the exasperation she felt. There was a warm sense of melting through her body.

If I go home with him he can talk me into anything. A clear flash of their lovemaking came into her mind, a rush through her body, his face over hers . . . how could she give this up? Whatever he asked, wasn't it worth it?

And this is how half my clients get into the impossible situations I hear about every day, thinking with their emotions and glands instead of their brains. She started to pull away; his hand was hard on her wrist. He wasn't going to let go. His other hand was still clutching the wineglass, and Leslie watched, in shock, as the wineglass flew up, free of his fingers, dashing the entire contents full into his eyes. He coughed and spluttered, releasing her, snatching up a napkin to wipe his eyes free of the stinging fluid.

"Damn! How did *that* happen?" He mopped, scrubbing at the collar of his shirt, his soaking tie. She scrambled to her feet, still not believing what she had seen.

"You didn't have to throw it at me, Leslie! My God, have we come to this, that you have to wrestle yourself loose?"

But the glass was in his hand, not mine. I didn't have my hand anywhere near it. He'll never believe that. Maybe I did somehow grab it out of his hand and throw it at him. But her teeth were chattering, and all she could see was an ashtray, out of Eileen's reach, flying through the air to draw blood. The waiter was there now, solicitous, pressing fresh napkins on Joel, apologizing—Leslie could not imagine for what. He snarled and pushed the waiter aside.

"It was an accident, Joel, I'm sorry," she said, hearing her own teeth still chattering. "I didn't mean to. Is your tie ruined?"

His hand was possessive on her arm again as they walked to his car, but the mood had been broken and they both knew it.

"I'd better take you home," he said. "Poor girl, you do look exhausted. That job of yours, all those crazies, and house hunting too. No, never mind the tie, it's one my aunt gave me, I've always hated it, I'm glad to get rid of it. I can soak the shirt in salt water, that will take out the stain."

He would know things like that. It was all part of the old-world, gracious-living thing that was so important to him. Cold shuddered down her spine, remembering the glass coming free of his hand. He was editing reality. Her hand had not been anywhere near it. She had not touched it, she had not. She had not touched the ashtray either.

Not Eileen, then. Not Eileen at all. She had done it herself.

"Take me home, Joel. I—I think I must be coming down with something."

Coming down with a bad case of poltergeist. *And what do I do now, call a shrink? I am a shrink!* She let him help her into the car and take her home.

WHEN THE ALARM SHRILLED at seven, Leslie moaned and hid her head under the bedclothes. She had heard the clock strike three, then four, and her eyes burned as if she had not closed them all night, despite fitful dreams in which the bedclothes crawled off her like sinuous reptiles and wrapped strangling around Joel, who stood fighting them. Her impulse was to crawl back under them and not put her head out again that day.

A hot shower restored her at least outwardly to normal; she dragged on skirt and sweater and went down to put on the coffee.

Normally she limited herself to a single cup, wanting to be prudent until all the evidence was in on caffeine, but this morning she poured herself a second cup and was halfway through a third when the phone rang. She reached up to the yellow extension on the wall, and heard the buzz of the dial tone with angry frustration. That was all she needed, a telephone out of order. But when she hung up and checked, the dial tone was normal; she called the recorded weather service to make sure. Damp, more rain predicted; the spring rains had hung on longer than usual. Outside there was thick overcast and fog, and San Francisco would be worse. Did she really want to live in the foggiest city in the world?

The way things seemed to be going with the real estate agents, she might not have the chance. She hunted for a piece of bread to put into the toaster. All she found was a dark, appallingly solid-looking loaf whose wrapper proclaimed that it was made with nine organic grains, and sprouted wheat, and when she put it into the toaster, smelled like it. Emily had been doing the shopping again. Sniffing it distastefully as Emily came in, she inquired, "Don't we have any real bread, Em?"

Emily's wide blue eyes were disbelieving. "What's wrong with this? It has a higher protein-to-carbohydrate ratio than any other bread on the market, and there's no refined flour or refined sugar in it *at all.*"

"I'm perfectly sure of it," Leslie said glumly. "It smells like it." She reached, sighing, for the butter.

"And it's a new kind of margarine made only with polyunsaturated fats," Emily told her, just as she took a mouthful and found out for herself.

"Are we so broke we can't afford real butter, Emmy?"

"No, but I was reading the studies on saturated dairy fats, and I thought this would be healthier. What's the matter? Don't you *like* it?"

The dark organic bread really wasn't bad, once you got used to the heaviness of it. Anyhow, nothing would have tasted good to her this morning. Emily put on the teakettle, rummaging in the canister where she kept a dozen different kinds of herb tea; she never drank tea or coffee, and, looking at Emily's perfect skin and glowing hair, Leslie had to admit that whatever she was doing, it seemed to be working. She put a piece of the organic bread into the toaster. Her tea smelled faintly of lemon but looked like mouthwash or cherry Kool-Aid; Leslie looked at it and shuddered. Emily dug enthusiastically into a carton of cottage cheese.

"Want some of this, Les?"

Leslie didn't, but wasn't up to a lecture on protein this morning; she let Emily put a spoonful on her plate. What, she wondered, had happened to the good old days when teenagers lived on pizza, hamburgers, and various cola drinks?

"What was the telephone call?" Emily asked, her mouth full of organic toast, and Leslie grinned; that at least was predictable.

"Nothing; either there was a short in the system or it was a wrong number, hung up before I answered."

Emily stood by the sink, her hands overflowing with vitamin pills and brewer's yeast. "Nobody at all on the line? Maybe we ought to have the phone checked," she said. "It rang again a couple of times last night and nobody was on the line. At least it wasn't that crank caller again. Did you have a nice time with Joel last night?" She gulped the handful of vitamin pills. Leslie realized she ought to be grateful her sister was hooked on vitamins instead of uppers and downers. Or pot, like Juanita García. Juanita had been just Emily's age; the girls had actually known one another, though they moved in different worlds.

"Joel and I had a big fight," she said, and dumped the rest of the organic toast in the garbage can. Emily was already in the hall, grabbing her windbreaker, riffling through her backpack to check the books in it.

"I've got Music History at nine. That nerd we have teaching it keeps laying trips on us about the Romantic period. As if Mahler were a social disease, or something like that. I swear, he thinks music came to an end just before Beethoven. We spent three days, *three days* on Scarlatti, *Alessandro* Scarlatti that is, before we even got into *Domenico* Scarlatti, and then he made us look up all kinds of stupid operas by Bononcini, because he said the only reason Handel was the more famous was political. King George the third or somebody like that was queer for Handel and that's why we aren't hearing Bononcini at the Met. And he says the Romantic composers write the way they did because they all had tuberculosis or syphilis. Did they, Leslie?"

"Did who what?"

"Did the Romantic composers—the nineteenth-century ones—all have horrible diseases?"

"Well, there certainly was a lot of tuberculosis around then," Leslie said, struggling with vague memories of pale romantic young composers languishing in nineteenth-century prints. Emily had come back into the kitchen and was pouring a glass of orange juice.

"Tell me, Les, if they were unhealthy, does that mean their music has to be unhealthy? Or morbid?"

Leslie supposed there was something in it, but for the life of her she couldn't see why it mattered. She said, "I'd think it would depend on the music. A healthy body can certainly do some unhealthy and morbid things—I'm thinking of that young man who broke into a college dorm and murdered nine or ten young nursing students. He seems to have been a prime physical specimen, but the way his mind worked, I'm sure that if he had written music it would have been *really* unhealthy. In spite of his healthy body."

"I'm not so sure," Emily said. "Look at Charles Manson. I mean, *he* was supposed to be a musician, and look at him."

"*You* look at him," Leslie said. "I couldn't care less. I'm not arguing about the theory, it's *your* theory. Pour me some orange juice, will you?"

"It isn't *my* theory, it's Dr. Whittington's. How does a man like that get to be a full professor of music?" Emily leaned over with the glass pitcher of juice, tilted it into Leslie's extended glass. As she turned, her own glass went into the sink with a great shatter of broken glass. Leslie cried out, clutching her own glass.

"Damn!" Emily slammed what was left of the orange juice down on the table; Leslie moved it to safety. Emily was fishing for the broken fragments in the sink, and predictably held up a finger dripping blood. Then Leslie had to rush to find a Band-Aid—at least, she thought, the cut was clean—and Emily, clenching her jaw and swearing in language Leslie hadn't even known at her age, was rushing out, yelling that she was going to miss her bus. Leslie, fishing for the shards of the glass more cautiously, with a dishtowel around her hands, was still shaking. She told herself she had actually seen Emily's elbow brush the glass, but she was still shaking, all the same.

ALONE IN THE HOUSE, her heartbeat slowly returning to normal, Leslie finished her coffee (four cups! she scolded herself), called her answering service and cancelled all her appointments for the day.

If I am the poltergeist, what good can I do them? What little she knew indicated that poltergeists were formulated by hysterical girls, usually on the threshold of menses. But there was no hysterical young girl present, only herself.

Am I hysterical? Was I letting go of all my accumulated resentment against Joel? She wondered how many women had been bullied by psychiatrists into that kind of agreement with their husbands or lovers—even in her early days in psychology, the mental-adjustment people had been insisting that "emotionally healthy" women did not compete with men, and regarded their prime "developmental tasks" as being preparation for healthy heterosexual marriage. The women's movement had at least done away with that kind of thinking, and yet . . . and yet . . . was her subconscious giving her the message that what she really wanted was to give in, marry Joel, give up her work and her independence?

That was nonsense. If that was what she really wanted, why didn't she just agree with Joel to start with? More likely her subconscious was putting up a good healthy fight against letting Joel have the upper hand. She cursed the telephone as it rang again.

"Dr. Barnes? I think I have just the house for you. It came on the market only this morning. A nice quiet district, a few blocks off the Haight—and about the size you wanted. Can you come over and look at it right away?"

And if she hadn't cancelled her appointments for today, she wouldn't have received this call till she checked with her answering service at noon. "Eleven o'clock?"

As the fog burned off it turned into one of those rare perfect days when San Francisco justifies itself for three hundred or more days in the year of heavy fog and rain. Driving across the bridge, sea and sky reflected each other with brilliant blue; she had allowed for heavy traffic on the bridge, but it was unexpectedly light and she sped along, arriving in the Haight district almost half an hour before her appointment.

The former hangout of hippies and ecstatics had given way, in the late sixties, to gypsies and drug dealers, been briefly abandoned to slums, and was now entering a new cycle which someone had given the catchword *gentrification;* slum dwellings and ancient crumbling Victorian gingerbread houses were being bought up cheaply, restored, repainted, and lived in by the well-to-do. As she looked at the houses, freshly painted in gay colors— she especially liked one in Wedgwood blue, wooden-carving trim picked out in ivory—she thought it would have been a tragedy to let houses like these crumble away. Anything which preserved these beautiful old buildings had to have something good about it.

An artist's supply shop had displays of brushes and canvases, and several little bookshops were opening their doors, setting out racks of discards marked 3/$1 or EVERYTHING ON THIS SHELF, 50¢.

Leslie looked over a rack idly. Lurid-looking books about flying saucers and the Bermuda Triangle, another proclaiming the disasters which would attend the coming of comet Kahoutek. Leslie leafed through it idly; the writer identified the comet with something or other in Revelations, foretelling the end of the world. She remembered that Kahoutek had come and gone uneventfully near the end of the seventies. No wonder the book had ended its life on a 50¢ rack. One of her professors in her training class had called this kind of thing *psychoceramics.*

Replacing the book, she brushed another broken-spined paperback: *Those Incredible Poltergeists.* Blinking, she picked it up and riffled pages; despite the lurid cover, the author had some respectable initials from a respectable university after his name, and was, so the blurb said, a practicing psychologist who had encountered several poltergeist entities in his practice. What could she lose for fifty cents? She carried it inside.

Of course, it might be no more than sensational rubbish.

The woman behind the counter was slight and pale and middle-aged; but she had extraordinary eyes. Leslie had the disconcerting sense that the woman could read contempt in the way she held the book in her hands. The woman took Leslie's proffered two quarters, and said, "That's not at all a bad book. Are you particularly interested in the poltergeist phenomenon?"

Suddenly Leslie remembered her own face, sprawled across the centerfold of the *Enquirer.* "PIGTAIL KILLER, TRAPPED BY PSYCHIC!" In a place like this, they probably believed that kind of thing. A book called *Psychic Self-Defense* was propped up on the counter. Her skin crawled at the thought that she might be recognized from that story. She said stiffly, "I don't know much about it. Is this book—er—reliable?"

The woman had a good-natured smile. She said, "I'm out of the Margrave and Anstey monograph just now, and that—" she gestured to *Psychic Self-Defense*—"goes back fifty years, though it's very common-sensical. I have Nandor Fodor's *On the Trail of the Poltergeist,* if you want to wade through a lot of psychoanalytical twaddle."

Leslie did know the name of Nandor Fodor; he was one of the classic writers in psychology, and certainly could not be tinged with the label of sensational or crackpot. "I'll take that one," she said and dug in her pocketbook. While the woman went to find a copy in the back room, she looked uneasily across the shelves. Margaret Murray: *Witchcraft: Its Power in the World Today.* A book called *Seasonal Occult Rituals,* and another called *Magic: Its Ritual, Power and Purpose.* There was a book called *Occult Psychology,* and another called *Sane Occultism,* which struck Leslie as a contradiction in terms, next door to a shelf of Carl Ransom Rogers, whose work she knew and admired, a similar stack of Abraham Maslow, and such classics as James' *Varieties of Religious Experience,* piled up beside Jane Roberts's *Seth Speaks,* a couple of books about Lost Atlantis, and a huge display of a blue-jacketed book called *Drawing Down the Moon;* on the cover a young woman in a long cloak, armed with a sword, appeared to be performing some kind of ritual.

The woman came back with a battered copy of the Nandor Fodor book as Leslie was looking through a book entitled *Twenty Cases Suggestive of Reincarnation,* by a psychologist whose reputation was known to her. Could he possibly believe all this? Somebody had. There was a whole shelf of books on reincarnation. The woman was wearing a small silver circlet around her neck, inside of which was a five-pointed star. A pentagram? She had read something about witchcraft cults and even a Satanist church here in San Francisco. Wasn't the pentagram the sign of the witch cult? Well, Fodor was a reputable psychologist, not some occult crank. She paid for the book and hurried out. In Sacramento she would not have dared to be seen coming out of the Ancient Mysteries Bookshop. She saw in the window a display of a book titled *Adventures of a Psychic Detective.* There was a foreword by someone attached to the Los Angeles Police Department. That was what the *Enquirer* had called her; "Psychic Detective." She had had all kinds of weird calls, parents of missing children, wives with missing husbands, there had been nothing she could say to any of them.

Who did the woman in the shop think she was, to speak so condescendingly of "psychoanalytic twaddle"? She glanced through a few pages of a chapter on the "Baltimore poltergeist" where Fodor explained solemnly that "Twice in the preceding year, the decorative balls on the Christmas tree had exploded with no known reason; I thought he must have a strong grievance against Christmas." The psychoanalyst went on to explain that Christmas was a birthday symbol, and that the boy's own birth trauma was being relieved by the poltergeist.

Birth trauma! That old Freudian nonsense! She read on; the Baltimore poltergeist, it seemed, was a creative and gifted boy, and the psychoanalyst had managed to exorcise the poltergeist by encouraging the boy's grandmother to allow him to write and publish an amateur magazine, thus releasing the blocked creative "genius" which had supposedly created the poltergeist.

Which seemed no help at all to Eileen's situation, or to hers. If anything, Eileen's father was encouraging her creativity, perhaps too much, so that all Eileen wanted was freedom to be a normal teenager. As for herself, she was frustrated neither creatively nor sexually; she had a good job that she liked, was making money, had a lover, and even a younger sister who satisfied any random maternal impulses she might feel.

Fodor, of course, would probably have diagnosed it all in the antiquated Freudian jargon: penis envy, the female need for sexual submission, rejection of her proper female role model. Psychoanalytic twaddle was the right phrase, all right. Was she supposed to deny all her perceived needs, do violence to her conscious self, and marry Joel now, just to shut up her supposedly raging subconscious?

No way, she told herself, borrowing one of Emily's pet phrases, and thrust both books into her briefcase bag, heading toward the corner where the real estate agent would meet her.

A little street curved upward around a park Leslie had never noticed before, and was quickly lost in a labyrinth of side streets, courts and little cul-de-sac alleys. The agent stopped his car before a small brown-shingled house with a pair of matched bay windows on either side of a recessed door, and waved his hand. Leslie got out of the car and walked up the flagged driveway.

The door and steps and the painted trim were as fresh as if they had been decorated yesterday, though the house must have been built before the San Francisco earthquake. Inside, a fanlighted arch cast light into an ivory-painted foyer, and on either side a broad white door led into a pair of rooms separated by glass doors. She stepped into the set of rooms to the right and could immediately visualize Emily's baby grand piano and the concert harp that was still in storage. Beyond the window was a wilderness of green leaves. On the other side of the foyer, an identical set of rooms waited, running almost the length of the house.

"Miss Margrave had these rooms soundproofed," the agent said. "I thought right away of you wanting the rooms for your little office, Dr. Barnes."

A Tiffany lamp in many colors hung at the center of the larger room at the front. Through the glass doors was a smaller room, with a broad window at the back. The old-fashioned wallpaper, striped gold and white, was surely too new to have been the original wallpaper in the house, but its formal elegance belonged to another day. Perhaps too formal for troubled clients?

"Nice view from here," the agent commented. Leslie looked from the back window at the city falling away below in a blue distance to the wide panorama of the Golden Gate, the narrow graceful curve of the bridge spanning sea and sky. Behind her the room seemed a silent pool of peace.

Surely this very view would bring rest to the troubled; she felt at one with nature and city, sky and sea.

Nevertheless she tried to sound indifferent, not wanting this view adding thousands to the price.

"It would be too bright on a sunny day; I'd have to curtain out the glare," she said. "And anyway they'll probably build half a dozen skyscrapers down here in the next ten years, and where's the view then? I'll need to see the kitchen; if we have to use this for an office, and the rooms across the hall for a music room, we'll have to eat and maybe entertain in the kitchen."

But the kitchen, though it was huge in Victorian fashion, was big enough to eat in, with space for washer, dryer and half a dozen children underfoot; it had been extensively remodelled with striplighting, and a modern range and refrigerator.

The kitchen led out into a fair-sized garden. Although it was choked and neglected, there was fragrance drifting through the dampness. Against the back wall a lemon tree, dark branches sheltering white blossoms and yellow fruit, cast a sharp scent and shade.

The garden's lonely. It wants me to work in it. Leslie felt a sharp tug of homecoming. This was her house. A white cat hopped down from the back wall and vanished under the castor bean bushes.

"Does the cat come with the house?"

"Cat? I didn't see a cat; must belong to one of the neighbors," the man said. But the cat looked perfectly at home. Leslie had always wanted a cat. The place was perfect; it must cost four times what she could afford.

"And here is a remodelled garage apartment, with a separate entrance and half bath," said the agent. "You could use it for an office; it was done over for an artist's studio, I think."

Maybe Emily would like a separate apartment, though she had seen the second double-room suite as a music room. Oh-oh, she thought, I knew there had to be a catch, and here it is. Despite three large windows cut in the wall of the old garage, it was dark and dismal, shaded on the garden side with a heavy growth of some vine that cast a sickening smell. Where every room inside the house had been shining with cleanliness, the agent frowned disapprovingly as he hit the light switch here. In the center of the room was a potter's wheel, covered with the slimy remnants of damp clay; a broken cup oozing discolored fluid had been dropped in the middle of the mess. Leslie shuddered with distaste; the room was cold and dank, completely lacking in charm. The cold fluorescent lighting, which added gaiety and a modern touch to the kitchen, here gave the place all the charm of an abandoned warehouse. The small fireplace did nothing to cheer it, choked with ash and dirt.

Ugh, great for a Hallowe'en party; chill your friends and spook them out! Then Leslie warned herself not to judge too soon. A coat of fresh paint, cheerful furniture, could do wonders; that, and cutting down that ivy, or whatever it was, shading the garden window. She turned her back on it, shivering, inspected the half bath with distaste—it was clean enough but smelled neglected and foul, as if a broken sewer somewhere had backed up.

"We'll have all that stuff cleaned up for you, of course," the agent apologized, leading her back into the main house and upstairs. The stairs were hardwood, the curving balustrade a shining dark wood. There was a mirror at the corner of the stairs.

Yes, this is my house. I've come home. Now go away and let me alone, she thought, but dutifully inspected hall closets, the bath in the upper hall, a small bedroom which would make guest quarters—the agent called it a maid's room—a spacious master bedroom looking out on the same sky and sea view as the downstairs office, with its own bath in delicate shades of blue tile.

The agent led her across the hall to a second large bedroom where an opened casement window wafted the scent of jasmine from the garden. She breathed it in with pleasure, then recognized the scent as the same which had smelled so dank in the garage room.

The agent scowled. "How did those windows get open again? Have those damn kids been climbing in here?" He pulled the casement closed and examined the latch. "This isn't the first time we've found windows open!"

Now she was reminded to ask some of the questions which, fallen under the house's spell, she had forgotten. "What is the neighborhood like? Malicious kids, teenage gangs?"

"Oh, no. This would be little kids—climbing. This is the worst damage we've ever found—a window not staying shut. May need a new latch or lock. Notice there are grilles on all the ground floor windows, even in the garage room; they were put up when there were all those gypsies and junkies in the Haight. Listen—so quiet up here, you'd hardly know you were in the City."

It was so quiet that Leslie could hear bees and insects humming in the fragrant garden. In the rental house where she lived now, there were traffic sounds from a nearby street, twenty-four hours a day. Here it was a distant murmur. She felt that she would buy this place if it took her last cent. She asked the price, prepared to haggle all afternoon to bring it within reach.

She heard it, unbelieving. It was actually a couple of thousand less than she had been prepared to pay for the little jewel on Russian Hill— and this house was twice the size, with a garden. Granted, it was not such a fashionable address, and property values in the Haight had gone down during its years as a slum, but even so—

"Is it full of termites or dry rot? Am I going to have to spend another fifty thousand to bring it up to the building code?"

"I have an architect's report in the folder. You can see it in the office. You could move in tomorrow."

"Then what's the catch?" she asked skeptically.

"For you, none, Dr. Barnes. They want to settle the estate fast—get the place off their hands. The fact is, it's been sold three times in the past year, and every time the sale fell through. The old lady who owned this house died very suddenly; she'd lived here fifty years, had no children, and the place went to some distant cousins in Nebraska or South Dakota. They put it up to sell, and a series of unlucky coincidences— I think they're convinced the place is a jinx, and they brought the price way down. First, an old couple bought it, and the very day the escrow was to close, the old man dropped dead, and the widow didn't feel she could live here alone. Then a family bought it, but a month afterward—" he hesitated. "The mother of the family—well, she committed suicide, so they forfeited their down payment and their first mortgage payment and there was the place back in the hands of the owners again."

Somehow she felt sure the woman had committed suicide in that dank studio, a perfect haunted room if she had ever felt one—firmly Leslie reminded herself not to be superstitious. "You said three times . . ."

"The woman just changed her mind; lived in the house a month, then did the same damn thing—forfeited her down payment and walked out one day—you saw her junk in the studio. So the owners have already made some profits they didn't expect; now they just want the place off their hands!"

Now Leslie thought very seriously about it. Some houses did have an atmosphere that was difficult for a sensitive person to live with. And so far the place seemed unlucky. Did she really want a house with that history?

"Did the old woman who owned it die in the house?"

The agent hesitated. He evidently didn't want to tell her this. "She did," Leslie guessed, and, reluctantly, he gave a little nod.

"Was she murdered in her bed or something? Tell me; I'll only imagine something worse."

"Oh, no, nothing like that! She fell off her piano stool, downstairs, and lay here in the house, dead with a broken skull, for a couple of days. The police investigated—even questioned a few of her friends. But they finally agreed it was just a bad accident. A lady that old just shouldn't have been living alone," he added with real indignation.

No wonder the distant owners felt the house was jinxed! A mysterious death and suspected murder, a second death, a suicide and a disappearance—maybe they think they've got another Amityville Horror on their hands! The thought made her smile. Their loss was her gain. She would take it before they came to their senses and found out what a house like this should bring!

"I'll put a deposit down today," she said. "Subject to the architectural report—" for she knew that the verbal assurances of a real estate agent were no more legally binding than those of a used car salesman, and she wanted to see it in writing that the house was sound—"I'll take it."

Downstairs again in the room she had mentally christened the music room, imagining Emily's piano and harp here, she wondered if the old woman who had died here had kept her piano in that corner. She thought perhaps so. She had had to come to terms with the knowledge that she was psychic; but this was not the terrifying thing it had been when she saw Juanita García, bloody and violated, under a drainage ditch. It was the faintest whisper of sound, almost music. A benevolent presence; an old woman ready to die, struck down quickly by a stroke or heart attack at her beloved instrument. The very way a musician would wish to go, surely.

But just the same, she thought, as the agent was writing out the receipt for her deposit, she would not tell Emily that old Miss—what had her name been? Graves?—no, Margrave, that was the name—had fallen from her piano bench and died in this same room where Emily would put her own piano.

''AT THAT PRICE, THERE'S got to be something wrong with it,''
Emily said. Even after Leslie retold the set of unlucky coincidences which
had led to three cancelled sales, she remained skeptical.

"The whole thing could be a criminal plot, you know. Those Nebraska
people. Maybe they sell the house, then scare people out of it, so they get
forfeited deposits and down payments and have it to sell all over again.
They could make a lot of money that way."

"I think you've missed your vocation, Emily. You ought to write whodunits. You'd make a million before you were twenty. I think I'm just
lucky." She chuckled and added that if anyone turned up trying to scare
them out, she'd leave it to Emily to catch them, then offered her own
theory.

"They probably think they have some kind of Amityville Horror on
their hands and want to get rid of it before the story spreads."

Emily said coldly that she believed the Amityville incident had been exposed as a fake and nobody with an ounce of brains would ever have believed in it, and fetched a carton of yogurt from the refrigerator. The phone rang, and she started toward it, but Leslie was closer.

"Dr. Barnes's residence."

"Is that Leslie Barnes?" asked an unfamiliar voice, and Leslie let out her breath, realizing that she had been tensed for the heavy inhuman breathing of her crank caller.

"Yes, this is she."

"Dr. Barnes, you don't know me, but Sergeant Beckenham of the Sacramento police gave me your name and address. This is Lieutenant Charles Passevoy, Santa Barbara Homicide, and we have a very puzzling disappearance down here. A young child. Would you be willing to fly down here and see what you could do to find her? We heard how you found that young girl when the Pigtail Killer was killing young girls in Sacramento—"

Leslie's throat closed with panic. It was happening again. Damn Nick! Damn Nick for giving out her address, damn the *Enquirer*, which had made it likely that this kind of thing would happen again and again. . . . She said thickly, "I'm sorry. I really can't. I can't do anything like that, please. I don't want to—"

"Look, Dr. Barnes," said the pleasant deep voice on the other end of the phone. "I honestly understand how you feel—"

"You can't possibly—"

"Doctor, we can promise you. No reporters. No publicity. But this is a little girl, seven years old, disappeared from a parked car—"

Leslie felt her throat closing again with dread. She didn't want to know. Before her eyes she seemed to see a small girl with Dutch bangs and twin gaps in her teeth. Imagination, she told herself; what she was seeing was a generic seven-year-old. *Phyllis.*

"—the mother is sitting here in my office. Will you just talk to her for a minute? We're prepared to pay your plane fare and expenses down here—"

"It's not a question of money," Leslie began. "It's only that—that I can't do that sort of thing, I have patients here, I can't leave—"

Suddenly there was a new voice on the telephone, a woman's voice, crying, almost babbling.

"Dr. Barnes, listen to me. My little girl. Phyllis Anne. She was just— just seven years old. I was buying her birthday cake when she disappeared right out of my car in the parking lot. I went in to get the cake and she was gone—listen, you come down here, and if you find her, I'll give you a thousand dollars—" She heard the woman swallow. Leslie said coldly, "It isn't money I want—"

"Oh, God, I know that, I don't mean to insult you, I promise you, only I know I couldn't leave my work just like that, I thought it would help you decide—" The woman gasped. "She's so little—and those crazy, crazy people, if some sex fiend's got her—" She stopped cold as if paralyzed and Leslie could feel the horror coming over the phone to her; she spoke quickly to stem it, not knowing what she said until she heard her own words.

"She's not dead. She's all right. A man has her." At the sound of the faraway gasp of horror she added, "She's eating her birthday cake right now. She calls him Daddy." She swallowed hard as she heard it but heard her own words racing on.

"Her father has her. She's all right. He bought her a—a pair of red patent leather shoes—"

She heard the indrawn gasp on the other end of the line.

"She begged me for them and I said they weren't practical. She really wanted them. But her father? Her father *refused* custody, he didn't want her—he would never kidnap her—"

"Well, he has," Leslie said bluntly. "He took her out of state. Look for her in—" She hesitated, groping for a picture of desert sand, cactus, but at the other end the woman whispered, "He's working in Phoenix—"

There was a sense of *rightness* to it which Leslie could feel. She repeated, "Phoenix. She's there . . ."

"I'll be on a plane tonight," the woman gasped. "How can I thank you?"

"Just don't tell anybody," Leslie said, weakness flooding through her whole body; she hooked a chair close with her foot and fell into it. "Promise me that; I don't want money or anything else, just never tell anybody—"

She could not bear it if this was going to start again. She could not bear it, her face smeared over the tabloids, lunatics coming out of the walls. She would call Nick and threaten him with lawsuits, injunctions—but Nick was her friend, he knew how she felt. What could she do?

Lieutenant Passevoy was back on the phone. He said quietly, "We'll check it out, Dr. Barnes. Right away. Can I call you back?"

Leslie said frantically, "No," and slammed down the handset. She covered her face with her hands, and Emily, who had stood watching, yogurt forgotten in her hands, whispered, "What was that all about? Did you really see—something?"

"A little girl. Disappeared—" Leslie felt that she could not bear for this to touch Emily. "I wouldn't have said anything. The woman—offered me money." As she spoke the words, Leslie felt that sickening sense of having been dirtied by the offer. "Only she was—was afraid the little girl had been raped, kidnapped by some lunatic—I couldn't stand it, I had to relieve her mind. Oh, God, Em, now if they find her dead or something I'll want to die, how do I *know*—" Already the awful sense of certainty, of pressure, was fading and she was unsure.

"You mean you just told her the first thing that came into your head to get her off your back?" Emily looked horrified, and Leslie said, distracted, "No, no. I was sure while I was saying it, perfectly sure. I would have gone into court and taken an oath. Only now it's all fuzzy again—"

Emily patted her shoulder lightly. "Well, if you're going to have psychic flashes, I should think it would be better to have good ones than bad ones, better to see something nice than something horrible. Maybe this time you were lucky too."

"Lucky!" Leslie covered her face with her hands again.

"I'll make you a cup of tea," Emily offered. "Valerian? It's a natural tranquilizer and very soothing—can't possibly hurt you. It's been used for nerves for centuries, Les."

"Let's just forget the whole thing, Emmie. I'll call Nick and tell him if he ever drops anything like that on me again, he can forget he ever knew me."

"Would you like me to get you a drink? There's some wine in the cupboard. You really do look sort of pale, Leslie."

"No, it's all right."

"You were telling me about the house—"

With relief, Leslie seized the opportunity to change the subject again.

"I put down a big deposit, and I can make a down payment of over half the cost, with Grandmother's money. That means I'll be paying less, even with interest rates what they are, than we're paying for this place. There's a big room you can have for the piano and you can get the harp out of storage—the woman who owned the house was a musician too. And there is this beautiful big room, soundproof, that I can have for an office," she went on, as she began to scrub vegetables for a salad. Emily grabbed a small carrot and stood munching it. She had finished the yogurt, Leslie noticed. At least, for all her food faddishness, she had a normal teenage appetite.

"Can't I have the soundproofed room? Then I could practice even if you had a client."

"I really want that room for an office, Em. I've fallen in love with the view. But it amounts to the same thing—if the office is soundproof, you can practice anyhow."

Emily cocked her head and frowned. "Why would an old lady soundproof a room?"

"Maybe she was a music critic and liked to play records at the top of the sound level. Maybe she was into primal therapy and liked to go in there and scream at the top of her lungs. How would I know?"

"Well, it sounds funny to me," Emily said darkly. "People don't go around soundproofing rooms for nothing."

Leslie chuckled as she took a chop out of the refrigerator. "That sounds like the old New England theory that if people drew their shades at night, they must be doing something they were ashamed of. Want one of these, Em?"

"Oh—no thanks; I'll make myself a grilled cheese sandwich. How you can go around eating pieces of a dead animal—!"

"Better a dead one than a live one," said Leslie equably. They had had this argument before.

"There are three bedrooms upstairs: a little one that we can use for a guest room, and you can have your pick of the two big bedrooms. Want to drive over and see it tonight? We could be back by ten."

"I'd like to, but I can't; I'm playing for the choir Sunday and I have to practice. Why don't you pick me up after my Music History class Friday, and we'll see it then?"

Leslie ran mentally over her Friday schedule. Eileen Grantson again and no chance to read up on poltergeists. Not that Fodor and his outdated Freudian twaddle—a very satisfying word, that—was likely to be much help. And if she herself was the poltergeist, how could she be any help to Eileen?

"Friday is all right," she said. "But we'll have to be back by five for a client, all right?"

She talked about the house while the chop was sizzling, while Emily took apart the waffle iron, reversing the waffle plates to make them into grilling surfaces and grilled herself a sandwich. She gulped a glass of milk and grabbed an apple, then went into the living room. After a moment, Leslie heard her run a series of arpeggios, then settle into heavy chords that sounded like Liszt. Maybe she should give Emily the soundproof room after all.

She should locate the books on poltergeist phenomena, Fodor and the other one, who at least had credentials from someplace respectable. But she sat without moving, listening to Emily practice, knowing that she was reluctant to enter again the world of unreason which had driven her from Sacramento, and now had forced a break with Joel. Was her subconscious telling her loud and clear that Joel was not the right man for her? But she would miss him.

She heard the telephone and started for the hall extension, but heard the piano stop and surmised Emily had already grabbed it. After a minute her sister called, "For you, Leslie. It's that policeman in Santa Barbara."

"Tell him I can't come to the phone," Leslie said, coming slowly back into the kitchen. Emily repeated that, listened a minute, and said, "Oh, but that's wonderful! Les, listen to this, they found that little girl right where you said they would." She handed her the extension.

Leslie took it. Lieutenant Passevoy's voice said in her ear, "I wanted you to know this right away, Dr. Barnes. We found the kid—Phyllis Anne Chapman—right where you said. We had the Phoenix police go check out her father, and sure enough, the kid was there eating her birthday cake. Her father said he flew in to ask if he could take the girl for her birthday, and when he found her alone—damned idiot—said he thought he'd give his wife a little scare, and just said, 'Let's surprise Mommy.' He said he was going to call his ex-wife in the morning. He never thought she'd be dumb enough to call the police. Personally I think the guy's a sadist, but the kid is fine. She talked to her mother on the phone and the father said he'd put her on a plane to Santa Barbara in the morning. So what could we do except give him a lecture about rules of child custody, and ask him nicely not to do it again?"

Leslie let out her breath. She had not known she was holding it. She did not hear any of Lieutenant Passevoy's repeated thanks and praise; she only knew that sometime later she was huddled in the kitchen chair, the receiver was back on the hook, and Emily was playing Liszt again in the living room.

It was reaching out for her again, all the insanity that had driven her from Sacramento. And if she, a mature woman with awareness of her own hostilities and weak points, was terrified by it, what would it do to fourteen-year old, emotionally troubled Eileen?

The Fodor book had not been in her study. Had she left it in the living room? Emily was still coaxing great resounding chords from the old baby grand. Leslie listened for a moment, thinking that Emily was really good. Of course, she was prejudiced in favor of her sister, but she sounded better than most of the players Leslie had heard at concerts. The girl cocked her head like a small bird in a fountain, listening to a spill of notes like spraying water; listened and repeated the phrase like beads slipping down a string, then saw Leslie and stopped with a martyred look.

"What is it now?"

"Did I leave a book in here? Or did you borrow it? Nandor Fodor, *On the Trail of the Poltergeist.* . . ."

Emily looked at her blankly. "What would I be doing with it? I didn't know you owned a book like that."

"Okay, I just thought I might have left it in here." Leslie went out, hearing the same spilling phrase repeating again and again. *I wonder if she ever woke up enough to know what it was I asked her?* Yet it had been foolish to ask. Except for stark necessity in schoolwork—and Emily was an indifferent student at best, in everything but music and languages—Emily read very little, spending every free moment in the ballet studio or at her piano, and professed to think reading was a waste of time. Emily might have noticed a book if she found it on the piano keyboard. Or, just possibly, if she stepped on it.

Fretting, she checked the briefcase again; then realized that after that call from Santa Barbara, the very last thing she wanted was to read about a poltergeist.

She sat in the hall and listened to Emily practice. The phone rang again; she grabbed it quickly.

"Leslie Barnes here."

"Alison, is that you?"

Leslie frowned. "What number are you calling? There's no Alison here," she said and hung up. Immediately it rang again, but this time there was no one on the line. She repeated, "Hello? Hello?" But it did not have the empty echoing sound of a vacant line. She could hear breathing. Oh, God, not that again.

"If you don't get off this line," she said sharply, "I will report to the telephone company!"

"You'll be sorry, bitch," said a thick and indistinct voice. And then there was a click, and the dial tone.

The piano had stopped. Of course. Emily could not bear to think she might miss a telephone call.

"Who was it, Les? For me?"

If it had been for you, I would have called you, she thought irritably, but there was no need to snarl at Emily. "Just our friendly neighborhood crank caller," she said, trying to make her voice light.

"You ought to report him," Emily said, wandering back to the piano in a daze, and Leslie called the business office, to get a recorded message that she could call at nine o'clock the next morning. When the phone rang again her hand shrank from picking it up.

"Dr. Barnes's residence." She waited, cringing internally, for that thick, fundamentally inhuman voice. Instead it was a light, almost childish voice.

"Dr. Barnes? I hate to—I mean, you said I could call you at home if anything went wrong. I did it again. I mean, I'm sorry to disturb you—"

"It's all right, Judy," she said, recognizing the voice as one of her teenage clients. Judy Attenbury. Anorexia; fifteen years old, she had grown too big-boned for the ballet she loved, had retaliated by self-inflicted starvation, lost almost thirty pounds, and could not resume normal eating no matter how she tried.

"I did it again, Dr. Barnes. I ate, Mom nagged me until I ate some chicken and salad and then I started eating mashed potatoes and I ate and ate and I couldn't stop." Judy was crying almost hysterically. "And I felt like such a pig. I felt so *gross,* I couldn't stand it, so I went and threw up. . . ."

Thank God. A real caller. A real problem. Then Leslie was dismayed that she could feel this pleasure when one of her clients was in deep trouble.

"First of all, try and stop crying, Judy; it isn't the end of the world. Now I want you to tell me just how you were feeling when you took that first helping of chicken. What did your mother say. . . . ?"

"She wanted me to eat. She kept nagging me to eat. And when I started eating mashed potatoes she said, Either you starve yourself or you overdo it, don't you? You can't seem to do anything sensibly. And I felt so *gross*. I'm such a pig—" Judy's words tumbled over one another.

Judy's mother could not bear the fact that she, perfectly preserved and slender at forty-five, could have anything but a perfect daughter. She had been the one really traumatized when Judy had been kicked out of the ballet school. A superb dancer, Judy simply did not have the lean, stripped frame of a ballerina. She had nagged her and nagged her to lose weight all the time Judy was growing.

She managed to quiet Judy, to call Mrs. Attenbury to the phone and ask them to come in for a joint session the next day, then spent the evening packing books in her study. But the Fodor book did not appear.

Leslie got up early the next morning, resuming the packing of books in her study into grocery boxes and labelling them, but by the time she heard Emily come down to breakfast the Fodor book had still not surfaced; by now she was fairly sure it was not in her study. She had checked the car to be sure she had not left it there. She came into the kitchen, preoccupied with the problem of getting packing boxes for kitchen items.

She reminded herself not to be too definite until she had a chance to study the architect's report; she had looked through it casually in the agent's office, and everything had seemed to be in order, but she wanted to give it a careful reading, just because she had so completely fallen under the spell of the place. She thought it would break her heart for the deal to fall though now.

That tells me what my priorities are. Joel hasn't called since that fight we had, and I wouldn't blame him if he didn't call at all. After all, I threw a glass of wine at him—one way or the other. And here I am talking about heartbreak, but only if I lose my new house. So much, I guess, for Joel. And if that's what he wants in a woman, or a marriage, good riddance. But it made her sigh. She missed him. And in her busy life she had little time to meet men.

Now I sound like Mother. She was always encouraging me to try to meet men.

Emily was standing at the counter, stirring spoonfuls of wheat germ into a carton of yogurt, and alternately sipping from a cup of thin yellow tea from which issued fragrant lemon-scented steam. She looked up. "Something wrong, Les?"

"Oh, no. Just hoping the architect's report says the house is as good as I think it is."

"Sounds as if you've fallen in love."

"That was just what I was thinking. With Joel out of the picture, maybe the house will turn out to be the great love of my life after all. A grand passion, maybe."

"Well, there's one good thing about that kind of grand passion," Emily retorted. "It will never give you VD or get you pregnant!"

Blinking, Leslie commanded herself not to register shock.

"I can't wait to see this marvelous dream castle," Emily went on. "I don't suppose we could manage today instead of Friday?"

Mentally Leslie ran over her calendar. "What time are you finished today?"

"I have Music History at nine and a lesson with Dr. Agrowsky. I'll be through at one-thirty. Do you want me to meet you there? Or can you pick me up at the Conservatory?"

"I'll pick you up. Put some toast in the toaster for me," Leslie said, fiddling with the coffeemaker. She sniffed appreciatively at the steam from Emily's tea. "That smells nice. What is it?"

"Lemon grass. Want some? It's very soothing."

"Not this time, thanks." She slid into her seat, and blinked. "I see you found that book I was looking for."

"What?" Emily turned. Lying on Leslie's place mat was a grubby and water-stained paperback. The garish title, smeared across a dark background and a string of lights like the flying saucer chase sequence in the Spielberg film *Close Encounters,* was *Those Incredible Poltergeists.* She had forgotten that she had bought this book, too, in her search for the Fodor volume.

"Thanks, Em, but that wasn't the one I really wanted."

"Don't thank me," Emily said. "I never saw it before. I wouldn't put anything that filthy on the *table!*"

"Then how did it get on the table? I certainly didn't put it there," Leslie said, picking it up fastidiously between thumb and forefinger. "Are you trying to tell me it got up and walked?"

"I'm not trying to tell you anything. I don't know anything *about* it," Emily said. "What would I want with a book on—" she craned her neck and read the title, "Poltergeists?"

"Emily, if this is a joke, damn it, I'm not in the mood this morning!"

"Don't you dare use that tone of voice to me," Emily flared. "I don't think it's funny either."

"It damn well *isn't* funny, Em. Come on, if you put it there for a joke—"

"I already told you I didn't! Why are you so upset?"

"Because, damn it, I *know* I didn't put it there, and now you tell me you didn't, so who does that leave?"

Emily flung down the yogurt carton so hard that it bounced off the table and fell to the floor. "Maybe it was one of your fucking poltergeists, then! You're the one who believes in all that goddamn psychic garbage, aren't you?" She stormed out of the kitchen, slamming the hall door, and a moment later Leslie heard the bathroom door bang shut.

Dazed, Leslie picked up the yogurt carton, wiped up the smear on the floor, and sat down to have her coffee, shoving the offending book to one side. She wondered if she was losing her mind.

The question, even as she formulated it, snapped her out of it. She had heard it so often from her clients.

She formulated the answer she would have made to a client.

Why do you think you're losing your mind?

Well, there was this book on the table. . . .

Do you think you're imagining it?

She reached out hesitantly to touch the stained and dirty cover. *No, it's real enough and Emily saw it too.*

Folie a deux? No, Em's a pretty together kid, and I was thoroughly analyzed before I went into this business. I think we can take our relative sanity as a working hypothesis. But what's the answer, then?

Emily reappeared, dressed for class. She reached for her lemon-scented tea and sipped uneasily at it. "I'm sorry I yelled at you, Les. You okay?"

"I guess so. Sorry, Em. I know you don't lie."

"It's all right. If I'd had any sense I'd have lied this time and said I did it; I had no idea you'd get this upset."

A dull fear was pulsing through Leslie's mind again. *All that psychic garbage.* She said, "So what's the answer? Do we have elves? Or maybe gremlins?"

"What's so upsetting about a book on the kitchen table? Maybe it wants you to read it. Oh, damn, that was my yogurt that spilled." Emily rummaged in the ice box; started to eat cottage cheese out of a carton.

Leslie said stiffly, "Books can't *want* anything. And they cannot move unless they are moved by some outside force."

"The Force is with us," Emily quipped with her mouth full of cottage cheese. "If anything *was* going to move without somebody moving it, I should think it would be a book on poltergeists, wouldn't it? Maybe one of us is walking in our sleep. That makes more sense than believing that one of us is making like a poltergeist without knowing it." She dropped the cottage cheese carton into the garbage can and scribbled *cottage cheese* on the list on the refrigerator. "Hey, I've got to run or I'll be late." On her way out she called back, "Pick me up at the Conservatory at one-thirty, right?"

Leslie poured herself a second cup of coffee, staring at the lurid cover of the book. Maybe one of us *is* walking in her sleep. Probably me. Her mind was full of ashtrays flying across the desk, red wine splashing into Joel's eyes. Emily didn't know; it had been a shot in the dark.

Maybe it wants you to read it. She found a paper towel, scrubbed the surface dust from the book, and stared morbidly at it. Certainly her brief foray into the pages of Fodor had produced nothing but Freudian twaddle. She began to leaf one-handed through the stained, dog-eared pages.

The poltergeist is generally a product of emotions in a state of chronic tension, usually but not always centering upon a girl at the threshold of menses, less frequently a disturbed adolescent boy or a pregnant woman. The awakening sexual forces combine with family hostilities and resentments to create a force which expresses itself in knocks, bangs, broken china, and objects moved about without visible cause. Frequently the ambiance is that of a naughty child; the girl is frequently eager to maintain adult status and disclaims responsibility for any childish resentments, thus creating strong tension between the unconscious need to behave like a child, and the conscious desire for adulthood.

Poltergeist phenomena are mostly brief and transient. If enormous family drama is produced around this phenomenon, however, the young girl will begin to use this drama to get the attention or special treatment which she cannot obtain in any other way. (This is one reason for early observations of poltergeist phenomena centering upon hysterical maidservants or nursery governesses whose status was low and whose emotional needs were ignored.)

Occasionally, however, the poltergeist may take on a more

serious tone, shifting heavy furniture or other objects; the flying china may not only make a gratifying noise, but may inflict injury; and an occasional poltergeist may begin to set fires. These developments should be taken seriously, whereas the minor phenomena of breaking dishes and moving objects can safely be treated as of mild interest, neither ignored nor overdramatized, but as a symptom of some underlying emotional trouble.

A relatively serious problem among poltergeist children is the young girl or boy whose emotional needs are so gratified by the attention surrounding these strange phenomena that she turns from involuntary poltergeist activity to deliberate manipulation when the first wave of activity begins to die down, throwing china or other small objects secretly while denying knowledge of it (and some children may actually do so in a state of somnambulistic dissociation) or even secretly setting fires. This, of course, is a problem for the psychologist or mental health worker rather than the psychic investigator. Poltergeists, voluntary or involuntary, should never be ignored or taken lightly; it goes without saying that they should not be punished for it, shamed or derided, and should never be accused of pretending the phenomena, since, whether the occurrences are due to hysteria, somnambulisms or true psychic force, they are not under the child's control and are never caused by deliberate mischief or "naughtiness."

Yet another kind of poltergeist activity may be the expression of psychic force in tension, not around a hysterical or maladjusted child, but around a relatively well-adjusted adult. When this occurs, there is some unresolved psychic force in action; it could be said that the Unseen is coming in search of the individual concerned, and this does not, strictly speaking, come under the scope of this book.

In addition to the case histories in this book, consult Carrington and Fodor, cited elsewhere, as well as the monograph by Margrave and Anstey, in the Autumn, 1983 issue of *The Journal of Unexpected Phenomena,* reissued by Silkie Press, San Francisco, as *The Natural History of the Poltergeist.*

Impressed, Leslie put down the book. It seemed that her instincts had been good, to try and calm Eileen, while not allowing her to make a drama out of it. Interesting that she had found nothing in the psychoanalytic literature, except Freudian nonsense about birth trauma—an exploded theory by now—while she found, in a sensational paperback, a serious and rational analysis of the problem, with sensible hints for handling it.

But why was there nothing serious in the literature?

Maybe there was; she hadn't by any means exhausted psychological writings. Or maybe the whole profession was so shocked by this non-rational subject that they had an emotional need to ignore it even when it happened.

She re-read the phrase in the book: *it could be said that the Unseen is coming in search of the individual concerned.* But that was not, the author said, within the scope of the book. Well, Leslie resolved that if the Unseen, whatever it was—she *hated* that kind of fuzzy language—was coming in search of her, it would have a good hard look.

Anyway, my unconscious was telling me what it thought of Joel. Leslie scanned the page again . . . *whose status was low and whose emotional needs were ignored.* I never realized it before, but Joel evidently thinks women *are* lower in status, assuming that I would naturally give up my work and dedicate myself to his career. No wonder I threw a glass of wine at him, either in a sort of somnambulistic state of dissociation, or else— Her mind sheered off from the enormity of thinking that her mind alone, unassisted by any physical force, could have flung the wine.

Nothing was to be gained by going over and over it. She would try and find the other references, even if she must go back to the odd little bookshop and question the woman with the pentagram about the other references. Meanwhile, she would try the suggestions in the book about Eileen's poltergeist, when she saw her again. And now she had to brace herself to talk to Judy Attenbury and to her mother.

CHAPTER

Four

SULLEN RAIN CLOUDS HOVERED over the city. Driving over the Bay Bridge, Leslie saw small whitecaps whipping up on the face of the water; if it was like this in the sheltered Bay, what was it like out at the ocean? She pulled up in front of the Conservatory and Emily ran toward her through the first splattering drops and slammed the car door. Suddenly the rain was coming down fiercely, a whipping, gusting wind beating against the car so that she had to fight the wheel, and the wipers could not clear the glass. Leslie pulled the car to the side of the street.

"It will let up, it never comes down this hard for more than a minute or so," she said, watching people scurrying to shelter through the downpour.

"Good thing you picked me up," Emily said. "I have my old poncho in my backpack, but my hair would have gotten soaked. And I'm ushering at the recital tonight."

"Do you have to go home first, then?"

"No, I keep my black dress and heels in a locker here," Emily said.

"I've got to stop at a drugstore, though; my last pair of pantyhose has sprung a run. Hey, there was a lot of excitement around here this morning. They're putting new locks on all the doors; some creep busted into the orchestra room and smashed a cello and put his foot right through the tympani!"

Leslie felt her breath catch in shock. Vandalism at the Conservatory, the most peaceful place in the City? It frightened her to think of Emily there, exposed to the unreason of the mentally disturbed—for surely anyone who could smash musical instruments, intended for no purpose except to give pleasure, must be deeply disturbed. The rain was slackening off and she put the car into gear and drove away.

"Is there any clue to who did it?"

"Nothing. Nothing at all." Emily hesitated. "I don't suppose you could come in and try to—well, to find out, could you?"

So even Emily was willing to let this irrationality intrude on her. She felt her throat closing almost convulsively, and Emily, seeing her face change, said, "Hey I'm sorry, Les. I—I guess I know how you feel about that. Only I know the girl who owns the cello, and you should have seen her this morning. It's insured, sure, but it was her father's. And if I could catch that creep. I'd—I'd—" she floundered, "I'd skin him alive, maybe. He may be a sick person, but dammit, he'd be sicker when I got through with him!"

Leslie sighed. "It wouldn't do any good to punish him, Em. You'd have to find out why he did it, and not just keep him from doing it again, but keep him from *wanting* to do it again."

Emily said brutally, "I'd settle for putting him someplace where he *couldn't* do it again! Preferably dead himself."

"That's the way most people feel. And that's why we have such a violent society," Leslie said. Punishing the violent had never done anything except convince them that the world they lived in was a violent world and make them determined to *inflict* violence, rather than *suffering* it. But how could she make Emily see this?

"Only, if you're, you know, psychic, wouldn't that be the way to figure out why people do this kind of stuff?" Emily fumbled. "Like that man who killed all those girls up in Sacramento. You couldn't cure the Pigtail Killer, but if you could find out why he did it, maybe you could keep some other guy from whatever happened to him to make him start killing them."

"We already know that," Leslie said grimly. "But there's no profit in preventing crime, just in punishing it." She fought her way through the rain, which had slowed cars and streetcars to a crawl, while Emily fiddled with the dial of the radio, switching it back and forth between the two classical music stations.

She drew up before the house, turning into the short concrete driveway. She had seen it before with sunlight streaming across the twin bay windows; now, with rain streaming down the panes and dripping from the gutters, it looked lonely and desolate.

"At least we'll find out today if the roof leaks," Emily said.

"Bite your tongue!" The hallway was dark and damp; she fumbled for a light switch. But either the bulb had burned out or the electricity was off at the main. In a few days the deal would go through; rapidly, because the title search had been completed with the previous aborted sale. Then she could call P.G. and E. to have gas, electric services, and telephone hooked up. She would need an extension in her office, and another for her answering service, as well as the regular house phone. Should she give Emily an extension in her own room? She turned to put the question and found that her sister had wandered away. She found her in the room she had already christened the music room.

"I thought we could put the piano and harp in here, Em, and you could have this room to yourself. Do you want a telephone in here, or would you rather not be interrupted while you're practicing?"

Emily gestured impatiently for silence. Her head was cocked in that listening gesture, and for a moment Leslie too felt that she could hear the faint, almost inaudible music of a piano—or was it a harpsichord?—playing a Bach prelude.

Then Emily turned white as a sheet and crumpled to the floor.

"THAT'LL TEACH ME TO skip breakfast," Emily said, lying back on the windowseat, her head pressed to the rain-washed glass.

"You had breakfast. I saw you."

"I didn't finish. I should have stopped for a muffin or something, but I forgot. And that creep Whittington went on and on about the aesthetic sense of the rococo, whatever that is. He thinks Romantic music is a social disease. So I was late for my piano lesson, and I knew Dr. Agrowsky would have had fits if I was ninety seconds late through his door, and old Auntie Whitty kept us. I swear, I wanted to *throw* something at that guy."

After her morning's reading on the subject of poltergeists, Leslie didn't feel like talking about throwing things. "How do you feel now?"

"I've got a splitting headache."

"There's some aspirin in my bag, and I think the water is still turned on."

"Ugh, aspirin! What good will that do? What I need is to *eat* something! I don't suppose you have a candy bar or anything in your bag, dieting all the time the way you do?"

Rebuked, Leslie said, "As it happens, I do have a roll of Life Savers; my throat gets dry driving," and scrabbled in her pocket. Emily thrust two or three of the candies into her mouth.

"This is a bad thing to do," she said, "eating sugar. It forces the body to dump insulin into your bloodstream, and then when the sugar rush wears off, you crash, *whump!* But I guess it's better than popping aspirins. I wonder if that deli we saw over on the Haight would have something like an egg and avocado sandwich?"

"Probably," Leslie said. "If you asked politely, I suppose they'd even put sprouts and yogurt and wheat germ and kelp on it for you." She had seen some of the concoctions Emily called organic sandwiches.

"I suppose you'd rather have pastrami all full of salt and nitrates and chemicals," Emily demanded crossly. "You're a doctor, and you put all that garbage in your body and laugh at me when I don't!"

"Em, I was teasing you! Have anything you want to eat, whether it's organic sandwiches or Twinkies! You want to go get it now? Or you want to lie here and rest while I go and get it for you?"

"I'm sorry, Les," Emily said, pulling herself upright on the window-seat. "I guess my blood sugar was awfully low and that's what made me so grouchy. I'll be fine. It's just that I should eat something sensible soon. But this candy ought to hold me for a couple of hours." She crunched another handful. "Let's look at your lovely house."

She shouldn't complain about Emily's sharp awareness of her body, and of suitable food for it. She had seen, this morning, with Judy Attenbury, what the lack of that kind of body awareness had done to another young girl. Of course it didn't help that Evelyn Attenbury had been conditioned to believe that you could never be too thin or too rich.

Emily said, "I love this room, but are you sure? I mean, it isn't fair for me to have the nicest room in the whole house—"

"I have one just like it on the other side of the hall, only mine is soundproof."

"Oh, hey, Les, want me to take that one? Then you won't have to listen to me practicing all the time—"

"No, no, I love listening to you," Leslie said, "and if I have the sound-proofed one it won't disturb my clients anyhow—that's going to be my office."

"Let's see that one," Emily said, crossing the foyer, and Leslie, following thoughtfully, thought that again she could hear the faint whisper of Bach. Surely it was her imagination, she knew that the woman who had lived and died here had been a musician. It could only be coincidence that Emily had fainted at the very spot where the old lady had died at her piano. . . .

She told herself angrily that she was being an idiot. More likely, old Miss Margrave had kept the soundproofed room for her piano. She followed Emily into the connected rooms she had already begun to think of as her office and study. Emily stood by the bay window, looking out into the streaming rain.

"It's coming down hard again."

"I wanted you to see it in the sunshine. The back window, there, has a view of the whole Bay Area and the Golden Gate Bridge—we're pretty high up on this street."

"Good practice for me, walking up from the streetcar," Emily said. "I'm supposed to get in training by walking up steps, and hills. My teacher says a pianist ought to be in as good training as any athlete. I was thinking of taking ballet classes again."

She wandered back across the hall into the music room.

"I really love this place. Did you say the lady who lived here was a musician? That's why the place seems so peaceful and calm, I guess. Did you ever notice that old musicians, old pianists and conductors, look like saints, or angels? So wonderfully peaceful. I remember seeing Menuhin playing on television, and thinking that he looked as if he was already in heaven. And the pictures of Toscanini. They say he was such an old bastard, screaming and yelling at the orchestra. But in his pictures, he looks as peaceful as Saint Francis!"

"You think you'll be happy here, then?"

"I already love it," Emily said, looking with delight and pride at her domain. "The piano here, and the harp over *there*. I wish I had a harpsichord. But they're fantastically expensive. You can get kits, though, and build them. Maybe someday I can do that. And no chairs. Just cushions on the floor."

Leslie thought it sounded ghastly, but Emily should have her music room the way she wanted it; she was the one who would have to live with it.

"I can just see it, no furniture at all, just enormous cushions, and the piano and harp. Mommy said I could have that old Japanese screen Dad brought back from Tokyo after the war. We can drive up to Sacramento someday and bring it back; it will fit on the top of the car. Let's go see the kitchen." Emily bounced back along the hall. "Oh, this is nice and modern, this house is so old I was afraid the plumbing would be all Victorian and horrible."

"It was remodelled by one of the people who bought the house and gave it up."

"I can't imagine anyone who lived here being able to give it up." Emily opened the kitchen door, standing sheltered by the overhang. "Oh, Les, a real garden!" A fresh smell of rain on green leaves, herbs, and plants stole into the kitchen.

Emily sniffed ecstatically with her eyes closed. "Why, there's rosemary, and mint, and sage—why, it's an herb garden, Les! Fresh herbs! Peppermint tea is good for everything, stomach upsets especially, and there's fresh basil, and cilantro, and thyme . . ."

"Are you going to Scarborough Fair, Parsley, sage, rosemary and thyme," Leslie hummed, and Emily joined in the chorus softly for a moment. Her voice was sweet and true, though untrained.

"Just think. You can cook with fresh herbs, Leslie. We could grow chives, and shallots, and fresh garlic for pesto to put on spaghetti, and there's camomile and golden seal—why, the old lady who owned this place really must have been into organic herbs! What's that door over there?"

"It used to be a garage. It was remodelled into a separate apartment, but used as a studio, I think—"

Emily flung her sweater over her head and ran; Leslie followed with the key. The rain was slacking off and the smell of rain on the garden filled the air with a sweet and pungent fragrance, evocative, haunting. For a moment, as Leslie fumbled the key into the lock, she had a sharp sense of *déjà vu;* surely she had stood before this door like this, the fragrance filling her nostrils, but suddenly the sweetness was a stench, harsh and nauseating, and she felt herself shaking with rage that filled her until she wanted to vomit. *How dared they do this to her beautiful house, her lovely dedicated place?*

"Les? Are you all right? I bet you skipped breakfast, too. Here, give me the key, and you have a couple of those peppermints," Emily said, twisting the key expertly. She stepped inside, while Leslie put the candies in her mouth.

"Yuck! There's something dead in there. Or the plumbing's on the blink," she said, sniffing in distaste.

"I can't smell anything but peppermint," Leslie said. The mess of the potter's wheel had been cleaned away, and when she stepped into the little bathroom it seemed tidy enough, but she flushed anyway.

Emily was still sniffing around. "Maybe that white cat I saw outside got in here and shitted—shat—whatever. Cat shit stinks worse than pigs, that's why they put all that deodorant stuff in kitty litter. It's awful." She stepped out into the drizzle. "We've got to do something about that, Les."

"I did see a cat when I was here. Maybe that was it." Outside the smell of jasmine was sweet and fresh again, not the cloying, nauseating stench it had been inside. "Come up and see the bedrooms. Since you have the garden view downstairs, you can have the bedroom with the Golden Gate view up here if you want it."

"I can't see anything but rain," Emily said, looking around, "and fog coming in. You can have it, if you like it. I like the garden view and all the herb smells. And my room would be over the music room, so one side of the house could be yours and the other side mine, sort of." She led the way into the second bedroom over the garden. "Just breathe that! When the window is open like this, you get all the herb smells."

Leslie stared, appalled and angered, at the wide-open casement.

"He said he'd fix that lock." She went and pulled it shut. "If those wretched boys have been climbing in here again—"

"I don't see any muddy footmarks," Emily said, coming to the window, "and they'd have to do some climbing. That trellis isn't very strong—and anyhow, they'd have to be in training to be a human fly, or a circus acrobat, to get up here. I couldn't climb it."

Nevertheless, Leslie thought, *an active ten-year-old could climb almost anything, and the latch looked strong enough that it wouldn't simply blow open. She had better get a more effective window lock.*

"You're sure you want this room? The other one has its own bath—"

"If there's only the two of us, I'll have the other bath to myself anyhow." She trailed Leslie down the stairs, still chattering about what she hoped to do with all the space at her command. She had never before let Leslie guess how cramped she felt in the ex-closet which had been all Leslie could give her for a bedroom.

"And we can put a television in the little room when we get one."

"Do you want a television set, Em?" Leslie had never felt the need of mechanical entertainment.

"Not really. But sometimes I get to feeling as if I was in another world or something. When people mention something everybody knows but me." Emily's voice was tentative. "Like when I was in high school, and all the kids were into rock. It was like they were all on one world and I was on another."

Leslie listened without speaking; her sister might share a moment of vulnerability, but would never forgive Leslie if she offered sympathy or even comment.

"They thought I was some kind of snob. I got so lonesome. That's why I'm so crazy about the Conservatory. Even old Whittington. He's nuts but he *cares* about things, even if what he cares about is a little crazy. Hey, can I go over now and get that sandwich? I'm starved. And I need some pantyhose if I can find a drugstore."

But before they got into the car, Leslie walked around outside. The high window of the garden bedroom looked inaccessible, even to an active child. The drainpipe was too far away and looked as if it would hardly support the white cat, which she saw again, slipping through the garden. Did the cat belong to a neighbor, or should she try to make friends with it?

In a small bakery restaurant, Emily got her egg and avocado sandwich, piled with a number of unidentifiable organic ingredients, which she tackled with a grin of delight and plowed hungrily through; but she let herself be persuaded to have a piece of pecan pie afterward. Leslie discovered she was hungry too—or was it only watching Emily eat?—and ordered onion soup, which turned out to be excellent. A salad loaded with raw vegetables came on the side, and Emily leaned over to snatch carrot curls and onion rings from the salad top.

"You ought to eat your onions, Les. They're good for you."

"That's supposed to be my line. I'm the grown-up and you're the kid, remember? I have a couple of clients this evening. Am I supposed to breathe onions all over them?"

"They'd probably live through it. Everybody would be better off if we didn't worry so much about smells."

"You were complaining loud enough about the smells in the temple— I mean, in the studio, the garage!" Emily shrugged that off.

"That was an *unhealthy* smell. Something dirty. Onions are a nice clean organic smell," she stated uncompromisingly.

Leslie didn't feel like getting into one of Emily's arguments about organic things. She handed her sister a bill and said, "Go get your panty-hose. Get me a pair, too, and please remember this time that I wear medium instead of tall. I'll meet you at the drugstore."

The sky was still threatening, but for the moment, at least, it was not raining. As she passed the bookstore where she had bought the poltergeist book, remembering it had given her the first useful tip she had found so far, she went inside, hoping to see the white-haired woman, who seemed to know what she was talking about.

But this time the customers were mostly young; the place was crowded, as if they had flocked in here out of the rain; long-haired, in brilliant cottons, they looked like early flower children before hard drugs and persecution had wrecked the movement. One young woman in a tie-dyed skirt, long fair hair to her waist, was leafing through a book on herbs; in her backpack a bright-eyed blond child was chewing on a raw carrot.

"Is that a good book?" Leslie asked. "I want to get a book on herbs for my sister." Emily evidently enjoyed the herb garden, and might as well be encouraged to look after it.

The girl with the baby nodded. "Yes, very good. I know the woman who wrote it; she comes in here sometimes. When I started breast-feeding Timmie, she gave me some kind of tea that helped my milk supply. No, Timmie," she admonished, as the baby tugged at her hair. "Eat your carrot, like a good girl. Do you live around here?"

"I just bought a house in the neighborhood. A few blocks up there." Leslie picked up a copy of the herb book from a stack on a table. "I was in here the other day; there was a woman behind the register—a tall woman with blue eyes—about fiftyish—"

"That's Claire Moffatt," the girl confirmed. "She only comes in on Mondays and Fridays."

"I wanted to ask her about a book——"

"Frodo can tell you most anything you want to know," said the girl, indicating the young man behind the counter. He was tall and emaciated; he wore a green smock or Russian blouse, embroidered in brilliant colors, and there was a gold earring through one earlobe. His hair was as long as the girl's, held back with a beaded headband. *Frodo.* She wondered what his parents had christened him. Probably Melvin, or something worse. Then, for an unexpected instant, it was as if a film dropped from Leslie's eyes and she saw him as the girl had seen him, an elvish creature incongruously indoors, a wild thing; she could almost see the shadow of antlers over his brow. Then the flash was gone, and he was only an outlandishly costumed youngster again. He waved to the girl.

"Hi, Rainbow! How's Timmie coming along? I heard she'd been sick."

"Just a tummy upset. She may be allergic to bean curd. The doctor said, give her apple juice and Jell-O and clear tea, no solids for a day or two, and now she's fine. She just loves camomile tea. She's drinking from a cup all the time now, but she has a bottle at bedtime, and I put camomile tea in it. She just gobbles it down!"

Emily, Leslie thought, would love this one. Frodo asked, "Are you coming to the Beltane picnic? I'm going to set up my booth and read Tarot there. Hey, guess who crawled out from under a rock the other day?"

"Who?"

"Simon Anstey. He was in here Monday."

"Simon?" The girl's mobile face wrinkled in distaste. "What's he doing in town?"

"Another operation, I think; his hand was bandaged. Or maybe he's teaching a class somewhere."

Rainbow's eyes narrowed—or was it only that Timmie was tugging at her hair again? She said in a whisper, "Colin must have been livid."

"He wasn't here. Lucky. I think he would have busted a chair over Simon's head, or something like that."

"Frodo, I never saw Colin lose his temper——"

"Well, I did. When Simon was giving out his spiel about black and white magic being a narrowminded, moralistic, racist concept."

"I heard about that. Colin said that whatever they called it, black magic was something he didn't want anything to do with. And you know, I agree with him."

"Who wouldn't?" Frodo asked, and answered his own question. "Anstey wouldn't, I suppose. You know the way he has of talking—this time, Monday, he got on to Colin, called him a sanctimonious old fraud—"

"That must have gone down well with Claire, if she was here," Rainbow said.

"Oh, it did." Frodo wrinkled his face up in a grin. "She said, 'Simon, you are a damned fool, with the emphasis on *damned*,' and turned her back on him."

Frodo was a good mimic; Leslie could see the woman Claire, hear her very voice. Yes, this was the woman who had offered her Fodor's book with the telling comment about psychological twaddle. But Frodo had lost the grin and was serious and angry.

"I wish Colin had been here to throw him out. I can't stand that guy. Seriously. He gives everyone in the pagan community a bad name. The very idea of comparing that—that bastard with somebody like, oh, you, Rainbow, or Earthlight, or Claire, or Colin, or the Carmodys, or Alison Margrave—"

"Alison collaborated with him," Rainbow said seriously. "There must be some good in Simon somewhere."

Alison Margrave? Then Leslie thought she must have mistaken the name. The young man Frodo had seen her, standing with the herb book in her hand. "Oh, excuse me, ma'am, I didn't mean to keep you waiting." She had intended to say something about having bought a house belonging to a Miss Margrave and ask if it was the same one. But Frodo's tone put her firmly back in the older generation. "That'll be seven-fifty. Can I show you something else, ma'am?"

"No, thanks." If the woman Claire had been there, she might have asked her about poltergeists. Or would poltergeists come under their definition of Black Magic? She smiled a farewell at Rainbow, who said politely that she hoped Leslie liked living in the neighborhood and that her sister would enjoy the book on herbs, while Timmie waved a cherubic bye-bye over Rainbow's shoulder. She left, feeling suddenly old, as if she had moved on in Time and grown old while these young people had remained in the sixties.

But no, that wasn't fair. The sixties were a memory to her, but these young people were finding their own version of that idealistic time.

She could come back sometime when Claire was here and explore at her leisure.

But by that time, maybe, I won't have to be worrying about poltergeists.

When she dropped her sister back at the Conservatory, Emily hesitated before getting out of the car.

"Going straight back to Berkeley?"

"Not yet. I bought a tape measure, and I'm going back to the house and measure the windows—I need to know if the curtains and shades we have will fit, or if we'll need new ones. You want to meet me down there and ride back? I have to start back by four at the latest—" Eileen Grantson would be at her house at five. Emily shook her head.

"Remember, I'm ushering. I'll probably be late."

Leslie hated making noises like a mother hen; Emily was almost a grown woman. But she admitted, if only to herself, that she would be glad when they were on this side of the Bay. She hated to have Emily make the long commute alone, especially at night. She headed back to the house. The rain had started again, a bleak dreary drizzle. A delivery truck was parked on her street, blocking the entrance to her driveway . . . how quickly she had become possessive, *her* house, *her* driveway! She parked across the street and walked toward the house with the bay windows, just as a man came down the walk, a tall, broad-shouldered man with greying hair. At first glance Leslie thought it was the real estate agent and ran to catch him before he drove away. But the man was a perfect stranger; she knew at once she had never seen him before. She would have remembered that profile, the aquiline features, heavy grey eyebrows, the way his arm angled away from his body as—no, it was actually in a sling. There was a long scar down the side of his face, running into his neck, and a patch over one eye. What had he been doing on her sidewalk and in her driveway? He had come from inside the garden, surely. What had he been doing there? Leslie hesitated then; he was a large and powerful man, and there was something menacing about him. By the time Leslie convinced herself the man was a harmless meter reader or something of the sort, he had climbed into a long grey car at the curb. As he was turning the corner, the car idling for a moment against cross traffic, he turned, and Leslie could feel his gaze on her; for a moment they stared at one another. The eye contact could not have lasted fifteen seconds, if that, then the car slid away and Leslie drew a long breath and went around the house, into the garden. There were trampled patches on the grass; and looking up at the window of the garden-facing bedroom which would be Emily's, she could see the casement standing wide.

I feel like Mama Bear, she thought. *Somebody has been sitting in my chair. Eating my porridge.* She stared at the slender lattice covered with climbing roses. There was no way a man of average size could climb that lattice, even with the aid of the drainpipe. Not even an acrobat. And the intruder had been six feet or over. She thrust her key into the kitchen door and ran upstairs. Her heart was pounding. The door had been locked, but there were damp footprints on the rug and a whiff of some faint scent—incense? Some burning herb? Emily's window gaped wide and she pulled it shut and locked it again. *Somebody, said Mama Bear, has been sleeping in my bed.*

She never knew what prompted her, after latching the window, to run downstairs, through the garden, out to the garage. She stepped inside; it was dark and the dank stench hit her like a blow. Then for an instant, as she blinked, she saw the man she had just seen getting into the grey car, tall, eye-patch, the strong eagle-nosed profile. He was standing in the center of the room, his hands raised as if in invocation. Leslie blinked again, crying out, "Who are you? How did you get in here?" Before she had finished, the figure melted away.

At the back of the studio, two panes in the window were smashed. Not as if anyone had used them in climbing out—they were too small and too high for that—but as if someone, in rage or sheer need to destroy, had put his fist through them. She ran mentally over her picture of the intruder, but there was no sign of blood or cuts on hands or face, only the white seam of a long-healed scar.

Leslie had lost all impetus to measure for curtains. She would call the real estate agent and tell him that someone had a key to the house and that she had actually seen someone leaving; she would insist that all the locks be changed before she moved in.

She locked the studio securely and went to her car.

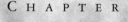

CHAPTER

Five

EILEEN WAS ALMOST TEN minutes late, and when she did come in she came sullenly, turtling her head down inside a cowl-necked sweater, sidling into a chair and snuffling.

"Have you a cold, Eileen?"

Snuffle. "I guess so."

"There is a box of tissues right there."

Eileen took a handful in silence and blew her nose.

Silence. Snuffle. Leslie usually allowed a client, especially a teenage client, to choose what she wanted to talk about, but finally she said firmly, "Have you been having any more trouble with broken objects?"

I need to know whether she is the poltergeist—or I am!

"Yeah," Eileen said at last, "I broke about half a set of dishes the other night. My *father*—" she made it sound of venom, "said he was sick of it and he was going to take it out of my allowance, so he only gave me three dollars for the week, three lousy bucks, and when I told him that wouldn't even buy my lunch he said to take sandwiches from home, so I made a roast beef sandwich and old lady Mattison—that's that shitty housekeeper who comes in—she yelled at me because she wanted to have the leftovers for supper. So I fixed them all—" Her eyes glinted with malice. "I called my mother three times long distance. So he grabbed the phone and yelled at my Mom that she could pay for my calls, and I wanted to talk to her again but he hung up!"

She stared, red-nosed, out of her high collar. The father, Leslie thought, was playing into his daughter's hands, allowing her to manipulate the household, then handing out punishments when it was too late.

"You were very angry at him when he did that?"

"Yeah. I got a right to call my own mother. It isn't as if we were going broke, for Godsake! I ate up the roast beef and old Matty said I'd have to take peanut butter tomorrow. So the jar fell off the counter and smashed all over the floor, and the old creep yelled at me to clean it up, and I said, That's what my Daddy's paying you for, and I walked out of the kitchen. He got mad at that too and said if I got her mad enough to quit I could do the housework myself. He can't make me do that, can he? There are laws, like, about child labor, aren't there?"

"I don't think that applies to housework," Leslie said tactfully. "It might not be a good idea to push him far enough to find out. Did you knock over the peanut butter on purpose so you wouldn't have to take sandwiches?"

Eileen looked scared, but still defiant. "She said I did. She said she saw me knock it over, only I didn't." Eileen looked fearfully at Leslie. "If I was going to do anything like that, I'd have cracked her over her big fat head with it, the way she was hollering at me, but I wasn't within two *feet* of it. Like last time. Like—" She twisted her body fearfully in the chair to stare at the ashtray. "Remember?"

Leslie nodded. "Yes, I remember, I saw it. It really happened, Eileen."

Eileen's composure broke. "What makes it happen? It *did* happen, and my father didn't believe me. The dishes, I mean. If I was going to break something on purpose it wouldn't be my Mom's dishes. I mean, I *love* them. She had them when I was just a little girl. They're like willow ware, only they're this sort of deep rose pink." She began to cry. "I wanted to throw something, only not Mom's dishes. I thought, if she came back they'd be there for her." She was bawling loudly. "Only they smashed, right in the sink, one after another, they slid right down in the sink and smashed—"

Her voice stopped, smothered in phlegmy sobs. She grabbed another handful of tissues and blew her nose again and again, weeping. "And now I suppose you won't believe me either!"

"I believe you," Leslie said quietly. "One part of you wanted to hear something smash and break up your mother's dishes. You are very angry with your mother for leaving you, aren't you?"

Eileen raised her head and looked fearfully at Leslie.

"Yeah. Sometimes, I think if she came back I'd—I'd spit on her and say *I don't need you,* and sometimes—"

"And the other part of you was being grown-up and responsible and telling you not to take it out on your mother's dishes. Only the baby part of you was mad at your mother too, and she wasn't here. So even when the grown-up part of you was telling yourself to stop it, the baby part of you kept on smashing things. Why don't you smash your father's things, if it's your father that you're mad at?"

"I don't do it on purpose," Eileen shouted. "I thought you believed me!"

"I believe you," Leslie said. "I didn't say you threw them—"

"I didn't! I got scared and wanted them to stop and I stood there and screamed, *Stop it, stop it,* and they kept right on smashing—" Her face was white around the reddened nose.

"I know you didn't touch them. But some part of your mind wanted to smash them. Like the ashtray," Leslie said quietly. "I know you didn't touch that. But something in you threw it. Even when you were scared and horrified at what was happening."

Eileen nodded, shakily. "Yeah. Like I stood back and watched myself throw them. What causes it, Dr. Barnes? What makes it happen?"

"Even the greatest psychiatrists in the world don't really know why it happens. Maybe between us we can find out why it happens to you, though. It happens to a lot of people, usually girls about your age. It's called a *poltergeist. . . .*"

"There was a movie about that. I saw it," Eileen interrupted, and her face was white. "Do the—the other things happen? Do you think our house is somewhere old ghosts are buried or something, and I could get—get trapped? It was real scary, really awful!"

Firmly, Leslie shook her head. "Whoever made that film just liked the name *Poltergeist;* he threw all kinds of psychic phenomena in one big mess, and shoved them all in the movie. A poltergeist isn't like that at all. The word means *noisy ghost,* but it isn't a ghost at all, they do know that much, it's just something your mind—people's minds do."

"It really happens?" Eileen was crying again. "I was so scared. I thought I was going crazy or people were all lying about me. Or everybody else was going crazy saying I did all this stuff when I *knew* I hadn't, and then I started to wonder if I did it after all and I was crazy and didn't know it. It really happens? To people who aren't crazy and don't— don't—" She stopped fearfully and peered sideways at Leslie.

"Go ahead," Leslie encouraged.

"Who aren't, I mean, people who aren't all screwed up and don't have to see a shrink all the time to be straightened out?"

The words lay in the silence between them, and Leslie thought, *If that's what the kid thinks, no wonder she's so hostile!* Yet she knew it was the unstated message between all parents and all counselors: *"Here is this son or daughter of mine who is not behaving the way I want her to. Take her and make her over into the kind of son or daughter I want her to be!"*

It would do Eileen no good to rush into a defense of her profession, its strengths and shortcomings.

"One of the things we do know about poltergeists is that almost everyone associated with them has some problem in their life that they can't solve. If they could handle their problems any other way, their unconscious minds—what I called *the baby part of you*—would *do* something about their problem. But they are usually in what they call a double bind, where anything they do is going to be wrong. Like you; you are very angry at your mother for leaving you, and at your father, only you can't leave them and be on your own because you're only a little girl and you still need parents. People in this kind of double bind can't handle their resentments any other way, and so they create a poltergeist to do it for them."

"You're saying I did it myself? Only I wanted it to stop! I—I *screamed* at it to stop—" She was quiet, thinking. "Only maybe I sort of wanted to scare them. To fix them."

Leslie was quiet, encouraging. She had been afraid that she had thrown it all at Eileen too quickly.

"Like in the orchestra. Those violin strings. I was so mad at those kids. And at the teacher. Only I couldn't tell him or he'd throw me out of the

orchestra. And I need to stay in orchestra because it's too late in the semester to drop a class without getting an F for the whole semester. I was
glad when the strings kept breaking and they could all *see* I didn't do it."

And then she was scared again. "But now it happens when I'm not
really mad, and keeps on happening! How can I stop it?"

*Who am I to talk? If I'd had the guts to tell Joel off, or even to throw the
damn glass of wine in his face, I probably wouldn't have had to resort to poltergeist
activity either!*

She said, "Why don't you take your mind back, Eileen, to exactly how
you felt when it was happening. It seems to me you were in a classic double
bind; whichever way you went, you had gotten yourself, or someone around
you had gotten you, into a situation where whatever you did was going to
be wrong . . ."

Eileen was saying, snuffling, "I see what you mean. Like whatever
I did, somebody was going to be mad at me, and if I sat there and
didn't do nothing, then I was going to be mad too, because I was just
letting them dump all over me, and there was nothing I could do that
would be right—"

"And you felt you couldn't face having them get angry with you any
more—"

"Because last time everybody got mad at me, my Mom went away.
And my father got mad because he was stuck with me, and he really wanted
me to go off with her—"

Leslie listened as Eileen rehearsed the overfamiliar situation yet again.
Inwardly she could blame neither, the freedom-demanding mother nor the
father who, after years of emotional escape from his home, hiding in his
work, was suddenly landed with the total responsibility for a difficult and
emotionally starved daughter. There should have been emotional alternatives for all three of them, but in this society, committed to the nuclear
family as the ultimate structure, it was inevitable that the mother should
leave and remarry, the father should stay and work, and the daughter
should be caught between them.

"I love my Daddy. But he wishes I was out in Texas with Mom."

"Why do you think that, Eileen?"

"Well, he yells all the time." She paused. "But anyhow he's stuck with
me, isn't he, when he doesn't want me at all? And he's paying the bills
for my school and violin lessons and everything. I guess maybe it's hard
on him."

With that moment of detachment, Leslie had to be content. Perhaps Eileen's insight would grow, or perhaps it would be sunk again in Eileen's enormous self-pity; the knowledge that her father, whether he loved her or not, was at least doing his duty by her, while the mother, who professed to love her, had for all practical purposes abandoned her daughter. Perhaps Eileen would understand her father's resentments and her own, and perhaps not, but she had had a glimmering of the truth. Eileen had reverted to her fright at the snapping of violin strings, the crashing of dishes and launched into another tirade of self-pitying defensiveness. Leslie listened quietly. Eileen had had a tiny moment of insight, and perhaps that was enough for one day. All Leslie could do for her now was to listen to them—and it was a crime to live in a society where people had to pay somebody to listen to their troubles—but at least she listened conscientiously. At the end of the hour she gave a brief suggestion.

"Next time anything like this happens, try to control it. Try to *direct* it and make it happen the way you want it to. It's yours; you ought to be able to tell it what to do, instead of letting it scare you."

Eileen only looked at her glumly and said, "See you on Tuesday."

She thought again what a crime it was to live in a society where people had to pay someone to listen to their troubles, while she was listening to her only other client that evening. Leonard Hay had spent four months in her office, alternately insisting that he was proud to be a homosexual, and that he felt guilty about abandoning the woman whom he had married, for all the wrong reasons, in a last-ditch attempt to prove his manhood and to have someone to care about him.

She listened to his repetitive complaints, thinking that there was very little the art of counseling could do for him; she could lend a sympathetic ear, of course, but part of his trouble was the social conditioning which meant that a man in his situation couldn't find an old school buddy or a sympathetic relative to take serious interest in his plight without fearing to be tarred by the stigma of being themselves homosexual.

"What I hear you saying is that you simply can't come to a decision," she said, as she had said at least every other session.

"That's it, Leslie. That's exactly it. Anything I do is going to be wrong."

"And if you don't do anything, that's going to be wrong too," she said, knowing he was not ready to hear that yet. If he avoided a decision, at least there would be nothing for which anyone could blame him. And the inability to accept responsibility for his own decisions was what had brought him into her office in the first place; about the most she could do for him would be to help him realize that he must take responsibility for his own indecision as well.

"What would happen if you made a wrong decision?" she asked him, only to start another tirade about how terrified he was that what he would do would be wrong, that anything he did would be wrong, that what he did was always wrong and at least if he did nothing, he was doing no harm; that a wrong decision would wreck his life. He was already wrecking his life, she thought, and heartily cursed the childhood training which had taught him never to take any risks. But until he could realize that he was creating his own chaos, she could never tell him.

And even if he did realize it, part of his trouble would always be the society which tried to demand that everyone force himself into a neat little pigeonhole, manly versus weak, heterosexual as opposed to homosexual, right against wrong. She could help her clients make their own decisions, but never reform the society which insisted that they must live inside these pigeonholes.

As she let Leonard out and locked the door behind him, she felt that perhaps her double bind with Joel was only symbolic of the double bind she was in with her profession.

Why can't I really do something for these people except listen to them? She went into the kitchen to fix herself some supper. As she sat at the table, nibbling scrambled eggs and sliced tomatoes, she went back gloomily to assessing the dead end of her profession.

Well, she was giving them a sympathetic ear, without nagging, criticizing, or pressuring them to make decisions. She was keeping them off the couches of Freudians who would keep them exploring infantile sexual repressions for five to fifteen years without ever examining the symptoms that had driven them to a counselor in the first place. The phone rang, but when she picked it up there was no one on the other end. Wrong number? Almost immediately it rang again; this time there was the heavy, almost inhuman sound of breathing. She slammed it down, and when it rang again this time she let it ring, reluctant to touch it again. After twelve rings there was quiet.

But when it rang again at a quarter to twelve she sighed and picked up the receiver. She couldn't refuse to answer a phone at night when Emily was out.

"You'll be sorry, you bitch," said the thick voice on the other end of the line, and Leslie stood with the handset still in her hand, hearing the dial tone.

What in the world was that all about?

Joel? It was not unlike his voice, but she simply could not believe he would do this. Not even when he was drunk. She was sad that he hadn't called, but if he felt that way, better to find it out now than later, or even after marriage.

A prank. Some hostile youth with a hate for women. She glared at the phone, daring it to ring again, and went to make herself a final cup of tea before bedtime.

It rang again shortly after midnight, and she picked it up, braced for further abuse, but sighed with relief when it was Emily's voice.

"Les? The concert ran late; didn't want you to worry. I'm at the Civic Center BART station and I'll be there in about half an hour."

"Okay, honey, thanks for calling." She left the kettle on *warm,* one of Emily's herb tea bags on a saucer, and a handful of cookies on a plate, and went up to bed. As she was falling asleep she heard steps on the stairs.

"Emily?"

No answer. Suddenly alert, she got up, hurried to her bedroom door. No one on the stairs, certainly. Had she heard the sound outside in the quiet street, someone walking past? *Oh, hell, am I turning into the typical old maid, looking under the bed for imaginary burglars? I heard somebody passing in the street and imagined it was on the stairs.* Then she noticed that one of the "Take me upstairs/Take me downstairs" baskets, which she and Emily kept for items which had to go up or down, had overturned. Spare shoes, books, odd stockings, clothes or dishes stashed for safekeeping until they could be returned to kitchen, hallway or laundry room, were scattered up and down the top five or six steps.

Who upset that basket? She dismissed the possibility that she had done it herself when she came upstairs—if she had kicked over a basket loaded with dishes, books or shoes, she would have noticed doing it. Had someone actually come up the stairs, hidden quickly in the bathroom or in Emily's bedroom? She checked the stairs, the door of the linen closet—things like this *did* happen. But surely she had locked the deadbolt when she came up—she picked up the scattered junk thoughtfully, carried the basket down and set it in the hall, then checked the door. Yes, it was double-locked, the deadbolt set from inside. She went out to the back to check the kitchen door. It, too, was carefully locked and bolted.

Yet the basket *had* been overturned, after she heard steps. Inclined to laugh at herself, nevertheless she found the good, heavy rolling pin she had brought from the Sacramento house and went quietly upstairs, determined to check every room. Armed with the hefty implement, she could handle any intruder unless he happened to have a gun and was trigger-happy. She would not have a gun in the house herself— Most guns, she knew all too well, were eventually used not against burglars or intruders, but against family members, by mistake or in a family quarrel.

There was no one on the stairs. No one in the hall. Leslie could hear the sound of her own breathing on the landing. She had carried the basket up again, and set it down on the landing; she opened the bathroom door carefully, and peered inside, snapped on the light. Nothing out of place except Emily's sopping towel from this morning. That should have been taken down to the dryer. She flung it into the basket at the stairhead and went into Emily's tiny room.

There was nothing out of place; remembering the disaster area of her own teenage room, Leslie thought that at least the form Emily's rebellion took was easier to live with than its opposite. Her breath caught; there was a heavy thumping on the stairs—*steps! Footsteps!* Clutching the rolling pin, she cried out.

"Emily!"

Silence.

Her knuckles were white, felt strained on the rolling pin. She could hear her own breathing again, the only sound now in the entire house. The basket which she had set at the landing was overturned, the towel halfway down the staircase.

She remembered a glass of wine, flying up into Joel's startled face. Her poltergeist again? It must have been. She retrieved the basket and the wet towel.

Steps again. Footsteps. Inside the house or outside? She held her breath as the doorknob turned.

"Emily?" Her voice sounded ridiculously small from the landing.

"Who do you think it would be at this hour? Prince Charming?" Emily said, carefully locking the door behind her. "What are you doing up, Leslie? Waiting up for me?" She looked tired and cross, and even before she turned, she slipped her high-heeled pumps off her feet and threw them into the basket at the foot of the stairs. "Ouch! My feet are really killing me. Why they have to require high-heeled shoes for ushering, I'll never know. It's discrimination against women—the men would strike if they made them do ushering in anything like that!"

"Well, maybe the women ought to get together," Leslie said, coming down. Emily stared at the rolling pin in her hand.

"Les, what's the matter?"

"Nothing; I thought I heard footsteps in the house; must have been somebody going by on the street." Leslie, turning so Emily would not see her white face, went to put the rolling pin in the kitchen. Emily trailed after her.

"That's not like you, Leslie. Your nerves are really shot, aren't they? You ought to take valerian capsules. Natural tranquilizer—can't possibly hurt you. I've got some."

Leslie shook her head. "No, thanks. I'm all right now."

"Oh, good, the water's hot." Emily poured it over her tea bag and grabbed up a cookie to munch. "Well, let me make you a cup of camomile tea anyhow. It's very good and soothing." She did not wait for Leslie to answer but fetched a second tea bag from a jar on the shelf and poured water into a second cup. She handed it to Leslie. A sweet, haylike fragrance stole out from the teacup. It did indeed smell soothing. Leslie sipped and found it surprisingly good.

"Camomile, you said?" Rainbow, in the bookstore, had given it to her baby. "It's good. Thanks, Em."

"What happened, anyhow?"

Leslie told her about the overturned baskets, the sound of steps on the stairs.

"Must have been somebody going by on the street. The acoustics here, or something."

"It's never happened before," Leslie protested. "I could almost feel the stairs vibrate. And the overturned baskets?"

Emily shrugged. "I don't know, maybe we had a little teeny earthquake. This *is* California, after all. Not enough to rattle windows, but if the basket was close enough to the edge of the stairs, any little thing might knock it over." She rinsed the cup and set it in the dishwasher, yawning. "All okay now? Not nervous any more?"

Leslie rose to put her own cup in the sink, feeling that she had been foolish. They were leaving the kitchen when the telephone rang, shrilling imperiously through the silent house.

"At this hour? God, maybe it's Mommy!" Emily raced back into the kitchen, almost knocking Leslie off her feet. She grabbed up the receiver.

"Hello? Hello? Damn you, is anybody *there?*" She slammed it down, her face white.

"Some *creep!* Les, we ought to have an unlisted number! I was sure Mommy had had a heart attack or something—" She swallowed hard; Leslie came and put a hand on her shoulder.

"I can't get an unlisted number, Em; people have to be able to reach me. I could report it to the telephone company, but there isn't much they can do. It's not even as if he'd made any threats or said anything obscene." And then she remembered, the cold voice, muttering.

You'll be sorry, you bitch. There was no need to frighten Emily further. Someone with a real or fancied grudge, against her or against the world. Probably more a victim than a victimizer, one of the hundreds of thousands of men so brutalized by society that no reasonable person could hold him responsible; but she wished, whoever he was, that he would take his grudge out on whoever was *really* to blame.

She reminded herself that there was no evidence that most crank callers ever committed any acts more violent than this; they were fearful people, afraid of confrontations.

And who was she, after her own poltergeist activity, to judge others for their unconscious aggressions? "Forget it, Em. No harm done. Let's get up to bed."

Emily turned out the kitchen light and followed. They were halfway up the stairs when the doorbell, shockingly loud in the quiet house, buzzed its summons.

At this hour it could only be something important. The police. Accident . . . She ran down the stairs, peering out through the glass pane. There was nobody on the porch. Emily hurried down after her.

"Who is it, Les?"

"Doesn't seem to be anybody there."

"Well, somebody had to ring it," Emily protested. "Unless your stupid poltergeists ring doorbells. Do they?"

A mixture of fear and anger seemed to claw, like an icy hand, at Leslie's heart. *Poltergeist. Am I doing this to myself, to Emily?* She said, "More like some idiot kids playing practical jokes. Unfunny ones." She turned out the light and went upstairs. Emily trailed her close, looking uncharacteristically shaken.

"Leslie, suppose there is really someone out there? I mean, you hear about it in big cities. They ring your doorbell and hide and when you come out to see if anybody's there, they jump you. Muggers, rapists . . ."

"Well, since I didn't open the door, they'd have a hard time mugging or raping us," Leslie said gently. "And I don't intend to open the door for anybody unless I recognize him. Don't worry, Emily. Some crank—"

"How can I help worrying? Do you know how white you were, and that big rolling pin in your hand? And then a crank caller, *and* the doorbell and nobody there. If somebody's doing this, *why?* And *who?*"

Leslie shook her head. "I don't think so—"

But she wondered. *Campaign of terror? Or her own unconscious hostilities, concentrated into a poltergeist? Had I better see someone about it? And who could I see? Most therapists would laugh their heads off—or assume that I was paranoid and wholly out of touch with reality.*

The telephone rang again. Emily snarled out something obscene and reached for it; put it down with a sigh of resignation.

"*Him* again," she said. "Creep. I'm going to leave it off the hook, Leslie; we've got to get some sleep."

Knowing it was the coward's way out, Leslie nodded agreement. The sound of that cold, muttering *bitch* still iced her blood. But at least it was proof that she was not wholly paranoid. Emily had heard the man too. She was not doing it all to herself. She went into her room, ignoring the buzz of sound from the telephone, the loud recorded voice, *Please replace your telephone receiver,* and the silence that followed. At least this way she would not be awakened several times during the night.

THE ROOM WAS DARK, WITH grey wisps of fog. Leslie lay in the darkness, feeling the fog on her face. There was a pale eerie light shining through the room, and she could make out, dimly, the outlines of paintings on the walls. They had surely not been there when they moved into the house; they were hardly more than crude and obscene graffiti; a scrawled sketch of a woman, legs spread, vulva gaping a filthy crimson; a heart pierced by many swords; bewildered, Leslie turned her eyes from them. She felt too sick and sluggish to move. The fog was greenish, twisting in slow coils.

She was paralyzed. The fog licked at her throat. She could not move . . . she was *tied!* She tried to struggle, to cry out, but the cords cut into her flesh, pain biting at her wrists and ankles, a gag drawing back her dry mouth, and then some monstrous faceless *darkness* was hovering over her, closer and closer, only blank where features should be, and she felt herself struggle, fighting hopelessly . . . pain . . .

And then, abruptly, she was awake. She heard the telephone in her study jangling, the other line, her answering service: but she was safe in her own bedroom and her own bed, and knew that it had been a nightmare. In her office the telephone rang again, and she knew she should run down and get it; it might mean some patient in desperate trouble, a suicide attempt, even a nightmare such as her own. Leslie still felt the sick nausea that swept through her when that dark *thing* was hovering over her. She ran down the stairs, not bothering with slippers or robe, but the phone was now silent. In the dark she dialled the familiar number.

"This is Leslie Barnes. Did you ring me just now?"

And the surprised, bored voice on the other end of the line.

"Why, no, Dr. Barnes. There haven't been any calls for you."

Of course not. Would this night of terror never end? Glancing at the clock, Leslie saw that it was only four-thirty; but it was unlikely that she would be able to sleep again. She turned on the light, stole silently up for her robe and slippers, found a comfortable chair in her office and sat till dawn reading the dryest professional journal she could find.

CHAPTER

Six

LESLIE SIGNED THE CHECK; the agent looked at it, put it away in a folder, and then, rising, shook her hand.

"I think you've got a nice house there. The escrow and title search and all that will be nothing but a formality. Strictly speaking, legally, you'll have three days to change your mind—the state law requires that for any sale of real estate. But there's no reason now that you can't move right in. By the end of this week, just check with me, by telephone if you want to, just to be sure no legal glitch has developed, then you can move in."

Leslie nodded. The sooner she moved, the better; the last three nights had been made hideous by continual ringing of telephone and doorbell. Finally, at Emily's insistence, she reported it to a politely skeptical police officer, who had written it down and instructed her to try and keep the calling party on the line so the call could be traced. *But how can you keep a calling party on the line when there is never anybody there?* Another skeptic from the telephone company had checked out every one of her telephone extensions and reported them in good order, saying that perhaps the dampness of the long rainy season had caused some short or failure in the equipment relays. About which, of course, nothing could be done. She had even considered having the telephone taken out.

But that wouldn't stop the doorbell. Anyhow, what could I say to my patients? She had tried to program herself to ignore the jangling bell, but she knew she had reached a point where she jumped every time it rang.

And what if I am doing it to myself? What if some force—poltergeist?—in my own mind is causing the noise?

She had gone to the public library in Berkeley, and when that produced nothing of interest about poltergeists or psychic phenomena, to the University library on the Berkeley campus. There she had pored dutifully through the works of Nandor Fodor and J. B. Rhine, the former providing only elaborations about what she had begun to think of as "psychoanalytical twaddle." The latter provided many statistics about the calling of cards imprinted with simple symbols, which, although fascinating and convincing evidence of either telepathy or extrasensory perception, gave no real light on how to handle either Eileen Grantson's poltergeist or her own. Emily, as jangled as herself by the incessant noise of doorbell and telephone, still insisted that the cause had to be faulty electrical equipment.

Still Leslie compelled herself to answer it—because at least a third of the time it was a patient or a business call; once, when Emily came in and found her on the phone, she set it down with a sigh and said fervently, "I never thought I would be relieved when a phone call turned out to be someone trying to sell me insulation!"

However, when Eileen Grantson came in, on the afternoon of the day when she had signed the check for the new house, she found Eileen, for once, smiling and excited; at a skating rink she had skated with some relatively high-status boy from her high school orchestra. "He plays string bass. He doesn't really play any better than I do, but his father's the basketball coach and all the girls are just crazy about him. Those jerky girls were all watching us, they just *died* when he came up and skated with me again," she informed Leslie gleefully. For the first session in four weeks now, Eileen had not a word to say about the noisy intrusions in her life of the poltergeist phenomenon. It seemed that her new friend, whom she named only as Scotty, had done more for Eileen than she could herself.

Most high school problems come down to peer status anyhow, no matter what any psychologist or educator says; the kids who have it get along, and those who don't, don't, Leslie thought, and, not for the first or the fiftieth time, wondered if she had chosen the wrong profession. Maybe a successful psychologist was one who could help people make the right compromises for that kind of peer status.

And this kind of thought was hardly helpful, she thought, just when she had just put the only small capital she was ever likely to own into the new house. Emily's share had already been put into a trust fund to complete her expensive conservatory education with a small amount left to give her a shot at a concert career, or to cushion the shock of readaptation if she found out that the concert career wasn't going to materialize.

And sooner or later, Mom's money is going to run out, and we're going to need to find a place to move her into. Or bring her down here to live. So far, Dad's pension keeps her all right. But if she gets sick or senile, we're all in big trouble. So there was no real option to change her profession at this late date. It was the contemporary trap for young people, she thought: you trained, at great expense and time, for a profession into which you went, all bright-eyed and bushytailed and eager to do good in a world where good was not greatly valued—and after four or five years, you found out that it was like trying to empty Lake Shasta reservoir with a bucket. There was so much misery in the world, and what little good she *could* do was limited to the people who could pay for it.

Maybe she should have married Joel; she was beginning to sound like what he had said in the first place, that she was spending her life with losers and whiners. . . .

But she *was* doing some good, she reassured herself firmly, as she smiled at Eileen.

"You know that in two weeks I'm moving over to my new office in San Francisco. Will you be able to manage getting there?"

"Sure," Eileen said. "Daddy said I could ride over on BART and take the Haight Street bus up to your office."

"Actually there are three buses that go about two blocks away," Leslie said. "I'm having a card printed up for all my clients—I'll give you one next time." She let Eileen out, and stood on the steps watching her.

But this is serious. If I am having doubts about the only profession I was trained for, what then? I can't afford to throw it up and take something else because I've lost faith in my ability to do any good with this one. The telephone rang;

she picked it up, hoping against hope that it would be a real call, or at worst, silence. Anything was better than that dull heavy breathing, or the muttering words of her heckler.

Silence. Nerve-jangling silence; because of what was perhaps behind it, her own imagination peopled the silence with the lurid newspaper accounts of mass murderers. No, she thought, the silence is peopled only with my own imagination.

"Damp weather," Emily said, coming into the hall behind her. "Maybe the electrical system's working better in San Francisco and the phones won't be doing this all the time. Les, guess what?"

"I don't know; what?"

"I'm going to audition in three days for an appearance with the San Francisco orchestra. Rachmaninoff's Second Piano Concerto—"

"Do I know that one?"

Emily hummed a phrase, which Leslie instantly recognized. "Isn't that Tschaikowsky?"

"Not unless the people who print the score have made a mistake," Emily said, "but it's Rachmaninoff, all right. I had to listen to a lecture from old Aunty Whitty when they gave out the announcement this morning. He thinks they should have done a Mozart concerto, I guess. Or better still, something by Scarlatti." "I don't care. I *like* Romantic music, and I went right out and bought the score—the piano part, that is. I'm glad you like it; you're going to hear me practicing it a lot in the next couple of days. Three days, my God. I've *played* it but I've never *studied* it—"

Leslie asked soberly, "Are there going to be a lot of students auditioning?"

"Eight or ten, I guess. And one of the judges is going to be Simon Anstey, that pianist who was brilliant but he lost two or three of his fingers in an accident. And I heard a rumor that he doesn't like woman pianists. So the competition's going to be really tough." She drifted into the music room.

Leslie followed her and said, "I saw the real estate people today. We can move in anytime. I already gave notice here at the end of this month, but how about next week?"

"Huh?" Emily's eyes were already buried in a score, and when Leslie repeated herself, she said vaguely, "Well, don't have the piano picked up till after the audition, will you?" and sat down at the keyboard. Leslie felt that Emily had already gone into that magical world where she could cut off all concerns and worries.

I wish I could get away from things that way. Then Leslie reminded herself to be fair; Emily had other problems, maybe worse ones; auditions, the tremendous competitive world of pianists, and judges who were prejudiced against women. She stood for a moment in the doorway, listening to Emily playing the spacious opening bars of the adagio.

There was an old popular song—Mom said it dated back to the forties—to that melody. "Full Moon and Empty Arms." Maybe that's my trouble. A new man did wonders for Eileen. Maybe I ought to call Joel. She stood for a moment, listening to the haunting melancholy of the sound, until the telephone rang again.

"Is it for me?" Emily called.

Leslie slammed the reciever down.

"No," she called. "Just your friendly neighborhood poltergeist!"

"That's not funny any more," Emily said.

"Damn right it isn't," Leslie said, but Rachmaninoff was already filling the house again; Emily had lost interest.

The telephone rang six more times, shredding Leslie's nerves raw, before she finally gave in and took it off the hook. There was never anyone on the line, and a fragment of sanity told her that at least this was better than the menacing presence of the breather on the other end. At least this way she could blame it on the wet weather or the elusive short in the line. She applied herself grimly to finishing the packing in her study, and when that was done, she went into the kitchen and started wrapping glass casseroles in newspaper. Three times the doorbell jangled, sending her hurrying through the hall to open the door on an empty, rain-slashed porch.

After the fourth summons by a nonexistent ringer, finding herself with a screwdriver in her hand (she had been unscrewing her spice rack from the kitchen wall), she grimly unwired the doorbell, leaving a loose wire dangling, and lettered a card with a felt-tip marker:

PLEASE KNOCK.
DOORBELL OUT OF ORDER.

That'll fix it, whether short or poltergeist, she thought, affixing the card to the door with masking tape, and went back to the kitchen.

The telephone rang again. She would have sworn she had taken it off the hook. There was no one on the line, and she sighed as she replaced the kitchen extension—she would go and take off the one in her office, so she wouldn't have to listen to the maddening buzz here in the kitchen. The sound of the opening chords of the Rachmaninoff filled the house as Leslie got out butter, sourdough bread, cups and plates, and started tearing lettuce for salad. Tonight she would pack the dishes and get paper plates and cups to use until they were settled in the new house.

The phone rang again. She would have taken oath in court that she had left it off the hook. She let it ring. But it went on and on, and then her nerves snapped as she picked it up.

"Why are you doing this to me?" she shrieked into the receiver.

"I must say that's one hell of a way to answer a telephone," said a laughing, rebuking, *familiar* voice, and Leslie let out a long-held breath.

"Joel. Oh, God, I'm sorry. I've been getting calls from a crank, and the phone has been ringing every five minutes for an hour, and I'm all on edge."

"Poor love, it sounds as if you've been having a rough time," Joel said. The piano had gone into the melancholy tune of the adagio again. *Full moon and empty arms,* it sang in the background, as Joel went on. "I've missed you so damn much, I never figured I could miss anybody so much, and our argument was pretty dumb when you come to think of it. Will you forgive me, and have dinner with me tonight?"

"Forgive you? I acted pretty badly myself," she heard herself say, her ears stinging with heat at the thought of red wine dripping off his face. "But dinner—I don't know, Joel, I have our dinner all ready, and Emily's practicing—and I'm busy packing."

"You're busy—*what?*"

"Packing. We're moving a week from tomorrow."

There was a momentary silence on the other end of the line.

"Moving?" he said at last, "and you were going to go without calling me?"

She said, reluctant, "I think I would have called you." She was not sure. Something in her had wondered: losing Joel, was it only clearing the decks before a fresh start in the new house? He sounded pained.

"You only *think* you would?"

"I'm a stubborn bitch," she said, contrite, "but I'm glad you called. Is that good enough?"

"Where are you moving?"

"San Francisco. I bought a house over in what used to be the Haight-Ashbury district."

"So you bought the house." Disapproval was still a ghost in his voice. But finally he said, "Well, with property values what they are, I suppose it could be a great investment just about now. I suppose you were right about that, it doesn't make sense to rush into things."

She knew this was as close to an apology as Joel would ever come; considering the circumstances it was astonishing he had come that close. And he was right; it made no sense to rush into things, or out of them for that matter—to wipe Joel out of her life under this kind of crisis and tension. She was always telling her clients not to make life decisions under great stress.

I'm learning all over again what kind of person I am. I'm beginning to suspect I'm in the wrong profession. How do I know whether or not I want to marry a man like Joel?

"I'd ask you over to share our cheese sandwiches, but do you *really* want to listen to Emily practicing Rachmaninoff all evening?"

"Can't we send the kid out to a movie?"

"If she was still fifteen we probably could, but she's all worked up about an audition Monday; she's trying out for an appearance with the San Francisco Symphony."

"She'll get it, or something better," Joel said. "The kid has lots of talent. But I must admit the idea of sitting and listening all evening to Rachmaninoff isn't my idea of a great time. And I still owe you a celebration from last time. Friday night?"

"I'd love to," she promised fervently.

"Tell me about the house," he said generously, and they talked for another twenty minutes before he reconfirmed the date.

"Tomorrow night, and dress up. I'll take you to the Claremont. Love you, Les."

"Love *you*," she said softly, and replaced the receiver. Maybe things weren't all bad. She would be getting out of this house, with its jangling telephone and doorbell rung by no visible hand, its falling baskets and flying ashtrays; she would have a new telephone number to confound heavy breathers.

She put the sandwiches in the grill and called Emily. Her sister drifted out, her eyes fastened on the score in her hand; walked to the table, dished up salad with one hand.

"Look out, Em, you don't want mayonnaise on that, do you?"

Reluctantly Emily reached over and put the score on the counter, digging into her salad. Leslie took out the cheese sandwiches.

"Good supper, Les. Thanks. I should have helped you—"

"Forget it. You have the audition."

Emily said with her mouth full, "Did I hear the phone a while back?"

Trust Emily to notice even through a blur of Rachmaninoff. "It rang half a dozen times. I left it off the hook for a while. But Joel called."

"Oh."

After a moment she elaborated. "I thought that was all off. Is it on again, then?"

"He called up to apologize," Leslie said stiffly, then caught sight of her sister's wrist. There were small dark spots circling the narrow, small-boned wrist.

"What happened to you?"

Emily pulled nervously at the dark sleeve of her sweater.

"Old Agrowsky twisted my wrist," she said.

"He—" Leslie broke off. "Does that kind of thing happen very often at the Conservatory?"

"I guess not. I mean, he didn't really twist it on purpose. He said I was holding it wrong and grabbed it and held it," she added, twitching the sweater down over the dark spots. "Don't fuss."

Leslie was inclined to be indignant, but Emily was not an eleven-year-old to be protected. It was for her to complain or not, as she chose.

Emily squirmed under Leslie's eyes on her arm. She said, "He doesn't take many people for lessons. I'm one of the lucky ones, that's all, and I'm not going to rock the boat."

Leslie reflected that "luck" was not the word she would use for a piano teacher who included wrist-twisting in his course of instruction, but held her peace; she knew that Dr. Boris Agrowsky was a world-renowned musician.

"He was Simon Anstey's teacher," Emily went on, "and he says if I do all right in this he'll sign for me to take Anstey's master classes this summer."

"Isn't that awfully short notice? For anything this important, I should think they'd give you more time to prepare. Weeks, anyhow. Maybe months."

"Oh, they do. The *symphony* audition is in September. But a batch of us have to play for a piano faculty jury Monday to see which of us are going to be allowed to audition *for* the symphony, and Agrowsky didn't say I could play for them till this morning. Damned old sadist!" She rose and drifted to the counter. "Any chance of another sandwich?"

"Sure. Want me to make it?"

"I'll make it. Don't get up." Emily spread her organic bread thickly with a double layer of mayonnaise, sliced cheese liberally on it, then nosed inquisitively in the refrigerator. A handful of sprouts went on top of the cheese, while Leslie shuddered, then Emily said, "Oh, goody, ham!" She piled two slices of ham atop the sprouts, buttered the outside of both slices of bread and stuck it into the grill.

"Want one, Les?"

"I've had plenty, thanks." The appetite of a teenager was, Leslie knew, a bottomless pit; nevertheless she felt compelled to ask, as the enormous sandwich began to sizzle inside the grill, "Changed your mind about being a vegetarian?"

"Well, no." Emily looked sheepish. "But I have this *craving* sometimes, and maybe my body's trying to tell me something." She lifted the grill, surveyed the browned buttery crust with satisfaction, pried it off and transferred it to her plate. "Listen, Les, if I get to sign for Anstey's master classes it's going to cost about three hundred dollars extra."

"It's your money, Em. If you want to do it, I'll sign for it." She was trying to remember where she had heard the name Simon Anstey. After a minute she said so.

"Oh, he's been around just about forever. He won some tremendous prize when he was only about sixteen years old and played all over the world. I had some of his records when I was only a kid. He's made two or three movies too—he was awfully good-looking in a sort of slicked-down fifties way—and he's sort of—oh—elegant. He was awfully old, thirty or even thirty-five," Emily added, munching ham and cheese while Leslie shuddered at her definition of senility.

"Anyhow, Les, it was in all the papers—he was in this ghastly accident, he lost a couple of fingers and his face was all sliced up. He was in the hospital just about forever—he hasn't played since—but now he's teaching all over the world, giving master classes. I think he does some conducting, too. And Agrowsky said he'd sign for me to take the class if I do all right on Monday." She giggled. "I've heard Anstey's a holy terror—makes Agrowsky look like Santa Claus." She patted her bruised wrist with a grimace.

"Anstey's disabled, then?"

"He lost a couple of fingers and maybe he's blind in one eye. But his master classes are always jammed."

Leslie was sure that she had heard of Simon Anstey in some other context; a memory was nagging at her brain. Well, it would probably surface.

"Is Joel coming over, Les?"

"He wanted to, but I told him you were practicing. Anyhow, I have to get the packing organized, so I can call the movers first thing tomorrow."

"Be sure to call Mom and tell her," Emily reminded her. "Les, if there's an extra bedroom, shouldn't we move Mom down here? I worry so much about her, up in Sacramento all alone. If she had a fall and broke her hip or something. I feel so guilty, I really ought to have stayed home and gone to college up there in Sacramento. But I just couldn't find the right teachers—"

"Nobody, not even Mom, expected that, honey," Leslie reassured her, because it was what Emily needed to hear. But even while their father was alive, she knew her mother would have preferred them both to marry and stay in town, dutiful daughters; she had not raised them, she had reminded Leslie often, just so they could go away. Nor could either of their parents understand why Leslie should want a career more interesting than teaching school, and Emily's passion for performing, first ballet and then piano, had appalled them. They had given both girls ballet and piano lessons, but only because these were respectable accomplishments for young girls in their class; but pursuing them seriously as a career orientation was not. Leslie, like most of her friends, had been content to abandon them both when she went away to college—she still played the piano for her own pleasure, but only when Emily was not in the house.

Emily was different, had always been different, but neither parent could understand why Emily couldn't find a piano teacher in Sacramento, or even why, when she could play any piece of music set before her, she needed a teacher at all. Why, their mother had said, she could even teach piano herself! Both of them had been scarred by the battle even to let her apply to the Conservatory; Leslie knew their mother still secretly blamed this battle for their father's heart attack. Leslie knew better; he was the classic success-oriented type who clawed and scratched his way to success. His survival into his sixties had surprised her.

"Emmie, your job now is to concentrate on your work, and this audition. Mom's fine where she is, and I don't think a whole delegation of guardian angels could persuade her to move down here, away from all her friends. She has her life all arranged the way she wants it, and she knows we'll arrange ours the same way." And if she doesn't, Leslie added to herself, she'd better learn it. Emily was nosing in the refrigerator again and came back with a huge thick-skinned navel orange.

"Want one? Had your vitamin C and potassium today?"

Leslie laughed and accepted an orange; the kitchen was filled with the sharp sweet smell of orange peel as they sat tearing away the thick rind. Emily absently pulled the Rachmaninoff score toward her again and sat studying it, absentmindedly cramming orange sections into her mouth. Leslie's mind was on the minutiae of moving, but she sat and studied her young sister for a moment, the eyes untouched with makeup, the fluff of dark hair escaping from the right braid. Her slender neck and poised head gave her the look of a ballerina. She would have wonderful stage presence someday. No wonder their mother had felt like a domestic hen contemplating the swan she had hatched. She reached for the telephone pad and began to make notes. Real estate was always a good investment and could only go up in value. She need not stretch herself financially, nor extend her office hours that much; rent would be offset by the mortgage payments. She could even spare an hour or two, perhaps, for work at one of the public health clinics, or take a free patient or two referred by the public schools. Or was she just cushioning her conscience for being one of the propertied classes?

The telephone rang. Leslie cringed, and Emily said, "I'll get it." She listened a moment, then said, "Fuck off, bastard," and slammed the handset down with a grimace. "That's the only way to handle these creeps. Give them as good as they dish out."

"Heavy breather?"

"Well, I couldn't quite make out what he was saying, but I don't think it was Happy Birthday or Hare Krishna."

"One thing: at least after we move we won't have to cope with that particular nuisance. I'll get an unlisted number and just give it to my patients."

"You think maybe it's an old patient with a personal grudge, then?"

"That, or somebody who picks at random and noticed that this number is only answered by women," Leslie said. That thought was preferable to the feeling that there was nobody there at all, that some uncanny and inexplicable force was invading her life, out of the blind chaos of the dark.

As for the doorbell, or the telephone jangling even when she left it off the hook, well, a prolonged rainy season could do strange things to electrical systems.

The doorbell rang; Emily jumped up and ran to the front hall. After a minute she came back frowning.

"Nobody there. That damned short in the wiring, again, I suppose. Oh, well, at least it wasn't the Jehovah's Witlesses coming to try and convert us."

And then Leslie's nerves snapped.

"Emily, I *unhooked* that doorbell! It *couldn't* ring! Just come and look at it," she cried, and pushed back her chair, which crashed down behind her. She ran through the hallway, pointed at the wires dangling from the doorbell button.

"Look! Look, I unwired it. What's happening to us? Oh, God, what's happening?"

Tears were pouring down her face. Emily patted her shoulder, troubled.

"Don't be silly, Les. How can you say it couldn't ring when we both heard it? You got the wrong wire, that's all, and it's still hooked somewhere inside." She pushed the doorbell button.

Silence.

"You see?" Leslie cried.

Emily didn't know about the poltergeist—Eileen's that sent a heavy ashtray flying through the air to draw blood, the power that flung a glass of wine in Joel's face, sent baskets cascading down the stairs. Emily was resolutely pushing the silent doorbell again and again; she gave an experimental tug at the hanging wire.

"You must have partly unhooked it so it doesn't make a good connection. You should call an electrician—you could get electrocuted messing around with the wiring." She gave the loose wire another casual yank. "Why do you let these things get on your nerves like this, Sis?"

"You just don't realize—"

"Damned good thing I don't," Emily stormed. "If it makes you act crazy like this! Anybody would think you wanted to believe in all this crazy psychic crap—psychics and poltergeists and the police calling you—Who do you think you are, Uri Geller or somebody? I think you've been around too many patients with a screw loose in their heads and it's beginning to rub off on you!" She yanked at the doorbell wire until it came free of the wall and flung it down the steps, then stormed inside.

Leslie was speechless. Emily's view was, of course, the one any rational, enlightened adult would have to take. How could she, an educated and intelligent woman, specially trained in the use of the mind, justify defending psychic attacks or poltergeists to her normal, rational sister? Slowly, she went back inside, locked the door. She would have to have the doorbell rewired before they moved away.

"Emily, I'm sorry. I guess I've been letting it get on my nerves."

"You've had a lot on your mind, what with moving, and fighting with Joel," Emily said. "Now you've made it up with him, everything's going to be all right. You'll see."

Leslie opened her mouth in outrage and shut it again; Emily had already disappeared into the music room, and the crashing chords of the Rachmaninoff concerto were echoing through the hall. Emily didn't understand and it was probably a good thing that she didn't.

She could even be right. Even Eileen, now she had a new boyfriend, had not mentioned the poltergeist. Fodor seemed to think that frustrated sexual energy was at the basis of the poltergeist. Of course, he was a Freudian and they thought frustrated sexual energy was at the basis of everything. But maybe in this case they were right.

Maybe the conventional wisdom is right and all I need is a man.

Well, she was seeing Joel tomorrow night. Leslie scraped sandwich remnants and orange peels into the garbage can, put the dishes in the sink, and went to the basement to find the original carton from the blender and a cardboard box to pack dishes. While she was busy packing the dishes, she forgot the doorbell and the telephone, neither of which rang again that night.

IT WAS A RELIEF, the next day, to start checking off the list of telephone calls she had to make, to visit a printer and order cards for her new business address, to draw a little map showing her patients how to get there on public transit, to search for a new answering service based in San Francisco. By the end of the day she had located a moving company that would come one day next week for an estimate, and a separate specialist to move the piano, which would not be picked up till after Emily's audition. She barely had time, through the blur of Rachmaninoff that had crashed and thundered all afternoon through the house, to shower, wash her short hair and blow it dry and brush it up into a short flip. She scrambled into her best dress.

Emily surfaced long enough to say, "Hey, you look great, Les. Have a nice time, say Hi to Joel for me," before drifting back to Rachmaninoff.

Joel heard the music when he knocked at the door, and while his eyes brightened at the sight of Leslie in the red-and-gold dress.

"She plays so well. But doesn't it get on your nerves, hearing the same thing over and over when she's practicing?"

"I don't mind it, but some of my clients get a little edgy, so I can't let her practice when anybody's here." Emily had been hysterical about that today, with the audition coming up, but Leslie had had to be adamant. "The new house has a soundproofed suite I'm going to use for my clients, so she can practice whenever she needs to. The former owner was a musician, I understand."

"Anyone I'd be likely to know about?"

"I doubt it; I think she was a dedicated amateur. She was a professional psychologist—what do you think of *that* for a coincidence?"

"Truth is stranger than fiction, they say," Joel said unoriginally, opening the car door for her. "Do you remember her name?"

"Margrave. Alison Margrave."

He raised his eyes and pursed his mouth. "It's a small world, they say. Smaller than you'd think. Dick Carmody, at the office, was one of her lawyers; she was old, but very sharp, and she and the Carmodys were involved in some kind of nut-cult together, I think—I don't know the details. Some screwy religion, anyhow. Not the kind that goes after your money, though. Spiritualists or something. Seances. Anyhow, there was a big flap when the old lady changed her will—she'd left everything to some adopted son, or something, and all of a sudden she left the house to some distant cousins in Omaha or Wyoming or some godforsaken spot, people she'd never seen. And then old Miss Margrave—she must have been nearly ninety—died very suddenly, and there was an inquest and they questioned the adopted son, or whatever he was. Only he'd been in an accident and was actually in a hospital when it happened, being operated on. Awful thing, that; he *was* a professional musician, a famous pianist or something.

THE INHERITOR | 101

He's lost an eye, and the fingers of one hand or some such; I remember thinking at the time what a terrible thing to happen to a musician."

"My God, the coincidences are really flying around tonight," Leslie said. "You don't mean Simon Anstey, by any chance?"

"I guess that was the name. The house was all locked up tight when the old lady died, and I gather he was one of the only two or three people she'd given a key. And you bought that house?" Then the lights of the Claremont came in sight, and they hurried into the great antique foyer with its nineteenth-century glamour. Dinner was perfect, and afterward they danced, snuggling closer and closer as the evening went on. Without any particular moment when one asked or the other answered, halfway through the evening Leslie knew they were both taking it for granted that she would go home with him and spend the night. She was content to leave it at that. She had missed him, not least the good sex that they had together. Nor did he again bring up the subject of marriage.

But waking early in Joel's bed while he slept, she found herself listening in the dark and wondering, not without guilt, if she had agreed to come home with him, at least partly, to escape a house where telephones rang when one extension was off the hook, and an unwired doorbell jangled as an unfortunate reminder that something was going on that she could neither understand nor rationalize.

She would not lie here going over and over it again. She snuggled into Joel's side and nuzzled her face into his neck until he woke. And then she did not have to think about anything at all.

CHAPTER

Seven

THE MOVING MEN CAME with an estimate on Saturday morning; and the rest of that day, while more and more household items disappeared into boxes, and furniture was shoved into locations for the moving crew who would come on Tuesday, Leslie thought that there was so much chaos that a poltergeist could do his worst and no one could have noticed.

She packed her bureau drawers and asked Emily to do the same, but Emily hardly heard her.

"I have to practice. I'll do it Monday night when this is over, okay? Just let me alone," Emily muttered, barely lifting her eyes from the keyboard. She returned to a phrase, repeating it again and again. Then she realized Leslie was still standing in the door.

"Want something, Les?"

"Just listening."

"Well, don't," Emily snarled. "Haven't you got work to do? I have," and before her fierce scowl Leslie fled.

She was so absorbed in the hard healing physical work of moving that she hardly cringed when the telephone rang, and a cheery half-remembered woman's voice said, "Les? It's Margot."

"Oh, where *are* you?"

"Sacramento, of course," Margot said. "Nick and I decided to call you and let you be the first to know. We're being married in June—yes, I got the wretched degree—and of course Nick wants Joel for his best man. And I want you for my bridesmaid. It won't be a big wedding, we'd both hate that, but a nice little one with some of our best friends."

"That's wonderful, Margot!" She was delighted for her friends. And how wonderful that they had called today, after she had made it up with Joel. How miserable it would have been to tell them that she and Joel were not on speaking terms.

"Will you like being a policeman's wife?"

"I'll probably hate it," Margot said candidly. "But Nick is a policeman and that's all he ever wanted to be, so I guess I'll be a policeman's wife and learn to like it. How are you liking private practice, Leslie?"

"It beats the school system." It wasn't the time to burden her friend with her own qualms about the state of the art of counseling, or her recent self-doubts. Although Margot was one person, she thought, with whom she could share those qualms. And perhaps someday she would be able to do so. But not now, not when her friend was thinking about marriage.

"Margot, I just bought a house in San Francisco!"

"Wonderful! But isn't it awfully dangerous in the City? Isn't it safer in the East Bay?"

How could she explain the spell the house had put on her? She simply said, lightly, that she had fallen in love with the house, and that Emily would be safer, without the long transbay commute.

"That's right, she's studying at the Conservatory now, isn't she? Listen, I ran into your mother in the library yesterday—"

"How did she look?" Leslie asked, and they chatted for several minutes about family and mutual friends, before Margot said, "Listen, Nick wants to talk to you," and after a moment she heard the hearty baritone of her old friend.

"Hi, honey. Margot told you our great news?"

"She did, and I think it's wonderful, Nick."

"It is; I can't wait. Listen, Les, my friend Chuck Passevoy, down in Santa Barbara, called to tell me you found the Chapman kid. That was so wonderful, that you could do that, that it turned out to be a comedy of errors, and not some awful tragedy, this time!"

Leslie had almost managed to block the Chapman episode out of her mind. Now, with renewed anger, she protested. "I wanted to talk to you about that, Nick! How could you do a thing like that to me when you knew how I hate it?"

"Les, Chuck was all shook up; he was afraid he had something like the Pigtail Killer on his doorstep. Whenever a little girl disappears, cops get edgy. And the woman had seen your picture in the *Enquirer* . . . she knew what you could do."

Leslie took a long breath, trying to fight panic. She said, "No. No, I won't, I can't. Please, Nick, never do it again. Never."

"I won't promise that. Such a gift, it's a crime not to use it. Yes, I said a crime, Leslie."

"Nick, I can't argue with you about it. But I can't do it, either—"

"Have you thought of all the good you could do with it, Leslie?"

"I didn't do Juanita García any good, did I?"

"Maybe no one could have. Maybe it was just her time to go. But suppose he'd come after Emily next? Or somebody else's kid sister? And the Chapman kid—"

"The Chapman child was never in any danger. Her father would have brought her back in a day or two—"

"But meanwhile her mother was going through the tortures of the damned! Leslie, we've got to talk about it when you come up here for the wedding. Tell me about your house—" And the dangerous subject was avoided again for a moment. But Leslie was still shaking when she put down the phone. She would not, she could not go in search of that irrationality. It was wrecking her life, and all she wanted was to be free of it.

Her mind flashed again on the introduction to the poltergeist book.

Psychic force in tension, not around a hysterical or maladjusted child, but around a relatively well-adjusted adult. She had every right to think herself so. *When this occurs, there is some unresolved psychic force in action; it could be said that the Unseen is coming in search of the individual concerned, and this does not, strictly speaking, come under the scope of this book.*

Was the Unseen coming in search of her? She wondered if Claire, with her knowledge of psychology, and her apparent ability to take such irra-

THE INHERITOR | 105

tional things as poltergeists for granted, could answer that question for
her? Or would she, like Nick, urge Leslie to develop and use her gift for
police work?

That afternoon Joel brought his station wagon, which was bigger than
Leslie's car, to transport the first load of books and files for her office, with
a few boxes of kitchen items. On the way across the Bay they talked of
Nick and Margot's wedding plans. As they drew up in front of the house,
Leslie realized that she had dreaded coming here alone. The memory of the
man standing in the garage studio was still with her. But he had not been
there at all.

It was like the silly song she had heard as a child.

> Last night I met upon the stair
> A little man who wasn't there.
> He wasn't there again today;
> Gee, how I wish he'd go away.

Nonsense; with all that had been happening, and the absurd conversation she had overheard in the occult bookshop—and it served her right
for going into the place to begin with—she had imagined him, had a
hallucination; the man had come down her driveway, a harmless meter
reader or workman, and she had imagined him inside the garage. Anyhow,
the place was empty and quiet, and Joel, carrying a load of books, whistled
appreciation of the art deco stained glass, the parquetry of the hardwood
floor.

"You must have paid a fortune for this place, Les!"

"Not quite. It was going cheap." She explained the repeatedly cancelled sales, and even Emily's theory that it was a plot to scare people out
and resell the house at a profit. Joel laughed as heartily at that as she had
herself, so she put forward her alternative theory: "I think they wanted to
get rid of it before people jumped to the conclusion that they had something like the Amityville Horror on their hands."

"Oh, that!" Joel took it lightly. "Well, their craziness is certainly your
gain. I'd say it was worth half again what you paid for it, maybe twice the
price, but maybe in Nebraska they don't know what property values are
like out here on the coast. It's a good investment; you're a smarter busi-
nesswoman than I thought."

She laughed a little. "Actually, I fell in love. Come on, I'll show you around. Dump that box of stuff on the kitchen counter." She led the way through the kitchen, drew back the inside bolt and stepped out into the garden. The afternoon sunlight was weak and pale, and clouds were lingering—there would be more rain, later in the day—but the mingled scents from the herb garden were damp and pungently sweet, and the lemon tree against the wall gave off an intoxicating fragrance.

Inside the kitchen she heard water running. Joel called, "Les, did you know the water was still hooked up?"

"Good, that means the toilets will be working, so we can skip one problem on moving day. Come out and see the garden."

"Somebody put a lot of work and energy into this," he said, stepping out to survey it. "Money, too; a lot of rare plants here. Hibiscus, and those striped fuchsia there are very unusual. And the lady must have been an enthusiastic gardener; look at all those herbs," he added, kneeling by the little patches of green. "Comfrey, camomile, sage, peppermint, foxglove—that's this pink stuff that's running wild here and choking out all the other things—verbena, lobelia, thyme— all the standard ones, and plenty I don't recognize."

"Yes, Emily was very impressed, she's very interested in herbs."

"Is that a garage?" Joel asked, pointing.

"I think it used to be; they remodelled it as a studio. There was a potter's wheel and some artist's junk in there when I first saw the place."

"You might think about remodelling it right back into a garage; there's going to be less and less street parking in any big city in the next decade or so, and a house without a garage is going to be a liability."

"Well, there's a good long driveway, and in this climate a car can stay outdoors," she argued, but he looked pessimistic. "The crime rate's going to go up, too. I'd want a good locked garage."

Leslie shrugged. "It's a thought. The place is fairly dark and dismal for a studio. But they rebuilt it with a half bath, and a fireplace, and it would be a lot of trouble to tear that all out. A separate apartment is a good investment, I suppose." She took her key and unlocked it. Joel sniffed distastefully.

"Something dead in here. I hope you don't have rats."

Leslie let out her breath. She had not known whether she would see something inside, maybe the strange man who had not been there. "It was inspected for termites, and I'm sure the report would have mentioned any sign of rats. But one could have gotten in somewhere and been trapped, I suppose."

Joel was prowling around the walls, looking inside the bath and the closet next to it. "These cardboard cartons—is this stuff you moved in?"

"No, not mine; must have belonged to the former tenant. I'll call the agent; if he doesn't want to take it away, I'll send it to the city dump. What's in it, anyhow?"

Joel lifted up the flap. "Artist's stuff—paints, brushes, clay—what's this? Candles? Sticks of incense—smells like that stuff the Hare Krishna people sell on the street. Some old pottery. I wouldn't think anyone would abandon perfectly good art supplies these days, with what things cost." Leslie was reluctant to touch the box; there was a faint sickly smell, which must have been the incense.

Looking at him kneeling by the carton, his hair windblown, Leslie thought again that she really enjoyed him; she bent and kissed him quickly on the forehead.

He looked up, smiling. "What's that for?"

"I was just thinking how grateful I am that you called me. It's a good thing I didn't have the phone taken out when I was getting all those crank calls, after all."

He scrambled up and hugged her.

"That goes double for me, sweetheart. Show me the rest of the house. I must say I'm not impressed by the studio."

HE STOOD IN THE middle of the bay-windowed office, turning his head appreciatively from side to side. She came to stand beside him, looking out at the panorama of sky and sea and the thick fog rolling in like waves through the Golden Gate. The lower supports of the bridge were already knee deep in fog and only the graceful curve of the suspension span remained.

"Pity to waste this place for an office. It would make an elegant formal dining room."

She didn't want to argue with him about her work. "And look, across the hall there's another suite just like it, where Emily can practice as much as she likes. The two suites are identical, except that I have this wonderful bay view, and hers looks out on the herb garden. Plenty of room for the piano, and our grandmother's old concert harp."

"She's a lucky girl, I'd say, to have a sister like you; luckier than she deserves. Had you considered using this room for a living room and putting the piano out in the studio? She'd have even more privacy there for practice."

"I wouldn't do that to her. The place is too damp for the piano, anyhow. And it's horrible and depressing."

He shrugged. "So put in some heat. Why give her the nicest room? You're doing enough, I'd say, sending her to the Conservatory. You spoil her."

"I'm not paying for the Conservatory; she has some of the same money that bought me this house," Leslie said. "But she has to live here because she couldn't commute from Sacramento. And this, of course, will make it easier. There's a bus line a couple of blocks away which will take her right by the Conservatory."

He frowned, seemed for a moment to be listening.

"Did you hear anything, Leslie?"

"Nothing at all," she said, enjoying the silence. Even the sound of traffic was blessedly distant.

"I guess I imagined it. But there's a draft in here—is one of these windows open?" He went to the front bay window, to the smaller, narrower window beside it. "No, of course not. And look, metal grilles over the ground-floor windows; good idea that, with so much street crime and burglary these days, even in good neighborhoods." He was moving around, frowning a little. "There *is* a draft in here. And yet the hall door is closed."

He was standing exactly where Emily had stood the first day when she fainted, Leslie thought. But that was ridiculous. Emily had skipped breakfast and fainted from hunger. She came to stand beside him. Yes, it seemed as if a cold wind was blowing. And yet when she stepped away she could not feel it.

"Must be a draft somewhere," he said. "None of these old houses are really weathertight. Let's go and see the upstairs."

The same cold draft seemed to attack them on the stairs. "There's got to be a window open somewhere," Joel said, and plunged into the bedroom already designated as Emily's. "Aha! Here we are!"

Leslie looked frowning at the window standing wide open again. "The real estate agent said something about kids getting in," she said, "but I don't see how any kid could climb up there."

Joel came to her side. "Kids can get in anywhere. Bobby tells me stories that would make your hair curl. They'd have to have a ladder, I'd think. I'll bet you'd find ladder marks down there somewhere, but in this mud, after all the rain we've had lately, they might be hard to find. When you're living here, of course, if you hear anything like that, you can call the cops and catch the little buggers red-handed."

Try as she might, Leslie could see no marks in the smooth dirt of the herb garden which would indicate intrusive feet or ladder marks. "Maybe the house isn't balanced right and the window swings open," she said. "This kind of casement window doesn't always latch."

Or maybe, the thought crossed her mind, *it's like the doorbell that rings when it's unwired.* Angrily she dismissed the thought from her mind. Joel tested the latch again.

"It's shut now anyhow," he said. "Is this going to be your room?"

"No, Emily liked the view of the herb garden," she said, and led him across the hall to her own room, the old-fashioned wallpaper and antique door moldings. She had already mentally arranged the furniture.

"It's beautiful," he said, drawing her to the window to look down on the same sky and sea they had watched from the office suite below. "There's only one thing wrong with it."

"What's that, darling?"

He put his arm around her; they stood close together. "It ought to be ours, the place we'll move into after our wedding."

"Is there any reason it can't be—someday?" she asked, knowing that she was still not sure. But you had to take risks sometimes. "Not yet. But someday."

His face contracted. He said quietly, after a moment of silence, "No reason at all, except that I told you, I'm—old-fashioned. I feel it's my responsibility to provide the place where we'll live after we're married. But I guess we can work something out. I guess we'll have to."

And she knew that for Joel, that was as near to complete capitulation as he would ever come. The moment lasted, was prolonged, closer than a kiss. Then he drew away a little. "You've got a screwdriver downstairs. Let me check that latch in Emily's room. We'll try fixing it from inside."

The telephone rang. Leslie started in shock before remembering that she was in the new house and it could not be her persecutor. A telephone was frequently left hooked up in an empty house—there had been one hooked up when she moved into the place she was now renting. Yes, the extension was here in the little dressing room.

She picked up the handset. Cream-colored, she noted, slim and modern. "Hello?"

"Alison?" asked an unknown voice. "Alison, is that you?"

Alison. This again. Then, abruptly, she made the connection.

"If you are looking for Alison Margrave," she said sharply, "I believe she has been dead for a year." After a moment she added, "This is *my* house now," and heard the person on the other end of the line replace the receiver. But she stood, gripping the telephone in her hand until the knuckles turned white.

She had received the first crank call asking for *Alison* the day *before* she had seen this house. Alison Margrave's house. *Once is coincidence. Twice is happenstance. Three times is enemy action.* But who was the enemy and why? The Unseen, coming looking for her? And why?

It's not the house that's haunted. It's me.

CHAPTER

Eight

AT THE BREAKFAST TABLE, mentally going over a checklist, Leslie
raised her eyes as Emily came in. She was already dressed; a black leotard,
and black skirt over it, gave her the quality of a black-and-white snapshot
of herself; all color seemed to have been withdrawn from her face. She
moved like a zombie to the teakettle and made herself a cup of tea. Her
hands stretched nervously. The steam was odd-smelling even for Emily's
herb teas.

"What's that, Emmie?"

"Valerian. My nerves are shot." Her smile barely stretched her mouth.
She sipped, poured it in the sink with a grimace and rinsed the cup. "Too
shot for the taste of valerian. Can I have some of your coffee?"

Leslie poured her a cup without a word. This was no time to make fun
of Emily's herbal tranquilizers. "Want me to drive you in? I cancelled all
my clients till Wednesday, because of moving."

"I'm a big girl, Les. I don't need my hand held." Emily sipped the coffee and made another wry face. "Ugh; I can't decide which tastes worse, this or valerian!" She poured the coffee out. "Lemon grass, I guess. Nice and soothing."

"Sit still. I'll make it for you." Leslie went to the canisters of plainly marked teas and found the lemon grass. She poured water, sniffing the fragrant steam, and shoved it in front of her sister. "Save your energy for the audition. Why fight rush-hour traffic?"

"Would you, Les? I mean—"

"Sure. Take it easy. What time do you have to be there?"

"Nine-thirty to take a number for auditioning. I may not get to play till noon—"

"That's all right. I don't have anything else to do this morning."

"And the movers coming tomorrow?" Emily gave her a shy smile of gratitude. "I'm the only freshman auditioning. Most of them are seniors and graduate students. Only Agrowsky wanted me to play for the jury. There's no way, with some of those people auditioning, that I'm going to get the Symphony appearance. It's just that if I do well, I can get into the master class." Emily was spooning down yogurt, but her hands were shaking.

"Emmie, go and put on some lipstick. And some blusher on your cheeks."

The girl said savagely, "They're going to judge me on how well I *play,* not on how cute and sexy I look!"

"Do you want them all to know how scared you are? Your face is dead white! You ought to look normal, at least."

"Okay." Emily paused and said in a very small voice, "I don't own any."

"Try my dresser." They were close to the same coloring, and putting on makeup would give Emily something to do besides thinking of her nervousness. Emily came back looking far more like herself. She tucked the piano score in her backpack, but all the way across the bridge she kept digging it out and looking through it obsessively.

"God, I hope I get to go first or second. Or else last. Only I'd hate to sit there and listen to all the rest. We were told to prepare the whole thing, and the jury would ask us each for one movement at random. I can be brilliant and technical all right. But if I get the adagio—I don't know how to go all romantic, and my legato is putrid. If they ask me to play the adagio I'll get right up and run out—"

"No you won't. You'll sit down and play it the best way you can. You'll be all right."

"What the hell do you know about it?" Emily snarled.

"Not one thing. But I know a lot about *you,* Emmie."

"Oh, God, Les, stop the car. I think I'm going to throw up—"

"I can't stop the car on the bridge. If you have to, roll down the window." She made her tone hard; Emily rolled down the window, but she did not vomit; she lay back, letting the icy stream of sea-fog blow through the car.

The hall was cold and barren; down front there was a table with four chairs. Emily whispered, "The jury will sit there. That's Dr. Agrowsky." She tilted her head a little to indicate a thick-set man with hunched shoulders and a sleek bald bullet head. He looked menacing to Leslie until she saw the laugh lines around his mouth and eyes. He nodded to Emily, and Leslie thought he looked encouraging, but she was not even sure her sister had seen. The world-famous teacher went down and took a seat in one of the four empty chairs.

Students were drifting in; Leslie had not realized that the auditions would be open to all students, but after all, it made sense; even a student should get used to playing for anyone who cared to listen.

A tall man came from the back, to a stir of small sounds in the auditorium. Leslie surmised this must be the famous visiting musician, and turned to look. With a sense of inevitability she saw the eye-patch, the arm in the sling, the scarred face, the aquiline profile. She had last seen him getting into a grey car in her driveway. No; she had last seen him— or imagined him—standing at the center of the dank remodelled studio room at her house. Simon Anstey paused, as if her thoughts could reach him, and his single eye, blue and blazing, met hers as it had done before her house. Leslie grabbed the edges of her chair.

Then he gave a curt nod and strode on down the aisle, taking the last of the vacant chairs at the jury table.

A man stood up at the front.

"Good morning," he said. "Will the candidates please come up to the table and take a number at random from the basket."

"Wish me luck," Emily whispered, and went. She was back in a minute, looking dazed, a slip of paper in her hand. "Number five. About the worst slot I could have."

"Well, it's a challenge," Leslie whispered back.

"Number one. Please come up here, state your name and we will ask you to play."

A heavy-set woman in her thirties, in a tight white skirt and sweater, strode aggressively to the center stage.

"Joan Paddington."

"Mrs. Paddington, let us hear the adagio, if you please."

"Fat pig," Emily whispered. But the fat pig played like an angel; Leslie, listening, began to enjoy the concerto, but Emily was tearing a Kleenex to shreds in her hands.

The audition went on. When number five was called Emily wet her lips, clutched her music and went forward.

"Emily Barnes."

It was the tall, scarred Simon Anstey who said, "Let us hear the first movement, if you please, Miss Barnes."

Emily wadded up the Kleenex in her hands, wiped her palms surreptitiously on her skirt, and sat down at the keyboard. Leslie heard the eight crashing chords which opened the concerto, beginning *piano* and rising to *fortissimo,* as she had heard them a hundred or a thousand times in the last days, then moving into the first opening melody.

Emily had chosen an unabashedly romantic interpretation. "Rachmaninoff *was* a romantic," she said. Under Emily's skilled fingers the lush music sounded pure, emotional, without a hint of sentiment or schmaltz.

Agrowsky, Leslie thought, had done wonders for her; but of course she was in no position to know what standards the jury would apply, or to hear them if she did. All the students sounded equally professional to her, and Emily no less than the others, though she was the youngest by some years. She certainly looked lovely at the piano, slender, with her straight back and delicately poised ballerina head and shoulders; but of course that was irrelevant too. She looked young to Leslie, and fragile.

At least they didn't ask her to play the adagio. When she had finished, it was Anstey's deep voice that said, "Thank you, Miss Barnes. Number six?"

A tubby young man in blue jeans came up and said hoarsely, "David Lenney," and Emily, very white, came back to Leslie, and slid into her seat. "Jesus, did I blow it," she whispered.

"Do you want to go?"

"Do you mind? I'd rather sit here and listen to the rest of them, now it's over—I feel fine."

There were three more candidates. When the last one, a bearded young hippie who reminded Leslie faintly of Frodo in the bookshop, had played the first movement again, Dr. Agrowsky rose and said, "Thank you all very much, young ladies and gentlemen. If you will return at four this afternoon, we will announce our decisions." The students began to stream out of the auditorium. Leslie gathered up her handbag and Emily's backpack and they went out.

"Shall we go somewhere and get some lunch?"

"I couldn't eat, Les."

Leslie shrugged. "Then let's go shopping for those cushions you wanted, and take them over to the house. And while we're there, we'll decide where to put the furniture."

AS LESLIE HAD HALF expected, once they were away from the Conservatory, Emily decided she could eat an egg and avocado sandwich, and they went to fetch it, while Emily talked volubly about the other candidates.

"Jo Paddington is one of Agrowsky's pupils too. If she wasn't so fat, she'd be marvelous. But she's such a slob. They wouldn't pick anyone like that. Personally I think they'll pick Dave Lenney. He's one of Dr. Milhauser's pets, plays for the orchestra at rehearsal. God, did you hear Anstey? That *voice*. Basso profundo. And that ghastly eye. That must be what they mean when they talk about the evil eye, isn't it? He stares right *through* you, doesn't he?"

Leslie put that down to the state of Emily's nerves, and discounted it. "He's the one who's teaching the master class?"

"That's right. God, I don't know if I want to get in it or not. I'm simply *petrified* of that man. Evil Eye Fleegle."

Leslie had been so preoccupied with Emily's ordeal that she had put her own emotions on hold. Now it all rushed over her again. What did it mean, that she had seen Anstey at her gate? Even more, what did it mean that she had seen his shape, his *doppelgänger*, inside the studio? She could just manage to believe that perhaps a man killed by violence might manage to give off a wraith, like some kind of visual recording, of his death, and this was what was called a ghost. But a living man?

She told herself again that she had certainly been hallucinating. The story Joel had told her had given her a reason for his physical presence there; he had known Alison Margrave, and he might have wanted to see again the house where his old friend had died. And he had, or once had had, a key. She had called locksmiths and the locks would be changed by tonight, so there would be no question of Anstey's turning up there again; or if he did, he would find he could not get inside.

The locksmith's truck was actually there when they arrived, and she pocketed two new sets of keys with satisfaction. When she went upstairs, the window in Emily's room was open again, but the locksmith had installed a chainbolt rather than the simple latch on the casement; Leslie bolted it shut and chained it.

"Did you call the storage company about the harp?" Emily asked.

"They'll deliver it Wednesday. Emmie, do you want the old bow-front dresser in your bedroom?"

"I guess so," Emily said vaguely. "I ought to have a music cabinet in the music room, Les. I wonder if they have any lobelia in the garden? Somebody told me it was a tranquilizer, too."

"I wouldn't know. Just be sure of what you're picking." Leslie followed her down into the garden to check the key to the studio.

"Does the white cat go with the house, Leslie?"

"I don't know. But I've seen it here often enough, it's certainly making itself at home in the garden." She called softly, "Here, kitty, kitty, kitty . . ."

"Where did it go? Leslie, can we put out some tuna fish?"

"It probably belongs to one of the neighbors, Emmie."

"Then they don't deserve it; it looks half starved. I'll bet the former owner just went away and abandoned it. People who do things like that ought to be *shot!*" Emily opened the studio door, and wrinkled her nose at the rush of dank air.

"I bet it's been in here to crap. Maybe we ought to put a litter box in here for it. Maybe it was used to finding one in here."

That could, Leslie thought, be one explanation of the smell.

"Open a window, and we'll air the place out." A coat of quick-drying paint in a cheerful color, she was thinking; the old rocker from the Sacramento house; her sewing machine and the old dress form, and there was room for an ironing board and a cutting table. Bright curtains; sunshiny yellow, she thought. It would do wonders for the place. She was making a shopping list when Emily yelped, "Oh, God, it's quarter to four, I wasn't watching the time, you'll have to drive me, Les!"

The auditorium was locked and students were milling around waiting for someone to come with a key. Simon Anstey, head and shoulders above the crowd, striding for the door, came face to face with Emily and looked down at her from his great height.

"Miss Barnes. I heard you play this morning. You are very young, of course, but I shall be happy to have you in the master class."

Emily gulped. "Thank you, Dr. Anstey."

Anstey looked straight at Leslie, and the silence became so obvious that Emily muttered, "My sister. Dr. Barnes."

Leslie raised her head and looked directly into the steady stare of his one eye. Did the man mean to be rude, or was it a function of impaired sight? She felt an inner surge of anger. It was he who had trespassed on her property, not she on his. "I think we have met, Dr. Anstey."

His scarred smile was bleak. "I believe so, yes. Are you a medical doctor, Dr. Barnes, or a colleague of Dr. Margrave's?"

"The latter. Although I never had the privilege of knowing Dr. Margrave, I heard the other day that she was a psychologist. That is my profession also."

"Oh?" The one-eyed gaze was unflinching. Leslie reminded herself that probably the man did not mean to be offensive; he might have no control over his eye. "I was sure that Alison Margrave must have chosen you, and seeing you here, I thought perhaps you were also a professional musician. Alison was the greatest living student of the harpsichord, though she was better known for her writings about them than for her stage career, which was brief. She never appeared on any concert stage after 1953; she said she had not the temperament for a stage performer, though I think she was mistaken. She was well known for her transcriptions of Bach and Scarlatti manuscripts. I was—" he hesitated briefly, "a protégé of hers. I know the house well."

"I am sorry; I know very little of music, and I do not play. Emily is the musician in the family."

"I am sure Alison is glad to have your talented young sister in the house, Dr. Barnes," he said, bowed slightly, and went into the now-unlocked auditorium.

Joel had called him an adopted son of Alison Margrave; he spoke of himself as a protégé. The students were crowding into the auditorium; Leslie and Emily found a seat. There was a brief conference at the front, then Boris Agrowsky stood up. Emily was pale and stricken at her side.

"Mr. Lenney, Mrs. Paddington, Miss Hadley have been chosen to compete with entrants from other music schools on August fifteenth. In addition, Miss Barnes, Mr. Kalergapolis—excuse me—Kalapergos?— yes—thank you; Mr. Kalapergos and Mr. Stainer may enroll in the master classes given by Dr. Anstey. Thank you. If the candidates will come to the front when we have finished and take your adjudication papers."

Emily went up and returned with a handful of scribbled papers. As they were leaving the auditorium she studied them in a daze.

"Agrowsky said I should work harder on *legato*. What else is new? He's been telling me that for months. And what do you know? Anstey says I have a nice feel for Rachmaninoff's music without being sentimental."

He was right; Leslie herself had felt it, but Anstey was in a position to know. But Emily, though she hardly lifted her eyes from the papers all the way back to the East Bay, volunteered nothing more, and Leslie did not ask.

CHAPTER

Nine

THE LAST NIGHT IN the rented house, Leslie hardly slept; the telephone jangled until she took both extensions off the hook, and the doorbell roused her twice out of sleep. It was not much after five when she finally gave up trying and came down to clear the refrigerator and pack a final few odds and ends to be taken in the car.

At the first light she dispatched Emily, with the spare set of keys, to await the arrival of the harp from storage, and the special movers who would come to pick up the piano.

By noon, the furniture had been moved across the Bay and was stacked in the new house, in a chaos of boxes and cartons. The bedsteads had been set up by the moving men, and Leslie managed to get her room habitable, her clothes in drawers and on hangers, and to carry the file boxes from her office into the soundproofed study, where desk, chairs and lamps had been dumped by the movers. She went into Emily's room and hung clothes in the closet—her sister could rearrange them later, the important thing was to get them off the floor, and Emily was, of course, busy in the music room with the six-foot concert harp that had belonged to their grandmother, tuning it, replacing a couple of snapped strings. She heard the piano arrive and ran down as they were maneuvering it through the door and into the music room, re-attaching the legs and unwrapping the protective padding. Emily hovered like an anxious mother watching her sick child being given a dangerous or painful treatment, and while Leslie was paying off the piano movers, she heard arpeggios and went back into the music room to see Emily grimacing over the keyboard.

"Did you find a piano tuner on this side of the Bay, Leslie?"

Leslie hadn't. She had not yet readjusted her priorities to the realization that a piano tuner was as much a necessity of life as the nearest supermarket or drugstore. "Good grief, Emmie, the piano was tuned not three weeks ago—"

Emily said with an energetic grimace, "But it's been *moved!* Well, never mind—" with a martyr's sigh, "they must have a list at the Conservatory. I guess it can wait till tomorrow morning."

"Maybe you ought to learn piano tuning at that," Leslie commented.

"It would certainly help. I don't like to go a whole day without practicing."

"How did the harp survive storage?"

"I think it's going to be all right," she said, moving to the harp and lovingly running her hands over the gilt molded upright. "It has a lovely tone. I sometimes wish I'd chosen the harp as my primary instrument. I can tune it and look after it myself."

Leslie thought of her grandmother playing it when she was very small. Emily sat down and swept her fingers over the strings.

"But there isn't that much solo literature for the harp. Unless I wanted to specialize in Irish folk music or something—" Her expressive grimace suggested that was not much better than playing in a rock band. She began to play, and Leslie said, "I remember Grandma playing that. What is it?"

"Debussy. *Danse sacre et profane,*" Emily said, and Leslie shook herself awake.

"I love it, but this isn't getting us moved in. I put the bamboo pattern quilt on your bed, Emmie."

"Fine," Emily said without listening. "I wish I had a harpsichord. There's plenty of room for a small one in here. It's impossible to find antique ones without paying a small fortune, but nowadays they have kits

THE INHERITOR | 121

that you can build them with, for a couple of thousand dollars, and I'm good with tools. I wonder what happened to her harpsichords?"

"Whose harpsichords?"

"Alison Margrave's. You said this was her house, didn't you? There was a piece about her on the bulletin board in the keyboard department. She had nine harpsichords. I wonder where she put them all?"

"I'm sure some of them must have been in here once," Leslie said, remembering the day she had heard a ghostly tinkle of music in here. That kind of psychic flash didn't bother her at all.

"Hungry, Emmie? Neither of us had much chance for breakfast," she reminded her sister.

"Oh, is the kitchen all hooked up?" Emily asked absently.

"There was nothing to do but turn on the gas and electricity, and they came around ten," Leslie said, trying not to sound impatient. "We can boil water for tea, but almost everything's still in boxes; I was thinking of sending out for some sandwiches. What kind do you want?"

"That place where we were the other day has super egg and avocado ones," Emily said, coming out of her trance eagerly, "and they have egg-plant parmigiana too. Want me to hike down and get some? What kind do you want?"

"Egg salad is all right. But please, tell them to hold off on the sprouts; I know they're supposed to be good for you, but I just can't stand them!"

"I'll get them on the side and eat your share," Emily offered, slid her feet into sandals and went down toward Haight Street.

Leslie went into the kitchen and started to unload dishes onto shelves, to hang saucepans on the pegboard, to unpack the blender and the grill for Emily's eternal cheese sandwiches. She should have asked her to bring back milk, butter and lettuce. She started making a grocery list to hang on the magnetic board on the refrigerator. Once she stopped, thinking Emily had come back, but it was no more than a ghostly whisper from the music room. With that kind of haunting, she told herself, she could live very easily. Anyway, it was probably a radio next door. The kitchen was big enough for a dishwasher when she could afford one. She was remembering one of the biggest fights in the Sacramento house, shortly before she had left home. She had told her mother that she should have a dishwasher.

"I *have* a dishwasher," Constance Barnes had said, smiling fondly at her younger daughter, then fifteen. "Her name is Emily."

The rumpus had not subsided for the better part of three days. And it had been foolish. Her mother could perfectly well have afforded a dishwasher, or even a part-time housekeeper. It was only that she had preconceived notions about the normal duties of teenage girls, and felt that it built Emily's character to have household duties.

Leslie went into the study and began unloading boxes of patient files, stowing them in the lockable cabinet. A labelled box marked DESK TOP had been so carefully packed that she had her desk, within ten minutes, looking exactly as it had looked in the Berkeley house. She put up her wall calendar, placed her appointment book in its accustomed place, stationed the new telephone extension where it belonged; a new, slim, cream-colored one which coordinated perfectly with the elegance of the walls and windows. Her scarred old desk looked faintly out of place, but it would settle in as she did. Someday she would afford a good one. She stood looking out at her cherished view of sky and sea; the ocean was brilliant, the sky blue with a few scattered pillowy clouds, and the view seemed to be welcoming her.

Leslie sighed with pure content and resumed her unpacking.

A box on the study floor, under some of the books, held Emily's hairbrushes and an assortment of tights and leotards. That shouldn't have been left down here—it was clearly labelled EMILY'S ROOM. She would carry it upstairs to the second bedroom right now.

On the landing she discovered her sister's door opened wide. That was right; she had carried an armload of clothes through here and hung them in Emily's closet. As she set the box on the floor, there was a shadow across her eyes and she saw the white cat, noiselessly scrambling out through the wide-open casement and down over the sill.

Well, that settled one thing: the problem of the old casement latch coming open. Not a mischievous child or teenager bent on vandalism, but a cat, accustomed to coming in and out by the trellis, bumping its nose against a latch it knew how to dislodge from the outside. At least with the new chain bolt they would not have that trouble. But she had better chain it up again; Emily might not want a strange cat coming in and out by her bedroom window. She heard the soft chime of the doorbell—how much less troubling than the harsh buzzer in the Berkeley house—and ran down to welcome her sister with a big bag of sandwiches.

"Let's go and eat in the garden," Emily said.

They perched on the low wall, munching sandwiches in companionable silence. Leslie saw the white cat, slipping silently along the corner of the garage studio, and remembering, ran inside, hunting out a box of canned goods and opening a can of tuna fish; she put some in a saucer.

"I'm going to feed it," she told Emily. "It belongs here, evidently; I found it in your bedroom just now."

Emily looked at her vaguely, stuffing sprouts into her mouth; when she had chewed and swallowed them, she said, "Well, it didn't get in the casement window; I left it chained shut."

"You didn't, honey; the casement was wide open, and I saw the cat climbing back out."

Emily shrugged. "You must have opened it to air and forgot about it. Maybe the moving men did when they carried my bed up; the place could have been pretty stuffy. Speaking of stuffy, did the movers put anything in the garage, studio, whatever we're going to call the place?"

"The sewing room, I guess; I had them put the machine in there and Mom's old dress form. But I figured the place could use a coat of paint before we use it," Leslie said. "I don't have any clients coming till Thursday morning; we can paint it tomorrow. You're handy with a paintbrush, and so am I."

Emily wrinkled up her nose. She said, "Have you thought about turning it back into a garage? Anyhow, if we're going to be working in there, we'd better air it out." She went and unlocked it. "Yick, I'll bet that cat was in here again."

"Leave the door open; we're going to be in and out of the yard all day," Leslie said, and went to explore a tiny ramshackle structure at the far end of the garden. The padlock yielded to one of the keys on the original ring the agent had given her, and inside she found an old, but serviceable lawnmower, a rake, a trowel, a coiled garden hose, and an assortment of lawn tools.

"Look what we inherited!" Leslie called, and Emily came to inspect them.

"I'll hook up the hose right now and water these flowers; they look as if they could use it. There's a lot of weeding and work to be done in the garden," she said, fixing the hose to the outlet near the studio door.

"You'd better close that door, at least partially, so the sprinkler won't get it all wet inside," Leslie said, and Emily went to obey, then cried out. Leslie, shaken, ran to see what was wrong, but Emily was laughing nervously.

"Thought I saw someone in here. I guess it was the dress form," she said, indicating the battered shape draped in an old gingham dress, but Leslie's peace of mind was gone; she remembered coming in here and seeing Simon Anstey's fetch, or astral body, or *doppelgänger,* or ghost, standing in the center of the room. She told herself not to imagine things, and went out again. She had put the saucer of tuna fish under the overhang near the porch. The cat was probably too shy to come and investigate while they were there. Then she saw it, slipping along the castor bean bushes at the back of the garden.

"Here, kitty . . ." she called softly, but the cat vanished into the shadows.

"Are you sure you want a stray, Leslie? It may have gone feral; trying to feed and tame it could be a waste of time."

"Hello there," called a voice from the front gate. "Are you getting moved in?"

Leslie went around to the front, and saw the girl Rainbow from the bookstore, with Timmie in her backpack, and the long-haired young man she had called Frodo. They were carrying something green in a clay pot. She opened the gate to let them in.

"Emily," she called, "our first visitors! Are you neighbors?"

"Frodo lives down in the Haight," Rainbow said. "I'm around the corner here, on Buena Vista. We remembered you said Miss Margrave's house." She remembered intending to tell Rainbow that; she did not remember that she had actually done so. "And you said your sister was interested in herbs, and I was re-potting some aloe vera, so I brought one over for her. It's really good to put on little cuts and scrapes—helps everything heal better." She proffered the pot, in which an odd-looking succulent, almost like a cactus but without the spines, straggled every which way.

"Oh, thank you!" Emily said, taking the pot with as much delight as if the ugly succulent had been a precious orchid. "I've been wanting to get some aloe vera, but I didn't know where to look for it."

"This is Rainbow, Emily, and this is Frodo. I'm Dr. Barnes. Leslie."

"Come around and see the herb garden," Emily said and led them back into the yard. Rainbow set Timmie down on the walk, then hesitated.

"Is there anything here she shouldn't get into?"

"Not that I know of, though probably you don't want her getting all wet, and the sprinkler is on—"

"That's all right; it's a hot day and she's not wearing anything special,"

Rainbow said superfluously; Timmie had on only a pair of cotton panties. "I have a couple extra pairs of training pants in the pack, so if she gets wet I can pop her into dry ones."

Emily set the aloe vera in its pot on the steps. "Should we leave it in the pot, or transplant it into the garden?"

"I'd leave it in the pot for now," Frodo said, "but when it gets big you can transplant it. Just keep it in the sun."

"We haven't had time to do much with the garden yet," Emily said, "but the herb garden is marvelous! There are things I don't recognize, but Leslie got me the most wonderful book on herbs—"

"I know," Rainbow said, smiling. "I was there when she bought it."

"Kitty!" Timmie cried, and began to scamper back toward it. Leslie, who vaguely remembered that castor beans were unwholesome if not actually poisonous, started after her.

"I'd forgotten the castor beans," Rainbow said, hurrying to reclaim her daughter. "Alison used to keep them cut down, but they grow back awfully fast, and I don't think the people who lived here this last year had any little children. Play here on the grass, Timmie."

Timmie fretted. "Kitty! Want kitty!"

Rainbow shaded her eyes with her hand. "Do you have a cat? I didn't see—"

"There's a white cat hanging around," Leslie said. "I put some tuna out for it. It's been coming in the house, I think—"

"Claire said something about having given Alison one of her kittens, years ago," Frodo offered. "Rainbow said you'd met her in the bookshop. She and Alison were great friends. And Claire has the loveliest white cats; if you want a kitten, she has kittens to give away every few months. But I suppose one of Alison's cats could still be here, hanging around, though I would have thought it would have gone to the SPCA when Alison died."

"Did you know Miss Margrave well?" Emily asked.

"I wouldn't say *well*," Rainbow said, "She used to come in the store sometimes. She was Claire's friend, really, not mine; she was *very* old. But we were all shocked when she died. She seemed so strong and hearty. That was why the police came, asking everybody who knew her if they had any idea what happened. Are you the one she chose to take her place?"

Leslie shook her head. "I never knew Miss Margrave."

"That wouldn't make any difference," Frodo said. "If you're the one she picked. What do you do, Dr. Barnes? Are you a medical doctor, then?"

Leslie shook her head. "A clinical psychologist."

"But that would have suited Alison just fine," Frodo said, "because she was a psychologist and a parapsychologist, too. People came from all over the world to consult her; I mean she was *famous.*"

"I thought she was a musician, an expert on—was it harpsichords, Emily?"

"She was," Rainbow told her, "but that was when she was younger. Oh, she still played; I came here with Claire one day and she played for me—she had all kinds of harpsichords, one of them in black lacquer, painted all over with gilt figures and inlaid with mother-of-pearl."

"I was wondering what happened to her harpsichords," Emily said.

Rainbow's voice went flat and impassive. "I think she left them to a friend of hers. A man who used to be a musician. I really didn't know her that well, as I told you."

Emily sighed. "I'm thinking of trying to build a harpsichord," she said.

"Alison would like having one in the house, I'm sure," Frodo said, "and she did say once that she wouldn't let anyone live in the house until the right person came along. And see, now there's another musician in it, Rainbow! We'll have to tell Claire!"

"That's right," said Rainbow, looking at Leslie with delight, "she must have saved the house for you!"

Leslie laughed uneasily. "I think that's ridiculous." They were charming young people, but this was insanity.

Rainbow glanced at Timmie, splashing in the mud around the sprinkler. "It was sold to people who couldn't live in it for one reason or another, until you came along. A musician. And a psychologist. I know that one woman lived here and couldn't stay. She told me the place was haunted. But Alison would never hurt anybody; it was just that the place wasn't right for her. This woman was an artist, and maybe she thought that would be right for the house, only she could never work here, and finally the house drove her out—"

Emily's eyes were wide, and for a moment Leslie felt real anger. They would be nice friends for Emily. But not if they were going to tell these mad stories about her new house. She said angrily, "I heard about that from the agent. The woman was obviously neurotic—"

"Oh, she certainly is," Rainbow said with a smile. "Alison would really have hated having her here. But it doesn't matter," she added quickly. "The important thing is that the right kind of people are living in the house *now*. And I'm sure you'll be lucky in it, and happy here. Emily, I have some cuttings of dittany of crete, and it's hard to get; would you like to have them?"

"I'd love them," Emily said, and the conversation turned to herbs; Emily invited them in to see the new music room, and Leslie excused herself, saying she had to unpack her study. She left the door open, listening to them talking about herbs, music, organic foods; she came out once and saw Rainbow and Emily giving Timmie an impromptu bath in the kitchen sink. Later they were all sipping one of Emily's herb teas at the kitchen table, and later still she heard the sound of the harp from the music room. After a time she heard the familiar sound of Emily practicing, and when she came out they had gone. After a time Emily joined her and said, "I like them."

"I do, too." *Even if they have crazy ideas,* she thought.

"Listen, Frodo asked me to go to a concert tonight with them."

"Oh?" She would have thought he would be interested only in folk guitar. Emily said, "Yes, there's an outdoor concert in Stern Grove up in the park. He used to play classical flute. He knows a lot of people up at the Conservatory. He and Rainbow are coming by for me at seven." She hesitated. "Unless you really need me to unpack, or something—or to do a lot of shopping—I really should have asked you, shouldn't I?"

Leslie shook her head. "Go and enjoy yourself, dear. I can manage. Would Rainbow like me to babysit with Timmie?"

"No, she's bringing her along, and a blanket," Emily said. "We'll just put her to sleep on the grass. Sometimes Timmie's father keeps her overnight, but he's playing tonight—second violin."

So Emily had found some friends who loved her own kind of music. That would help. Leslie said, "Well, have fun."

"You won't mind staying alone in a new place? Honestly?"

"I won't mind at all; I'll spend the time unpacking my study," Leslie said. "But you can go and pick up some groceries first. I'll give you a list."

Darkness came earlier on this side of the Bay; the fog began to sweep in through the Golden Gate, rolling across the Bay and the hills like great waves of cloud, and soon the sky was thickly overcast and a few drops of drizzle began falling in the garden. The tuna was untouched, and Leslie saw the white cat again, called and tried to coax it, but it would not come. She wondered if the creature was hurt or sick; she saw a darkness across its front and for a moment the stain looked like blood. If she could not tempt it out in a day or two she should notify the SPCA that there was an injured and starving animal near here, to be picked up and taken to an animal shelter.

Emily left with Rainbow and Frodo, and Leslie, carrying her simple supper of soup and crackers into the study, spent the evening settling her study and enjoying the peace and quiet. No telephone jangle disturbed the stillness, which, after the poltergeist-induced strain of the last few days, seemed blissful. She even went into Emily's music room and spent a quiet half hour at the piano playing the simple first movement of the *Moonlight Sonata* (she had never been able to handle the rapid chords of the second movement) and a jaunty little Bach minuet. As she finished the Bach, she heard a tiny spray of notes, like an echo from a harpsichord, and thought of Miss Margrave. Was she really pleased to have two women who shared her interests in the house she had loved? She told herself that she did not for one moment believe Rainbow's story, but it was pleasant to imagine the soft echo of Alison Margrave's harpsichord in the room she had loved.

And if I am truly psychic, and Nick insists that I am, perhaps I am simply picking up a sign of her welcome. She went back into the study and leaned back comfortably in her chair. Tomorrow this quiet would be invaded by patients, but for tonight the place was all hers. Perhaps it was truly a gift, not a curse. She turned off the light and went upstairs. She was arranging clothes in her bureau drawers, and had just heard the study clock, with its tinny cuckoo note, striking ten, when Emily came in and up the stairs.

Leslie came out on the landing. "How was the concert?"

"Fine. They played some Mozart, and a Haydn symphony, and afterward we all went over to Frodo's, and he played the flute for us—he did that solo from *Orpheus and Eurydice*—'The Dance of the Blessed Spirits,' I guess." She hummed the gentle baroque melody. "And Dr. Anstey was there."

"At Frodo's?"

Emily giggled. "No, silly, at the *concert*. They said he was going to conduct some of the concerts this season. I'll bet that man is a holy terror on the podium!" She shuddered. "Old Evil Eye Anstey, that's what he is!"

"Emily!" Leslie rebuked. "The man can't help his deformity!"

"I think it must have been his karma or something. He just *fits* my picture of somebody with the evil eye," Emily said.

Leslie sniffed; a curious haze hung around Emily. She inquired sharply, "Emily Jane Barnes, have you been *smoking?*"

"Pot, you mean? I took a whiff of a joint," Emily said. "Relax, Les, I'm a big girl now. You know I don't like it; it makes me too muzzy to practice properly. But they were handing it round and I took a tiny puff and didn't inhale. Just to be sociable."

That was, Leslie supposed, the best she could expect; Emily was inevitably going to encounter the stuff socially, and if she had already made up her mind how much she could handle—and nothing which would inhibit her musical judgment was acceptable—then all Leslie could do was trust her.

"You'd better take a shower before you go to bed—the smell is all over you," she said, wrinkling her nose.

"Oh, come on, we were all out in the park. Maybe you smell Frodo's beedies—you know, those herbal Indian cigarettes; he smokes them for his asthma, but they're harmless; they smell like cinnamon," she said, turning to her door. "No, wait, I smell it too. Oh, God, is something on fire?"

"No, or the smoke detectors would go off," Leslie said, but she ran downstairs to the kitchen. All was quiet, with no trace of smoke or smell. But in the upstairs hallway she could still smell faint fragrant smoke, blue wisps thinning out on the landing.

"It's frankincense," Emily said, "but where's it coming from?" She followed the scent along the hall, and together they searched the upstairs, but without result.

"Maybe somebody's burning it in the house next door," Leslie said. "Your window's open; maybe it came in there."

"I thought I left it shut," Emily said, "but it's been a long day, and I'm not sure. Anyhow it's shut now." She went into her room for bathrobe and slippers. "I'm going to take a shower. Goodnight, Les. Sleep well."

"Good night, dear." Leslie went into her own room and presently heard the hall shower running. It was good not to have to share a bathroom. Before the shower stopped running, she was asleep.

LESLIE SAT UP IN bed, confused, with no idea what had wakened her. Fog rolled white outside the window. Had she heard the jangle of the telephone? Then she heard Emily's cry across the hall, almost a scream; she ran across the hall barefoot, and found her sister sitting up in bed, her eyes staring, her mouth wide open in a scream.

"How did he get in?"

"Who, darling?"

"Dr. Anstey," Emily stammered. "He came in by the window—"

The window was open, streaming cold fog, white and curling. Leslie took her sister's hand.

"You dreamed it, Emmie. There's no one there. See?"

Emily shook herself, came wide awake with a dazed whimper. "But it was so real," she whispered. "It woke me up, the sound of the window coming open, and see, it's open! And he was standing right there, Les. Staring down at me. It was *him,* Les! That hand of his, and that awful eye, *glaring.* . . ."

The white cat flowed over the windowsill like part of the fog and was gone.

"That was what you heard," Leslie said sensibly, "that cat getting in again." She went to the window and drew the bolt firmly shut.

"I guess so," Emily said, but she still didn't sound too sure. "Only it was so real. He was standing right there by the window. Staring at me. And his eye was so—well, it sort of blazed at me. Only it's dark," she said. "I couldn't really have seen it, in the dark, could I? I guess it was a nightmare," she concluded, in an unsure small voice. In her flannel pajamas she looked about ten, her hair flowing loose on her shoulders.

"You're letting him get on your nerves, honey. After the strain of the audition, and all that," Leslie comforted, and Emily briefly clung to her, then let herself be persuaded to lie down, staring at the closed window and the streamers of fog flowing past it.

"Are you all right now?"

"Yes, of course, Les. I don't know what got into me. I'm so sorry I awakened you—"

"It's all right, dear. Sleep well." She went back to her own room, puzzled.

Emily's not the only one who lets that man get on her nerves, she said sensibly to herself, lay down again and slept peacefully till morning.

CHAPTER

Ten

THERE WERE STILL A hundred things to be done around the house, but Leslie, sipping coffee and nibbling on a piece of toast at the breakfast table, reflected that she could not get to any of them before this afternoon. Susan Hamilton, her first client in the new office, would be here at half-past nine, and Eileen Grantson in midafternoon. Emily came down and, as she ate her way steadily through two pieces of organic toast and half a carton of cottage cheese, announced her intention of making a start on the ex-garage studio.

"I've been so caught up in the audition that I've been letting you do it all," she said. "I've been a selfish pig. As soon as the paint store opens this morning, I'll go and get the paint, and start putting on a coat of a nice cheerful color. Canary yellow?"

"Sounds good," Leslie agreed. "I don't really swallow everything they say about the healing properties of colors, but it couldn't hurt to make the place a little less gruesome. How are you going to get four or five gallons of paint home? Take a taxi? And you'll need rollers and paint pans and brushes—"

"Frodo's going to bring his old truck and help me. He said he doesn't work in the bookstore till two o'clock today, and he likes painting. He gave me a card to figure out how many gallons of paint I'll need, so I have to go measure the place." Emily swallowed the last of her mouthwash-colored tea and disappeared; after a moment she came running back, her face white.

"Les! That white cat—"

Leslie rose hastily. "What is it, Em?"

"It's lying in the studio, all over blood—"

Leslie said, "Just let me grab the first-aid kit," and hurried after her sister, the blue-and-white box with its red cross under her arm. She wasn't that experienced, but during her training in the crisis intervention service, she had had to earn three first-aid certificates. She ought to be able to do something for a wounded animal. Emily flung the door open and stopped with a cry.

"It's gone!" She stood staring at the empty room, the old sewing machine and rocker and the shrouded dress-form stacked in a corner. "It was lying right there. In the middle of the floor."

"Maybe it dragged itself into the garden—a hurt animal will do that sometimes—"

Emily was very pale. "Les, it *couldn't!* There was blood all *over* it—"

"Did you touch it, Emmie? Are you sure it was as badly hurt as all that? Blood looks like a lot more than it is to an amateur," Leslie said, and Emily shook her head.

"It was just lying there in a pool of blood. I was afraid it was dead; I took one look and ran for you. I figured—" her voice started shaking, "you'd know what to do."

Leslie said, "I don't see any blood. If it was that badly hurt, Em, at least there'd be some drops of blood around—"

Emily knelt in the middle of the floor, shivering. "There's got to be blood. Les, it was *covered,* it was lying there in a *pool* of blood—" But the grey linoleum was clean and without a single bloodstain.

"I'm going to look in the garden, Emily. If it was as badly hurt as that, it couldn't have gone very far."

"It couldn't have *moved,* Les, I swear. I—I'm beginning to wonder if I saw it at all. Only I don't—I don't imagine things like that. Do I? I wonder if there really was a cat at all—"

"Nonsense," said Leslie, more brusque than she felt. "I saw it too, last night in your room. I've seen it four or five times. It's a real cat, all right."

"I'm not so sure." Emily was so shaken that she wobbled when she got up. "There was so much blood, Les. Or I thought there was—and we've *seen* the cat but we can't touch it. It didn't even come for the tuna. A real cat would."

"Emily, you're getting all worked up about nothing," Leslie said sharply. "Maybe it doesn't like fish. Maybe the people who own it have trained it not to touch food except from its own dish—"

"You can train a dog like that. I never heard of a cat that wouldn't take food wherever or whenever it could get it." She was searching the brick walks, looking under the castor bean bushes, the tangled blackberry briars. "No cat. Les, I don't think it was a real cat. I think it was a ghost."

"Oh, for heaven's sake!" Leslie, exasperated, stood on the steps of the porch, the first-aid box still under her arm. "It probably crawled into the next yard to die."

"No. Really, Les. The lady who owned this house—Miss Graves, was it?"

"Margrave—"

"Rainbow said she had a white cat. Only that friend of Miss Margrave's who works in the same bookstore as Frodo—Claire?—came to take it home with her after Miss Margrave died, and she couldn't find it. And has that cat ever made a sound? Les, I tell you, it was lying in a big pool of blood; if anything had caught it, a dog or anything, we would have heard *something*."

Leslie was re-examining her memories of sighting the white cat, trying to remember if she had heard it make the slightest sound. No; a preternatural silence seemed to surround the animal. It had made not the faintest noise even climbing over the windowsill last night. Granted, the noiselessness of a cat was proverbial, but its claws must have made some sound at the window. But there had been none. She felt the hair rising on her forearms. A woman had been frightened out of this house and another had committed suicide here.

Alison won't let anyone live in this house unless she likes them. But her mind revolted against the notion.

"I can—just maybe—believe in a ghost of a human being, Emily. Not the ghost of a cat."

"What do people really *know* about those things, Les? Would you have believed you could see a dead woman, or a little girl eating her birthday cake in, where was it, Denver?"

"Phoenix," Leslie said automatically, her whole body feeling cold. Emily went back into the studio and looked around, wrinkling her nose. "Yick. And that smell is here again—"

"And, you said, like cat shit," Leslie reminded her, "and a sick or dying animal would have fouled the place—"

"But the smell comes and goes. Like that incense on the stairs. And there was so *much* blood, Les. If it had really been there it couldn't have moved without leaving a single drop of blood around."

"Ghost cats! Phantom incense!" Leslie said disdainfully. "Em, you ought to write for the *Enquirer*."

"Remember how I said maybe the people who sold the house try to scare people out of it again?" Emily inquired, "Do you think we've bought an honest-to-God haunted house?"

Leslie had been beginning to wonder that herself. She had seen Simon Anstey in the studio, and last night Emily had seen him in her bedroom.

But surely that was psychological. She's frightened of the man, and no wonder. That audition was a terribly stressful thing for a girl her age.

But what about me?

Then she reminded herself that Simon had known the house, had evidently been an intimate of Miss Margrave's, a fellow musician. And coincidences like this were the stuff of which fakes made their living.

"Let's not get all worked up and jump to conclusions, Emily. I'll visit the houses on either side and ask if they saw the cat, and call the SPCA to take it away if it's dead or hurt."

"I'll bet you don't find it," said Emily, and departed in the rattletrap pickup truck which Frodo pulled into the driveway.

Alone in the kitchen, Leslie jumped when the telephone rang, then remembered she was in her new house.

"Dr. Barnes's residence."

It was her answering service. "Mrs. Hamilton asked you to call about her appointment. And there is a message from Mr. Beckenham."

For a moment Leslie went cold inside, wondering if Nick was calling from Sacramento to entangle her in some new unreason. Then she remembered that she had not known her new telephone number to give to Joel.

She called Susan Hamilton; the telephone rang five times and the woman's voice sounded choked with tears.

"I'll be late for my appointment, Leslie; I have to get a sitter for Chrissy."

"She's not in school?"

"She was, but her program teacher called and I had to bring her home. They said she bit another little girl and when the teacher tried to restrain her, she hit another teacher and blacked her eye. She's been so good lately, I was beginning to hope—"

Leslie waited, but the woman was silent, with the bleak silence of despair.

"How is she now, Susan?"

"How do I know? She's quiet. She just sits there. The terrible part is, she can't tell me what happened. They say she just bit the other child without warning, but how do I know? Maybe the other kid was hurting her, teasing her— If a normal child gets into a fight in school, they can find out—but with Chris I never know—" Her voice died again. At last she said, choking with tears, "I've always been a religious woman. But how could God do a thing like this? What did I do to deserve it? Or even if I did—even if I committed some sin, slept with David before we were married, why would God take that out on Chrissy? And all I get from the minister is that God's ways aren't for me to question."

There was nothing Leslie could say to that, and Susan Hamilton expected no answer. She said in a dull voice that she would call when she knew when she could keep her appointment.

"You can come anytime before noon; if you can't make it before that, call my service," Leslie said, and hung up, her heart aching for the woman struggling under that monstrous burden. Her professional training had taught her to keep detachment, but she had gone into counseling out of a desire to do something for people like Susan, and what could she do? It would require a direct pipeline to God to do anything for the Susan Hamiltons—or the Christina Hamiltons—of this world. She sighed as she dialled Joel's office.

"Hello, darling, how's the new house?"

She wondered what he would say if she told him about ghost cats, phantom incense, excremental smells in the studio, and the ghostly figure not of a dead man, but of a living one. "Fine," she said.

"Listen, I have to be in court tonight in San Francisco, and I'd like to drop in and see what the place looks like with the furniture. Okay?"

"Come around five, and have supper with us. You can be our first guest."

"Okay, if Emily doesn't cook," he agreed good-naturedly. "I don't like yogurt or alfalfa sprouts."

"I'll grill us a steak," she promised. The prospect had brightened her somewhat, and she went into her office. The fog was beginning to burn off, and the view of the sea and sky was endlessly peaceful. She saw from the front window Frodo's rattletrap truck, and Emily unloading paint, brushes, ladders and a variety of equipment; she ran out.

"Did you buy all that, Emily? We're not painting the whole house!"

"No problem, Dr. Barnes," Frodo said, "I borrowed the ladder from my Dad. We'll have that studio painted by noon."

"Wonderful," Leslie said, and ran to answer the office telephone. This time it was Susan Hamilton herself.

"I found a sitter for Chris; I'll be over in half an hour, if that's all right."

"Yes, certainly."

Leslie stepped out to the studio. Frodo, on the ladder, was covering ceiling and upper wall with broad strokes of pale yellow paint; Emily was putting masking tape around the window trim and covering the glass and the light fixtures. She did not go in; they were deep in conversation about the operas of Gluck and Handel.

If there was a ghost, could it survive layers of fresh paint, and the attentions of young cheerful people? Even the question was ridiculous, in the brilliant sunshine that was beginning to burn through the disappearing fog. She went in to wait for Susan Hamilton.

SUSAN WAS A SMALL, harried-looking little woman; still in her twenties, her pale hair looked faded rather than just blond, and she was carelessly dressed. She came into the house as if sleepwalking, but immediately brightened when she saw the new office.

"What a lovely, peaceful place! I envy you, Dr. Barnes."

Leslie let her exclaim over the view and the decoration of the office for a few minutes, then asked, "How is Chrissy?"

"I just don't know." Susan shook her head. "I felt so guilty when I left her with the sitter after all that shakeup at the school. She looked so bewildered, poor little thing. The school definitely wants me to make other arrangements for her next year. They simply aren't equipped to handle a combative child. But she's never done anything like that before. There's intelligence there somewhere, if I could only reach it; all her therapists say so. She's not mentally defective. But she might as well be. I see signs she's coming along so well, and then something like this happens."

"Has she been making progress, then?"

"Everybody else says so. Once she said 'Hi' to me, just like any other child. Her teachers say that now and then she'll do what they tell her— really listening and cooperating, though she doesn't speak. And one time she went all the way up to the park all by herself and I found her where I'd taken her once, playing all by herself on the slides. Leslie, that's more than a mile away! How could she have found it? It was a naughty thing to do, I was absolutely terrified, I had the police out looking for her. But just the same it made me realize—there's some kind of intelligence in Chrissy, and if I could only reach it! What am I doing wrong?"

"We've talked about guilt before, Susan. Why do you think you feel guilty now?"

"I always feel guilty," Susan burst out, "and now on top of all the guilt I have for having her, you seem to think I should feel guilty about *being* guilty!"

"I hear you saying that you think it is reasonable to feel guilt, Susan, and that I am ignoring your feelings about it."

"Well, I must have done *something*. Maybe I didn't take good care of myself when I was pregnant. Or maybe that first doctor was right, when he said autistic children were being rejected by their parents—Only I didn't reject her! I didn't! David did, but only after they realized there was something wrong with her, not before!"

"Nobody has ever been able to say for certain that Chrissy is autistic," Leslie reminded her. "She is an affectionate child, which is certainly not autism; a truly autistic child ignores her parents. And you said Chrissy cried for her father after he left. Anyhow, 'emotional neglect' is only one theory about autism, and it's never been proven. Certainly you never neglected her, even when it would have saved your marriage."

They had been through this more than once, while Susan tried to untangle the labyrinth of guilt and misery. Her husband had blamed first himself, then her; they had tried to track down distant relatives with similar conditions; even reassurance that it was probably birth injury had not helped.

But I can't do anything for any of them, Leslie thought. *I can't even say anything.*

"No, seriously, Leslie—" Susan interrupted herself in the middle of her flow of words. "Not as a therapist. Just as a human being. I know you say professionally that I'm supposed to get rid of guilt—"

"Well, do you think it is a constructive feeling?" Leslie asked. "Do you think that if you gave up your guilt, you would be taking Christina's plight too lightly, that you would feel you didn't care enough about her?"

"That's part of it," Susan said slowly. "But I've been thinking about what I said on the phone. Why did this happen to me? I am a religious person. I'll never believe that life is all chaos and that there's no purpose for anything. If I believed in that kind of blind chaos, I think I'd take Chrissy in my arms and jump with her off the Golden Gate Bridge; it would make life easier for so many people."

"Have you been thinking about that?" asked Leslie. In her training, she had been taught never to ignore that first mention, even lightly, of suicidal thoughts. Susan was in very real trouble; not simply neurotic maladaptation, as so many of her clients, but a problem which had driven other women to suicide before her, and would again.

"Not really," Susan said at last, slowly. "I still feel that somewhere, somehow, there must be a *reason* for all this. A reason why Chrissy is the way she is, and why it happened to me. I know rationally it wasn't anything I did, and it can't have been anything Chrissy did, she's a *baby*—only I hear the kids these days talking about past lives, and karma, and all that. Do you suppose maybe Chris and I did something to each other in a past life, so that we're stuck this way with each other now? I mean, sometimes I think it's the only thing that makes sense."

Silence. The peace of sun and sky flowed around the two women in the quiet office, and Leslie was conscious of the tick of the cuckoo clock on the wall. Leslie knew that by all the canons of her profession she should say something to discourage this irrational notion; why should she allow Susan, who had enough guilt for one lifetime, to take upon herself the notion that there might be other troubles beyond this one life?

"I don't know, Susan," she said at last. "I don't think it's quite as simple as that. It's not a matter of being good or evil in one life and being punished or rewarded in the next. That's just one step beyond the simplistic religious notion that we pay for what we do by going to heaven or hell. I don't want to sound like your minister and say we mustn't question God's purposes; I think we have to question what happens to us. If I have any religion at all, it's that there *is* some order in the universe. Did it ever occur to you that maybe, before we come into this life, we choose what's going to happen to us?"

"Do you think I'd choose this?" Susan cried.

"I don't know," Leslie said again, while with one detached part of her mind she wondered why she was saying this; but she had never been so sure of anything in her life. "How do we know how things would look from the perspective of more lives than one? It's possible that for some reason you felt you needed to learn compassion for the handicapped; perhaps you felt you had been insensitive to the needs of someone. Or perhaps Chrissy, for some reason, felt that she needed to learn the lesson of being something other than perfect—a lesson of humility, perhaps, or of helplessness—and she came to you because you were the right parent. Some parents would have institutionalized a child like Chris as soon as they found out what was wrong with her. . . ."

"And even when David begged me to do it, saying it was the only way to save our marriage, I wouldn't," Susan said. "I felt it was unfair to make me choose between them, that he should share the burden. And I know now that he wasn't the kind of person who could. The way he reacted to Christina showed me that. If Chrissy hadn't been the way she was, I might have gone on believing David was right for me. Chris showed me that I couldn't trust David to put anything before his own comfort and convenience. I think I knew that all along." She stopped, thinking it over.

"What are you going to do now?" Leslie asked.

"I'm going to try and find another school for Christina," Susan said slowly. "I am beginning to realize that someday I may have to institutionalize her. Until then I'll do my best, I'll give her what I can, all the love I can. And when I can't, maybe I'll just have to go on to the next thing. If she has my—my support and love while I can give it, then maybe—" She stopped again, and said at last, "If she was born the way she was for a reason, then maybe her destiny isn't entirely up to me. I can only do so much for her before I have to let her—" She was searching for words now, slowly, thinking it over, "find out what her destiny is, even if it isn't to stay home and be my poor helpless baby."

Leslie nodded, but did not cheapen this insight with words. If only, she thought, their own mother had been able to accept this, that her gifted daughter had a destiny of her own, that Emily belonged to herself and her own talent, not to Constance and James Barnes, to gratify them as their wonderful child.

But when the cuckoo clock struck eleven and Susan had gone, still mentally chewing over her new insights, Leslie remained in the office, wondering what had gotten into her. She had never had more than the faintest intellectual interest in reincarnation as a philosophy. Yet from somewhere she had been able to find exactly the right thing to say to Susan at this impasse in her life. Where had it come from?

SHE WAS FIXING HERSELF a sandwich in the kitchen when she heard the sound of a guitar; Emily and Frodo, somewhat paint-smudged, were sitting on the garden wall, and he was playing the guitar and singing. She would have thought Emily's response to this would have been to put her hands over her ears and run away.

Maybe Emily had found a male for whom she would compromise her cherished opinions and prejudices? She knew Emily well enough to know she wasn't simply putting up with Frodo because he was a man who showed interest in her—she had seen Emily's uncompromising attitude toward boys who tried to interest her in such supposedly normal teenage pursuits as disco music or sports. But she remembered Emily saying that Frodo played classical flute. That, she supposed, made the difference; his opinions were therefore worth hearing, even, perhaps, on music. She stepped out on the porch.

"Want some sandwiches?"

"Oh, goody," Emily said. "Is there any cheese? Come on, Frodo, I'll make us some sandwiches before you have to go to work."

She came in and put some eggs in a pan to hard-boil. "Want lemon grass, camomile or Red Zinger tea, Frodo?"

"Lemon grass is fine," Frodo said. "Hello, Dr. Barnes."

"Leslie, please. Even clients my own age call me by my first name," Leslie said, smiling, and passed him the honey jar for his tea. She found that she liked this amiable young hippie.

"Les, *did* you find that cat?"

Leslie had half forgotten the animal. She was about to say she had not had a chance to look when Frodo pointed out the open kitchen door.

"You mean Miss Margrave's white cat? There it is, going along under the castor bean bushes—see?"

"But it can't be," Emily began, crowded to the door, and fell silent. At last she said, "I told you. It's a ghost cat. No sign of blood or anything."

"Emily, there are a lot of white cats in this city—" Leslie began, but Emily had already begun telling Frodo about the cat lying in its blood, this morning, in the garage. She was wryly surprised that Emily had not regaled him with the tale while they were painting. The stove timer sounded before she had finished, and Emily moved to take the eggs out of the pan, juggling them in her hands as she ran cold water over the shells in the sink. She began peeling them.

Frodo said, "I'm not surprised. There's something in that studio. Claire's friend said it all seemed to center around the studio. Candles went out. The fog kept coming in and she had nightmares about the place. Two or three times some piece of work she was doing on the potter's wheel was wrecked when no one was there. She said, by invisible hands."

"And you believe all that, Frodo?" Leslie asked curiously.

Frodo sipped at his tea and looked at her as if he was afraid that what he would say would be somehow offensive. "Sometimes I do and sometimes I don't. But the point is, I know Betty Carmody. She's not a nervous or hysterical woman, and that's enough for me. Did it ever occur to you, Dr. Barnes—Leslie," he amended, "that on any other subject, if somebody who's generally sane and truthful tells you they saw something, or felt something, you'll believe them? But on this one, we jump right away to the conclusion that people are lying, or freaking right out, or on drugs or something. And if Betty Carmody said this happened to her, it's like Rainbow or Claire said it; I'd believe them. Or her."

She had never thought of it that way. But it had happened to her in Sacramento. They had believed she was lying, or deluded, and some people continued to believe it even after Juanita García had been found dead, even after her description of the murderer had led them to a suspect they had questioned before, found the girls' bloodstained garments and locks of their hair in his possession; they would have preferred to believe that Leslie had somehow been his silent partner or accomplice.

There are more things in Heaven and Earth, Horatio . . . she refrained from speaking the cliché, and was reminded of the way in which an answer for Susan's distress had come to her when she needed it most. "Frodo, do you have any books on reincarnation in the store?"

"Lots of them. Good and bad. Why? You getting into reincarnation?"

"I'm—curious," she said.

"There's even one by a psychotherapist who used to counsel people on their problems by finding out what hangups they carried over from past lives," he said. "Miss Margrave used to swear by it; she wrote a preface to the paperback edition."

Oh. Really. That was very interesting, Leslie thought. "I'll try to get over to the bookstore. If you could hunt up a copy for me, I'd be grateful."

"Sure. No problem."

Emily demanded, "You want mustard on your egg salad, Frodo? Leslie, you want some of this? It's good," and the conversation veered away from the occult to the general. Leslie went to look into the studio; it was already covered with a coat of quick-drying paint, and Emily said that after lunch she would paint the trim. "But I think I'd better get in an hour or two of practice first, Les."

"Can I come over after work and bring my lute?" Frodo asked. "I really want to hear how it sounds with your harp, Em."

"I thought Emily said you played classical flute—I didn't know it was *lute,*" Leslie said, delighted. Frodo gave a deprecating grin.

"Oh, I play the flute too. And the piano, some, only not the way Emily does, not seriously. And drums, and I'm studying the sitar. And the cello, a little."

Emily said eagerly, "He played as a cello soloist with the Dallas Philharmonic when he was eleven years old."

Yes, Leslie thought, this is the kind of young man Emily can take seriously.

Soon after, Frodo shouldered his guitar and went off to the bookstore; Emily went into the music room, but while Leslie was scraping the sandwich plates and putting them into the sink, she reappeared again.

"Listen, Les," she said diffidently, "I think I need to see a doctor. Your gynecologist. Can I call up and make an appointment right away?"

"Sure, why not?" Leslie said. "Have you been having troubles, Em? Cramps, or something?"

"No. I mean, well, uh, I could just go over to the Planned Parenthood clinic, I guess."

Leslie was glad that her back was turned to her sister; she did not want to register surprise. Emily's confidence was precious. "No, call up Ellen Baring; she's very good, very sensitive. I've always preferred a woman gynecologist myself."

"Listen—" Emily paused. "Do you believe all that bad stuff they say about the pill?"

"No, I don't. I think ninety per cent of it is propaganda by the Catholic Church; all that's wrong with it is that it's really effective. Of course some people may be allergic to it, but every single side effect reported by the pill users was also reported by the people who took placebos. If you can't take one pill, chances are they'll find another one that agrees with you better. Personally, I wouldn't even consider using anything else. But she'll explain all the different alternatives to you."

"I'll go and call her before I forget," Emily said, and Leslie, hearing the telephone in the hall, wondered if it was Frodo's presence which had sparked this in Emily's mind or whether it was simply a part of the maturation process. It was none too soon; Emily was nearing eighteen, and she could not live her entire life encased in a cocoon of music.

No sooner was Emily off the phone than it rang again, and her sister called, "For you, Les," on her way into the music room. Leslie picked up the kitchen extension; the hall and music room were already filled with crashing chords that reassured Leslie unconsciously; Emily might be contemplating almost anything, including a sudden foray into adult sexuality, but her music was still her first love; she could always gauge Emily's state of mind by the vigor of her playing.

"Hello?"

"Dr. Barnes—I saw your picture in the *Enquirer,* how you found that girl's body." It was a shaky female voice. "Can you help me find my son? He disappeared six months ago—"

"No," said Leslie automatically, not even stopping to think. She put down the receiver, feeling her stomach knotting. *Not that again, please God, no, not that.* Would it always pursue her? She went out toward the studio, hearing it ring again behind her, knowing it was the same disconsolate female voice, feeling trapped and frightened by the intrusion of this irrationality into her world again. It went on ringing, but she did not care. She called over her shoulder, "Don't answer it, Em. It's someone I don't want to talk to."

Emily and Frodo had left the door open to air out the paint smell.

Leslie stopped on the doorstep; before her eyes splashed blood, shocking red against the grey, drab paint of the floor. In the welter of blood the white cat lay motionless.

Leslie blinked, heard herself cry out. Even as she stared it melted like vanishing fog. This, then, was what Emily had seen; and she would have denied its very existence except for Frodo's common-sense words.

But there was nothing there now. Grasping at straws of sanity, she thought; but we all saw it—

There are hundreds of white cats in the city, I'm sure. Probably the cat was killed here—messily—and the shadow, the psychic image, remains; the same process by which, looking at Juanita García's dead body, she had seen the girl's murderer.

And now she could not doubt the evidence of her eyes, or she risked the same kind of intellectual dishonesty that had been quoted in her training.

On any other subject one-tenth the evidence would already have convinced me; on this subject ten times the evidence would not convince me.

In any case the phenomenon was transitory; it was gone now. Maybe it only showed itself once to any person. As for the white cat that came and went in the garden and Emily's bedroom, she was far from admitting that it was the same cat. Or ghost.

Emily had left some color-sample chips on the swaddled sewing machine. When she went to the bookshop for that book on reincarnation— and she did want to know something about it; why had she suddenly found it in her mind to counsel Susan that way?—she would buy some suitable material and make covers for the cushions of the old rocker. She had been nursed in that rocker; one of her clearest memories of her tenth ysitting it when the newborn Emily was put into her arms. *That's my baby,* she had said to her mother. *That's not your baby, that's my baby.* Her mother had only laughed, but after this morning she wondered. Emily had always been a misfit in their family, and neither their mother nor their practical father had ever understood her or felt comfortable with her. *Only Grandma. And me. Maybe Emily needed a family that wouldn't be too sympathetic. A family that would make a fighter out of her. And even if I have children of my own someday, Emily will always be my kid. Maybe she came to me the same way poor little Chrissy came to Susan. Only I was luckier.*

Then, in a fit of revulsion, she slammed the whole thing out of her mind. Reincarnation! That was worse than the superstitious idiot on the phone, begging for the help of a psychic whose name she had read in a lurid tabloid, to find her lost son! She went angrily into the kitchen and fetched the tape measure, to measure for the cushions of the rocker. The damned woman had probably driven her son away from home by trying to make him live as if he were still ten years old. Most mothers did—look at her own family! Trying to force Emily into a teachers' college! She measured the tattered old cushions, pulling the rocker into the center of the floor and unloading the layers of drop cloths.

She rummaged for a pencil and paper to write down the sizes. She would need about two yards. A nice, sunshiny yellow print. She had seen some fabric with daisies. She glanced back; was the rocker rocking by itself? Oh, damn, she was seeing ghosts in every corner now; soon she would be seeing them under her bed, or consulting the *Enquirer!*

Although for all the good she was doing her patients, she might as well be an astrologer or a psychic. At least the psychic or the astrologer could give them the illusion of hope, instead of giving them mental health to go out and live in an insane society which would probably bomb itself to shreds before the century ended. Maybe she should take up practice as a psychic! She was certainly at a dead end in her profession, and it was the second one she had had; she had failed as an educational counselor, and now she was so discouraged about the prospects for her patients that she doled out spiritual advice about reincarnation! In a fit of depression, she flung the pencil away. What difference did it make whether she covered the old rocker or not? She couldn't afford to stay in this house unless she found some new patients, and it was dishonest to take anyone on, knowing as she did how little a counselor could do for anyone. Maybe she should marry Joel and give up the whole business. It would certainly be more honest. At least, as Joel's wife, she knew what she would be giving and what she would be getting.

INSIDE THE OFFICE, LETTING the soundproofed calm enfold her as she waited for Eileen Grantson, she felt better. When the telephone rang again, she picked it up and heard the woman's voice again.

"Please, Dr. Barnes, don't hang up. Won't you please let me come and talk to you? I can't just give up on my boy. He's the only one I've got. I just need to know whether he's alive or dead. If he's dead I can stop worrying about him, and if he's alive at least I'll know."

Leslie was about to refuse again. But the note of desperation in the woman's voice made her hesitate. She said, "Do you live in the city?"

"I live in Marin County."

"All right. Come and see me tonight." Joel would be here. Perhaps he could talk the woman out of it. "Seven o'clock?"

"That's wonderful. Oh, thank you, Dr. Barnes, thank you, God bless you—"

Leslie cut off the woman's repeated thanks, almost curtly, and watched Eileen Grantson walk up the driveway. Now, she supposed, she would be subjected to an hour-long discussion of poltergeists. A cat's ghost, psychics, reincarnation—well, it served her right for moving into a haunted house!

Eleven

BUT TO LESLIE'S SURPRISE, again Eileen did not once mention the poltergeist, breaking china, or any similar subject; she spent the whole hour talking about Scotty, an argument she had had with her father about what time she should be in after dates, and how she felt about a proposed visit to her mother and stepfather in Texas. Watching her run down the steps, Leslie did not know whether to be relieved or frustrated. For Eileen's own sake, she was glad the phenomenon had subsided and was perhaps ended for good.

For her own, she still wished that she knew what had caused it, and whether the cause, and the purpose of the visitation, was the same in her case as in Eileen's. In the new house, she had seen no evidence of poltergeist activity—unless the window in Emily's room, which seemed to open itself rather more often than she could account for, was an example. Of course, if a cat was getting in . . . but the cat seemed to be a ghost. Nonsense,

Leslie told herself, the city was full of cats and a good proportion of them must be white.

Eileen's poltergeist seems to have cleared up when she found herself a boy friend. Sounds suspiciously Freudian, Leslie told herself; I shouldn't assume cause and effect without proof. And when she had resumed her affair with Joel and started sleeping with him again, her own poltergeist phenomena—if that was truly what they had been—had if anything grown stronger. It was certainly not as clear-cut as frustrated sexual energy.

Maybe she ought to go over to the bookstore and get Miss Margrave's book. She had, after all, asked Frodo to choose something for her on reincarnation. But there was hardly time now; Joel was coming at five for the steak she had promised him, and she still had to go out and get one.

She noticed that there was no sound of the piano inside the music room. Had Emily gone out? No, from the kitchen window she saw the studio door still open; her sister must be out there, painting.

Emily, in cutoff jeans and bare feet, was listlessly stroking cream-colored paint on a windowsill.

"This room's going to be really nice when we get it finished, Emily," Leslie said. Her sister barely raised her eyes.

"Yeah. I guess so."

"Want some help doing this? Or I can finish it tomorrow, honey, if you want to practice. There's no rush."

"It doesn't matter," Emily said, still mechanically painting the same piece of windowsill. "It's all right."

"Em, is something the matter? Shall I go away and let you alone?"

"No, it's okay. It's nothing you've done." Emily moved to the next level of window sash. "I'm just fed up, that's all. Practice five hours a day for the last six years and where the hell am I getting? You saw those faculty jury papers." (Leslie hadn't.) "I looked at them first off and thought they were so good. Only one of them criticized the way I sat, too low, said I was losing energy. That's the kind of thing you say to a nine-year-old, criticize her *posture,* for Godsake! Dr. Anstey said I had a nice feel for Rachmaninoff—couldn't he find anything to say about my playing and technique? I guess there was nothing good to say, not even what I was doing *wrong.* And then that fat pig Paddington gets a chance to audition for the Symphony, and if she is better than I am, I must really be god-awful—"

"But Simon Anstey came up and complimented you personally," Leslie said, wondering what had suddenly touched this off. "I didn't notice him doing that with any of the other students!"

"Yeah, and he made a point of saying how young I was, like I was a child prodigy or something! Do I look *that* young? I think he just meant I was too immature to be in a competition like that."

"But you got into his master class," Leslie pointed out, "and I doubt if he takes absolute beginners into that—"

"So did that ham-handed freak Steve Kalapergos; he took all the fucking incompetents," Emily raged. "Maybe he thinks we're so bad we *need* his rotten master class! And stop trying to cheer me up! Shit, Leslie, my goddam career is over, before it ever really started." She threw the paintbrush on the floor and burst into tears. Through sobs Leslie could hear confused imprecations, making out only a few connected words.

"Spend your whole lifetime working . . . not worth a damn thing . . . not good for anything . . ."

"Emily! Stop it!" Leslie took her sister's shoulder and shook her lightly. "There's no reason to get hysterical!"

"I'm not hysterical," Emily shrieked. "I'm just trying for once to look at things realistically! Making sense instead of listening to all these people who stand around telling me what a fuckin' genius I am!" She wrenched herself away from Leslie. "An' you're about the worst, pushing and prodding me and telling me I deserve a goddam career. What good has it done you? Mommy was right! You got the career woman bee in your fuckin' bonnet and now you want to ruin my life too!"

Leslie took a long breath, reminding herself that Emily was not making a considered judgment but was obviously hysterical.

"Fine," she said crisply. "You can sell the piano if you want to, and the Conservatory term is up in a few days; you can enroll in San Francisco State for summer school and take courses in typing and data processing."

Emily stood there and blinked at her.

"What?"

"I was suggesting that you have other options, after all. No one has sentenced you to a life term. Your life is obviously your own; stay off the subject of my personal life, will you?"

"What do you mean? For Godsake, what did I say to set you off like that?" Emily demanded, in such absolute sincerity that Leslie felt confused. She took another deep breath.

"I think you're tired, Emmie, and overreacting. Come in the kitchen and I'll make you a cup of tea. And did you remember to eat something?"

Emily rubbed her eyes. Her face was blotchy with tears.

"Yeah, I guess I'm just too tired. It just all rushed over me all at once, how hopeless it looks. I'm at a dead end. My hands—" She spread them out before her. "They feel stiff and horrible. I kept making all kinds of stupid mistakes while I was practicing. Agrowsky said that everybody goes stale now and then, only I thought he was just trying to cheer me up. And he's going to Switzerland for six weeks, and over the summer I'll get into all kinds of bad habits."

Emily snuffled, covering the paint cans. "I can't imagine what got into me. I just exploded. Only I don't think it's all hysterics, Les. Do you seriously think it's worth all this time and money, when I don't have a ghost of a chance at a concert career and I'll probably wind up teaching piano or playing the organ in some fucking church."

"That would be quite a church," Leslie said. "Listen to yourself sometime, Emmie." And Emily hesitated, replayed her last words in her mind, and gave a tentative giggle.

"I guess I do want some tea," she said, and followed Leslie into the kitchen. "Only you don't have to make it. You spend too much time waiting on me as it is. I'm just sponging on you all the time. I don't even do my share of the dishes—"

Leslie shrugged. "You can look after me when I'm old and feeble," she said, deliberately keeping the tone light.

"No, honestly, Leslie," Emily said, when she was seated at the table with a cup of tea and a cookie in her hand. "What I asked you before. Do you really think it's worth all this time and money on just the off chance of a career as a concert pianist? Living like this, and—and never doing any of the things other people do—"

"Emily, how do I know? I'm no expert. I think you play marvelously well, but with that and sixty cents you can get a ride on the streetcar. If you want an expert opinion, go to Dr. Agrowsky or to one of the people in the Conservatory."

Emily drew a long breath and let it out, half sobbing. She said, "Agrowsky's making a lot of money teaching me. He's supposed to say he's ripping me off?"

"Then go to Dr. Anstey. He doesn't even know you; he only heard you play once. And you don't even like him, so you couldn't say his opinion was anything but disinterested."

She snuffled again. "Maybe I will. Is there any Kleenex, Les?"

"There's a box in my office," Leslie said, and Emily went to fetch it.

"Be sure to put it back when you're finished," Leslie reminded her, and Emily said with a shy giggle, "Do your patients cry all the time?"

Leslie said lightly, remembering something in her training, "When I was studying, one of my professors said that all nondirective counseling could be reduced to a handy box of Kleenex and a series of sympathetic noises every few seconds. But it's true that when people are trying to explore their feelings—well, a box of Kleenex is helpful."

Emily blew her nose and nodded.

Emily's sudden disillusion at her chosen career hardly surprised her. She had felt very much like that, sometime this morning, feeling that she was at a dead end in her profession, hopeless, that she should have married Joel—suddenly she remembered *where* she had felt that way.

"Emily, tell me, did you get to feeling down about your playing, and quit practicing and go out to paint? Or did you go out and start painting and then get fed up about your career?"

Emily swallowed a mouthful of peanut butter cookie. She said, "Oh, I felt fine while I was playing. I felt I was really getting along wonderfully, and I was all excited over Anstey's master classes, because usually freshmen aren't eligible. Then I felt guilty at leaving the painting unfinished, because I was afraid the rollers and pans would get all hard and horrible, so I went out to finish up, and while I was working in there, I got the most awful sense that I'd been fooling myself, that I was all washed up, wasting my time, that I'd never be any good for anything again. . . ."

Leslie said deliberately—it was time they faced this thing together—"I was out in the studio alone for a while this morning. And I got to feeling very much that way about my own career . . . as if it was a total waste of time and I couldn't do any good to anyone, that I'd wasted my whole life. . . ."

Emily's eyes widened. She said, "And Frodo said that was why that woman who was here before us—Betty somebody—was driven out of the place! Because she said the studio was haunted by something that hated her . . . hated her art especially! So my worrying about the piano—" She broke off to think about that.

"Leslie! If the place is haunted, do you think that Miss Margrave—she was a musician herself—do you think it's a case of, she's jealous because I can still play and she can't?"

Leslie said, "I can't imagine it could be that." Several times she had heard the faint echo of the harpsichord in the music room or the hall. And her office was a haven of peace and contentment. "Have you ever felt anything like that anywhere else in the house? In the music room, for instance?"

Emily shook her head. "Never! When I'm playing, I feel"—she smiled sheepishly, "that she likes having me there. The way Dr. Anstey said. Once I even thought I heard a harpsichord for a second," she confessed, "like a little echo. But I probably imagined it."

"I've heard it too," Leslie said. "But whatever it is, I don't think it's the same thing. From the first day I came here, I've felt that the studio was—" she hesitated, then said the word that was in both their minds, though neither was willing to say it in the eighth decade of the twentieth century, "haunted."

"What are we going to do, Leslie? Just shut it up and not try to—to go in there?"

"It was all right when we were both in there with Frodo this morning," Leslie reminded her, and Emily nodded. "Yes. Even after you left, Frodo and I were just fine. Maybe it only hits people who are alone in there."

"That's easy, then," Leslie said. "We'll fix it up as a party room, and make sure there are always lots of people there. Somehow I don't think whatever's in there would have much luck haunting a party of people laughing and having fun." She patted Emily on the shoulder. "I have to go over to the market and get a steak. Joel's coming for supper; he has to attend night court or something over here."

Predictably, Emily wrinkled her nose.

When she came back, as she had half expected, Emily was making herself a grilled cheese sandwich in the kitchen. She said, "Rainbow asked me to go with her to a thing over in the bookstore. I'll be out late. In case, I mean, if Joel wants to stay over—"

Leslie laughed. "He has to be in night court, I told you. But thank you, Emmie."

Emily, on the way out, gave her a quick, lopsided kiss on one cheek. "I'm sorry I yelled at you, Les. Honest."

Twelve

THE STEAK WAS WONDERFUL, done the way Joel had taught her, with grains of fresh-ground black pepper pounded into the surface. Joel approved the music room with harp, piano and the garden view, and her peaceful, elegant office. She took him upstairs for a glimpse at the bedrooms (Emily had left the window open again), and in her room he pulled her down on the bed. "We've just about got time," he urged, moving his hands to excite her, but Leslie pulled regretfully away, moving to the dressing room to straighten her hair.

"Love, I'm really sorry, but I have this crazy woman coming at seven. Listen, there's the bell; go and let her in for me, will you?" She heard what she had said as she went down the stairs; how could she so blithely toss around words like "crazy," she, a worker in mental health? But she did not regret her harsh label; people who went to psychics were mad, and that was that.

And what about the psychics?

Mrs. Chloe Demarest did not look like the conventional definition of a madwoman. She was fiftyish, controlled and composed, an ordinary suburban matron complete with hair rinsed in an attractive shade of blue. She herself brought it up when she was seated in Leslie's office.

"You must think I'm a little crazy, coming to you like this, Dr. Barnes. Only a friend of mine told me how you found the body of that poor girl in Sacramento." She looked uneasily from Leslie to Joel's tight-lipped, skeptical face.

Leslie said quietly, "You must realize that I can't promise to help you."

"Oh, I'll pay your fees whether you can help me or not," the woman said quickly, and Leslie felt a surge of real anger.

"I charge my patients; you are not my patient. If I can possibly help you, I will, but I can't accept payment. Tell me about your son. Has he left home before this?"

"No. Never. He was such a good boy, he never wanted to worry me. David would never do a thing like this—" she began, and Leslie sighed inwardly, tempted to tune her out. It was the common lament of mothers without the slightest idea what their sons were really like at all, thinking of them still as obedient toddlers when they were twenty or thirty. But then Mrs. Demarest said something that made her listen.

"And even if he didn't care what I thought, he wouldn't do this to Mary—that's his sister; she's blind and he's always been terribly close to her. And he left his dog in the boarding kennel, six weeks now without calling me or Mary to go and get her back and look after her, and he knows we'd be glad to do it."

That made her think. If he was the kind of youth who would spend time assisting a blind sister and fail to make arrangements for a cherished pet, possibly he had actually met with foul play.

"The police found his car, empty," she said. "A little crashed but not bad enough to kill him, and where was his body if he was killed?"

"You brought his picture. May I see it?" Leslie asked, sure without knowing why. From some remote, silent corner in her mind she knew that the irrational, inexplicable state was stealing over her again, and hopelessly resented it. But she was as powerless to stop it.

She took the photograph in her hand and even before she turned it, to look into the kind, unremarkable, bespectacled face of David Demarest, she knew he was dead before his twenty-seventh birthday, dead and peaceful, his face unmarked, his glasses unbroken on his face.

"He went south," she said. "Another man was driving. The man who crashed his car. Afraid he'd be charged with a hit-and-run. South. South and—yes—west. Route Five. He died and the man put him out of his car." She heard the woman moan, but went relentlessly on.

"Get in touch with the police in a town—" She stopped, trying to focus her erratic vision. "Oil wells. And towers—" The maddening wisps of vision were clearing. "By the ocean. Oil wells in the water." She had a fast glimpse of Phyllis Anne Chapman's face and knew the city she had seen. "Santa Barbara. Ask the police in Santa Barbara if they have an unidentified young man." Abruptly the pictures were gone from her mind, and she handed the living face of the dead man back to his mother, feeling drained and cold. "I'm sorry," she said. "I'm so sorry. I wish I could have had something better to tell you. Has your son ever been fingerprinted?"

"No. He was never—his footprints were taken when he was a baby. In the hospital. Would that still be any good?"

Leslie didn't know. She said, "Telephone them. If they have an unidentified body it might be worth going down there to—to identify him." In the back of her mind, a tiny picture in living color, she could see the woman pulling out a morgue drawer, fainting with a scream of recognition; she would go to Santa Barbara, would find her son there. Rage surged in her against the unknown man the police would never find, who had done this rather than face the nuisance of an inquiry, a possible minor charge of vehicular homicide or reckless driving, who had failed to find his victim medical attention, then callously put a corpse out of his car in a strange city. And then it was all gone, like a fading dream, and Leslie wanted it to go, to go far away, never to come near her again. (But it would. She knew it would. Again and again. Resigned, she sank hopelessly into her chair, where another woman had sat before her.)

Joel was gathering up the woman's belongings, ushering her out of the house. Leslie wished he had not, she should at least have offered the woman a drink, a cup of coffee, time to gather herself together after the bad news she had had to give, but she felt too exhausted and drained to move or protest.

"I got rid of her for you," said Joel, coming back. "How much of that stuff you gave her was for real, and how much of it did you make up to get her out of here?"

Outrage did what compassion could not; Leslie sat up straight in her chair.

"Joel! You can't believe I'd do a thing like that!"

"Anything's fair with a kook like that," he said. "You ought to have told her that your fee was a thousand dollars. Or five thousand. That would get rid of them faster. No, seriously, Les, I mean it. If you let it get around that you do this kind of thing for free, they'll never let you alone, and judging by the look on your face, you can't afford to do it too much."

Her strength was coming rapidly back to her. She remembered feeling like this, seated in the police car, near a drainage ditch where a young girl lay dead.

"I'd have had to tell her what I saw, or if I didn't see anything, anyhow. I wouldn't feel right about taking money for it. It—it just comes, it doesn't cost me anything—"

"Except your time and energy. You should see yourself, Leslie. That's worth anything you could charge for it."

She drew a long breath. "If it was the only living I had, Joel, I suppose I'd have to. It isn't. Joel, I don't want to talk about it."

"That's fine with me," he retorted at white heat. "If I never hear of it again, I'll be happy. Why do you keep on letting his kind of crap happen?"

Because I can't help it. Because it's what I am. Because there has to be a reason why it came to me. She did not say any of these things. "Why does it upset you so, Joel?"

"I'm a lawyer," he said. "I see enough of the crummy things that happen when people don't use their minds, when they start giving way to the irrational, letting their emotions take over. Greed. Superstition. Religion. Fear. And people like you and me have to pick up the pieces. And how can we do it if we let all this—this outmoded garbage—take over? Goddam it, Les, logic is a *religion* with me. I haven't any other. I can't live with this kind of stuff."

What about me? I can't live with it either, and I'm the one it's happening to. And you're no help at all. She only said, "But it's true, Joel. You don't think I'm making it up, do you?"

"Oh, God, Leslie, I don't know *what* to think," he confessed.

"That makes two of us," she said, and heard the bitterness in her own voice.

"Is there a drink in the house?"

"There's a bottle of Scotch in the kitchen." Neither of them was much of a drinker. He went and fetched the bottle and poured a couple of generous drinks. He tossed his off at once, but Leslie shook her head. She had an unresolved feeling from somewhere, that it might be dangerous, leave her mind open to the unknown forces of the Unseen, hovering perilously near at this time.

"Drink it, Les."

"I can't. I'm near enough to losing control as it is." At his angry look she pleaded, "Don't you think I'd like to get drunk and forget all about this—this—" She broke off with a helpless gesture.

"Les, I'm scared for you," he said. "One of the senior partners at the office—Carmody—he's that kind of wacko. One reason I took night court for him was—" he made a wry face, "he was going to some kind of crappy seance or something tonight. Some kind of occult bookstore over in the City. Okay, so the senior partner cops out, I get a chance to jump in and take over, that's great. Then I find the same damn thing here—"

Emily's words were in her ears: *Rainbow asked me to come to a thing at the bookstore.* Coincidence? No. There's a reason all this is happening, she told herself, and did not inquire what she meant. Joel was not listening anyhow.

"I wish I could stay with you, Les. But I have to rush off to court—"

Two weeks ago, she thought, wondering at herself, she would have begged him to stay and somehow he would have arranged it. Now she did not care. Why didn't it matter any more what Joel thought of her? She thought, *It will be a shame to miss Nick's wedding*, and was shocked that this was all the valedictory she could make for Joel.

I was right. Moving over here was just clearing the decks for a new life, she thought, and wondered what she had meant by it.

Next morning she confronted Emily before her sister could tell her.

"How was the seance?"

Emily started, almost guiltily. "How did you know?"

"I'm psychic," Leslie said flatly. Only after she said it did she realize she did not sound as if she was joking. "No, Joel told me. Was it interesting?"

"Sort of. That woman Rainbow was talking about, Claire, was there. She's nice. She said she'd seen you in the bookstore and hoped you'd drop in someday. One of the mediums was a Mrs. Carmody. She's the sister of that woman who used to live here. She had a message for me from Grandma; she was glad I had her harp, and I ought to have a harpsichord. Only I knew that already. Sort of." Emily stared at the tablecloth.

"Anything *really* unusual come over from the other side?" Leslie knew her voice was harsh and ironic.

"No. Not really. A couple of other people got messages. She looked sincere enough. Only the messages she gave could have suited anybody, anyhow. One man told his wife she shouldn't trust her lawyer. I mean, through the medium."

And Carmody was a lawyer, and his wife a medium. Oh, sure. I bet the medium will be all ready to recommend a good lawyer. Like Manchester, Ames, Carmody. . . . Nothing real. Nothing that could ever be verified. "No messages for me about how dangerous this house was, from her sister?"

Emily stared. "No. The sister isn't dead. She's living in San Jose. Only then it really started to get interesting. The other medium was a funny, fat, horrible woman with dyed red hair, talking a lot of stuff about Summerland, and we sat in the dark and held hands, and then things started to happen. I got the creeps. Because there was ectoplasm floating around, it was sort of green and gruesome looking, oozing all over the place, and her tambourine levitated, and I was sitting there with gooseflesh all over me, and then that friend of Claire's—his name was Colin, an old man, awfully nice—turned on a light, and there was the medium with a bamboo rod tied to her toes, moving it around. And all this thin cloth coated with luminous paint. So we all laughed at her. I was sorry for the poor woman, even if she was so awful, because she cried, and said it was all real. Only people wanted to see this kind of thing, and it was her religious duty to help convince them how real it was. She said people wanted signs and wonders. Les, are there any real mediums, or are they all fake? Mrs. Carmody didn't seem like a fake, only kind of silly. And the other woman, the fakey one—"

"I don't know, Emily," Leslie said. "It's always someone else who's seen the real ones, or knew somebody who saw the real ones. There may be real ones somewhere." After a minute she added, "Maybe it's like the cat's ghost. Even when you see it yourself, after a while you don't believe your own senses." This morning she had only the vaguest, most dreamlike memory of the surety which had sent Chloe Demarest to the police in Santa Barbara for her lost son. She could, she knew, develop an obsessive need for verification, proof, if only for her own sanity. Would it someday drag her to providing the kind of visible evidence as that unknown medium felt compelled to do?

She thought not. She was secure in her own integrity. But living on the edge of unreason, what could it do to her?

"No message from Alison Margrave about how happy she is that we're living in her house?"

"No," Emily said. "Mrs. Carmody tried to reach her but she didn't come."

"Sensible woman," Leslie said. She was sure that if personality survived death, the spirit had something better to do than to go to seances. But as the days went on, she began to catch her breath again. There was no further evidence of unreason. Now and again she sniffed the phantom incense on the staircase; the white cat continued to prowl in the garden. She put out cat food or tuna for it, and sometimes the tuna remained untouched and sometimes in the morning it was gone. The City was full of cats. Did it matter? Emily complained that her window opened when she did not leave it open; but Emily, engrossed in the master classes held by Simon Anstey, hardly knew what was happening on the ordinary plane. Or did she? One night she told Leslie offhandedly that she was spending the night with a friend; Leslie suspected the friend was Frodo, but she did not inquire; Emily was a big girl now and entitled to her privacy. She saw a packet of pills in Emily's bathroom closet, but that didn't necessarily mean anything.

And then, near the end of June, she opened the door one afternoon to the door chime and found Simon Anstey on her doorstep.

"Dr. Barnes?"

She blinked and greeted him. His scarred face was smiling and friendly, his single eye intent on hers; on his left hand he wore a black glove.

"I have your sister in my class," he said, "and I would like to speak with you."

She invited him in. "Shall I call Emily?" The sound of a Bach prelude filled the hall, and he smiled.

"Not just yet, if you please. I used to know this house well; I confess I am curious to know what you have made of it. And—" The flicker of a smile touched his lips, which were thin and somewhat austere. "I am not unaware that you have had all the locks changed. I confess that I retained my key and on one or two occasions made use of it, before the house was regularly inhabited again. I felt it did no harm."

She felt he was trying to charm her. She said, "I will let Emily show you the music room herself, when she finishes practice. But you're welcome to see the kitchen and the office. The soundproofing has been very helpful with my patients." She conducted him inside, and he nodded approvingly.

"You have made the room very peaceful," he commented. "You said you were not a medical doctor? You have none of the paraphernalia of an ordinary surgery—?"

She shook her head. "A clinical psychologist."

"Not a Freudian, I hope? Alison rather despised the Freudians. She had actually met Dr. Freud and several of his disciples, and had been unimpressed." His smile was quite droll.

Leslie smiled in response. "No. Not a Freudian. Not nearly."

Emily came across the hall. "Les, I heard the doorbell—" and broke off, in surprise and shock. "Dr. Anstey!"

He bowed, urbane and smiling.

"Your sister has been kind enough to show me her office; I was remembering it as it was in Alison's day. She kept the finest of her harpsichords here; a museum piece, a sixteenth-century Venetian one in lacquer and gold. It is now in the Metropolitan Museum; and Alison left the other museum pieces to the Smithsonian and to the Juilliard School of Music, where she had studied. The others, the ones she actually played, she kept with her piano across the hall. I was wondering if I might see the music room?"

Emily caught her sister's eyes. She had known it was the music room. She led Simon across the hall.

"You have a Knabe; Alison had a Bechstein," he said, "but the Knabe is a fine instrument. And the harp, of course, is almost a museum piece itself. Do you play the harp as well?"

"A little."

"You said once in class that you were interested in the harpsichord, Miss Barnes—Emily. Alison left me her other six harpsichords; I would like to lend you the small one, so that you may see how well you like the instrument. I cannot play all six at once, and the harpsichord is not really my instrument. And it is a crime to let all six of them stay in storage, unplayed." Leslie saw the black glove on his left hand twitch and wondered if his disability was truly hopeless. What a tragedy for a musician! "I offered one to another friend, but I think he was superstitious—possibly he thought the bad luck which has pursued my career might rub off on him."

"Dr. Anstey—" Leslie could see that Emily was almost speechless with delight, but she still hesitated. "If something happened—I would really be afraid of the responsibility—"

"They are insured; I am charged a fortune for insurance on them wherever they are," Anstey said almost indifferently. "It will cover them here, in case of fire or, God forbid, burglary or vandalism. I know you will guard it as you do your own instruments, and that is all I can possibly ask. If instruments are not safe even in the locked orchestra room of a conservatory, I doubt if an archangel could keep them any safer. So, unless you really do not want to try it—"

"Oh, Dr. Anstey, I really don't know what to say—I'm simply overwhelmed—" Emily was all but babbling.

"Say that I may have it delivered later this week," he said. "We will regard it as a long-term loan; when I go abroad again, I will be glad to know it is in loving hands. And I should like to hear you play it, sometime, if I may come. I spent many of the happiest hours of my life in this room; my mother was an old friend of Alison's, and Alison actually introduced me to the harpsichord before the piano; she never, I think, overcame her disappointment that the harpsichord appealed to me less." He sat down at the keyboard. "May I, Emily?"

"Oh, please do—only I didn't know—"

"That I could still play?"

"I heard—" Emily stopped, knowing whatever she said would sound tactless. He smiled up at her.

"I *do not* play—not before a concert audience, although perhaps an uninformed audience would hear nothing wrong. But I know; I must—I am not sure how to say this—the racing driver Sterling Moss said once, in his book, that after a head injury, he could still drive, but that he had to *think* about it; it was no longer a reflex, a perfect union between himself and the car. I do not want the critics making allowances for me, nor do I want their pity and condescension. I am already a rich man—two movie appearances saw to that—so I can please myself. I have not yet lost hope that one day—with luck and determination and perhaps the help of the medical profession—or something more—I will return." Leslie saw fierce determination and anger tighten his mouth. "Sit here, Emily; it would give me pleasure to play for you."

She sat beside him on the piano bench. Slowly, he pulled the glove from his hand. The fingers were whiter than those of the other hand, the back crisscrossed with lines and scars.

"A medical miracle," he said indifferently. "One finger was actually severed at the first joint; fortunately it was not lost."

He had made himself vulnerable before them, Leslie thought, and wondered why. He began to play; the eight chords, beginning with the caressing *piano,* increasing inexorably to *fortissimo,* of the Rachmaninoff concerto Emily had studied so long. Leslie felt she had never heard it before. When he finished the first movement, tears were rolling down Emily's face.

He sat motionless at the keyboard, his fingers moving slowly to pull the glove on his hand again. Abruptly he stopped; bent forward somewhat, the fingers of his good hand moving to cover his eyes; Leslie could see the clenched jaw, the twitching of the fingers. She heard him draw a long breath and knew he was in agony.

"Dr. Anstey—"

"Sometimes there are pains in this eye," he said, letting his breath go.

"I hope you haven't tired yourself—" Emily said, and he laid his hand on her shoulder, smiling.

"No, child. It was a pleasure. May I see that garden?"

EMILY INVITED HIM TO stay for supper, and was delighted when he confessed that he was a vegetarian. Leslie had to see a patient and left him to Emily. Away from the fascination of Simon Anstey's presence— and she too had fallen almost completely under his spell—she was aware that for some reason he had moved in on them. She told herself not to be ungenerous; she knew well enough that a concert musician had a lonely life, and a companionable pupil, even one a third of his age (for Simon, as he had entreated them to call him, must be well into his fifties), was not the worst of friends, especially if she lived in a house where he had once been cherished almost as a son.

Emily led the way into the kitchen. He asked, "Can I help?"

"You can peel these cucumbers," Emily said, getting ready to slice tomatoes. "I'll make a salad."

"I usually leave the peel on, myself," he countered, smiling; took off his finely tailored jacket and hung it over a chair, rolling up his sleeves. "But I try to slice them paper thin; will that do?"

The doorbell interrupted them; Leslie went to let in Leonard Hay.

"Am I late? I had to park a couple of blocks away—there was a car in your driveway—"

"My young sister has a guest," she said. "Go into the office, Leonard, I'll be with you in a few minutes; actually you're about eight minutes early." She showed him into the office.

"Your sister has some ritzy friends," he said sullenly. "A Mercedes?"

"He is one of the teachers at the Conservatory," she said. "Sit down and make yourself comfortable. There are some magazines on the table." She went back to the kitchen; Leonard frequently came early or tried to stay a few minutes extra, subtly demanding extra attention, and she tried to make it clear she would not be manipulated this way.

Simon, in shirtsleeves, was perched on the kitchen counter, arranging fine slices of cucumber around elegantly carved radish roses. "Someday," he said, "I must make you one of my cheese soufflés."

"I can never manage them," Emily confessed, laughing. "They fall down—flat! I make good quiche, though. Or did you read that silly book that says real men don't eat quiche?"

Simon chuckled. "On the contrary," he said, "I am exceptionally fond of quiche, when well made. Should anyone doubt my credentials of manhood, I am sure I could find someone to provide them for me, but I never felt the need."

In the garden the white cat slid silently along the back wall, under the castor beans. "Simon," she asked, "did Miss Margrave have a white cat?"

He followed her glance and she saw the tendons in his neck standing out like steel cords above his open collar, but his voice was casual. "She always had a white cat; in the last year of her life she had the last of several."

He saw it too, Leslie thought. And he was perfectly well aware that it was no ordinary living cat. It would have been normal to say, *What, that cat in the garden?* or, *Yes, there it is now,* or *Yes, she did, but that's not the one.* But could ordinary rules apply at all to a man like Simon? He was taking cucumber slices from a bowl with his gloved hand; suddenly it slipped and fell on its side, and Simon exploded.

"Filthy blood thing!" he shouted, and the metal bowl went flying from the counter, spraying cucumber slices as it went, and skittered to rest halfway across the kitchen. Simon went, she thought to pick it up, and gave it a savage kick; it *clanged* and Emily looked up with a cry. Simon's face was transformed with rage; but abruptly it melted away; she heard him let his breath go as he bent to pick up the bowl. His voice was neutral and impassive again.

"I am sorry," he said. "I was—swearing at my own clumsiness; there are times when I—suddenly lose my grip. It does not happen when I am playing, not usually." He stood opening and closing the gloved fingers, and his face was pale.

"Have I wrecked your salad, Emily?"

She shook her head. "No, no, just rinse them off under cold water. I scrubbed the floor myself this morning, it's clean." Simon went to rinse the vegetables, and Leslie wondered if she had imagined that moment of terrifying rage.

She said, "I'll see you two when I finish with Leonard; save me some salad," and went toward her office. She heard a burst of laughter behind her in the kitchen and could not help feeling that Simon was as much at home in the house as she was herself; perhaps more so.

SIMON TELEPHONED THREE DAYS later, saying that he had arranged for the delivery of the harpsichord, and asking if he could come and supervise the installation. He watched over the carrying in and unpacking, inspected the instrument meticulously as it was set up, then stripped off his jacket and set about tuning it. He did not remove the black glove, but touched all the little jacks and hammers almost as dexterously with it as with his bare fingers.

"This is going to be a fairly long job," he said. "Don't feel you have to stay here."

"I'll leave you alone if you'd rather," Leslie said, "but will it bother you if I stay and watch?"

"Not at all, unless you start chattering at me about something irrelevant," he said bluntly.

She sat on the harp stool and watched in silence. His free hand was fine, strong, exquisitely articulated and muscular; Leslie had been brought up on the myth that long narrow delicately fingered hands were "musicians' hands," but had learned better; the hands of a pianist were as muscular as those of an athlete. After a time he took off the glove and flung it impatiently aside. He raised his head, saw her watching and said curtly, "There is a splint in the outside of the glove; it's troublesome when I am doing fine work." Without the glove, the left hand curled shut, the little finger and fourth finger actually touching his palm; but, she noticed, he could hold the fingers open when he tried. The glove was an adjunct to therapy, then. Without it, though, the tuning went faster, and after the better part of an hour, Simon was satisfied, and closed the instrument.

"Is it a very old harpsichord?" she asked.

He shook his head. It was about half the size of a piano, with two manuals, unevenly placed one over the other; the body of the instrument was some smooth, gleaming wood, highly polished.

"This one was built in the early part of this century," he said, "in Austria, I believe. It is not particularly valuable, as harpsichords go. But it has a very pleasant tone." He pulled the piano bench over before the harpsichord, sat down and began to play a Mozart minuet.

"I think that's Emily now," Leslie said, and he broke off and moved to the window. Then Leslie saw the clenched look she had seen before move over his face; rage, or the extreme of pain? He was watching Emily climb out of Frodo's rattletrap truck, take farewell of the boy with a careless hug. But as Emily ran up the steps, she thought she had imagined it.

"Leslie?" Emily called, but it was Simon who answered.

"In here, Emily; I have a surprise for you."

She came through the door, and her face flushed, as if the sun had come out behind her eyes; she drew a long ecstatic breath.

"Oh—oh, Dr. Anstey—oh, *Simon!*"

"It seems happy here," Simon said gravely. "I hope you will enjoy playing it. And I am sure Alison would be pleased to see this one in its old place, where I took the liberty of placing it."

"Oh—" Emily couldn't speak; she simply stood and stared at it, her face ecstatic.

"Will you try it?"

She drew a long breath, moving to the instrument, and then stared at her earthy fingers. "Let me run and wash my hands first; Frodo and I were grubbing around in his garden." She ran out into the kitchen and Leslie heard water running.

Simon said softly, "It was worth it to see that look on her face. What a lovely girl she is. She lights up from inside. That, not any technical capability, is the mark of the true artist."

Emily came back, her hands shining clean—a curious contrast to her rumpled jeans and sweater. Remotely, Leslie thought she had never seen

Emily disheveled before; was Frodo teaching her to be more relaxed, less precise? She looked at the harpsichord with a sigh of sheer delight.

Then she sat down at the keyboard, saying gaily, "I knew there had to be some reason I had to sit through old Auntie Whitty's lectures! Otherwise I might not know any Rameau or Scarlatti!"

Simon was shaken with a gust of laughter.

"Oh, dear, do the youngsters still call him that? I think I invented that name for Doctor Whittington—the dear man, he has the best heart in the world, but he does let his enthusiasms carry him away."

"Doesn't he just," Emily agreed.

"Do you know Rameau's *Rappel des Oiseaux,* Emily?"

"I grew up on your recording. I studied it when I was still in Sacramento."

"But the tone is very different on the piano," he warned. "You must not treat the harpsichord like a piano. The touch is completely different."

She nodded soberly and began to play. Leslie stood, spellbound by the delicacy of the music; it was a new Emily she heard, as if the instrument brought its own music to her natural gift. The touch was still exploratory, cautious, as if she and the harpsichord were taking one another's measure; but somehow it fitted the fastidious precision of Emily's hands, combining the delicate perfection of the ballet she had once loved, and the music of the eighteenth, that most deft and precise of musical centuries.

When she paused, looking up insecurely at him, he said, "Emily, I think you have a natural gift for the harpsichord. Tell me, what do you intend to do this summer while Boris Agrowsky is in Switzerland?"

Emily sighed. "I don't know what to do. I know he deserves a break, a vacation. But I hate to lose ground this way."

"Of course you must not interrupt your study," Simon said decisively. "While Agrowsky is abroad, I will continue your lessons. When he returns—well, we will see."

She looked up at him, stunned and delighted. He patted her cheek.

"Play some more Bach. Play as much Bach as you can; it will teach you more than I can about the harpsichord."

Emily hurried to the piano and brought back a book of Bach sonatas. She sat down at once and began playing. Simon listened for a moment, then put his hand on Leslie's shoulder.

"I think we are superfluous," he murmured, "and I never interfere in a love affair. I think the girl's fallen in love. Shall we?" He moved her into the hall.

"I suspect she's safe for four or five hours," he said, with a droll smile. "Would you have dinner with me, Leslie? I have an orchestra rehearsal tonight; would you care to attend the rehearsal? Or—" He hesitated. "I don't know; I have been assuming that you shared your sister's love of music—"

"How can you ask, Simon? I'd love it. But—" she hesitated, "Emily would enjoy it so much—"

He laughed, his hand still warm on her shoulder.

"Emily is a lovely child. But there are times when I feel the need of more adult companionship. Would you honor me, Leslie?"

It was the first time he had used her name. She smiled up at him.

"Just let me run up and change into something suitable—"

"You are perfect as you are," he said, "but I know that women enjoy a chance to dress up. Go gild the lily, if you must, and I'll leave a note for Emily."

Leslie realized, dressing, that she had been wondering if his interest in Emily was personal after all; it was not unknown, after all, for a famous man of mature years, handsome and virile and carrying all the glamour of the limelight, to captivate extremely young women; Stokowsky and Balanchine had both had that reputation, not only for pursuing but—repeatedly—for marrying them. With this invitation he had disarmed that suspicion too.

When she came down he was holding the telephone; he had on his jacket and the black glove.

"I took the liberty of using your telephone to make a reservation. Emily didn't even look up when I sneaked in to get my jacket and glove; she's playing Bach as if she'd invented him." He urged her toward the door.

"Our reservation is for six. That's early for dinner, but I must be at the opera house at seven-thirty. I hope you like the Mark Hopkins."

"I've never been there," she confessed. All she knew was that it was fabulously expensive.

"Then it will be my pleasure to introduce you to the Top of the Mark; one of the most beautiful sites in this beautiful city." He offered her his arm.

The grey car was a Mercedes; Leslie felt like a princess as he handed her into it. She thought, *He must really be fantastically rich, then*, and remembered he had spoken of movie appearances. Yet he was not limited to that world; she had seen him in shirtsleeves, slicing cucumbers on her counter, kneeling on the floor tuning a harpsichord. He was a man who knew his own world and could get down and work hard in it, with his bare hands. And the phrase reminded her of the glove on his hand. She glanced at it, knowing now what it concealed; and later that evening, when they were laughing as they looked out over the city lights from the high room at the Top of the Mark, she saw him squeezing something in his jacket pocket. She knew he did not think she had seen. Therapy again for the injured hand? She knew his savage determination and admired it.

They had to hurry a little to get to the rehearsal; he said he could not keep the orchestra waiting. He found her a seat, and then she knew he had forgotten her.

She watched Simon, calling forth music from the massed instruments with the tip of a slender stick, stopping them again and again with his steely voice:

"Thank you; that is quite wrong. Can I have more definition from the violins, if you please? The sound is mushy. Mr. Andrews, take it again from the viola solo—" As the evening went on, his voice grew harder, but his meticulous courtesy never wavered; she felt it must be more difficult to endure than the most bullying abuse. What was it Emily had called him—a holy terror? Unholy, rather!

But if he demanded much of his players, he demanded even more of himself; when finally he thanked them and dismissed them, she could see that sweat had soaked through his jacket and that his hair was drenched. Even the black glove on his damaged hand was soaked. As they streamed out, one or two stopping to speak briefly with him—he was all amiability now, smiling and shaking hands—he lifted his eyes and met Leslie's. His glance clearly said, "We'll be out of here in a little while." And absurdly she felt her pulse beating faster.

At last he came toward her, smiling, letting out his breath in a long sigh.

"You must be tired to death, Simon!"

"No, I'm—high; exhilarated," he said. "It takes me forever to wind down from this kind of thing." He shook his wet hair. "We can go somewhere and have a drink, if you like; but as you can see—I should run back to my apartment and shower!" He laughed. "Want to come with me, and wait? I'll give you a glass of a fine Liebfraumilch and you can sip it while I wash off the rehearsal! And then—who knows?" He met her eyes, and Leslie suddenly knew what she was being asked. Then he added gravely, "Or, if you wish, we can have Irish coffee somewhere and I will take you home and leave you with a chaste goodnight kiss."

She knew she was being carried along on the same high that bore him, and she did not care. She laughed as she said, "I'll come back with you."

His eye lighted from inside, and his hand was eager and demanding on her arm as he hurried her out to his car. It had started to rain lightly; over her protests he took off his jacket and flung it over her as they hurried across Van Ness Avenue toward the parking garage.

But as he bent to unlock the door on her side of the car he stopped suddenly and stood bent over; she saw his face twitching, and again the tendons in his neck stood out like knotted cord. She could see cold sweat breaking out on his forehead.

"Simon—" she said softly.

"It's all right. Don't take any notice. I'll be all right in a minute," he said through gritted teeth, and then, with that sudden way of making himself vulnerable, his clenched hand in the black glove tossed the keys to her.

"Would you drive, Leslie?" She heard him let out his breath. She took the keys and unlocked the car, slid into the driver's seat.

"Tell me where to go."

HE HAD A FIVE-ROOM condominium in a high-rise building up on Twin Peaks. The spasm had subsided before they arrived, and he had recovered his gaiety; he flung the keys to the night attendant of the garage to park for them, and conducted her ceremoniously to the elevator, which he operated, not with a key but with a slim plastic computer card.

The main room of his apartment was furnished with elegant austerity in black and white; a nine-foot grand piano, a harpsichord somewhat larger than the one he had loaned to Emily; a glass coffee table. Through an arch she could see a gleaming modernistic kitchen in chrome and steel and hardened glass. He brought her wine in a glass of Swedish crystal.

"I'm going to shower. I'll join you presently." But he lingered a moment, then bent, raising her face to his, his mouth closing over hers. There seemed a feverish heat in his kiss; he lingered a moment, then broke away.

"Not now. Later."

Leslie sipped at the wine, which was so smooth and mellow that she knew she was not qualified to say just how good it was. She only knew she had never tasted anything quite like it.

She heard the shower running and knew that he had left the doors between open so that she could hear, and imagine his naked body, hard and lean and virile, under the hot water and steam; she knew this with the same sureness with which she had known the whereabouts of Chloe Demarest's dead son. She let herself enjoy the image fully. Why not? She was a grown woman, here by her own choice and conscious desire.

She walked to the window, looking down over the lights of the city fourteen stories below. Complete contrast to her own house; that was the graciousness of the past, this was the cutting edge of the future; both in complete harmony.

On a heavy pale wood shelf were a line of heavy books; she went to examine them. *The Great Book of Magical Art.* One volume called *Magick and Will.* She raised her eyebrows; more of the curious coincidences which had seemed to surround her? What was she getting into? Clinging to the binding of the books was a faint, bitter, almost familiar scent; after a moment she identified it as the whiff of phantom incense she had briefly smelled on her stairs; the pungent dry harshness of it stung her nose. There was a book with Latin letters in such an eccentric script she could not read it; but there was something familiar on it nevertheless: a curious interlaced five-pointed star identical with the one which Claire, in the bookstore, had worn on a chain round her neck.

The shower had stopped running. Simon, bare to the waist, came into the living room, came up and lifted the glass she had left on the table; drank a sip of the wine, then came and kissed her; his mouth too tasted of the same fruity tang of the wine.

"I saw you looking at my books," he said, drawing back from the kiss, "and now you will be thinking me a black magician?"

"I have no idea what you would mean by that, Simon."

He smiled fiercely and said, "Magic is like music: the art of the trained will. It is like yours as a trained psychologist; it is another name for the same thing, Leslie. I learned long ago the art of surrounding myself, structuring my life so that everything around me supports that trained will. You noticed at dinner that I did not drink a cocktail."

That was right; he had not, though he had urged her to have one if she wished.

"I never drink strong spirits. Wine is different; it is the most refined essence of the fruits of the earth, and its aura purifies and sensitizes. It is for the same reason I am a vegetarian; not from some sentimental love of animals, nor an overconscientious ethical sense, but because red meat desensitizes, and as a musician I wish to remain open to the small vibrations of the universe. And at present—" he moved the gloved hand, deliberately, "I have a use for my will. There is no limit to what the trained will can accomplish. Even the mundane behaviorists are beginning to prove that to themselves, with the foolish crutches of biofeedback machines and such things. Medicine has done for me as much as it can reasonably do," he added. "The rest I shall accomplish with mind—and will."

"Amen," she said softly. She could only imagine what it must mean to Simon, to have had his concert career shattered by violence in this way. She had known cases where the will to live had meant the difference between life and death. Who was she to say it could not accomplish a similar miracle in restoring a damaged hand to function?

"But for now I have something else on my mind," Simon said softly, bending to kiss the bare nape of her neck, sliding his arm around her waist. "If it is your will as well as mine—"

She nodded. He whispered, "Bring the wine. We'll drink it together. Afterward," and led her into the inner room.

It was as stark, as austerely furnished as the living room, with a single difference: in a corner near the window there was a table fitted as a small altar, with a single light, glowing red in a candle cup.

"Would you like to shower first? There is a robe on the door that you can use," he said, holding her close for a long kiss, and releasing her. "There is no hurry. Sex is never anything to be taken lightly, Leslie. The coming together of man and woman, no matter how careless, casual or even commercial, creates a—how shall I say this? Living in Alison's house, I know you understand me on one level, even if you do not consciously know what I mean—creates a psychic vortex, a special bond. Some people laugh at that, which is why I choose women as carefully as a violinist chooses his instrument. Or will you laugh at me, Leslie? If this seems absurd to you—" and his eye glowed with that fierce light, "then we can have another glass of wine, and I will take you home."

She felt, instead, that he had put into words something which had been at the back of her mind for a very long time. Another thought she did not confide to him, which surged into sudden awareness; this was what she needed to break the now-unwelcome bond with Joel; to create that bond with another man. . . .

She went into the shower. For a moment, when he had said there was a robe she could use, she wondered: *Was he one of those self-conscious sensualists who entertained women so often he kept such things for the convenience of any woman who might come along?* But the robe was evidently one of his own, a cotton Japanese kimono in a man's pattern, too large for any woman, folded on the bench just outside the shower. She found curious thoughts floating through her mind as she stood under the pounding water, as if she was washing off Joel's touch on her body and memory, observing some kind of ritual preparation for him; but at the last moment she was unwilling to undergo that mark of possession, wearing Simon's robe; she wrapped herself from neck to knees in one of the enormous thick bath sheets.

Simon waited for her, naked, his back to her; he was crouched before the altar, but rose to his feet as she came in. She recognized the drifting scent; a clean, dry bitterness, not what she would have considered sensuous. He turned to her and held out his arms.

He was immensely strong. He lifted her bodily and laid her stretched on the bed, pulling away the towel and bending over her. He traced a symbol, with his right hand, on her belly, and it seemed that an electric blue light followed his hand; she could almost feel the electricity crackling between them as he lowered his mouth to kiss her breasts, her belly, to tickle the edges of her pubic hair with his tongue. Then, with a low laugh, he was astride her, pulling her against him with all his strength. Confused images of a priapic God spun in her mind as she raised herself wildly to meet him, and again it was as if lightning crackled round them as he entered her.

On the altar behind them the red-eyed candle cup raised itself eight inches in the air and came noiselessly down. But neither of them saw.

THE SHOWER WAS RUNNING in Emily's room as Leslie came softly up the stairs. The smell of the phantom incense was drifting on the stairs again—or was it the scent of Simon's incense clinging to her hair? As she opened her bedroom door, Emily stepped out on the landing.

"Leslie, I've found something awfully funny in my bedroom and it's in my bath too. Come and see."

There was only one small window in the bath, high in the wall; Emily pointed wordlessly. Below the sill, deeply incised in the wood with some sharp instrument like a nail, was the pentagram sign:

She had seen it on Simon's altar, and on one of his books. And Claire in the bookstore had worn it around her neck. Emily led her into the bedroom; under the dormer window at the far end was another of the pentagrams, but beneath the casement window which was standing open, a crude attempt had been made to obliterate the same symbol.

In the upstairs hall, at the little window in the wall, the same symbol was chalked in pale crayon, almost the same color as the wallpaper; and in the third room they had designated for a guest room. In each of these places pains had been taken, it seemed, to make the marks all but invisible and put them in places where they would not be noticed easily. Now roused to real curiosity, they searched the house. Over every door to the outside, even over the ladder leading to the attic (folded up behind its storage panel), the same mark was chalked; and under the sill of every window. Once the first one had been noticed, they were easy to find.

"But who put them there and why?" Emily asked, finally settling down to breakfast, yogurt into which she had stirred large teaspoonfuls of wheat germ; Leslie looked at the concoction and shuddered. She could have stayed and breakfasted with Simon, but she had a client coming this morning, a new one who had called for an interview; Leslie didn't know what her problem was. She was sure that Simon's idea of breakfast would have been something luxurious beyond belief. She thought she could easily get spoiled by the kind of life Simon could offer to his associates. On the other hand, she should keep it in perspective, and not be overwhelmed by his lavishness and generosity; he could bestow a harpsichord worth God knows what on a long term loan with no more sense of deprivation than she could have loaned one of her clients a towel. She put the coffee on, and sat at the kitchen table, smiling to herself.

"Was he good?" Emily asked.

"What?"

"Simon. Is he good in bed?" At Leslie's look of shock, she said, "Well, you go out with him, you come home at half-past seven in the morning, and somehow I don't think you were sitting out on Mount Tam looking for UFOs. What do you *suppose* I think?"

Leslie said in shock, "I haven't asked you any questions about Frodo, have I?"

Emily looked away from her. "Oh, Frodo's a darling. But I guess I just haven't made up my mind yet, that's all."

"There's no hurry," Leslie said. "It's a good idea to be really sure. Not let yourself be stampeded into a decision."

"Frodo isn't the kind to stampede anybody," Emily said with a gentle smile. "I'm awfully fond of him, Leslie. But I want to be sure I want to get in that deep with anybody. How old were you, Les? How did you know it was the right person?"

Leslie sighed. "Sixteen and a half," she said, "and even then I knew it wasn't the right person. It was just something I felt I had to do. An act of—well, rebellion, I suppose. I was so sick of hearing everybody make such a big *thing* out of it. I wanted to get it over with."

"So in the long run you were glad you did—what did you say—get it over with?"

Leslie shook her head. "No," she said. "Even today I'm not. I think it ought to have meant more than that. Since then, I've been downright fussy. And if you don't mind, I think that's just about enough of my love life."

Emily traced a restless finger over the pentagram below the window just above the table where they sat. She said again, "I wonder who put these here? And why? Shall I ask Frodo what they mean?"

Leslie said, staring at them, "They could have been here since Alison Margrave lived in the house. Or that crazy lady who thought the place was haunted. Carmody? They have something to do with the occult. And Alison Margrave wrote a book about poltergeists. I ought to go and pick it up, and that book Frodo said he'd find for me."

"He's going to be there this afternoon," Emily confirmed. She glanced up at the clock and yowled.

"Aargh! I'm going to be late! I have my final exam in Music History today! Just think, after today I never have to listen to Auntie Whitty sounding off about the baroque as if it was the only kind of music God ever made and the devil wrote everything else!" A minute later the door slammed.

The telephone rang; it was her answering service.

"Dr. Barnes, please telephone Eileen Grantson's father. He called at eight twenty-two this morning."

Leslie went into the study and looked up the East Bay number. After a time the voice of Donald Grantson came over the telephone.

"Leslie Barnes here," Leslie said. "Is something wrong? Is Eileen sick?"

"That's not what you'd call it," said the man in an aggrieved tone.

"Things have been fairly quiet around here for a few weeks, since Eileen's been seeing you, Dr. Barnes. But suddenly all hell's broken loose in this house, and I thought I ought to call you and see if you can tell me what the devil is going on!"

"Mr. Grantson, I think I told you when Eileen began seeing me that I could not discuss the progress of her therapy with you. Her sessions are confidential. If you would like to set up a joint appointment where you can talk together in my presence, you may be able to communicate—"

"Communicate be damned," the man shouted. "I want to keep the girl from breaking up the whole house! There isn't a dish left unbroken in the house—I had to go out and buy some paper cups! She kicked a hole in our television set, and denied it!"

"Was she hurt?" Leslie asked quickly. She simply could not believe Eileen could have kicked a television set in without landing in the hospital.

"Hell, no, she just stood stone-still in the middle of all the flying glass and said she didn't know anything about it." Donald Grantson was almost shouting. "She's got worse since she started coming to you, and I want to know what you're going to do about it."

Oh, dear God, Leslie thought. She vaguely remembered from the small amount of reading she had done that the poltergeist sometimes started up again, more fiercely than ever, after a lull. She had been a fool, or so troubled by her own poltergeist problem that when Eileen's subsided, she had behaved in typical ostrich fashion, hiding her head in the sand.

"Mr. Grantson, listen to me," she said quietly. "I have reason to believe that your daughter is possibly the focus of a poltergeist—"

"Christ almighty," he said in disgust. "I saw that movie on the Late Late show! If you're trying to tell me—"

"No, no," she said quickly, heartily damning Steven Spielberg and all other makers of horror movies. Then she heard him say, "Listen, we're not even Catholics, but I do know a priest, would it help—"

"No, nothing like that. Mr. Grantson, don't do anything yet. Just send Eileen in to see me at—" briefly, she consulted her calendar, "four this afternoon, after school. You can come with her if you like, but I really would prefer to talk to her alone this time. And please don't panic. These phenomena are not nearly as uncommon as you might think, and they are almost always short-lived; they usually go away of their own accord." *Unless she should start setting fires. But that's very uncommon.* Leslie prayed it would not come to that.

"It's easy to say that," Grantson said, sounding injured, and Leslie didn't blame him. "But I'm standing here in the middle of all this goddam broken glass I've got to clean up, and my housekeeper has quit, and now what am I going to do? I told Eileen she could do the housework for a while and clean up her own messes! I never spanked her, but damn it, I feel I ought to beat her ass black and blue!"

"That would be very unwise," said Leslie, as severely as she could. "I can understand how angry you must be, Mr. Grantson, but believe me, using physical violence on Eileen isn't the answer. She's not doing it on purpose. If you can get another housekeeper, one who isn't so hostile to Eileen, one who won't make her feel so threatened—your housekeeper, I understand, has not been kind to Eileen, and the girl—"

"I don't hire her for that," Grantson protested. "I pay her to clean house and cook!"

"Well, Eileen's unhappiness at home has been at least partly due to her hostile relationship to the housekeeper," said Leslie. "I'll talk with Eileen, and try to set up an appointment for the two of you to discuss your problems."

"I don't want to *discuss her problems*," the man said angrily, mimicking Leslie's tone. "I want her to stop making this house hell on earth, and I want you to straighten her out for me. That's what I'm paying *you* for."

"I think we had better have an appointment to discuss the aims of her therapy," said Leslie coldly. "If this is your attitude toward Eileen, perhaps you had better consider sending her to a good boarding school; it would not cost much more than long term therapy."

There was a shocked silence on the phone. Then Grantson said slowly, "Hey, listen, Dr. Barnes, you got me wrong. I don't want to get rid of the kid. You think maybe all this is because the housekeeper is mean to her and she thinks maybe it's my fault? I'm not the easiest man in the world to live with, and since Ruthie left me I know I've been like a bear with a sore tail, go to work, come home, yell at the kid, eat and sleep. Ruthie sure wasn't much of a mother, but I guess Eileen misses her. And when glass starts breaking all over the place and she stands there and *lies* about it—Ruthie was such a goddam liar, I can't stand to see Eileen cheating and lying—"

"Only she isn't lying," Leslie said. "That's what you must understand. She doesn't consciously have anything to do with it."

"For sure? God, that's scary," Donald Grantson said, and again Leslie reassured him. *I wish someone would try and reassure me. I think I'm getting in beyond my depth!* She agreed to talk to Eileen, and to set up a joint appointment later for the two of them, and hung up.

NO SOONER HAD SHE replaced the receiver than it rang again.

"Leslie Barnes here."

"You're too popular, my precious," said Simon's husky voice in her ear. "I have been trying to call, but your telephone was busy. So I sit here and squeeze my exercise ball between my fingers and wish they were caressing you instead. . . ."

She felt a shiver down her spine, but she controlled it; after all, she had to work today. "A patient in trouble, Simon."

"Ah, I woke up and you were gone," he said, sighing, "and I wondered if you had been but a beautiful dream! Shall we prove to ourselves tonight that it was no dream? I think Emily has her last lesson with Agrowsky for this term today before he goes away. Shall I steal you away for the afternoon?"

"I have a patient," she demurred, and he sighed.

"How unfortunate that I am such a model of perfection! Otherwise I could arrange to seek counseling from you . . . my dear Dr. Barnes. I am suffering unendurable pain and loneliness, because the most beautiful and fascinating woman in San Francisco—" his voice was just touched with drollery, but there was enough sincerity in it to make her shiver—"prefers the company of her patients."

"Simon," she said gently, "would you send a message to the orchestra saying that you had decided not to hold any more rehearsals before the concert and they were on their own?"

He laughed ruefully. "Well taken, sweetheart; unfortunately I grew up in a milieu where women were assumed to have no occupation but to give pleasure to the men in their lives. Perhaps we are well rid of those days, after all. Well, then; I am expecting that you and Emily will be my guests at the concert, and afterward, well, we will see. . . ."

They were the words he had spoken before, and they sent a prickle of delicious memory and anticipation down her whole body.

When she had hung up the telephone, though, she went into the study and thought it over for a few minutes. She had had no intention of letting this happen; on a whim, and more than a little glamoured by Simon, she had let herself be carried away, but she had never intended to become emotionally entangled in this manner. Was this what she wanted, a serious love affair instead of a little light romance to soothe her ego and her loneliness after she had decided Joel was not for her? Was she doing the same foolish thing she had done at sixteen, rushing into a sexual entanglement, ill-considered, under pressure that really had nothing to do with sex or affection?

Maybe, she thought dryly, I'm bewitched. It would be all of a piece with everything else that's been happening since I moved into this place. I wonder what Alison Margrave would think if she knew how my life and Emily's have become entangled with her protégé?

On the wall before her hung one of her treasures: a Wedgwood plate that had belonged to her grandmother. Amelia Barnes had given Emily the harp, and Leslie the Wedgwood plate. She had always cherished it, not because of its great value, but because from childhood she had loved the little dancing nymphs and dryads who ringed the edge against the brilliant blue. She had hung it here in a place of honor on her study wall. Now, as she looked, the plate joggled on its bracket, and before Leslie's horrified eyes, *lifted* from the bracket and sailed across the room. Leslie made a dive to catch it, but it fell to the floor and lay there, miraculously unbroken. When Leslie picked it up, it felt hot and tingling to the touch. Her hands were shaking so hard that she nearly dropped it again.

When she felt that she could trust her grip, she laid the plate on her desk. There might, she thought, have been a small earthquake. No; that was the same kind of intellectual dishonesty she deplored in others. Like Eileen Grantson, she was undergoing another outbreak of the poltergeist activity she had thought resolved. Why?

Insufficient data.

And she could not even investigate; her early client would be at her doorstep in a very few minutes. She didn't even have time for another soothing cup of coffee.

AFTER A MORNING SPENT with her patients, she set off for the bookshop. It had been a temptation to wait for Simon to call again. Somehow she had a strong feeling that if she had been entangled somewhat more deeply than she intended, so had he. Before she saw Simon again, she needed to do some serious thinking about herself and her own motives.

Her disciplined mind almost rebelled, as she stood on the doorstep, at seeking help in an occult bookstore. Yet she had found the one serious appraisal of poltergeists here. And Emily had told her that they had exposed a fake medium; at least they too were dedicated to honesty. If, in the words of the first book on poltergeists, the Unseen was coming in search of her, she wanted to know something about it from the best authorities she could find.

She had hoped to find Frodo there. Instead she saw the woman she had seen when first she came here, arranging books on a high shelf; and behind the counter, reading, a grey-haired, strong-looking man, who did not at first raise his eyes from the book in his hand.

Then he looked up, laughing in apology.

"I'm sorry," he said. "May I help you? I tend to get lost sometimes. I tend to get eyetracks over all the books before I sell them."

He was, she supposed, about sixty, but he gave an impression of height and strength, and his dark eyes were peaceful. She had the impression that while he took himself and everything else seriously, he could laugh at everything too, including himself.

Leslie quoted gravely, " 'I often wonder what the vintnors buy/One half so precious as the stuff they sell.' That goes for booksellers, too, I should think. I was in here the other day, and Claire?—Rainbow told me her name—said that she had some books about poltergeists—"

The old man raised his head and called, "Claire? I think this must be the lady you mentioned to me." He smiled at her and said, "Dr. Barnes, is it? I heard that you had moved into a house which once belonged to our dear friend Alison Margrave."

Another dear friend of Alison's. What am I getting into?

Claire came from the back of the store and nodded kindly to Leslie. She was, Leslie thought, somewhere in her fifties; carelessly dressed, her hair greying, about the age of Leslie's mother. She said, "The book you gave me on poltergeists contained the only sensible thing I had ever read about them. I came back to see if you had anything else."

"I'll start you with a monograph by Margrave and Anstey," Claire said, "and then I'll give you Alison's book. She was one of the great experts on the subject, you know." Leslie hadn't, but she was beginning to guess. She was less surprised to hear Simon's name.

Claire hesitated, looking troubled, as Leslie got out her purse to pay for the books. She said, "Your sister came to our seance a few nights ago; did she tell you?"

"She told me you had exposed a fake medium."

The old bookseller laughed heartily. "That's right. I can't imagine why that silly woman would try to fool us. She should have known better than that. She's known me long enough to know I wouldn't put up with that kind of nonsense."

"Colin," Claire said, reprovingly. "She was begging for help, I think. She wanted you—or at least a part of her wanted you to catch her, to stop her. I probably shouldn't ask this," Claire said, "it's none of my business. But I hope that your interest in poltergeists does not indicate that—" She glanced uneasily at the man she had called Colin. "How shall I say this?"

Colin said quietly, "What Claire is trying to say is that at one time we both knew the house well, and that ever since Alison's death there have been disturbances reported there. I had hoped that when you and your sister moved in—a psychologist and a musician—there would be no more disturbance. I knew that Alison would be unhappy with anyone living in the house who did not share her interests—"

"But that's preposterous," Leslie burst out. "You can't believe that! The dead—if they survive—why would they still be interested in what happens to what they left behind?"

Claire looked distressed.

"I hardly know what to say to you," she said. "I don't have any idea how much you know about these things."

"Nothing," said Leslie flatly.

"I find that hard to believe," Claire said. "Not if you are open-minded enough to investigate a poltergeist, and—forgive me, Dr. Barnes, I don't think much more of the *Enquirer* than you do, but there must have been *something* to the story they printed."

Leslie felt a sinking at her heart. So they had known all along who she was and how this monstrousness had come into her life. She bit her lip hard, feeling tears coming to her eyes. Colin said, "Claire, you are being too hard on her. Dr. Barnes, please forgive our unpardonable intrusion into your affairs. She came to us for books, Claire, not for unasked advice."

Suddenly Leslie realized that she was being foolish. Just this morning, she had been almost praying for someone who knew what might possibly be happening, to her house and to her life. And then when they came in response to that prayer, she held them at arm's length out of distaste for the sensationalism which a popular magazine had imposed, unnecessarily, on what was a very real thing.

She said, "Oh, please, if you know anything at all about this business— I'm at my wit's end! I was just thinking that I needed all the help I could get!"

"Has there been poltergeist activity in the house itself?" Claire asked.

"Among other things," Leslie said. "Although it didn't start when I moved into the house. I came here at first because one of my teenage clients had been showing poltergeist activity. I never knew it could go—go beyond that—" She was hesitating between the confidentiality proper to a patient, and the knowledge that she was really beyond her depth and needed to confer with an expert. Colin picked up on that at once.

"Dr. Barnes, a simple case of adolescent poltergeistry will subside soon enough; you don't need to be worried about it," he said. "I'm sure that the child and her family are suffering, but it is really not a serious matter. Trust me. On the other hand, when an adult becomes entangled in these phenomena, it usually means that the Unseen is reaching out for you, and you have really no choice except to know what is going on and why. Claire and I are committed, both of us, to find out the truth about these matters. We serve the truth and only the truth. And if either of us can help you, please consider us at your service."

"I don't even know who you are," she blurted out.

"My name is Colin MacLaren; I have been a student of these matters for half a century," he said. "Alison was my friend and colleague. This is Claire Moffatt, who has been an assistant of mine for many years."

She looked uneasily at the books in her hand. "I can't talk now. I have—the young girl—the poltergeist—coming in an hour from now."

Claire said, taking the books and ringing them up on the cash register, "Take these home and read them. And, if you like, I could come over this evening and try to see what is going on in your house."

"Are you a medium?" Leslie heard the hostility in her own voice.

Claire shook her head, unoffended.

"Ah, no," she said. "I do not try to intrude in the lives of people who have passed on to whatever lies beyond this life; I am only concerned with what trouble may be caused on *this* plane. Calling me a parapsychologist is as far as I would go. But I have had a little experience. I'm not sure I could find anything out for certain, but I do know the house, and I could try."

Leslie took out money to pay for the books. Colin said, as she opened her wallet, "If the cost is a hardship to you, Dr. Barnes, you can take them home and read them and return them at your leisure. We do sell books, but we also have a very firm policy that no one should go without their help if they need it and can't afford it, so we often lend books to people who can't buy them. Those books outside," he added with a friendly chuckle, "we put outside in the hopes that people will steal them; we are pleasantly surprised when anyone comes in and actually gives us a quarter for them."

Leslie joined in the laughter, but said she could perfectly well afford to pay for the books, and did.

"And if you wanted to come over and see what is happening in the house, Claire, I would be pleased. And grateful. Really."

"Good, then; I'll see you at five-thirty," Claire said, and Leslie went away feeling that perhaps she had found help after all. She sat down in her study and opened the book which bore the names of the woman who had previously owned her house, and the man in whose arms she had spent the previous night.

When the unknown and incomprehensible first comes into the life of any man or woman whose world has previously been governed by the ordinary laws of the material universe [so the first page began], their first emotion is invariably one of confusion and dismay. The laws of their old world seem to have been suspended; and the mechanics of their new, yet unquestionably real experiences have not yet been established. The world suddenly seems chaotic, without visible cause or effect. Yet the new world, they will discover if they persevere in a disciplined and realistic search for truth, is governed by laws as natural and discoverable as the old; only belonging to another order of experience.

Another order of experience. Leslie drew a long sigh of relief at this calm and rational appraisal of what had been happening, and sat down to read every word of *The Natural History of the Poltergeist* before Eileen Grantson should appear on her doorstep.

•   •   •

"EVERYTHING WAS GOING ALONG so good for so long," Eileen wailed. "I was having fun going out with Scotty, and getting along so good at school. And then all this—this—" She was wailing loudly. "Daddy said I kicked in the TV set, but I didn't, I swear I didn't, I wasn't standing near it, I was right across the *room!* And then all the light bulbs broke in their sockets, and Daddy had to turn off the house current to dig them out of the sockets—"

Leslie asked quietly, "Was anyone cut or hurt by the flying glass, Eileen?"

She shook her head. "I was scared they would be, but they weren't. But old lady Mattison quit, she said she wouldn't work in a place where people threw things at her, and so Daddy said I'd have to do the house-work—"

"I talked to your father, Eileen," Leslie interrupted. "He's willing to come in and talk over problems like that. We can make an appointment for the two of you to sit down together and talk things over reasonably. Now today I was talking to a man who knows a great deal about polter-geists; he said that they invariably—invariably, Eileen—went away by themselves. And I read another thing you ought to know, in a book by a woman who had made a lifetime study of them; it said that when there was a bad outbreak like this, after a long lull when you thought they were gone, that this is a last-ditch defense by the poltergeist part of you, just before what I called the baby part of you decides to settle down. So the very fierceness of this attack means it's on its way out. Have you any idea what might have happened, Eileen?"

She thought it over for a minute. "I was upset," she said, "because Daddy said sure, I could visit Mom, I could even go and live with her if I wanted to, and I thought that meant he didn't want me either. Because I thought it over—" she added shyly after a minute, "—well, and then she says in the letter she sent me, she's having another baby, and I thought—" She swallowed, but she did not cry. "Now, for sure she's not going to want me all that much. So I decided I wouldn't go and visit until I was sure how I felt, only I'd made such a fuss about going, I was scared to tell Dad I really didn't want to go. Only I guess what you called the baby part was making the fuss I didn't want to make."

"It sounds like it," Leslie commented. She was inwardly delighted with

Eileen's insight. "Tell me, Eileen, have you ever tried to move anything that way, with your mind, on purpose?"

Slowly, Eileen nodded. "I kept remembering what you said: it's mine, I ought to be able to control it. So I tried. That night when things had settled down a little. And I found out I could. Only it was hard. Watch."

She pointed at the box of Kleenex on Leslie's desk. After a moment it wobbled, fell over, slid a little and stopped.

"So perhaps the question ought to be, not, *can* you move things with your mind, but do you *want* to?" Leslie asked.

"I don't want to," Eileen said, and Leslie nodded, picking up *The Natural History of the Poltergeist.*

She said, "There's a story in this book about that," and read:

"A man came to one of the great Incarnations of Buddha, and said, 'I have spent ten years in fasting and prayer, and lo, I have learned to levitate myself over the river.' And the Buddha said, 'Foolish man, you have spent ten years in learning to do what the ferryman would have done for a penny, which you could earn by an hour of honest labor; and behold in those ten years you could have done much in this world to relieve the suffering of mankind.' "

Eileen listened in silence, and then she smiled.

"Did you say that you could make an appointment so I could come in with my Daddy and talk over what's happening?" she asked.

And as Leslie made the appointment, she suspected that the Grantson poltergeist had made its final appearance.

CHAPTER

Fourteen

CLAIRE ARRIVED AT FIVE-THIRTY, accepted a cup of tea in the shining kitchen, and said some nice things about what Leslie had done with the garden.

"I think perhaps we have young Frodo to thank for that," Leslie said. "He and Rainbow have been very kind about helping Emily get the herb garden back in order."

She nodded. "Frodo is a nice boy, and when he's a little older I think he may become one of the Seekers. I don't like to see young people commit themselves too early in life, before they know what *this* life is all about! Of course, some people are born old. Or born on the Path, and then they have no choice; if they do not go out in search of the Unseen, it will come looking for them instead, wherever they may try to hide."

"Claire, are you saying that we do not have free will in these matters?"

"I don't know," Claire answered, levelling her eyes at Leslie. "Colin and I would give you different answers about that. I'm convinced that we have absolute free will. Colin thinks that we have free will but that it's not always what we consciously choose; that we may have made the decision before we came into incarnation this time, and even if the circumstances of our mundane life and education move us away from the Path, we are guided by our inner selves to move back toward it. I just don't know. Why don't you tell me what's brought it up in your life?"

What Claire said made her think of what she had said to Susan Hamilton about a chosen purpose for her life and Chrissy's. Yet before this she had never even consciously believed in reincarnation. She said, "I hardly know where to begin. . . ."

"At the beginning," Claire said gently. But where was the beginning? When Emily was born and she had told her mother, *That's not your baby, that's my baby?* Or when she had found Juanita García dead in a drainage ditch? Or when first Eileen Grantson's poltergeist had manifested in her office, or when she had—or her mind had—thrown a glass of wine, without meaning it, in Joel's face? She told Claire about all these things, and about Phyllis Anne Chapman and her birthday cake and red patent leather shoes, and about the quarrel with Joel, and about the night when her telephone had rung when it was off the hook and when the doorbell had jangled after she had disconnected the wires. And then she stopped, wondering if Claire would think of her as she had thought of Chloe Demarest, a superstitious idiot.

"It must have been very frightening," Claire said.

"Bravo." Leslie's voice was dry. "Perfect non-directive counseling technique."

Claire laughed, a little abashed. She said, "I have done counseling. And I picked up nondirective techniques from Alison. She told me that if they do no positive good, at least that way I won't err on the side of giving unasked advice, as Colin said this morning."

"What sort of person was Alison Margrave? From everything I hear, she sounds like a perfect saint."

"She was certainly no saint," Claire said promptly, "though she was one of the kindest women I ever knew. If she had a fault, though, it was that she thought too well of anyone she tended to like. She had the temperament of a musician, which is not always the calmest, and she had very fixed opinions, which you contradicted at your peril; but I was very fond of her. Which brings me to one of the things I wanted to ask you. You said that you had observed—I don't know what to call it; disturbances, poltergeist activity—here in this house?"

Leslie laughed uneasily. She said, "There is a window that won't stay closed. Neither Emily nor I can close it and keep it closed, even when we chain the bolt. It's probably open now. There is something wrong with the garage; both Emily and I were ill with depression when we were in there alone. But the office was always a—a haven," she said slowly, only then realizing it. "Everything was always peaceful in there. Until this morning."

"What happened this morning?"

Leslie told her about the Wedgwood plate.

"May I see the office?"

As Leslie rose to lead her in there, Emily came running in.

"Oh, hello, Claire, I hoped you'd get over here! Les, did I get any calls? If Frodo calls later, will you tell him I'm over at Rainbow's? She asked me to babysit Timmie tonight and said I could have Frodo over. I won't be in for supper, all right?"

She ran upstairs, and Leslie called after her, "How was the Music History test?"

"A horror," Emily called back, "but I think I passed. I have to try and get in an hour or two of practice, though."

Claire sighed as Emily's door slammed. "I envy her energy! That's the only thing I regret about getting old; I used to work all day and play all night, and never care one way or the other about things like sleep or food or rest. I just can't do it any more."

"And I'm beginning not to be able to," Leslie confessed, "and I'm a good bit younger than you, I imagine!" She led the way into the study. Claire stood for a moment silent, as if listening. She looked at the tipped-over box of Kleenex, then at the Wedgwood plate. She asked, "May I?" and picked it up. She touched it with her fingertips carefully, touched it for a moment to her brow and temple, then laid it down.

"I don't sense anything wrong with it," she said, "and I think I'd know if there was any actual infesting energy. The office seems as peaceful as it did when Alison was here, and that is saying a good deal. I wonder," she mused, "if perhaps she was simply trying to call your attention to some-thing. . . ."

"If so, she certainly did," Leslie said frankly. "That was what brought me to the bookstore to ask for help. But I find it hard to believe that a—" she hesitated, "a dead woman should continue to be interested in what was going on in this life."

"That may be because you don't understand death," Claire said, "and after all, who does? Death isn't so much of a change as all that. And Alison died with her work unfinished, old as she was. When you reach Alison's level on the Path—"

"I don't understand what you mean by the Path," Leslie said crossly.

"It's a way of describing the search for truth. People who have a religious approach, those who are into Wicca or involved with the Mystery religions, sometimes speak of being 'in the Craft' instead of being on the Path, but it's the same thing: being aware of the road we all travel from life to life toward—whatever it is that you think we are sent here to accomplish. I am not really a religious person," Claire said, then amended it. "No, that's not true. I *am* a religious person. I just hate the enormous lot of rubbish people talk when they start talking religion, so I try to avoid that kind of jargon."

Leslie could certainly understand that.

"You said there had been disturbances in other parts of the house— could I see the window that won't stay shut?"

Behind the closed door of the music room, Emily had begun to play the piano; resounding chords. She led Claire quietly up the stairs, showing her, as she went, the pentagrams inscribed above or below every door and window. Claire nodded. "I set the wards on this house myself," she said, "when Alison was in the hospital after her first stroke. She wanted to be sure no one could intrude in her absence." She bent over the window where the pentagram sign had been rubbed out, scratched out, laid her fingertips gently on the sign, briefly rested her head on the windowsill.

"The window is certainly unguarded," she said, "but I don't have the sense that there is anything really wrong here. Neutral, if anything. You said something about a cat?"

"A white cat. Frodo said it was Alison's cat," Leslie replied.

"I gave Alison the first of a succession of white cats years ago. My old female had several litters of white kittens," Claire said. "I think Alison took the first one to save it from drowning, but she grew fond of them and always wanted one from every litter; she had half a dozen at one time, but she found homes for most of them. And in a city, some cats do get killed or lost." She straightened up. She traced with her fingertips the sign of a pentagram on the glass, another around the obliterated one on the sill.

"I can re-establish the wards," she said. "Of course, ideally, the whole house should be cleansed and re-sealed, and you should do it yourself; it will be much more effective that way."

"And it would keep the cat out?"

"If the cat is an ordinary curious kitty coming in an open window, probably not," Claire said. "If it's discarnate, perhaps the wards would keep it on its own plane of existence, and drive it off the earth plane. Not that the spirit of a discarnate cat is likely to do anyone any harm, no more than a living cat would; less, rather, for a discarnate cat won't scratch or leave any messes. Warding a house against the ghost of a cat seems like overkill, unless it had frightened someone."

Leslie shook her head. She was a little dizzied by the matter-of-fact way in which Claire spoke of discarnate cats.

"I think this particular cat met a messy end," she said, leading Claire downstairs past the music room; Emily was now playing the "Troika" section from Moussorsky's *Pictures at an Exhibition*. "Both Emily and I thought we saw the cat out here, lying in its own blood; Emily actually came running in, calling for a first-aid kit, but it was gone, and there was no blood on the floor."

"Well, if it had been run over, it might have come back, in spirit, to a place where it had felt safe in life," Claire said abstractedly, approaching the garage door. "Betty Carmody insisted there was something dreadful in the garage, but she never got around to asking me to come and help. I don't think Betty would ever have been right for the house. You understand," she added, "Alison had not trained a successor, as everyone who goes that far on the Path must do. She had begun, of course, and then discovered that the successor she had chosen could not be trusted. And she died before she could make a new choice." She stepped into the studio garage and recoiled as if she had been hit in the face.

"There is certainly something very wrong in here," she said, in a distant, withdrawn voice. "I don't know what it is. But it's horrible—horrible!"

"Both Emily and I—and the real estate agent, as well, and my ex-fiancé," Leslie said, "noticed a dreadful stench; we thought perhaps the plumbing had backed up. Or that the cat had gotten in here and misbehaved."

"It's worse than plumbing," Claire said. She was very pale. "I don't know if it's as serious as an earth elemental. But I sense—pain. And worse than pain, fear. No, not fear. Terror." She made a wry face, and swiftly plunged back outside.

"I'm sorry," she said weakly, "if I stayed in there, I'd throw up."

When they were back in the kitchen, she said, "I did tell you that Alison died without choosing her successor. She had actually begun to train him. And then she discovered that he had begun practicing black magic."

Fragments of a conversation overheard in the bookstore were surfacing in Leslie's mind. She said icily, "Are you by any chance referring to Dr. Simon Anstey?"

"Do you know him?"

"I do. He has been very kind to me and to Emily," Leslie said. Claire looked at her, troubled.

"At one time I was very fond of Simon myself," she said, "and when he had his accident we all prayed for healing for him; it was a very real tragedy. But nothing excuses meddling in the black arts. Simon had always been a little too—too interested in, and curious about the Left-hand Path for my taste, and eventually he went over the edge—"

"Oh, come, Claire," Leslie said, in disbelief, "you sound as if you were talking about Darth Vader—the Dark Side of the Force! You can't be serious!"

"I hope you never know how serious I am," said Claire. Her voice was level. "Where do you think all that about the Dark Side of the Force came from in the first place? It's a very real thing, and very dangerous. Even if you don't admit that magic exists, the power of thought is very real; if positive thinking can influence healing, and the growth of plants, what do you think negative thinking can do? I don't mind telling you: I don't trust Simon Anstey. I honestly believe that since his accident he has become unbalanced, and that he is a very dangerous man." There was a long silence.

At last Leslie said, "I'm sorry, Claire. I know you mean to be helpful. But I simply can't believe what you're saying, and I can't believe in black magic. I have enough trouble believing in psychic force, the ghosts of cats—"

"Maybe I'm to blame. Maybe I've been going—a little too fast for you," Claire said. "Perhaps you should talk with Colin. He really knows more about these things than I do."

"It seems rather underhanded, to talk about a man behind his back—"

"I would say the same thing to Simon's face, and I *have*," Claire retorted. "Listen to me, Leslie. I want to be your friend, and I don't want to influence you unduly. But be careful. Be very, very careful," she repeated. "Simon Anstey is a very dangerous man, and Emily is very young, and you are new to all this, and very vulnerable. Be careful, or you may find yourself deeply entangled in—in something you wouldn't want to be mixed up in if you knew what you were doing."

AT SIMON'S CONCERT, HELD a few days after Claire had come to the house, he insisted that Leslie and Emily should occupy the box reserved for the conductor. He had asked them to join him in the Green Room at intermission, but instead he appeared in the back of the box.

"Would you like a drink? And perhaps Emily would like a glass of champagne?" He smiled kindly. "She is old enough for that, I think."

"Not really," Emily said naively. "I won't be eighteen till next August."

"Well, I will not tell anyone if you do not," he said, smiling.

Leslie had believed it was most unusual for a conductor to appear in the halls during an intermission; but after all Simon was very much a law to himself. He seemed to read her thoughts.

"Could I deny myself the privilege of parading my gifted pupil, and the most fascinating woman in San Francisco, through these elegant corridors?" She thought, as she had thought before, that there was something Continental about his words and gestures.

Surrounded by the marble staircases and gilt chandeliers, they moved toward the bar, lined three or four deep with men in tuxedos, women in evening gowns and, even in July, furs; Leslie felt that her simple gown and Emily's were out of place in this setting. Yet the crowd was mixed, music lovers in ordinary business suits, even a few students in jeans or colorful hippie-style outfits which reminded her of Frodo. Simon looked at the crowded bar and said, "I'll brave the crush; wait here."

Leslie was a little hesitant to let him struggle with three champagne glasses alone, but she could think of no way to protest without humiliating him before Emily. She watched as his long, lean figure disappeared in the crowd near the bar.

"Oh, look," Emily said. "There is Claire Moffatt! I didn't know she was fond of music."

A phrase from one of the books Claire had given her surfaced in her mind: *What most people believe to be coincidence is the working out of cause and effect, but they operate by influences so subtle that they are not perceivable except at the very highest levels. The great adepts know that there is no such thing as chance.*

She wasn't an adept, whatever that might be, but she knew that her life was beginning to be surrounded by the most amazing coincidences. She did not believe they were meaningless. She greeted Claire and introduced Emily to Colin MacLaren.

"But we know one another," he said. "Frodo brought you to one of our seances. Are you enjoying the concert?"

Emily said, "Simon is my teacher; I'm studying with him this summer while Dr. Agrowsky is in Switzerland."

Leslie was braced against some tactless remark by Claire or Colin; they were, after all, Simon's enemies. But Colin said only, "I have always thought Simon would be a splendid teacher; perhaps the accident that so tragically destroyed his stage career was a blessing in disguise. The world has not lost a great concert pianist but has gained an equally great conductor and teacher. The career of a concert performer dies with him, but the teacher lives as long as his pupils, and the legacy of the great conductors transforms music for a whole generation."

Emily said indignantly, "I wouldn't say that in front of Simon if I were you!"

"I could never be so tactless," Colin said, "but how can anyone know what purpose there may be in these things? I don't believe there are any cosmic accidents. And Simon was Alison Margrave's chosen pupil; he would be as well aware of that as Alison herself."

"There is Simon now," Claire said. He strode toward them, three glasses of champagne on a cardboard tray; she might have known he would find some way to manage. She saw him stop for a moment and felt something turn over inside her; had he had another of those terrible disabling spasms? What would happen if it happened when he was actually conducting? She was shocked to realize how quickly her detachment had vanished.

Then he came on toward them, extended the gloved hand, bearing the tray, to Emily, then to Leslie.

"A most inferior vintage," he said, smiling, "but cool and wet. Hello,

Claire," he added, with the little inclination of his head which somehow gave the impression of a bow. "Colin. I'd forgotten you were music lovers. Or—" his face hardened to steel, "did you come to find out the extent of my disability?"

Somehow, swift in her mind, Leslie had the impression of a thrown gauntlet; but Colin's kind eyes refused the challenge. Claire said gently, "I'm very happy to see you conducting, Simon. I always thought you had a great gift for it."

"So you said at the time of the accident," he said, and his voice was silken, "but don't you give up on me too quickly, Claire. I don't happen to share your counsel of accepting some sort of divine will and settling for second best. You will see me on the concert stage again, and on that night—" he smiled, "I shall hope to see you sitting in the very first row and conceding defeat. You of all people should know the strength of the trained will." He raised the glass to his lips, then hesitated, touched it to Emily's. "Shall we drink to that?"

"If that day happens, Simon," Claire said, "I would be the very first to applaud you. Why do you think I wish you anything but the best? It was for your own sake that I warned you against certain methods—"

"Wait till you are where I am before you judge my methods, Claire!" he said. "Lose your own eyesight and your own livelihood and see if you are still babbling the same kind of old-maidish nonsense!"

"It doesn't look as if you had lost your livelihood, Simon. But is the eyesight so bad? I'm truly sorry to hear it; I heard they were still hoping to save the sight in your left eye—"

"They are, and they've spared me nothing in trying," Simon said. "They still aren't sure—"

"You know you will always have my prayers," Colin said quietly. "I've known you since you were a child, Simon. God knows, I wish there were some way I could give you my own hands."

"That's a safe offer," Simon said. "And this conversation is beginning to bore me. I have guests." He bowed again. "*Au 'voir.* Leslie, shall we—" They moved away toward the box.

"I didn't know you knew them, Leslie."

"I met them in the bookstore; Claire gave me the book you wrote with Alison. I didn't know you had so many talents, Simon."

He smiled and laid his good hand on hers. "Ah, the sins of my youth. I wrote that with Alison when I was hardly twenty. Colin was living in

New York and heading a small publishing house then, and Alison took me to help her investigate poltergeists. At that time I cherished delusions of being the true Renaissance man, a genius in half a dozen fields at once. Pianist, composer, conductor, writer, parapsychologist— Then, I suppose, I became hooked on the grandeur of the stage—" He smiled at Emily. "We are applause junkies, all of us who want to perform. That is what colorless people like Colin will never understand; when you have known that particular high, everything else becomes bland, ordinary, dead; you live only when you are before an audience, and everything and everyone becomes only part of an audience. The game becomes life." He ushered her into the box. A small, mellow-toned bell warned the audience to return to their seats, and he kissed Leslie quickly when Emily's back was turned.

"In the Green Room after the concert is over; I'll give your names to the doorman."

BY NOW SHE WAS prepared for the manic exhilaration which surged over him when the concert was ended. He was surrounded by fans asking for autographs, one or two people from the press, but he dismissed them quickly and came to her, laughing.

"Let's send Emily home in a taxi—and go home together!"

She drew a long breath, realizing that until that very moment she had not been sure the previous occurrence had not been an impulse on Simon's part, a one-night stand. Her ego could have survived that, since she had been there by choice, but she was gratified to know it was more.

I still think I am bewitched. But maybe it went both ways. Are there no coincidences even in physical attraction, either?

Despite the ritual solemnity of the altar, their lovemaking was filled with laughter, prolonged and tender. They did not sleep until the sun was rising.

She had never believed in love, certainly not in romantic love, and her training as a psychologist had made her very skeptical; either it was a fantasy of silly women, sentimental nonsense by which they strove to justify actions based on sexual passion, or else it was a myth invented to exploit those same silly women and sell them trashy novels, makeup and perfume.

She had never felt remotely like this. She had liked Joel, they had had good sex and shared interests, she had enjoyed dancing with him and being with him. She had accepted the cynical definition of love which she had read in a modern novel: *friendship with sex.* But lying awake at Simon's side, she knew that whatever abuses might be committed in the name of romantic love, somehow it had entrapped her. Sex was a part of it, a large part, but it was less and more than sex alone.

At her side he moaned in his sleep. Already if he was in pain it tore at her like claws; once during their lovemaking one of the terrifying paroxysms had come on him and she had held him till it passed. She held him now, and he wakened, staring about him with his uncovered eye, in terror and dread, then he recognized her and clung to her in sudden relief.

They lay side by side; after a moment he said meditatively, "I have heard rumors that Alison's house is haunted. I sometimes wonder if it is I who haunt it."

"I don't know what you mean, Simon." She curved her body tenderly around his.

"When I was in the hospital—drugged and in pain," he said, "I am sure that some part of me sought—that house where I had felt so sheltered and so happy. It had not occurred to me that my appearance there might frighten others, but of course with those who did not understand it would necessarily be so."

Was this, then, the explanation of all that had puzzled her so much? "It's not impossible, Simon. The night after Emily auditioned for you—" and she related how Emily had wakened, crying out that she saw him in the room. "And I saw you once, myself, in the studio."

"I hope you welcomed me," he said soberly, caressing her breasts with his scarred hand. He had removed the splinted glove that kept the fourth and fifth fingers extended, and they were curled motionless against his palm. "The doctors say I must use these fingers constantly if I wish to regain their perfect use." He moved them on her in a way she had not known how to desire before this.

"I didn't know you then. But Emily was frightened; she didn't know you then either."

"Being frightened will not harm her," he said indifferently. "Any strong emotion strengthens an artist's will; one is as good as another, love, fear, pain—"

"Simon, how callous that sounds!"

"I would not have frightened her deliberately, of course; whatever Claire or Colin may say, I have not become a monster. But after the audition, I was very tired, judging all those young pianists, good and bad, and I was also under considerable strain; I had an appointment with a specialist. As I told you, they are trying to save the sight in my left eye; the treatments are—" he hesitated, searching for a word, "they are excruciating; I will not harrow you with details. I rarely use drugs; they are dangerous for anyone of my level of sensitivity. But on that particular night I could not summon my usual fortitude, and I took a dose of chloral."

She had seen him now several times in those frightful spasms which reduced him to strained, tortured immobility.

"It is not impossible that during that period when my conscious will was suspended, I sought a place where I had been young—and whole. My spirit, if you will, fled to the room that had been mine, child and man, whenever I was in San Francisco. For many years it was my home; Alison was a friend of my mother's, and afterward—magic creates stronger ties than mere kinship."

Remembering the ritual which bound her to Simon, she could believe it. He sighed.

"Colin and I were dear friends once, and I am still fond of him, and of Claire. I am not sure why I have lost their friendship, but it was not my own choice." He was silent as the fog rolled against the window. It was not the time to repeat what Claire had said about black magic. She didn't believe there was any such thing; still less that Simon could devote himself to evil. Could they dare to condemn the fierce determination, the trained will that had set him to force healing from the unknown forces he believed in? Leslie no longer disbelieved that they might be possible.

He reached out for her. "But now," he whispered, "I need not face it alone. One of the things I have been lacking is a magical partner, Leslie. You will work with me, join your efforts to mine, to make me whole?"

Why at that moment did she remember Colin saying, *If it would do any good, you could have my hands.* She knew it was true of her. She would give her hand for his, and do it without flinching, and knew this was what was meant by love.

"I know nothing about it, Simon. But with everything that's been happening in the last days, I'm beginning to know that nothing is impossible. If anything I could do would help you, you know I would be more than glad."

He pulled her down on top of him; kissed her with savage intensity. His hands again traced the curious sign on her body. She recognized it now.

"I will not take you," he whispered, "but you must give yourself to me, Leslie." And in the silence she heard again the faint electrical crackling, almost visible between them, and then the almost inaudible chime of an invisible bell.

"The astral bell." His voice was soft and distinct. "We stand in the presence of unseen forces. What we say and do now goes beyond us two and through all the worlds."

On the altar Leslie saw the candle flare high; flame rushing to the very ceiling. A form of poltergeist activity? Simon was fully erect now, and again she heard the distant chime of the astral bell, the signal of the threshold between the ordinary world and the one on whose boundaries they stood. One part of her still disbelieved, one part of her said mockingly, *Right out of* Star Wars. *The Force is with us!* But the rest of her was all Simon's.

She whispered aloud, "I give myself to you," and heard the words echoing through some vast otherworldly silence as she took him to her.

THE FOG ENCIRCLED SIMON'S high windows when she woke; it was as if they were together on a high world, encircled by empty space. He rolled over to her and laughed softly.

"And it is a weekend," he said. "Today you need not steal away at the crack of dawn!"

"No." She stretched out luxuriously beside him. "But I feel guilty; there are so many things I ought to be doing at the house."

"We will go and do them together, later," he promised. "There is much you should learn. It would perhaps not occur to you that any house which you live in—psychic as you are—should be cleansed and resealed."

"Claire mentioned something like that."

"Claire should know; when Alison was helpless, she got in and sealed the house against me, hoping to keep me out. I am stronger, of course. But enough of that; I will teach you how to cleanse the house of all alien influences, to guard it against any forces except those which you yourself bid to enter, to seal and set wards upon every entrance." He was watching her carefully. "What is it, my beloved?"

"I can't help it; it still sounds like superstition to me."

"I see." He leaned on his elbow, regarding her. "Go on."

"I can accept the reality of psychism because I must; it happened to me. I *did* see that dead girl and her murderer—you know about that. I know what's happened to people I've never seen or heard of. I feel as if I'd stepped into the world of *Star Wars* . . . the Force is with us; an invisible different reality penetrating all the universe. . . ."

"Actually that is a very good way of putting it," he said. "We do live in the midst of unseen forces and influences. We cannot see radio waves, but if we had a radio here and tuned our dials to the proper frequencies, we could have anything from a broadcast of music by Brahms, a talk show where crazies call in and discuss flying saucers on which they rode to Venus and Mars, rock music that would blast our eardrums deaf, or a priest saying Mass in Latin. We do not have a radio and probably would not turn it on if we did—we have better things to do with ourselves." He touched her intimately, and she snuggled close to him. "But even without the radio, all those things, the Latin Mass, the rock music blasting, the babbling crazies, they are all around us somewhere in the air waves. Do you think we are unaffected by them, even though we have not tuned them in?"

"I never thought of it quite that way."

"Take my word for it; they do affect us, and other things as well. If you knew how to use your mind to its fullest potential, you would see everything, from this little room, that is happening in the City. Thousands of people flocking to churches and offering us prayers to their God, who said, 'Whatsoever ye shall ask in my name, it shall be granted unto you.' If we could tap into the force of all those minds, it could be an incredible force, but even they do not know how to tame it. If they did, then when they pray for—peace, for instance—none of the forces of war and human greed could possibly prevail. They say they want peace, but what they truly want is peace and a chance to achieve all their own petty little desires—for greed, mostly, profits. If you knew how to open your mind you could see every crime committed in this city last night—yes, you are right to shudder, that is the business of the police. But they should learn to tune their minds to the minds of those who break the law. They are afraid. They want to remain superior to the criminals and have power over them. But do you see what I am saying? All this is in the power of the trained will.

One of the great adepts—timid little people who did not understand him called him a black magician—said, *Love is the Law, love under will.* You have a trained mind, Leslie, and great natural gifts, but you must learn to use them or they will use you instead."

"What kind of learning?"

"Leave that to me. To begin, I will teach you to tend and refurbish the altar. At the level where we are, everyone must have a kind of shrine, a reminder of what is most important in life, whatever form it takes. It need not be a formal altar." He smiled, rolling over. "I am sure Emily's shrine is her music room, her devotions are her practice hours and the discipline of her hard work and passion, the dedication of her hands and mind."

She could in a very real sense see what he was saying.

"Come," he said, pulled her out of bed and brought her before the altar. "I have no graven images or idols, no hint of Satan or demons; I think all that is disgustingly vulgar; Satanists and such idiots are usually ineffective rebels who had a painful overdose of Catholic bigotry in child-hood and want to kick over the sacred traces. Although if God is what the Church thinks, I can hardly blame medieval rebels and anticlericals for defining the devil as a friendly fellow by contrast! Believe one thing for certain, Leslie, I have no truck with devil worship; I think those kind of people could call on their devil from now till Eternity with no more ma-terial effect than if they were reading the poetry of Edgar Guest, or Kahlil Gibran, or any other popular vulgarian. But the very idea of calling on some sort of anti-God would create the very ugly thing they called up. Satanists create their own devils, as pious religious people summon up their own God, and I want nothing whatever to do with either of them. Most organized churches call up thoughtforms of a God just as bigoted as anyone else's devil."

Then what in the world do they mean when they call you a black magician? she wondered, but did not yet have courage to put the question.

"What do you have on your altar, then?"

"Mainly, the four elements. Yes, when I went to school there were ninety-six elements and the learned scientists said there could never be any more; I grew up before the atom had been split or mankind inquired into nuclear mysteries. Now there are—what? A hundred and twenty elements and counting? The four elements—earth, air, water and fire, or, if you prefer, fire, wind, rain and soil—are metaphors for all the millions of things which exist in the Universe. Here we have fire, in the candle; salt and rock crystal for earth; incense for air, and a chalice of water. The altar is kept immaculate, and whenever you approach it, you must focus your will to encompass all the known and unknown elements in the Universe," he began. He took her hands and spread them over the altar; Leslie was not sure whether it was real or whether she had imagined it, but she could feel upswelling force palpable against her hands like a great magnetic field.

As he showed her how to cleanse the vessels, to replace the candle after cleaning the cup, to recharge the salt and water with the magnetic energies of her body, Leslie thought of the Japanese tea ceremony; it was like a meditation, a special exercise in mindfulness, a dedication of the will to the forces, seen and unseen, which permeated the entire world. But surely Colin and Claire were too intelligent to call this kind of thing black magic?

"And now," said Simon, when they had finished, "enough for a first lesson. One of the talents I attempted to pursue when I still cherished the ideal of myself as Renaissance Man was gourmet cooking; shall we try making strawberry crepes for breakfast?" He nuzzled against her. "Or shall we go back to bed and make the crepes later?"

By now she had no hesitation about wearing Simon's Japanese robe, or about taking it off. "Either way," she said, "we can't lose."

OVER THE NEXT WEEKS she sometimes found herself wondering about Simon's religion, or even if he had one. It was possible that, like Claire, he simply detested the jargon. The nearest he ever came to mentioning religion, on one occasion when she said carelessly, "God damn it," upon snagging a run in her pantyhose, he said lightly, "My darling, it seems absurd to condemn something to eternal theological punishment when what you mean is *How very tiresome.*" Yet on another occasion, when Emily ripped out a casual, "Oh, Christ!" he reprimanded. "Never take the name of God or devil lightly; you never know who or what may turn up in answer to your careless invocation."

Emily came home from her lessons with Simon either exalted to the skies or in the depths of despair; but she worked hard and incessantly, and seemed in good spirits. Sometimes the lessons were given in the music room in the old house, rather than at the Conservatory, and sometimes she heard Emily crying inside, or Simon shouting at her, but Simon frequently stayed for supper afterward and Emily laughed with him and teased him and helped him cook delicious vegetarian meals.

When June was nearly ended, he telephoned to ask if he might come over and keep his promise to help her cleanse and re-seal the house. Leslie had almost forgotten; the house had been perfectly quiet, and she had even spent some time in the studio/garage, hanging curtains and sewing cushions, without any sign of psychic difficulty. She was actually beginning to wonder if the whole thing had been due to hysteria, overwork and an overactive imagination.

"It's the summer solstice; the longest day of the year, which has had significance for the human race since people first investigated the measurements of time on this planet. It's a question of balancing the planet's magnetic fields and forces," he told her, "which is why it's a good day for it." When he turned up, he brought cuttings of various plants in his car.

"Juniper, and Scotch broom, and hazel; all the protective plants," he said, and insisted on gathering others from the herb garden.

"Where is Emily? I don't hear the piano or the harp."

"Emily's gone to a picnic with some friends," Leslie told him. Emily had left at dawn in Frodo's truck, Timmie perched in her lap, Rainbow and half a dozen friends roosting like brightly plumaged birds in the back. "It's the Solstice pan-pagan picnic somewhere in the East Bay."

Simon looked exasperated. "If she has time for that sort of nonsense, I must not be working her hard enough," he said.

"Simon, she's spent five to eight hours at the piano or harpsichord every day this spring! This is the first holiday she's taken! Have a heart," Leslie admonished. "She left us some devilled eggs; she was up half the night baking organic brownies with carob and honey, and mixing her own mayonnaise with safflower oil."

"I know some of the pan-pagan young people," Simon said. "They're a promiscuous lot; I hate to see Emily cheapening herself that way." He looked seriously at her. "My love, do you think I am jealous?"

"Well, I wondered," Leslie said.

"Emily is a lovely, gifted young woman, and if she were properly trained she would have psychic gifts equal to your own. But my interest in her is not remotely sexual," he added. "There is only one woman in my life at this moment in Time, and you know who she is." He smiled at her, a smile more intimate than a touch. "Like all women, Emily is an incarnation of the Goddess, but she has not yet, I think, found out who she is. I see her as the chaste warrior woman; Artemis, Diana the Huntress, Athena, the Valkyrie. Nor for words I touch upon or invade that powerful innocence. At present she pours it all, like a dedicated virgin priestess, into the service of her God, Music. Though she is very precious to me, I would no sooner think of her sexually than my own daughter if I were fortunate enough to have one. Shall we begin to purify and cleanse the house, Leslie? This is how we begin: we make a purifying water by steeping these herbs in distilled water; I had the foresight to bring a bottle from the grocery. You do not really want the emanations of the chlorine, and all the chemicals they pour into the city water supply, in the water you use to purify your house. . . ."

He spoke of the Goddess. Does he mean that literally, or is it a poetic metaphor, as with the four elements?

As a preliminary, working together, they swept every room in the house with bundles of juniper twigs, while Simon taught her some simple banishing formulas. They had nearly finished, and he had begun to ready the herbal solution for sprinkling, when he was seized by one of the crippling paroxyms of pain; he stood clinging to the wall, his good hand clenched in agony. When it was over, she could see the cold sweat on his brow.

But all he said was, "Fortunately that happened before we had seriously begun; we are supposed to keep full concentration when we are doing this, and it would have been—difficult to concentrate under those circumstances."

"Do you want to rest before we begin again, love?"

He shook his head. "Not necessary. But I wish the people who are so ready to advise other people to accept God's will for them could go through one of those spells. They might be less ready to condemn me for—" he hesitated, "for being ready to try *anything* to be whole again, and sound!" She flinched at the bitterness in his voice. But even before she could take in what he had said, he went on. "Now, everything must be done with the most concentrated mindfulness. Fill the chalice with the water steeped in herbs, and as we carry it through the house, sprinkling, form a clear image in your mind that we are purifying the place of any influences which we do not wish in our surroundings. It doesn't matter whether you visualize these unfortunate or unwanted influences as demons or as rock musicians; we don't want them here."

He took up the chalice and handed it to her.

"It is your house; it must be your force that does the cleansing and casting out."

"You said that Claire tried to seal the house against you. Were you serious, Simon? Could the house be sealed against a—a real person? Somehow I thought it would only work against—oh, psychic emanations, or ghosts—"

He said seriously, "If you were to seal the house against me, I could be made so uncomfortable that it would be difficult, supposing I were the least bit psychic, to remain inside. Of course, if you invited me in, that could override the sealing; remember in the book about Dracula, the vampire could not enter at first, but once he had been invited, then he could come in, however small the space. Writers of fantasy know these things instinctively; their unconscious minds stray into the spaces we call other planes."

"Simon—" she paused at the foot of the stairs, the chalice in her hands, "does all this have a physical, objective effect, or only a psychological one?"

"That implies that there is a difference."

"But there is a difference—isn't there?"

"I am not sure," he said seriously, leaning against the banister. "I know only that it works. If thoughts can affect the material universe, and I think the evidence is in that it can, then the work we do on the material plane—purifications, incense, protecting thoughts or prayers, whichever way you wish to define them—then these thoughts can spread out beyond this level where we are sweeping and cleaning and performing our rituals, to create a psychic barrier to unwanted intrusions from other levels of the Universe. I honestly could not say whether it is in fact subjective or objective, but I also believe it does not matter; results are what matter to me, and those I have seen." His face tightened into the lines of impatience she dreaded.

"Shall we go on?"

There was no reason for delay; she had her answer. They sprinkled the rooms with the herbs and water, carried incense through them, and when they had finished, together replaced the pentagrams. Finishing the task, he ushered Leslie out the door.

"Now walk in and see how it feels—?"

There was a freshness in the air which had nothing to do with the scent of herbs or the smoke of incense; it felt empty, silent.

"One thing," Simon said quietly. "If the spirit of Alison lingers here, in my mind I gave her special leave to remain. You did not want to drive her away, did you?"

To Leslie that was the final negation of the things Claire had said about Simon. If Alison had refused to trust him, if they had truly quarrelled, would he not have tried to exorcise even the ghost of Alison's presence from her house?

She said, "If Alison was happy here and wants to visit from wherever she is now, she's welcome," and smiled up at him. "What now?"

"And now—now you dedicate this place to the purposes of your will, Leslie," he said. "We must create fresh memories and joy, so the house will have not only a lovely past, unscarred by these recent disturbances, but a joyous present and a hopeful future."

She couldn't think of a better way to treat a house. They were still in the hall when she saw Frodo's truck pull up in front and Emily jumped out. Frodo leaned over to say something but Emily shook her fist at him, and even Leslie could hear her shriek, "You son-of-a-bitch!" as she ran up the steps. Frodo got out of the cab to follow; Emily slammed the door in his face and stood gasping on the threshold.

"Emmie, what's going on?"

"I told him to get lost," she said, gasping. "He said a horrible thing— horrible things about Simon—"

Simon stepped from the music room, encircled her shoulders with his arm, patted her cheek with his good hand.

"There, there, Emily, don't cry, my dear, do you think I care what some young yahoo thinks of me? He has been misinformed." He led her into the music room. "Sit here; yes, right here by me, on this cushion. I'll play for you."

Emily was still sobbing, but she sat silent as Simon drew off the black glove and began to play. The music, sad, intense and drifting, stole out and filled the room. Leslie watched Simon's face, drawn and still behind the eye-patch, which, at times like this, seemed a mask against expression. But the music spoke for him; when at last it was silent, Emily asked, "What was that, Simon?"

"The slow movement of my new concerto. I shall play it at my return concert."

"I didn't know you were a composer, Simon." She leaned against his knee.

"I had little time for composing on the concert circuit; but while I lay in the hospital, I found this theme in my mind. So that when I make a triumphal return to the concert stage, I will have something to perform which will be new and will prove to my critics that I have not wasted my time. There are critics who are so eager to see an artist fall—it is their business, I think, to create new sensations, and they lost no time in proclaiming me finished forever, as if I had no choice but to compose, or conduct, or teach, or any of those things which any second-rater can do—"

Emily cried out in protest.

"No second-rater could have written that concerto, Simon!"

"Are you sure? It seems to me derivative, second-hand Bruckner at best—there is no easy road for modern composers; how many can you remember offhand, except Gershwin, Vaughan Williams, Britten, Howard Hansen? Hundreds of others disappeared unknown; critics finished them off. Only an artist who can give his own work great performances can survive."

"Even that doesn't do it," Leslie protested shyly. "Who remembers Paderewskii, except other pianists? And Rachmaninoff would have been famous even if he had not performed his own work."

He rose from the piano, pulling on the black glove, his face impassive again. Emily came and snuggled against him.

"I told Frodo that if you were a black magician he ought to think seriously about studying black magic, because you were the best man I'd ever known!"

He caressed her hair briefly. "I'm touched, my dear. But if you have broken with that young man, perhaps you will have time to devote yourself to mastering the harpsichord's special touch; you still try to treat it like a piano. Mozart composed for the pianoforte because of the limitations of the harpsichord, but he wrote a great deal for the harpsichord with all its limitations and special characteristics; you must not play as if you were looking about with one foot for the sustaining pedal! At this stage in your life, my darling, you have no room for a love affair, except perhaps with Bach."

She smiled, a wavering sunshine. "Bach is the only man in my life at present. But can I be unfaithful to him with Handel and Rameau sometimes?"

"Indeed you may, child; that is one form of promiscuity that will never damage anyone's virtue," he said gaily, "but this is no time for a lesson.

Let us go into the kitchen and scrub some enormous potatoes and bake them with cheese or whatever we can find, and I will make you some of my superb strawberry crepes."

"Sounds marvelous," she cried. "I'm starved."

Leslie had already learned that Simon was invariably cheerful when he was cooking. Soon the oven was filled with the odors of baking squash and potatoes Anna, and while Emily, under his direction, beat a crepe batter, Simon removed his glove for the finicky task of hulling and slicing strawberries. She noticed that the weaker outside fingers curled against his palm, though he made himself deliberately uncurl and use them for slicing the strawberries. She wondered if he had tired himself playing, for the fingers trembled, and then she realized that she was staring and looked away.

"Filthy bloody thing, damn it to eternal hell!" Simon flung the knife across the room, his eyes blazing with rage, picked up the bowl with the strawberries and crashed it violently to the floor; it shattered into a thousand pieces, glass fragments mingling with crimson strawberries and strawberry juice. Leslie stared with amazement. There was a moment of absolute silence after the crash. Simon was standing over the bowl, fists clenched, and in that instant Leslie remembered a smashed garage window, another bowl that had not broken, being stainless steel.

Emily said lightly, "Well, it certainly *looks* like a bloody mess, there on the floor. What's the matter, Simon?"

He drew a long, strained, agonizing breath.

"My hand," he said. "It would not—serve me." He glanced around, half dazed.

"And I have ruined our beautiful supper," he said. "Come on, we'll clear away this mess and I'll take you out to supper."

"Oh, no," Leslie protested. "We can find something else, there's some ice cream—"

"No, no," he said, contrite. "I have ruined everything, I have upset you, I owe you that; run up and put on something festive, both of you. Has Emily ever been to the Top of the Mark?"

WHEN HE DROPPED THEM at their door that night, he told them he would be away for a few days. "My agent wants to arrange more lectures and master classes, and I must ask him instead to hold a block of time free for a return concert, perhaps next summer. Also, I have been asked to accept a position as artist in residence at an Eastern college, and I must find a tactful way to refuse. Fortunately I am not under financial pressure and I need not be stampeded into acceptance by thoughts of the wolf at the door."

But if his hand is so undependable, will that really come? Leslie castigated herself mentally for doubting it; if thoughts could materially affect what happened, doubts were wrong. "How long will you be away?" she asked, then wondered if she sounded plaintive, like a deserted woman.

But he seemed not to notice.

"No longer than I can help, my love; now there is a reason to come back to San Francisco," he said, kissing her.

SHE SAT LATE IN her study that night, enjoying the peace and silence. She had no doubt that Simon's work had cleared the house of any inimical presences, but even though Emily had gone to bed it seemed that she could hear, perhaps not with her material ears at all, a tiny drift of music from the room across the hall.

He had made no effort to exorcise Alison Margrave from these premises. They were hers before me and I am not unhappy to think that perhaps she is here, perhaps to counsel and advise me.

She was not even a little surprised to find the book on reincarnation, written by a well-known and controversial psychiatrist, with the foreword by Alison Margrave, lying on her desk. She had no particular memory of placing it there. Perhaps Simon had set it there to remind her to read it. Perhaps there was some less tangible influence. It didn't matter. She sat up late reading it, and when she had done, lay back in her chair, impressed and stunned with the evidence that had been presented.

The professors under whom she had trained would not have accepted it. No matter. They would not have accepted the evidence of Juanita García's body in a ditch, either, or of Phyllis Anne Chapman's birthday cake. But these things had happened to her and she no longer lived in that world. She knew now why she had been guided to this house, because of her disillusion and her feeling that she had come to a dead end in the counseling profession, that she could do very little good, and that only for people with the simplest problems.

Here in this very chair she had been led, without the slightest background or training in these matters, to ask out of the blue whether there might have been some purpose behind the birth of Chrissy Hamilton to her mother. One by one she began to apply it to all her patients. Leonard Hay, who could not make up his mind whether he wished to be homosexual or stay with his wife, might have become homosexual for a number of reasons. He might have lived many lives as a woman and not yet accustomed himself to the demands this society makes upon men. Or was that a sexist presumption, and the truth elsewhere? Possibly such men as Leonard rebelled against sexual stereotypes for men and were suffering this way to force more acceptance for individual life choices in society.

Judy Attenbury? If we choose what happens to us, why would she have been born into a body unsuitable for ballet, and yet have a passion to achieve status as a dancer? Maybe she needed a harsh lesson in fitting her choices to those really available to her? The conflict with her mother, the anorexia? Had she chosen a life which would force her to struggle for independence and to set her own standards? Or had she simply lost sight of her goals in the pressures of this life? Leslie began vaguely to see a new purpose in counseling. Perhaps what she could do was not so much to counsel adjustment to society and circumstance, but to try and help each client realize what was their basic purpose in life, and how they could achieve and work out that purpose. ("Karma" was as good a name as any.) Rather than flailing around blindly in the darkness of this life.

At least she could try. She supposed if she made any serious and radical changes at once, she would be read out of the counseling profession! Even the liberal state of California did not license counselors to help clients discover their true karma or the purpose of their present incarnation, she thought, laughing at herself.

But it was a new idea, a beginning, and at least she no longer felt completely hopeless about the work she had chosen. She put the book aside and went up to bed.

The faintest trace of incense and scent of herbs still lingered in her bedroom. She opened the window and let the fog roll through the room. She had found a little wooden end table that had been among the discards from the attic of the Sacramento house; she thought it might have been their grandmother's. She lighted a small candle in a red candle cup, lighted incense; earlier that day she had put water in a rounded scallop shell, and a crystal geode her father had brought back from a rock-hunting expedition, on the improvised altar, and she lay in the dark, thinking of Simon under the glimmering eye of fire. She was sure the effect was psychological, but she liked it. People had all kinds of private rituals; why not create one deliberately for its effect on your mind?

If her theory was true, if Alison's theory and that of the famous psychotherapist who had created the theory were true, then what was Simon's purpose in life and why had he come into her life just now? Even more urgent, what was the purpose of the accident which had lost him eyesight and hand?

Colin MacLaren had suggested one interpretation, that Simon's true influence should be as conductor, teacher, and tonight she had heard one of his compositions. If a conductor's influence can shadow an entire generation, what of a composer? The Bach Emily was playing had lasted more than three hundred years.

Yet Simon was experienced in these things; there must be a good reason he rejected Colin's explanation. And she herself had heard him say, *We only come to life before an audience.* Emily had that hunger, too. There were no simplistic answers. Even in conventional psychology there were none. How could she expect them in this?

Leslie remembered the first days after Simon had gone away as peaceful, with no hint of the shocking nightmare that was to erupt later. The morning after he had left, she answered her telephone to an unknown female voice.

"Dr. Barnes, I heard you've taken over Dr. Margrave's practice—"

"I'm sorry," Leslie began, but the stranger went on. "I heard you were living in her house, and I'm really at my wit's end, I can't think of anyone who can help me, and I swear, I'm ready to jump out the window—I just can't put up with it any more—"

She'd been taught in her work on the crisis lines: there are no phony suicide threats. She made the response which time had proved to be the only safe reply:

"Tell me about it."

She had no time for this, really. It would probably mean an hour on the phone counseling a distraught person who was not even her patient, but she had been thinking lately that perhaps she should do some volunteer work.

"I hardly know where to start—it's all so awful," the woman on the other end of the line said shakily. "That's why I called you. I heard that Dr. Margrave wouldn't laugh at me, only I heard she was dead and so I tried to put up with it, only he—he drove my kids away, and I'm all alone here and I just can't stand it . . . and I couldn't tell anybody. I tried one of those counseling hotlines and they told me to pull myself together—"

That phrase, Leslie thought, should be deleted from the English language, together with its twin, *Snap out of it.* It was the very inability to do that which brought them to seek help in the first place.

"I can't sleep any more, and all the time I hear him laughing at me. . . ."

An abusive husband, then. She had said he had driven her children away. After a while the woman finally ran down into a stupefied silence.

"I suppose you have asked him to leave?"

"Dr. Barnes, if I had a dime for every time I asked that man to leave, now *and* before—" she said, and again her voice faded into hopelessness. "I think he's tryin' to drive me crazy."

Persecution complex? Or a very real abusive husband, perhaps a battering one? Leslie knew how real that could be.

She asked cautiously, "Does he beat you?"

"Not now. But I know he wishes he *could.* He used to beat me, beat me all the time, even in front of the kids—and I tried to get away—I moved out and he said he'd never let me leave him—"

"You know, of course, that there is no law in the state of California which allows him to beat you. Have you made a report to the police?"

"I knew you wouldn't understand," said the defeated little voice on the other end of the phone. "I thought for sure you'd understand. The police can't do anything to help me." Leslie heard her sob at the other end of the line and she said with a little wail, "Pete died five years ago!"

Leslie said quickly, "I hear you, I'm listening. I'm not laughing at you." It was very important to keep the person talking, however irrational a counselor might think the client to be. A seriously deranged person, then, sane on every subject but that of her obsession. *Haunted!*

Yet Alison Margrave had been a parapsychologist. Had she then been one of these quacks who prey upon the gullible, encouraging the paranoia of the mentally disordered? That was not the idea she had gained, either from Alison Margrave's book or from the reports she had heard of her personally. Nor could a man of Simon's sharp intelligence have suffered a quack, whether self-deluded or preying on superstition. After a few more sentences, few of which she really heard—she was trying to absorb the concept—the woman paused again, she said, "I think you had better come in and see me."

She could at least appraise the woman's sanity, apply some of the standard perceptual tests. Then she could recommend a medical doctor, a hospital ward, a neurologist—or, if the woman's complaint seemed to be legitimate, possibly try some countersuggestion. She remembered, in the bookstore, seeing a book called *Psychic Self-Defense.* She herself had felt tormented by strange, inexplicable happenings in the Berkeley house and had wondered if she was losing her sanity. Who was she to say this woman must be insane?

She took the woman's name, Evelyn Sadler, and set up an appointment for her that very afternoon. It wasn't very long to acquire some information about people who were haunted, but Mrs. Sadler was in great distress and needed, at the very least, someone to talk to who would not laugh or deride her.

This morning she had an appointment with Eileen Grantson and her father, which she knew now would probably be about the amount of house-work it was reasonable to ask a fourteen-year-old girl to do—it was not as if Donald Grantson was disabled or on welfare, in which case there might be no alternative to Eileen's doing it all. They had had two or three sessions about this. But even under the pressures of the worst poverty, she felt it was unjustified to allow a girl of fourteen to assume responsibility for all household duties; to become, in effect, the woman of the house to her father. Unjustified, and unhealthy. At least there had been no further sign of the poltergeist to plague their final adjustment. After the Grantsons had gone she would try to find out more about hauntings by the ghost of a dead husband who would not let his wife live her own life after he had ceased to be concerned in it.

When they had departed, she had a spare three-quarters of an hour; she had scheduled it to work in the garden, but the needs of a client came first. She set out for the bookstore.

She realized that she was a little reluctant to meet Claire; she had made it clear that whatever this difference of opinion, of aims and goals, might be (Claire had called it black magic—how absurd), her own loyalties lay with Simon. The very thought of Simon made her warm, excited. How absurd, again, that she should be in love! *I never believed in it and it has happened to me.*

Like psychism?

At this hour of the day there were few customers in the bookstore; Frodo was arranging a display of books, and Colin sat behind the central desk, reading. Halfway inside, Leslie stopped; two cats, one black except for a small white patch on his chest, and the other misty white, were walking across a table covered with what a sign advised as BIG BAR-GAINS! She stretched out her hand to one of them, who came and sniffed at it; the other one came to nose his companion away.

"They're beautiful!" Leslie exclaimed, as the black cat twisted sensuously under her caressing hand, and Colin looked up and smiled at her.

"Dr. Barnes. What can I do for you?"

She felt foolish about explaining what she wanted and made conversation about the cats.

"What are their names?"

"They are the familiar spirits of the store," Colin explained good-naturedly. "The black one is Monsignor; see his clerical collar? But even as a kitten he was too dignified for an ordinary Father. Also he is celibate as a proper priest should be, having been altered as a small kitten."

Leslie chuckled. "And the white one?"

"Her name is Poltergeist."

"*Poltergeist?*" Leslie was sure he was teasing her.

"Poltergeist, because in her presence books fall from tables and ornaments topple from shelves without any intervention of human hands."

This time she actually giggled. "That's charming."

"They were both brought up in the bookstore; Claire found Monsignor as a stray kitten, starving in the street outside here; someone had kicked him. His leg is still a little crooked. Poltergeist was one of her own white cats. In general I have very strong feelings about harboring an unaltered animal; I can't bear the sentimentality which is too squeamish to spay or castrate a cat but thinks nothing of letting thousands of kittens and puppies die on the street or in animal shelters every year. But Claire is very conscientious about finding homes for her kittens. Alison had—" He stopped in midsentence and put on a stubborn look.

"But I'm sure you didn't come here to listen to me blather on about our pets. What can I do for you, Leslie?"

"Colin, everybody talks about Alison's white cats and won't say anything more about them. I think we have one of them, or maybe we don't." She told him about the elusive white cat, about Emily seeing it apparently bleeding to death in the garage. "I saw that, too, once."

He looked down at the desk top. He said, "I don't like to say anything. I didn't see it myself. But one of the reasons Alison quarrelled with Simon was that. Claire told you Simon was dabbling in black magic. Didn't she?"

"Yes, and I haven't the faintest idea what she meant by it."

"Believe me, you don't need or want to know," Colin said, "but among other things, I heard from Alison that he had sacrificed one of her white cats—ritually killed it, I understand. I knew myself it was not the first time he had done this sort of thing. He experimented with it as a boy."

Leslie stared at him, shaking her head. "I find that hard to believe. Simon is one of the most civilized men I have ever known. What could he possibly hope to achieve by it?"

"At that time? I don't know," Colin said. "I don't pretend to understand his motives. At that time I suspect it may have been nothing more than simple intellectual curiosity; he has far too much of that, and it often leads occult beginners onto the left-hand path."

This was the kind of fuzzy semantic statement which drove Leslie to distraction, and unfortunately Colin, despite his kindness and temperate intelligence, seemed much too fond of it. "As for intellectual curiosity, I can't think of a better reason for investigating parapsychological events. Or would you have people be what the sociologists call 'True Believers,' accepting the silliest things without trying to investigate them?"

"God forbid; the only person I like less than the skeptic who disbelieves without investigating is the true believer who believes without investigating. I believe Emily told you how I refused to tolerate that kind of fakery at a seance. But there is an enormous difference between intellectual *honesty,* which is essential if the whole field of psychism is not to deteriorate into fuzzy-minded nonsense, and intellectual *curiosity.* That curiosity is the most dangerous motive for doing anything. It has been used to justify everything from experiments with vivisection and Watson's experiments with behavioral psychology and operant conditioning, not only on rats but on living infants, to research in biological warfare and recombinant DNA."

There was, of course, something in what he said. She had even less respect for Skinner's behavioral psychology than for Freud's psychoanalytic jargon. Yet she challenged:

"What other motive could a scientist have for pure research except that one—the simple desire to know, just to know for its own sake?"

Colin leaned his chin on his hands. "I am disappointed," he said. "I thought when Alison led you to us, you would already know the answer to that. There is only one acceptable motive for any investigation, scientific or otherwise, and this is the only motive acceptable on the Path: *I desire to know in order to serve.*"

Something in Leslie responded to the words, as if they were in a language she had once known and was relearning, but the implied criticism of Simon outraged her and she changed the subject.

"Somehow it has gotten round that I have taken over Dr. Margrave's practice," she said. "Were you responsible for that, by any chance, Colin?"

Colin MacLaren looked up at her, his eyes singularly blue under his raised eyelids. He did not speak, but as Leslie met his eyes she knew the idea was absurd. She thought, *I know him better than that,* as if it was the most obvious thing in the world, as if she had known and trusted Colin all her life and beyond, with the trust usually given only to a father or a priest. And then she was confused again; she wasn't a Catholic and wouldn't trust a priest, and as a woman and a psychologist she knew that a father was often the last person anyone could trust . . . and she wasn't talking about exploded Oedipal theories either, but about simple family dynamics!

And she had known Colin less than six weeks.

Then Colin said simply, "On my honor, Leslie, no." In the few seconds she had almost forgotten what she had asked him. "Nevertheless, I suppose everyone who knew Alison took it for granted that she would not allow anyone to come into her house and live unless that person were her successor. Alison took her work very seriously. It was very important."

"Any work in mental health is important," Leslie countered. "But are you telling me that I am supposed to be a professional parapsychologist, a ghost hunter?"

"Leslie, I could never take control of your life that way. No one has that right; not Alison, not Simon, no one but you yourself can make that decision. But have you not already been forced into that by circumstance?"

"Splendid," Leslie said dryly. "The *Enquirer* calls me a psychic, so I have to be one?"

"The question, of course, is not what the *Enquirer,* or anyone else calls you, but what in fact you are," said Colin.

He's not too bad at this damn nondirective counseling technique either, Leslie thought, then was ashamed of the fencing, remembering what had actually brought her here.

"The problem is that I seem to be stuck with it, and I haven't any idea where to start," she said forthrightly.

"But this often happens with those who have natural psychism; they cannot learn to use it when they wish; instead it tends to use *them,*" Colin told her. "On second thought it is hardly accurate to say they cannot use it; rather, they are too lazy, or too afraid of the whole thing, to discipline themselves to use it. Either they let it control them and drift into trance mediumship and such nonsense, or else they pretend that if they ignore the whole thing, it will go away. The dangers in that—I don't want to frighten you, Leslie, but it can happen—can be as serious as possession."

"How do I learn?" she asked, almost in despair. "There's a woman waiting for me who is convinced that the ghost of her dead husband is pursuing her, making her life miserable. How do I weed out the kooks, the crazies, from the people who actually *are* being pursued by—by what you called the Unseen?"

Colin sighed. He said, "People like you often make the very best psychic investigators and consultants, Leslie, because, like Alison, they are natural skeptics, convinced against their will, and too intellectually honest to ignore the evidence. But every virtue has its own fault. I could give you all kinds of advice, but that would only tell you what has worked for me. And what you say is unfortunately one of the great pitfalls of this kind of work. The crazies."

"I thought you were trying to say that these things were real—"

"Oh, my dear, they are. But—I'm trying to think how to say this. Crackpots sometimes will say, 'They laughed at Galileo. They didn't believe Thomas Edison.' But the fact that these great men were laughed at does not mean that everybody with some absurd notion for an invention is an unhonored genius. Almost everyone who has a psychic experience goes through a time when he thinks himself crazy, or other people call him crazy. But that does not mean that everyone who thinks himself the victim of a psychic attack is necessarily sane. The very fact that we must be tolerant of eccentricity means that we attract eccentrics—and some of them are not harmless eccentrics but seriously deranged people; some harmless, some as dangerous as your Pigtail Killer. For every hundred or so people who hear voices, whether the result of real contact with the inner planes or of their own fantasies, telling them that all men are brothers and that they should live and love their fellow man—for every hundred of these there will be one or two whose voices, demoniacal or the voice of madness, will command him to slaughter the innocent or to persecute the helpless. 'Son of Sam' is a case in point. I do not know whether his voices were real, or came from somewhere in a chemically disordered brain, but whatever their source, the result was unholy. That is why it is so valuable when a trained psychologist will take up this work; differential diagnosis is possible, to know whether a given case is one for the medical doctor, the psychiatrist or neurologist, the police, or the psychic healer."

Some small voice in Leslie commented, *We always think an adviser is brilliant when he tells us what we already think.* She had been thinking along those lines herself. "But what do I say now? I have to go back and talk to her—"

"How long has this been going on?"

"Five years, and the woman is at the end of her endurance—"

"Most people are stronger than they think, if they have some hope of relief," Colin MacLaren said. "All you could do in a first session is to give a kind of psychic first aid, anyway; teach her to seal her aura and her private space—you *do* know how to do that?"

Remembering what Simon had taught her at the solstice banishing ritual, she nodded. He handed her one or two books.

"Take these and read them. No, don't pay me, not until you are sure they are what you need; then if you want to keep them you can pay," he said. "We'll write you up a charge account; anyone on the Path is entitled to that courtesy here. Frodo—" he raised his voice slightly, "come and write up a charge account for Dr. Barnes."

She reflected that this committed her to return here, either to pay for the books or return them, but the moment of immense trust in Colin remained, coloring her mood. You'd think I'd known him in a past life or something, she jeered at herself, but let him wrap the books without protest. Frodo looked up and said, "Oh, hi, Dr. Barnes. Is Emily okay and everything?"

"She's fine, but very busy." She had enough trouble running her own life without getting involved in Emily's, though she knew her sister missed him. Without Simon's intervention they would already have made up. But that was Emily's choice.

When she came home Emily was playing Bach in the music room with the door open. She came out as Leslie entered.

"There's a client in your office. I showed her in. We ought to have a waiting room somewhere, Les."

She had a point, though Leslie tried to stagger her clients.

Evelyn Sadler was small, dried-up and wispy looking, with clothes that looked expensive but seemed ten years out of date, her hair dragged back into a straggly bun. She said she was forty-seven, and looked ten years older. Colin's phrase, *psychic first aid,* rang in her mind as she encouraged

the woman to tell all about her husband and the progress of the haunting
from noises and lights and odd whispers to her husband's face appearing
out of nowhere. Her dog had run away. Her children had left home, though
it was not clear to Leslie whether the cause was harassment by the ghost
of their father, or intolerance for their mother's belief in it.

*I have to reserve judgment. But for the moment I will act as if it were true;
true or not, this woman is suffering.*

"You said it had gotten much worse lately. What happened to make
it worse?"

"It got so bad I went to a medium," she whispered in her scared little
voice, "and she said I ought to open myself to him, find out what he really
wants. So I did, but I found out what he really wants is to kill me. . . ."

True or a dangerous suicidal delusion? There would be time to appraise
that.

She said soothingly, "He can't harm you; he can only frighten you."
She wasn't absolutely sure, but it was safer for Mrs. Sadler to believe that.
"The important thing is to fill your life with so many things of this world
that it will make it harder for him to get at you."

"Well, I'd like to get out. But I haven't any place to go," Evelyn Sadler
said fretfully. "The girls are married, or away at college. I knew a lot of
people but they're all married and they aren't interested in an extra woman,
I found that out the year Pete died. So mostly I stay home with my memories."

"And that's the worst thing you could do," Leslie said bluntly. If the
haunting was real, then, like the seance medium's instructions, it would
open the way for the haunting entity to gain a foothold in the woman's
brain; and if it was an obsession, it gave her leisure to brood over it.

"But where can a woman my age go to do things?"

"Good heavens," Leslie said. "Any number of things. Join a church,
or a bridge club, or a swimming group at the YWCA, or take lessons in
tennis or macramé or short story writing—anything that will get you out
of the house and with other *people.* If your mind is full of real people, you
won't have time for ghosts."

"But I don't like playing cards, and I'm not interested in churches,"
she began, and Leslie realized that the focus of the session had shifted.
Ghost or obsession, here was a woman vulnerable because she was too
involved with herself. She let the woman go through what she called "the
YES, BUT sequence," explaining why it was impossible to take any of the

advice offered to get rid of her troubles. Then Leslie explained the sequence briefly to her, and then taught her a few of the psychic barrier and protective techniques Simon had taught her.

"Will these keep Pete away?"

"That depends on how much you want him kept away," Leslie said. "If you sit home listening for his voice and expecting to hear it, then you're calling him with one hand and telling him to go away with the other."

"But maybe he's lonely—"

"Do you think you have any obligation to keep him company?"

"No, by God," the woman exploded. "I put up with that man for twenty-two years! He's *dead,* dammit! Why doesn't he let me alone?"

"I don't know why he won't," Leslie said, "but you've got to make it clear that it's what you want, to be left alone. Have you thought of going back to work?"

"Yes, I have, but I haven't worked since before the kids were born—"

"Next time I'll give you some aptitude tests," Leslie said. "You probably have more skills than you realize; anyone who ran a house for twenty years and raised a family has plenty of skills, even if they don't know it."

"The kids don't want me to work; they say Dad left me fixed all right and I don't have to—"

Leslie said, "It's *your* life, Mrs. Sadler. You can sit home with a ghost, or get out and make such a full life in this world that it will discourage him. If you don't need the money, you can always do volunteer work. And meanwhile the psychic techniques I taught you will at least put up a barrier between you and make him realize that he's not on your plane any more." *And they will at least provide effective countersuggestion, if it's all in her mind.* The clock struck two, and she ushered the woman to the door, with a word or two about her billing practices. She would see her next week for some aptitude tests, and perhaps in getting rid of the woman's ghost she would also help her find a new life.

She returned to her office, glancing through the book on psychic self-defense techniques. The clock struck two.

Wait a minute. It struck before I let Mrs. Sadler out. . . . She wondered if she had imagined it. She looked up and saw the hands of the clock still at ten minutes after two.

Hell, I did imagine it. She returned to her book.

The clock struck two. This time it was *not* her imagination.

I thought Simon did a banishing in this place.

The clock struck again. Now the hands stood flawlessly, despite the noisy tick of the pendulum, at fourteen minutes past two. As she watched, the door opened and the cuckoo jumped out, crying, "Cuckoo! Cuckoo!"

Are you trying to tell me something, Alison?

She was waiting for another twenty minutes, her eyes on the clock; but it did not move, and struck the half hour with its single soft chime.

I thought all that was over now. It kept her jittery all through the afternoon, made her short-tempered with two clients, though she tried to conceal it, and later she felt angry that her office, her haven of peace, had been disturbed. What did Alison want with her? She refused to be driven out of her peaceful study.

Yet what had she counseled Evelyn Sadler? *You can sit home with a ghost, or* . . . She took the car to a nearby shopping mall and picked out a present for Nick Beckenham and Margot, since she would not be driving up to Sacramento with Joel for the wedding, and when she came back set herself to composing a note of polite regrets and good wishes.

That night at twenty minutes after six the cuckoo clock in Leslie's study struck twelve. She resolved to take it the next day to the repair shop. But why had it not struck this way at any time during the afternoon when Leslie's clients were here?

At twenty-eight minutes past seven it struck twelve again. In a rage Leslie raised her head and shouted, "Go away, Alison, this is *my* study now!" and then was glad of the soundproofing. Suppose Emily had heard her? But for the rest of that evening the clock struck only when it should, and Leslie, accustomed to the sound, hardly heard it.

THE FOG BANK HAD gone out to sea; an unlikely heat wave had brought San Francisco record-breaking temperatures in the nineties. Emily looked sleepless and weary at breakfast, sipping listlessly at her lemon-scented tea.

"I think I'll try to get Rainbow to go swimming today; we could take Timmie down to the beach," she said. "I haven't done much for fun this summer. Simon will be livid if I go a day without practicing—"

"Do a couple of hours this morning, and then go to the beach," Leslie suggested. "Simon would understand. All work and no play—you know the rest of it."

"Okay." The phone rang and Emily made a dive for it, listened a moment and handed it over with a sigh.

"For you, Les."

"Dr. Barnes? You don't know me," the voice said, "but I have something very important to say to you."

Oh, God. My daily crank caller? She said suspiciously, "I think perhaps you have the wrong Dr. Barnes."

"You're the one who's taken over Alison Margrave's house, aren't you?"

"Well, yes, I am, but—"

"Then it's for you," she said, "but I can't talk about it on the phone. Can I come and see you?"

Leslie sighed. "Do you want a full consultation? If so, you should call my answering service and make an appointment."

"No, no, it'll only take five minutes or so—"

Curiouser and curiouser! "All right," she said. "I have half an hour between eleven and eleven-thirty; you may come then." For the second day in a row her time for gardening had been pre-empted; she added in annoyance, "Just come through the gate; I'll be in the garden."

She had introduced Leonard Hay to the possibility that he might have chosen his predicament because of a situation left over from another life; unfortunately he had used this as just another "out" to encourage his life script, which read, "It's not my fault." Like everything else that had ever happened to Leonard, his karma was something that had been done to him against his will. Whether from this life or another, Leslie's task was to convince Leonard that in this life at least, he was still responsible for his own decisions or lack of them.

At eleven she closed the door behind Leonard and put a coverall apron over her dress. She had no time to change into jeans; another client was coming at one-thirty, a teenage boy whose parents could not convince him that going to school was more important to his life than playing games with his computer.

A small, gypsy-dark woman, with beads and bangles and a ruffled squaredance skirt, came around the corner of the house and stopped on the walk. "Dr. Barnes?"

"You called me this morning?" Leslie rose to her feet to welcome her visitor. She had the kind of eyes Leslie associated with hyperthyroidism; they seemed to pop from her head.

"That's right; I'm Kathleen Carmody. My husband's sister used to live in this house."

Leslie made a sudden connection. She said, "Your husband is a partner in Manchester, Ames—"

"Carmody and Beckenham; that's right," she said. "I don't know if you know, but I'm a medium—"

"My sister mentioned you." *She was nice,* Emily had said, *and I think she was honest, just kind of silly.*

"Well, you probably know, then, I tried that night to get in touch with Alison Margrave, and she didn't come through. But last night she came through to me, and gave me a message for you."

Leslie raised her eyes, but she only said politely, "That's very interesting." She was lying in her teeth. "What did she have to say to me?"

"The message was like this, Dr. Barnes. She said, Tell Leslie that the one she trusts, she shouldn't trust. Does that mean anything to you?"

"Yes, it does." Suddenly the steely taste of rage was in her mouth. "Who told you to tell me this?"

"Why, Alison did. A message came through me—"

"That's not what I mean," Leslie said. "I mean, who told you where to give the message?"

"Nobody. I knew where Alison lived, and when she came through to me, clear as clear, I wrote it down. See, here it is." In fine, especially clear handwriting, spider-lace elegant, the handwriting of a former day, was written, *Tell Leslie that the one she trusts . . .*

It was too pat. But there was no way to accuse this woman, who was, if anything, only an intermediary. She could guess who was behind it. She said, "Thank you," and waited for Kathleen Carmody to go. The woman looked at the garage with intense curiosity in her eyes, evidently dying to ask a dozen questions, but Leslie stared her down, and after a moment she said, "Well, thank you, Dr. Barnes, I had that message to deliver and I delivered it," and went away. Leslie stood with the paper in her hands, not knowing whether to tear it up with a yell of rage or to scream with laughter. She had told Emily: *my daily crank caller.* Maybe she should leave it at that. At least, today, the clock had behaved itself.

But anger carried her along while she went into the house, scrubbed the garden dirt from her hands and dressed herself in her crispest, most businesslike suit. This she would settle with the real culprit.

As she had hoped, the bookstore was almost empty; there was no sign of Colin, but Claire was behind the counter. As Leslie walked in, she smiled.

"I was so sorry to miss you the other day. What can I do for you, Leslie?"

Leslie set her teeth at the friendliness in the other woman's face. "You can stop trying to make trouble," she said, in her most clipped tone. "I had really thought better of you, Claire."

"Leslie, what's the matter? I don't know what you are talking about!"

"I suppose you didn't send your phony medium friend to the house with a convenient 'warning' against Simon Anstey? This isn't worthy of you, Claire!" she repeated.

"Leslie, I haven't the slightest idea—"

"And I suppose you'll say this is Alison Margrave's handwriting?"

She thrust it at Claire, who smoothed it out and read it, shoving her glasses up into her hair. She said after a minute, "Alison's handwriting? I really haven't the faintest idea. Leslie, I give you my word, by all I hold sacred, I don't know anything about this." She handed back the piece of paper. "Why do you think it necessarily refers to Simon?"

"Am I supposed to think it refers to Emily?" Leslie asked, still stiffly hostile. "If Alison Margrave has nothing better to do than send messages to the Carmody woman, well I don't admire her taste. If she is warning me about Joel Beckenham, which I doubt because he is a junior partner in the same firm Mrs. Carmody's husband belongs to, and they must know I've broken off with Joel, then she's about a month too late."

Claire gave her a troubled smile. "That's not impossible. Sometimes everything will be right about a prediction except the time element. They don't seem to know anything about time, on the other side. Maybe it only exists in the material world. Are you familiar with Dr. Dunne's writings about time? Something to the effect that all time exists simultaneously and we simply impose linear structure on events because it's the only way our brain can make sense of them?"

Leslie said, "I'm afraid that's too complicated for me. My mind works in past, present and future. What in the world would be the *sense* of warning me to break off with someone a month after I've already done it?"

Claire shrugged. "There's so much we don't know about these things. I'm sorry you think I'd be capable of something like that, Leslie. I really know nothing about it. I haven't seen Kathleen since the seance we had here."

"I'm sorry if I jumped the gun," Leslie said. She should have known Claire would not be underhanded. She had told Simon to his face what she thought. She wadded up the paper. "Throw this in your wastebasket. I guess it's like all oracles; it means any damn thing you want it to mean. I owe Colin for some books; I might as well pay for them now."

•   •   •

LESLIE DID NOT KNOW what had wakened her; she sat straight up in bed, hearing Emily scream. In a moment she was across the hall. Emily, wide-eyed, was sitting up in bed.

"Simon," she cried out, "it was Simon, here—"

The window, as once before, stood wide open, but Leslie saw only the tendrils of fog.

"It was terrible," Emily cried. "Oh, Leslie, his face was bleeding, it was ghastly, and there was blood all over his chest, and his hand—his hand—" She caught at her throat. "Les, it's *crushed,* it's just a lump of blood—oh, it's awful, awful—and then he was gone. . . ."

Leslie felt a creeping ice through her veins. What could this mean? Emily was sobbing.

"Do you think he's been hurt? Killed? Do you think his plane has crashed? Oh, Les, why would I see him this way?"

Leslie sat down beside her, holding her. She was numb and frightened, but she tried to speak with confidence. "You had a bad dream, darling."

If he was hurt, if he had been killed—with such a bond between us, surely I would have known. . . .

"Listen, Emmie," she said gently. "He said once that when he was drugged, in pain, he remembered—coming here. In spirit. And it must have been that."

"But—his hands—his face—the blood—"

She remembered Claire saying, maybe time only exists in the material world. "Possibly he was having a nightmare—about the time when he was actually in the accident," she hazarded, "and tried to escape by coming here. . . ."

"But what can I do? If he comes again—" Emily was shivering. "It's so terrible—it can't be real—"

There was a crashing sound, so loud that for a moment Leslie thought it was an earthquake. Then, with a splintering rattle, the glass in the casement window fell in shards to the floor. Emily screamed in terror. There was another splintering, crashing sound from below. Leslie drew her robe about her and prepared to investigate. Emily clutched at her.

"Les, no, no, don't go! It could be a prowler, a murderer—"

Leslie pointed to the glass shards on the floor. She said, "Was that a burglar? No, Emmie; it's not on this plane at all. I'm going down and see. Be careful; don't step in the broken glass—"

Emily came after her. "I'm not staying in this room alone! If he comes back—"

"Are you afraid of Simon, Emily? Maybe he came to you because he needs you," she said, trying to force down an immediate, jealous, *Why to Emily, why not to me?* She thrust her feet into slippers and ran down the stairs, twisted the lock and ran outside.

The garden was so thick with fog that she could hardly see her way to the garage. The scent of jasmine was heavy and damp, and she saw, without surprise, a light in the studio, pale and glimmering; candlelight? She twisted the handle. It was open. Surely she had locked it when she went to bed? She stepped inside, aware that Emily was on her heels. She heard the despairing cry of a tortured animal, but for a moment, by the dim red eye of the candle, could see nothing but a dark form, his arms upraised in invocation.

"Simon!" she cried out. "Simon, darling—where are you? What do you want here? Oh, Simon—"

Emily snapped on the light. The room lay bare and empty, yellow gingham curtains moving faintly in the wind from the fog, the dress dummy's headless form, the pale yellow walls untouched. The sewing machine had been left open with a half-finished rust cushion-cover folded on top.

"Look at the way the curtains are moving!" Emily swept them aside. The glass was smashed and lay in a circle on the floor.

She said numbly, "*Something* broke that glass. Something material. Maybe an earthquake?"

"Shall I call the police and report a prowler?" Emily asked.

And tell them that Emily's teacher, my lover, a famous concert pianist, appeared in her room, covered with blood. I can hear it now. She said, "I don't think it would do any good. Come on inside, Emmie, you'll catch cold in your bare feet. You'd better sleep in my room tonight. We'll cover the windows with a blanket, and call a glazier tomorrow."

"YOU CAN DRAG YOUR mattress into the guest room, if you want to," Leslie said, but Emily was still shivering, in shock.

"Do you mind if I come in with you? I'm scared, Les. Really scared. It *was* Simon, only—he looked like he was dying. Is that the kind of thing you see when you—" she still did not know how to say it, "when you do that psychic stuff? Do you suppose I'm getting it too?" She was hopelessly reluctant to go into the room where the smashed glass lay.

"We can't just leave it open, Emmie!"

"What good does it do to lock it, if some *thing* can get in and break the glass like that? It opens on the garden, not on the street anyway. And you yourself said nothing human could climb up there," Emily argued, holding back in the hall, and finally Leslie gave in. "We'll deal with it when it's light."

Emily's nightgown was wet with the garden dew. Leslie loaned her a fresh one; as she slipped into it she caught sight of the candle and walked over to inspect the altar.

"Good grief, what's all that junk?"

Leslie was not capable of explaining. "Some other time, all right, Emmie? Go to sleep."

Emily curled up against the wall and Leslie soon heard the regular breathing that told her the girl slept; but she lay awake, staring at the red eye of the candle on the altar. *Simon!* She ached for him, physically, but she was full of fear. If that dreadful vision were more than an overstrained girl's nightmare, a vision born of nerves, if Simon were hurt or dead somewhere, she might not know until she read it in the newspapers. She would not be informed; no legal tie, not even a casually acknowledged liaison bound her to the man she adored.

She tried to reach out, for the first time deliberately, and find him; but nothing happened, and as she stared numbly into the dark she remembered a phrase, casually spoken by a character in one of the books Claire had insisted on lending her:

"My psychism was usually reliable, except, of course, in matters where I was personally concerned."

So this was not an unusual experience; she *was* personally concerned, she was feeling her way tentatively through this new world. But what good was psychism if it could only warn her of dangers to people she didn't know or care about? She lay awake, staring into the dark and wishing she could cry without waking her young sister, until the sky began to pale.

And then she began, without being aware that she had slipped over the edge of sleep, to dream.

She was lying in a dark room, as now, with one red eye staring through the darkness, and dark forms hovered around her, hooded, robed, though she could not see them clearly. The incense was foul and suffocating, and she could hear the sound of chanting, but she could not move, because she . . . yes, she was bound hand and foot and could not even scream because she was gagged. And she remembered that somehow in a moment of insanity she had, for some reason, consented to this, and she could not remember why.

And what when this is over? Will they bundle me into that grey car and dump me somewhere in the Bay? He assured me it was only a game, an ordeal of terror to generate psychic force. I never refused to play that kind of kinky game before this! But I think now that this is serious. . . .

Humiliation and terror, he had said, a way to generate psychic force; as the ritual of the Mass generates power when properly done with full ritual by an ordained priest, so this Dark Mass generates power even stronger, because it goes to the unclaimed forces lying at the back of our civilization, ancient powers whose thought-forms have built up thousands of years of power, still unclaimed and waiting for anyone who can tap into them. But I thought he was just proposing a good excuse to play his kinky sex games. He promised I would not be hurt, but I've known enough of his kind to know I was in for something pretty rough.

This rough?

Hands were on her, harsh, demanding, a fierce and fiery pain; not fingers, nails—no, something metal, pliers—tweaked and tore at her breast; agony flashed through her, *No, No, I don't go this far,* but the gag was tighter than she realized; usually she had tricks to keep it looser than they thought, loose enough for escape if someone played too rough. She felt blood leaking from her nipples. The ropes forced her legs apart and she felt the slick touch of the oil there, and looked desperately up, struggling, even as she knew the struggles defeated her purpose, added to the psychic vortex which she could see through the electric dark, building around her.

I said I wanted to die. God knows I've tried often enough, pills, that overdose . . . but not like this. The warm gush of blood over her bare belly, the dying scream of the cat, that dreadful hand probing her genitals, smearing the blood there. Something, not an ordinary male organ, something unseen and cold and terrible, ripping and tearing into her.

Then she felt the knife at her throat and Leslie looked up in a moment of dying clarity into Simon's face and woke screaming.

•   •   •

ALL DAY THE DREAM worked inward, coloring her mood. It was absurd, no, it was obscene, to believe every nightmare must be a psychic flash. After such a disturbed night, it was normal to have nightmares, and between Claire's silly maunderings about black magic, whatever that was, and Emily's nightmare about Simon's accident—for that must have been what it was—no wonder she had nightmares, probably out of some forbidden trashy novel she had read during her days of exploring—and blocked from her mind. In memory it was right out of De Sade, or Mirabeau's *Torture Garden,* and her subconscious had obligingly placed the setting in her garage and grafted Simon's face onto it.

There was broken glass to be dealt with, both in Emily's room and in the garage. It was a relief to have something physical to deal with, and she swept it up, marvelling at the small size of the shards—the windows were not so much shattered as pulverized—and as soon as business hours opened, called a glazier. She cancelled her morning clients, telling them there had been a small earthquake or tremor in the street and some damage to her windows. The glazier came with gratifying promptness. He told her as he worked that this kind of thing was common, kids throwing stones through windows, and that she ought to get a lock on the garden gate, and she should have left it to him to take out the rest of the splinters from the frame. She was glad he had not seen the pulverized glass.

At five-thirty she saw Susan Hamilton struggling to get Christina out of her car. The child was skinny, with lank brown hair pushed to either side of her face; her jeans hung loose on her scrawny frame. When Leslie had first seen her, briefly, about a year ago, she had still looked much like any other small child; but now she had an awkward gait, flinging herself from side to side, almost lurching without seeming to notice where she put her feet, and her head twisted on her shoulders, staring first here and then there without apparent pattern. Susan held her by one arm, but the other hand was flailing at random.

"Chrissy, come now, be a good girl. Leslie, I'm sorry, I simply couldn't get a sitter. She can sit in the hall—she won't disturb anyone."

Susan should not have to worry about her child during her therapy hour. "She can go into the garden; there's nothing she can hurt there, or get hurt on, unless she pricked herself on a thorn—"

"She won't go near anything. I've never seen her handle anything alive, not even the potted plants in her school. She won't even touch a soft toy, only hard ones."

Leslie hesitated, remembering. "Maybe she had better sit inside; there are castor bean bushes there, and they are poisonous, if she found any of the leaves or berries—"

Susan smiled grimly. She said, "Since I've never been able to get her to eat anything but mashed potatoes or cream of wheat without a fight, she's not likely to put anything strange into her mouth. And if she did—" Her mouth tightened, but she did not complete the thought.

But she came back to it during the therapy hour.

"I couldn't help thinking—not that I want her to die—just how much easier my life would be if I could wake up some morning and find that she'd only been a bad dream. She was such a beautiful little girl when she was—oh, two years old. I never thought of anything like this. I'd seen some brain-damaged and retarded children, and they were grotesque, and Chrissy was so sweet and beautiful with those long lashes and big eyes. And now—she looks like—" Susan struggled to say it, "like any other retarded child. She's mine and she'll always be beautiful to me, but she's— she's—ugly. Empty." Susan was sobbing. "There are Kleenex on the table behind you," Leslie said.

"I try to keep telling myself, there has to be some kind of reason this happened to us. Only I can't imagine what it would be or what good it could possibly do either of us. And when you were talking about those poison bushes, I couldn't help thinking, what a mercy it would be if something did happen before she gets too big for me to handle and I have to—to put her into an institution."

Leslie kept her voice level. "Have you been thinking about that?" But her eyes strayed; she had heard a car in the street and it seemed that she recognized the sound of the motor. A grey Mercedes drew up in front of her gate behind Susan's battered blue Toyota, and Simon came up the walk.

He turned aside on the walk, so she knew he had not come through the front door but into the garden. Or was she imagining him again? So; she might hallucinate Simon, but not his car. She forced herself back to Susan Hamilton.

"No, of course you don't want to consider a state institution, not yet. There's no hurry, is there?"

"My family is giving me some pressure. They say I should do it before she gets too big to handle. But I won't give up on her yet, Leslie, I can't!"

There are always miracles. Yet could she in good conscience encourage Susan to hope for one? "Is that what you feel you are being pressured to do, Susan?"

"I've made arrangements for a special camp for her this summer. She'll have speech therapy again, and a good program. . . . I borrowed the money from my sister and God knows how I'll pay it back, and I get the feeling that Margaret was just doing it to humor me, hoping I'd come to my senses about Chrissy. She said I was still young, I could put the whole thing behind me, forget she ever existed, marry again and have other children. But I can't just wipe out Christina as if she never existed. And this camp—it's the first time she's ever been away from me. Margaret says she doesn't know the difference, she won't know or care. Maybe I do want to see how she reacts to being away from me . . . and of course I keep hoping that the camp will do her some good, help her care for herself a little, make some breakthrough. I know there is some intelligence there. If somebody could only reach it. Sometimes she does things that show real intelligence. . . ."

Susan repeated some of the stories which made her feel that somewhere within Christina there was real intelligence, if someone could only break through to it. Should she be encouraged to hope? The cycle of guilt, fear, renewed hope and despair was destroying her.

"Whatever you do, Susan, you mustn't be stampeded into making any decision until you know it's best for both you and Chrissy," was the only advice she could give, as she had given many times before. When the session ended she went with Susan to find her daughter in the garden. The child's sweater and jeans were smeared with dirt, but she seemed unharmed, kneeling on the grass and playing with some small stones. She fought to lift Christina and move her, resisting, to the car; Christina was limp, letting herself slide, as if boneless, through Susan's hands. She saw Simon come from the garage and stand watching the struggle for a moment; Susan looked up and saw the tall, elegant man watching her, and flushed. Then she managed to pick up Christina and carry her down the walk. Leslie opened the gate for her, and Susan set Christina on her feet; now obedient, the child walked to the car, and Leslie hurried back to Simon. He smiled and drew her against him, but he was still watching Susan fighting to get Christina inside and the seat belt fastened around her slumping body. As Susan slammed the car door, he shook his head and turned to Leslie.

"Hello, darling. Miss me?" He went inside with her, and as they went through the kitchen door, Emily dropped a glass and screamed.

"Simon! You're alive!" She flung herself into Simon's arms and began to cry.

"Here, here, what's this?" He held the girl at arm's length and looked down at her, extended one arm to draw Leslie close too. "I've missed both my girls, but why burst into tears at the very sight of me?"

"Oh, it was horrible—I saw you, bleeding all over—and your hand was just a bloody lump—and then the glass smashed, fell right out the window." Emily was almost babbling. "I was sure it meant you were dead somewhere—"

Simon stroked her hair tenderly with his good hand.

"I'm alive and well, and better than ever," he said, and then Leslie noticed, with a cry.

"Simon, the eye-patch!" For the first time since she had seen him he was not wearing it; instead he wore thick glasses which blurred the eye behind. He let Emily go, bestowing a final gentle pat on her hair, and drew Leslie close for a long, lingering kiss. He felt warm and real and very much alive; he pressed her tight to him, his gloved hand in the middle of her back, and she could just feel him hardening against her.

"Do the glasses spoil my romantic *image,* love?"

"Oh, no, but does it mean—"

"I *am* going to have sight in that eye. Not as good as it should be, I have about half normal sight. But at first they wouldn't even promise me I'd be able to tell light from dark, so this seems like a miracle."

"Oh, Simon, that's *wonderful!*"

"But it is not a miracle," he reminded her, smiling. "Nothing is impossible to the trained will." Reluctantly he let her go. "Now tell me about all these weeps and wails; why should I be anything but alive and perfectly well, and glad to be home again?"

So he thought of it as his home. For the first time, Leslie almost wished she felt able to marry; she sensed that he would ask her if she wished, and knew for the first time what her mother had meant when she said, *If she plays her cards right, a woman can get any man to marry her.* But she despised those feminine wiles—didn't she? Emily was telling Simon in detail about the vision, with gory details and all the crashing of glass. But Leslie said nothing about the obscene nightmare. Simon, warm and smiling, holding them both, was too real for that, and too dear.

"I'm starving, girls. Shall we cook something here or go out somewhere? Whatever you like. This—" he raised his hand lightly to the rim of his glasses, "deserves a wonderful celebration; on the other hand, we should plan something fitting. Can I help get supper if I promise not to lose my temper?"

Emily laughed at him and said, "I'll tell you what; you do the gourmet work like frying the crepes, and *I'll* be the scullery maid and hull the strawberries!"

And as they went into the kitchen, laughing, the nightmare melted away as if it had never been. By the time he drew a puffy baked omelet from the oven and set it on the table next to a bowl of cucumbers in yogurt, just fragrant with a whisper of curry, it seemed as if he had never been away; it was hard to remember he had not always been part of their lives. The crepes were stacked, dusted with powdered sugar, under a warm towel; the fragrant sauce steaming in a tiny saucepan. He had his own place at the table now, across from Emily.

"Who was that horrible little kid in the garden this afternoon?" Emily asked. "Mmmm, this is good, Simon," she added, taking a mouthful of omelet.

"Her name is Christina Hamilton."

"I did not know you worked with mentally defective children, love," Simon said.

"I don't; her mother is my patient. Susan couldn't find a sitter for Christina, so she brought her, and I thought she would be happier playing in the garden than sitting in the office."

Emily wrinkled her nose. "Poor woman, with a child like that! In any halfway decent society, they'd do something about idiot children! You look at a thing like that and it makes you petrified at the very idea of ever having kids."

"Chrissy isn't an idiot, or mentally defective as far as we know," Leslie said temperately, though she did not intend to be drawn into discussing a patient, "she is nonverbal, perhaps brain-damaged. She may be intelligent, but she cannot speak or communicate."

"I'd think a woman like that *would* have problems," Emily said. "Something like that ought to be in an institution!" She shivered, and Leslie reminded herself that Emily was very young.

"Chris isn't violent, or dangerous; why should she be institutionalized?"

"Because," Emily said vehemently, "she's never going to be the slightest use to society. One of the few things I remember from my political science class was some old guy who said the prime evil was to consume without producing, and that sure applies to defectives."

"I think it was Karl Marx," Leslie said.

"I don't care if it was Hitler or the devil himself," Emily argued, "that doesn't mean it isn't true."

"I don't think we can afford to make sweeping statements like that," Leslie said. "How do we know? Children like Christina may be of some value. I certainly wouldn't want the responsibility of saying they're not."

"Are you trying to say that old sentimental thing about reverence for life?" Emily demanded. "I haven't any reverence for life at all when it takes a form like that!"

"There is some precedent for what Emily is saying," Simon said. "It was Sparta where the law demanded that children who were not perfect should be exposed on a mountain and not brought up. The society was better for it; survival of the fittest is the law in every creature except man. In our great wisdom, what we call civilization has ordained that we can carry useless passengers and help the unfit to survive. I do not know if we are right or wrong. Can life have any meaning to such a child as that?"

Leslie didn't know, and admitted it. "I'm only glad that it's not up to me to decide," she said. "I honestly don't know how I would feel if she were mine. Hitler's Reich decided that children like that should be killed for the good of the state. Considering their other decisions, somehow I don't think it's a precedent we want to follow, not even with—was it Sparta?—as another example. Pass me the cucumbers, will you?"

"And why are we worrying about some idiot child who isn't our problem, anyhow?" Emily demanded. "Simon, tell us about your trip."

"I could not convince my agent to book me into Carnegie Hall for a return concert," Simon said. "He wanted more evidence from my doctor." Leslie was reasonably good at reading clues to his feelings now, even if his face seemed impassive; a twitch around his jawline, the whitening of the lines down the side of his nose. He was angry.

"I suppose it takes time," Leslie said, which seemed safe. "Shall I dish up the crepes, Simon, or will you?"

"I'll do the honors." The crepes slid onto plates; steaming hot, with the fragrant strawberry sauce over them. Emily tasted hers and wrinkled her nose.

"Ugh! I'm sorry, Simon, but I like them better *without* the Grand Marnier in them. Liquor, yick, who needs it?"

Simon smiled over her head at Leslie.

"I mean, it's very *nice,* Simon," Emily said, "but I guess it must be an acquired taste. Tell me about your agent. The bastard wouldn't book you into Carnegie Hall? Well, fuck *him,* there are other agents!"

"I would rather prove to him that he is wrong," Simon said. "It is true that the hand is not recovering sensation as I had hoped, but I am working with a new technique, self-hypnosis. . . ."

"I thought that was fakery," Emily said, taking another cautious experimental bite of the crepe and shoving her plate aside.

"No more so than biofeedback; with hypnosis I may be able to free myself of the fear and inhibition which keep me from allowing my hand to reach its potential," Simon said. "Because, like everyone else reared in a materialistic society, I have been brainwashed to accept its limitations. It might be a useful technique for you too, Emily."

"Hypnosis? Me? You're kidding! What for?"

"They have been using it on tennis players," Simon told her. "Because almost everyone holds back, one way or another, from releasing full strength. It teaches one to tap the reserve powers which are usually not accessible to the conscious mind. Some marathon runners are taught to put themselves into a light trance as they run. Do you use hypnosis in your practice, Leslie?"

"Sometimes." If a patient found it too difficult to talk about a problem, she occasionally used a light hypnotic induction, to ease the pain of reliving some trauma. It was especially useful with rape victims; she was also familiar with its use for athletes, but had never thought how it might help a performing artist.

But did she really want to think of him hypnotizing Emily?

Nonsense; if I cannot trust Emily to Simon, there is no one to trust in this world. She berated herself for allowing an obscene nightmare to dull the edge of trust or love.

LATER SHE WITNESSED THE first hypnotic session, calming her fears. Simon directed Emily to lie back and relax in a comfortable chair.

"Now go back. Go backward and backward until you have never heard of a piano, but your fingers retain all their knowledge and skill. Listen with all your attention."

He placed a record on the stereo player; the sound of Alison Margrave's harpsichord, light and delicate, the little spray of music she had heard in this room; a sudden blur of gooseflesh lifted the little hairs on Leslie's arms. When it trembled into silence Simon said quietly, "Now, with *your* skill, and your knowledge, go to the harpsichord and play that minuet, Emily. Play it as Bach himself would have played it."

Emily went to the instrument. Leslie knew too much about the mechanics of hypnotism to expect her to look "hypnotized" or as if she was sleepwalking, but her attention was so fiercely focused that she was oblivious to them both. She sat down, flexed her hands slightly and began to play, in a style which was uniquely her own, and yet sounded quite unlike anything Leslie had ever heard her play; delicate, touching the keys with a new sensitivity. When she had finished she clasped her hands in her lap with a faraway smile.

"Now you will waken, and remember everything perfectly, and when next you play the harpsichord you will remember that state," Simon directed, "and you will be able to reach this part of your mind whenever you sit before the harpsichord. Now I am going to count to five, and when I say *five* you will awaken and feel perfectly refreshed and relaxed. One, two . . ."

When he said "five," Emily turned promptly to him.

"I wasn't hypnotized. I heard everything you said. It was just I suddenly knew how it ought to sound, that's all, and how to get it."

Leslie, who had heard the same protest from her own clients, merely smiled.

"Of course," Simon said. "I only taught you how to focus on a certain part of your mind and memory, how to concentrate at a deeper level; that's all. Leslie can tell you that the common image of the hypnotist as a zombie being programmed by somebody else's mind is rubbish. All hypnosis is self-hypnosis; you are doing it to yourself. I only showed you how to access that part of you for yourself."

"Oh, *thank* you!" She flew to him and hugged him again. "Simon, I'm beginning to wonder if the harpsichord isn't going to be more important to me than the piano!"

"You won't know that for years, love. Just keep working," he admonished, and left her at the keyboard.

"Leslie, shall we go somewhere for a drink—or something?"

She knew what he wanted; his burning eyes told her. She told Emily, "Don't wait up, I may be very late," and went to get her coat.

WAKING IN SIMON'S HIGH room, surrounded by fog like the bridge of some ship drifting through interstellar space, wrapped in his robe as they breakfasted high above the Golden Gate, the nightmare again seemed obscene, intrusive. Yet it must be faced between them; she had experience enough to know what havoc it wrought, withholding fears and suspicions.

"This is nonsense, isn't it, Simon—all of Claire's talk about black magic? There's no such thing, I am sure. So what is she talking about?"

Simon poured her another cup of the excellent *café filtre* he had made in his machine. "Cream? Yes, I'm trying to fatten you up a little," he said. "I like my women a little better padded." Then he leaned back, his gloved hand automatically squeezing and releasing the exercise ball in the pocket of his robe.

"This thing about black and white magic is part of a very old scholarly controversy," he said. "I and mine are on one side, and Colin and his friends—and, I fear, Alison—are on the other. It is the age-old controversy between *theurgy,* which says that the less-known powers of the human mind must be used only for religious purposes, never for accomplishment, and *thaumaturgy,* which accepts no such limitations. The theurgically inclined, Colin for instance, consign any attempt at using these powers for personal accomplishment as belonging to the left-hand path; that is, the material universe, rather than leaving them all on some exalted astral plane. In short, they say that the magician who actually *does* anything, instead of leaving it all to God's will, is a black magician. A white magician, they would say, merely studies these things and learns about them, and makes no attempt to *use* them. Of course, Colin—I love the old man, but he is a pious old fraud—he sent Claire to put up pentagrams to protect Alison's house, and by his own definitions, that's black magic; who does he think he's kidding?"

He raised the coffee cup to his lips and drank. His other hand never ceased squeezing the ball in his pocket.

"I'm finding it hard to get used to these glasses. I've never worn them. They say that they can probably fit me with a contact lens for that eye when I play on the stage; it will look better. Or should I go all scholarly with horn-rims, darling? Well, then." He set the cup down and stared at her.

"Colin and Claire, and Alison, may her own God rest her, would say that I, as a thaumaturge—I like the term better than 'black magician'— seek to impose my will on the Universe rather than yielding to it as the Buddhists do in search of their Nirvana; but for better or worse I was born into the West rather than seeking the Light of the East, and this is a charge I readily admit. To my other crimes they would say that I sought to use black magic for healing after my accident, instead of meekly praying God to restore my sight and the use of my hand. And no doubt they have told you that I sacrificed animals. That white cat, for instance. I was shocked when I heard you had seen it in the garden, and when I saw it myself. For I killed it. I killed it myself, ritually on my altar, in the space I had made my temple, shortly after Alison's death." He raised his eyes and met hers. She noticed that there was a faint film over his bad eye.

"Does that shock you, Leslie? Why is it worse to sacrifice an animal than to—say—convert it into beefsteak or ham, and sacrifice it on the breakfast table? Assuming, that is, that I have a right to the animal? I would not steal someone else's pet and offer it up. That would not be honest magic; it would be no sacrifice to me. I had known the cat from a kitten; believe me, it gave me great pain to kill it, and it was my own pain, as well as the ectoplasm given off by freshly spilled blood, which created the power of the ritual."

Leslie drew a long breath. She might have known that he would be able to explain this.

"I still don't understand, Simon. Why would you—what good would it do to sacrifice an animal?"

"As I said; power," he told her. "I began years ago: I had heard of these things; was I to accept them without evidence? I experimented with the sacrifice of animals long ago, and I was not out of my teens before Colin delivered me his number-one lecture on the crime of intellectual curiosity; I'm sure he will treat you to it if you ask him." Leslie felt her face change, and Simon nodded. "Already? I thought so. I respect Colin's ethics, but not his attempt to impose them on others; in his own way he is as bigoted as any Catholic priest. I experimented and kept notes worthy of any scientist; someday I will show them to you. Was I to believe without verification? I sacrificed chickens; I found they were stupid, their nervous organization too slight. There was power in spilled blood, but I could get as much from the use of flowers and certain incenses; they, too, give off small quantities of ectoplasm."

"I thought ectoplasm was something faked by phony mediums." Emily had told her something about cheesecloth smeared with luminous paint.

"No, it is very real; someday I will demonstrate it in a way I am willing to subject to any test you would like to put. As I said; I sacrificed chickens, but they were too stupid. Warm-blooded mammals—rabbits from a pet store—more useful, and dogs and cats better yet. My own clairvoyance moved by leaps and bounds. But once my intellectual curiosity was satisfied, I let it pass, and did not try any of these things again until after—" he hesitated; took a deep breath, "after the accident."

He laid his hand on the table, letting the exercise ball roll away, and pulled off the splinted glove. Then he took off his glasses; the scarred face and damaged eye were newly shocking as he turned them to the light. She had not noticed that on one side of the damaged hand was the dead white of a skin graft.

"Look at me, Leslie. Really look at me."

"Simon—" she began to protest.

"You see with the eyes of love," he said, leaning across the table to caress her, "but I see myself as I am. Stage and movie idol—and *this!*" The bitterness in his voice made her cringe with pain.

"They told me I would lose—completely lose—the sight in my left eye," he said deliberately, "that there was no way to save it. They said that it was possible that the graft would not take, and that the left little finger, which had been completely severed at the first joint—" he stretched it out to her and she saw the line of stitches—"despite intricate microsurgery, might never develop motion and feeling again, let alone flexibility; it might even refuse to take, and drop off again. Then they said that it was likely, with this kind of eye injury, that I would lose the sight in the right eye too; they recommended I study Braille and prepare myself to be completely blind! That is what medical science told me, Leslie."

"But they were wrong," she whispered.

"They were not wrong," he said implacably. "That was when I told myself nothing was impossible to the trained will. I had taught myself magic—more than simply prayer, more than simply the tradition of meek acceptance of my karma! And so I sacrificed Alison's cat. . . ." He drew a long breath.

"That very day—that very day, Leslie, I saw the tip of this finger turning pink again and knew the circulation was restored. I had raised enough power for that. And that day, too, when they re-examined my eye, they told me that the right eye would survive and that I might even regain some sight, at least enough to distinguish light and dark, in my left eye. Could you blame me? Do you really think Alison would begrudge the life of a cat for *that*, Leslie?"

He truly believes this. But how could he know that he would not have healed anyway? But before the intensity in his voice she could only cry, "Oh, no, Simon! How could anyone who loved you—"

"Colin did," he said implacably. "I am sure they think I am damned, and if they knew the rest—" He gripped her hand with his good one.

"Leslie, could you still trust me if you knew the worst? If I said that the sacrifice of the cat had not been enough—? And that I did not stop at that?"

"You don't mean—human sacrifice—"

"I knew you would draw away with horror," he said fiercely, "but you are simply reacting emotionally. The life of a cat is surely of more worth than some men! That killer you helped to trap in Sacramento, the one who had killed four girls—what is he but a human sacrifice to a concept called Law and Order? I would rather spend the resources of this world lavishly on Alison's white cat than to allow that idiot girl-child in your garden today to go on draining the strength and emotions of its parents!"

It was a view she had heard expressed before this. She did not agree with it, but she knew some people passionately held to this belief. She could hardly blame Simon for holding it. How did she know that her own resistance to the idea was not a mere sentimental indulgence? Even Susan Hamilton felt that way sometimes. She, Leslie, did not have to live with Christina Hamilton.

"What would you think of some addicts, who are caught in a trap where they must steal three hundred dollars worth of merchandise and sell it to a fence every day to keep that heroin in their veins, or suffer the tortures of the damned? What of the women caught in the same trap, whose only option is to accept the lowest and most vicious of men? Women who have tried, sometimes, to kill themselves again and again but never quite succeeded? Doctors yank them back from the grave, then let them go out into the same world that exploits and befouls them! Leslie, if I were in that trap, I would be grateful to anything which sent me back to the source of being, to be reborn in a stronger, perhaps healthier body for a less agonized life!" His voice was fierce.

"Listen to me, my darling, listen with your mind, not your emotions. A life which was a terrible burden to her, a life she wanted to lay down. I did nothing I would not want someone to do for me; I told myself, if I was to be blind and lose one hand, I would pray for the courage to take a razor blade from *there*," he said vehemently, "and give one deep stroke *here*." With his scarred fingertip he swept his hand across the jugular vein, "And send myself back to the Lords of Karma, praying only that I would return as a musician once again."

I wanted to die. The pills, that overdose. But he was gripping her with both hands now.

"My beloved, it was that very day they told me that with treatment I could actually recover sight in the left eye, and my hand—you have heard me play, not as I did before, but now I know it, I *will* play again, I *will not* be a blind and crippled nonentity, groping my way through life, a cripple giving lessons to nobodies to stay off the welfare rolls! Do you condemn me? If that is black magic, my darling, then I rejoice at it! I am the heir of the great adepts, of John Dee, of Crowley . . . and I am proud of my heritage!"

Leslie was crying; how could she blame him, even if he was deluded? How could she judge what he had suffered? "Oh, Simon, Simon," she wept, "I don't care what you have done. I love you, I love you, I love you."

BUT SHE PAID FOR that blurted acceptance, replaying it over and over again in nightmares over the next month. Sometimes she was dragged into the temple to help Simon sacrifice a white cat, sometimes Alison herself, who had Claire's face. Sometimes it was herself, sometimes Emily, who lay bound on the altar; or one part of her watched in mute protest while the other part held the knife. She came to dread sleep, but waking, she told herself fiercely that Simon's life, his continued health, was certainly worth the life of some unknown junkie and prostitute. If it had ever happened; sometimes in the dream he told her that he had only been testing her, trying to see if she would accept the unspeakable. And she had accepted it. What was she to do? Speak to the police? What would prevent Simon then from laughing, telling them it had been some incredible bizarre joke? And of course he would never trust her again.

And waking she found herself facing Simon, knowing that whatever he had done she loved him and if the police were actually to come to her she would shield him. And whenever she looked into his eyes she found herself grateful that whatever his psychic gifts they did not actually include reading her mind.

Sometimes in her practice she had come across them, women who clung to, rationalized their love for a criminal, men who had committed every crime from wife beating to murder, men serving life sentences in San Quentin, women who had remained faithful to wholly worthless men. She could always tell herself Simon was different. But she had always condemned these women, feeling they were victims of low self-worth who had convinced themselves they deserved nothing better than these criminals. And now she was one of them. Or was she? Either Simon was a madman, an extraordinary liar, or else he had at least once committed a premeditated murder.

She pored over the pages of Alison's book about reincarnation; were she and Simon bound with some such tie as this? How else could she explain it? She wished Simon had never spoken, that she had Emily's innocence. She was Bluebeard's wife who had opened the forbidden door and must live forever with the results of her fatal question.

On the morning of the day when Nick Beckenham was to be married, she tore off the page of her desk calendar and saw the note she had made about the wedding. Had she ever believed that she loved Joel, had she, in her inexperience, thought that what they had shared was satisfactory sex? On that subject she had moved into a whole new level of awareness. She might as well, she thought, have come to Simon as a virgin.

She no longer believed in coincidence and was not surprised when Emily, eating a square of cheddar cheese on one of the crispbreads which Simon had introduced into their kitchen stock, called her to the phone, saying with her mouth full, "It's that nice policeman you knew in Sacramento."

"Leslie?" Nick's voice, just as she always remembered it. "Joel says you won't make it up to the wedding. I'm really sorry. I'd looked forward to having you as a sister-in-law, you know."

"Oh, Nick, I'm sorry." Shyly she said one of the things she had come, living in this house, to believe. "In a sense you *are* my brother; nothing can change that. We'll always be friends." *Perhaps for more than one life. What else could explain such things as Emily's gift, or love at first sight?*

"That's for sure," he replied. "When I went on the cops there was an old guy used to say to me, Your family you get wished on you by God;

but thank God he lets you choose your friends. But it would have been nice to see you."

"You and Margot can stay here next time you are in San Francisco," she offered.

"Thanks, love, we may take you up on that. Hey, Leslie, a friend of mine in the Frisco police department—" like all non–San Franciscans, he insisted on calling the city *Frisco*—"asked for your name, and I gave it to them—Okay?"

It wasn't okay. She still shrank from acknowledging it, but knew now that she could not refuse. She said, with resignation, "I'll be waiting for them to call."

"I really appreciate that, Les. Listen, I have to get going." She was tremendously touched that he had wanted to call her on this day of all days; more than any words, that confirmed that he shared her feeling that they were somehow bound.

"Give Margot my love, Nick. I wish you both every happiness. I really wish I could have been there."

If it was real that thoughts had substance and entity, she knew a part of her would actually be there, watching Nick married to her friend.

That afternoon Simon had a master class, which he had invited her to watch; she had two clients she could not cancel and had to decline, so he took Emily instead. For the first time in her life she had seen her name in a gossip column; not that she minded. *A famous musician with piratical elegance*—she supposed they were speaking of his eye-patch, though he had ceased to wear it—*has been seen about with a new lady; but does he want the Dark Lady or her teenage sister whom he squires about town with equal enthusiasm? Or is there safety in numbers? Who's chaperoning who, or do we mean whom?* People who had nothing better to read than this kind of thing always confused her. He would bring Emily back for supper; he seemed to love the kitchen here as well as the elegant modern one in his apartment. Perhaps she would go back with him and spend the night . . . the thought filled her with delicious anticipation, but she put it aside with stern discipline; she had to talk with Judy Attenbury, who was losing weight again, steadily but inexorably.

Perhaps only transsexuals were more resistant to therapy than anorexics, and for much the same reason; they believed they were right and the world wrong. What curious force of cause and effect, in this life or any other, would force a man to believe intractably that he was really a woman trapped in a man's body, or a teenage girl to starve herself, sometimes literally to death? What did conventional psychotherapy know about the human mind anyhow? Leslie wondered if it knew anything about anything. She felt she didn't.

She was having, she realized, a serious attack of self-doubt and there was no sense in giving way to it. Just the same she was relieved when her next client, a divorced housewife trying to create a new life after twenty years of finding her identity in a perfect house and perfectly brought up children, called to re-schedule her appointment. Leslie consulted her calendar to find the woman a new time, and went out into the garden. She was still finding flowers she did not recognize in strange corners, and the smell of herbs in the summer sun was heady, with bees humming over a strongly scented bush of lantana, and hummingbirds like tiny helicopters hovering and darting in around the honeysuckle. She found a heavy pair of pruning shears and began cutting back the castor beans. She had two hours before Susan Hamilton came in.

The garden was so peaceful, green leaves surrounding her with light; the very sky seemed to cast a greenish color over her. There was so much green here for a city built on sand dunes. But every blade of it, she remembered, even the exotics in Golden Gate Park, had been brought here by human agency, and cultivated blade by blade and leaf by leaf. Was there a lesson somewhere in that, that one could not leave everything to nature? Briefly she had a vision of the city stretching bare, waves of sand out to the sea.

She disposed of the castor bean leaves, stems, and poisonous pods in a heavy trashbag, and tied it up safely. Perhaps she should go to the animal shelter and get a cat to inhabit this garden. It seemed to need a cat. Perhaps Claire could give her a white one; Frodo had said she often had kittens to give away and would be glad of a good home for one of them. No, not a white cat, she was not Alison; she had Alison's house and seemed to have inherited her practice, but she would impose her own temperament and taste upon it. She would get a black cat, like the one Colin had called Monsignor, or a striped cat, or an orange tabby—she knew some people in the Berkeley hills who had a family of orange cats with a strain of wildcat, whose old tom had sown hundreds of orange kittens all over the hills.

She hauled the trashbag to the front gate where the trash cans sat, trying to visualize an orange cat in the garden, under the lemon tree. She stopped at the gate; a black and white police cruiser had pulled up in front of the house, and a uniformed patrolman came up the walk.

"There's no one in the house," she called. "I'm here in the garden. What's the matter, officer?" Her first thought, like anyone who has known tragedy, was fear; Emily was out with Simon—had something happened to her?

The burly officer came up the walk, a young policewoman in a khaki pantsuit at his side.

"I used to know the house," he said, "just checking to see it's lived in again. You're detective Beckenham's friend, aren't you? I'm Joe Schafardi."

She gave the little reflex start of rejection, though she had told herself she had accepted this. "I know him, yes," she said cautiously. The young woman was looking around the garden.

"This is one of the most beautiful gardens in the city. I'm glad to see someone living here who cares for it," she said. "There was a woman living here for a month or so, but I don't think she ever came into the garden. The real reason I stopped here was to ask if I might pick a lemon; when Dr. Margrave lived here she used to give me lemons, and passing by it occurred to me that there must be some on the tree, and if no one was living here, they would only go to waste. But of course if the place is occupied—"

"Help yourself." Leslie gestured to the loaded branches of the tree. There were more fresh lemons than even Emily could use for organic lemonade; she and Simon had been talking of making marmalade. "Take several, if you want them; I'm glad to know they won't go to waste."

The woman officer went and carefully chose three bright round fruits, carrying them back in her hands to the gate. Meanwhile Schafardi said, "Dr. Margrave was a dear old lady. Funny you should move into this place; *she* used to work with the department sometimes, you know—maybe Sergeant Beckenham told you? What's that thing they say, truth is stranger than fiction? She told us who did the Zebra killings, you know, only for political reasons we couldn't touch them. I never put any stock in psychic things, but the Berkeley police went to her, I heard, about the Patty Hearst kidnapping. . . ."

"You had some special reason for coming here today?" Leslie knew she sounded ungracious, and the young policewoman said, "Well, yes. We have a disappearance—we've done all the routine things, and we just need a place to start looking."

Leslie realized that this was a replay of one of her nightmares. Now they would ask her about a junkie prostitute, and she had no idea of what she would say—but the officer was telling her about a young man, a student at San Francisco State College, who had disappeared from his apartment without a trace, leaving no note or hint of his plans, on the eve of final exams—but he was a good student and had no need to be despondent. He had also abandoned his motorbike.

Leslie let out her breath slowly, hardly aware that she had been holding it.

"I'll do what I can. Of course I can't promise anything."

"Will you want to see his apartment? The landlady wants to rent it again, but I made her hold off another week so we could bring somebody around—if we just had some idea whether we're looking for a murder victim, or a voluntary disappearance—"

Leslie promised to come and see what she could divine. As they thanked her, she saw that Simon's car had drawn up behind the police cruiser, and he was helping Emily out; and she had a look at his face as he stood waiting.

He is living on the edge too, flashed through her mind, and she wondered later what she had meant by it. Then Simon came easily forward to the gate where she stood with the officers.

"Why, it's Dr. Anstey," Officer Schafardi said. "We came here when Miss Margrave—" he coughed, "passed away. We had to come see you in the hospital. How's the hand? I see you're not carrying it in a sling any more. Pat," he said to his colleague, "this is Dr. Simon Anstey. Officer Patricia Ballantine."

"Oh, I saw one of your movies, Mr. Anstey—" she said excitedly, and Leslie actually felt the quickly averted look at his gloved hand, searing Simon's nerves.

"Well, I'll see you this evening at the police station," the officer said. "Shall I send a squad car around for you, Dr. Barnes?"

"No," Leslie said, "I have my own car. I hope I can find your young man, and I hope alive rather than dead, but of course you know I can't promise anything." They thanked her again and went away with their hands full of lemons, and Leslie grimaced as she saw them drive away.

"I seem to have a new career whether I want it or not."

"Why do you let them come to you?" Emily asked.

Leslie sighed. "I don't know. I suppose because I feel sorry for them," she said, but she knew it was not all the answer. "What was it someone said about why they climbed Mount Everest? Because they're there, I guess."

Many things had surprised her lately; the calmness with which she had begun to accept this part of her life was one of them. There was a balance to everything. Simon and Emily had music to give the world. She had only such small skill as she could give to the troubled, and that was too little to justify all she had been given, so she must use this other gift too.

"We ought to pick the lemons, so many of them are ripe," Emily said, "I really want to try making marmalade. Will it work if we use honey instead of sugar, Simon?"

"If we use pectin to thicken it," Simon said, and she went off to the foot of the tree, calling back, "Do you want to fetch the ladder from the garage?"

"No," Simon said, and she laughed. "Lazy!"

"I will not put that kind of strain on my hand," Simon said fiercely. "There is no feeling in the outer edge; I would not know if I damaged something."

"Oh, Simon, I'm sorry," she cried, "I'll get it—"

She ran off to bring it, and Simon smiled his strained smile at Leslie. "Shall we go to the apartment and spend the night? When will you be finished with this tiresome business at the police station?"

"I don't know, love; they want me to go to some boy's apartment and check out a disappearance."

He shrugged. "Hundreds of young people disappear every year, and most of them have simply changed their address without the formality of leaving a new one. I hope it is no more than that."

With the memory of Juanita García's face under water in a ditch, Leslie hoped so too. If the young man was alive, she could forget him, and so could the police; it was no crime to move without telling your family where you were going, and she had been tempted herself when she left Sacramento. If it hadn't been for Nick Beckenham she might have been one of those statistics herself. But no, she would never have done that to Emily. To her parents, perhaps, but not to Emily.

"When must you be there? Have we time for dinner somewhere?"

"I have a client, Simon," she said regretfully. "I'll be finished at six-thirty; then I must get right over to the police station—I promised."

"And I have no claim on your time," he said, touching her cheek lightly. "We must talk about that, Leslie." He saw Emily coming back with the ladder under her arm and chided her.

"You should wear gloves; your hands are precious too, child. Run in and put on your gardening gloves."

Emily went off obediently, and Leslie wondered if she should be troubled by that. Emily never argued with or questioned Simon. Yet she had always been a fighter, never one to listen to authority.

Maybe it's just a stage she's going through. She helped Emily set up the ladder, then heard the telephone ringing inside the house.

"No, I must go, Simon, it might be my answering service."

But when she lifted the receiver, there was silence for so long that she felt a reflex tightness across her stomach muscles. Was this happening again? At last a timid voice said, "Dr. Barnes, somebody told me you'd taken over Alison Margrave's practice—"

"Well, I haven't," Leslie said shortly. "You have been misinformed. I have my own practice, and if you wish to consult with me, you should call my service and make an appointment."

"No, it's not that kind of thing—I was told you could help me, because I think I've been cursed—" The voice on the other end of the line stopped abruptly, as if the woman had heard herself speak and knew how insane it sounded. *What kind of world am I getting into? That's weird even for psychics.* She felt like slamming down the receiver.

What would Alison do? In a rage, Leslie wondered why she cared, even as she heard herself say, "Tell me about it." Was she to be no more than a dummy, a replacement for this wretched woman who had lived and died here?

Colin, she remembered Claire saying, insisted that we have absolute free will. She could tell these people to go away and be damned.

And very likely they would be damned, because if they were not they would not come to you in the first place. Was this what Alison was saying to her? The woman on the phone was telling her an involved story of money which had actually belonged to her daughter, which she had withheld because she disapproved of the daughter's husband. "Understand, Dr. Barnes, I had a right, a *legal* right, because my husband left it to me, and it was supposed to be for Margie at my discretion, my own choice, see? Only I didn't like her husband, so I told her I wasn't going to give it to her until I was sure he wasn't just trying to get his hands on Margie's money. I guess I wanted to see if he loved her enough to take it without that."

For some reason she thought of Joel, saying that lawyers existed to pick up the pieces after human beings had finished acting like human beings. She said, "Mrs.—Mrs.—"

"Terman," the woman said. "Peggy Terman."

"Mrs. Terman, it really sounds to me as if what you need is a lawyer. I really know nothing about wills—"

"Oh, no, that's not what I mean. You see, Margie, she died, and now I think she's come back to haunt me because I didn't give her her money—"

"And you feel guilty about it?" Leslie asked. Guilt could take the strangest and most astonishing shapes. Perhaps all this woman needed or wanted was conventional therapy.

"Would you like to make an appointment and come and see me? We can talk about your feelings about your daughter and the money—"

"No, that's not it," the woman interrupted. "You see, I *know* what to do with the *money*. There's this woman. After Margie died I dreamed about Margie three nights in a row, and this woman I know said the money was cursed and she could purify it for me. She only wants a hundred dollars, and she says she can take the curse off the money. All I have to do is give her a hundred dollars, and she'll wrap up all the money and seal it, and say a special service over it, and leave it all night under sacred candles in her church, and then I leave it three days and open it and it's all right again—"

"Wait a minute," Leslie interrupted. "Who is this woman?" But she hardly heard. She didn't know much about rackets and confidence games, but even she had heard of this one. She simply could not believe that in the final decades of the twentieth century there were still souls gullible enough to be caught by it.

"Mrs. Terman, don't you know that is one of the oldest confidence tricks in the world? Among other things, they call it the *gypsy switch;* when you unwrap the money—"

"But she said I could seal it myself," the woman protested. "She was never going to touch it; she'd give me back the package unopened—"

"And when you opened it," Leslie repeated, "you would find, perhaps, cut newspapers; but you would never see the woman, or your money, again. It's one of the oldest bunco games in the business."

"But she seemed so nice—"

"They always do."

"And all she wanted was a hundred dollars—"

And, Leslie thought, it would have been a cheap way to ease Peggy Terman's conscience; a hundred dollars. She repeated, "No reliable psychic would ask that kind of money." She didn't know what psychics charged, but she knew the honest ones set their rates reasonably, and it was a good rule anyhow, to stay away from anyone who wanted large sums of money for doing almost nothing. "Mrs. Terman, you really ought to go to the police and report this. To the fraud squad."

"I'd feel too much like a fool," Peggy Terman said. "How could I tell them about Margie and her money? And now—what am I going to *do* with Margie's money?" It was a wail of dismay.

"Why do you ask me? How do you know I haven't got some dishonest scheme for bilking you out of it?" Leslie asked. "You could give it to your daughter's husband—"

"That man! What's *he* done to deserve it?"

"Or to her favorite charity; or throw it in the Bay. You can even give it to the woman who offered to take the curse off," Leslie said dryly. "At least then you would never have to worry about it."

She supposed this was why there were so many fraudulent psychics; general reluctance to report that one had been taken in, human greed, human stupidity. Did she want to be associated with a field filled with such things? Maybe she should just leave the whole thing to magazines such as the *Enquirer.* She got a few more details from Peggy Terman. There was an old saying that no one could be swindled unless he was trying to get something for nothing, and the woman was looking for a cheap way to ease her conscience.

She hung up the phone, profoundly depressed. Susan Hamilton would be coming soon. Was any human problem, in fact, soluble? She felt overwhelmed with the weight of human misery. Why had she ever wanted to make a living at it? She went out into the garden, where Simon and Emily were picking lemons, just as Frodo's truck pulled up at the gate.

He came back through the garden, and it flickered through Leslie's mind that this was his setting, more than the bookstore; he looked like a very tall elf.

"Hello, Frodo."

"Hello, Dr. Barnes. I came to pick up my ladder; I left it here when

Emily and I were painting that day," he said. "I wouldn't bug you about it, but my Dad needs it. Oh, but I see you're using it?"

"I think they're about finished," Leslie said, feeling that perhaps this was a good sign. She hoped Emily and Frodo would make up their quarrel. He walked toward the lemon tree and the ladder and stopped.

"Hello, Emily. Oh—hello, Dr. Anstey."

Leslie wondered if Frodo knew how transparent his face could be. Simon nodded coldly to him.

"Hello, Paul."

Paul. She had wondered, and still wondered, why he had picked *Frodo.* Frodo explained about the ladder. Emily said, "Yes, of course, we won't need it again. Thank you for letting us keep it so long."

He tucked it under his arm. "The garden's looking really lovely. If you need any help with it—"

"Oh, thanks, but really, we've got everything under control."

He said, "You want to drive over to the East Bay and hear the Medieval Consort tonight? They're playing in the Greek Theatre, and they're using some of the instruments I built. There's a whole gang of us driving over, and plenty of room for you."

Emily's face lighted up from inside. "Oh, I'd love to," she exclaimed, then hesitated and looked at Simon. He gave a faint, almost imperceptible shake of his head. "But I'm afraid I really can't spare the time, Frodo. Thanks anyhow."

He advanced on them with an aggressive glare. "Listen, Dr. Anstey, does she need your permission before she goes anyplace? You adopted her or something? You're her guardian?"

"Certainly not," Simon said promptly. "Emily is perfectly free to do whatever she wishes. But I believe she has other plans for this evening."

"Frodo, I have to work. And if you can't even be civil—" Emily broke off and said, more politely, "I'm really sorry. Maybe some other time."

"Well, all right. But I wanted you to hear some of these instruments." He lingered and his eyes were fast on Emily. Simon asked curtly, "You're playing again in an orchestra, Paul?"

"No, not now. I wanted to take some time out and find out if that was really what I wanted to do with my life," Frodo said. "I like working with my hands, researching and building old instruments. You ought to understand that, feeling the way you do about harpsichords."

"Pure self-indulgence," Simon said. "Wasting the talent you have."

"That's what my Dad says. But I just can't see playing in an orchestra and having to get all dressed up in a monkey suit when I play. What does wearing a tuxedo have to do with whether or not I can play the flute? So damned artificial, as if music was a little playground for rich people. That's not what I think music ought to be."

Simon shrugged. "I've heard these theories before. I won't fall into the trap of calling them communist or even radical; they're simply a regrettable lack of discipline. What difference does it make what clothes you have to wear? The important thing is to play your best."

"That's just what I was trying to *say,*" Frodo said in frustration. "What does it *matter* what I wear when I'm playing?"

"I think, Paul, we're simply going to have to agree to differ on that subject," Simon said, and dropped a final lemon into the basket. "Emily, I shouldn't lift this; can you carry it in while I put away the garden tools?"

"Of course, Simon."

Frodo followed her, trying to take the basket and carry it for her. "Emmie, can I call later and talk to you? *Alone?*"

She lowered her eyes. "Look, Frodo, I don't really see any point to it. Okay? And I'm not a weakling, I can carry the damn basket!"

He went out the gate, carrying the ladder, angry, and Emily took the lemons to the kitchen. Leslie followed and saw Emily brushing away a tear. She said quickly, "I know he's no good for me. I can't help it, I still miss him." She put down the lemons on the counter and wiped her face. She went into the music room.

Leslie said, as Simon came in, "Simon, she needs young friends."

He said stiffly, "I'm sorry to hear you, of all people, preaching the gospel of social adjustment. Emily is different; I believed that you appreciated that."

"She really wanted to go tonight—"

"I know Paul Frederick well." After a moment she realized he was speaking of Frodo. "A gifted, a very gifted young man, but no ambition, no drive. One cannot waste or ignore a talent like his and ever expect to amount to anything. He and Emily live in different worlds; I should think you would understand that. Or do you really think that—that hippie—is right for her?" He went into the music room. Leslie started to follow, then sighed and didn't. He would have to make his own peace with Emily. It wasn't for her to interfere. It did not seem to her that lack of ambition or drive for success was such a fatal crime.

She went to let in Susan Hamilton, asking the routine questions about Christina's health and progress. When Susan was seated in her office, however, she asked a strange question.

"Leslie, do you believe dreams mean anything?"

Leslie had never believed the Freudian gospel of the value of dreams, far less the exaggerated importance, in New Age psychology, of "dream work." She tended to believe that dreams were simply a manifestation of REM sleep, a sorting mechanism to free the mind of the daily stresses; brain static while the nerve synapses flushed and recharged themselves. "Did you have a dream you wanted to tell me, Susan?"

"I dreamed about Chrissy," Susan said. "She was lost, she'd been kidnapped. And when I found her again, she was talking, she said, *Where's Mommy? I want my mommy.*" She was silent so long that Leslie asked, "What do you think the dream means, Susan?" Of course she knew how most of her colleagues would interpret it.

"Well, I've dreamed before this that she was talking, of course. I know that was just wishful thinking, dreaming she was the way I want her to be." A realistic insight, Leslie thought.

"But this was different. That was why I asked if you believed in dreams. I should have asked, Do you think dreams can ever be—what's the word I'm looking for—*precognitive?* Can tell what's going to happen. Because I'm beginning to think Chrissy's going to talk. And somehow after that dream I don't believe it was just wishful thinking. It was different somehow."

"Can you tell me how it was different?"

A year ago, Leslie would have dismissed this as what her own teachers would have called *magical thinking;* helping Susan to ignore realistic evidence about her failure to reach her child. But in the last few months she had had some hard lessons. Was Susan actually creating a fantasy to help her to ignore reality? What was reality anyhow?"

"Are you still believing there will be a miracle, Susan?"

"Not a miracle," Susan groped, "but some kind of breakthrough. She seems to listen to me more. To know what I'm saying. Like, the other day I told her to bring me her jacket when it was time to take her to her daycamp. And she brought me her raincoat instead, and I hadn't even noticed it was raining. But she made that connection."

"Then you think perhaps the dream was adding up, in your mind, some conclusion you didn't know how to put into words?"

"It could have been that, I suppose. I was packing up her things for camp, and for the first time she seemed to know what was happening."

"Then perhaps it's a good thing you haven't made any irrevocable decisions yet," Leslie said, ready to explore again Susan's guilt about sending her daughter away. But Susan had something else to say.

"She never seems to know me, and if she doesn't know the difference between being home and somewhere else, maybe I should do what Margaret says, and find her a place; because it wouldn't really matter if she was in an—an institution. But if she does know, if she knows me, if she wants to be with me—maybe something in Chrissy is speaking to me, trying to tell me not to give up hope yet. . . ."

That could be a dangerous illusion. That was the standard explanation, Susan refusing to accept good evidence about the realistic possibilities of hope for her child. How could Leslie be sure? She only repeated what she had said many times before at these sessions:

"You mustn't make any decision until you are really sure you can live with whatever decision you make; until you know it's what will be best for both you and Chrissy."

The cuckoo clock struck the half-hour, briefly. She looked up at it.

"We seem to be out of time, Susan. Next time we can talk—"

Theoretically at least it was possible, that the mind had an independent existence from the handicapped body. The imprisoned spirit of Christina Hamilton might use this way to communicate with her mother. A dream? Why not?

If this goes on, I might as well set up to counsel my clients with psychic readings, and send them to astrologers or tell them to try reading Tarot cards to solve their problems!

Susan thrust her arms into her sweater. The clock struck again, *"Cuckoo! Cuckoo!"*

But that's impossible, something inside her wailed in protest.

The cuckoo clock leaped off the wall and fell to the floor; the cuckoo flew across the room and crashed against the opposite wall. Leslie stood frozen, but Susan leaped forward.

"Oh, Leslie, your nice little clock! What could have knocked it off the wall like that?"

Leslie forced herself to laugh. "Well, you've got two choices," she said lightly. "An earthquake. Or our friendly household poltergeist. Take your pick."

"I didn't feel an earthquake," Susan said, puzzled, "but it could have been the vibrations from a truck in the street, I suppose." She gathered up the fragments of the shell, while Leslie picked up the small shattered bird, set the pieces on the desk—though she thought the clock was beyond repair.

What are you trying to tell me, Alison? She projected the thought with all her strength as she let Susan out, but there was no answer. She would come to some ridiculous medium, but not to Leslie? Was her legacy from Alison Margrave a new hope for her clients?

Or was it madness? In the music room Simon and Emily were still playing something by Debussy, she thought, piano and harp answering one another in waves of sound. Leslie knew they were not ready to interrupt their music for supper. But she could not force herself to go back in the office where the shattered clock lay on the desk. She *could* not.

CHAPTER

Eighteen

SHE MANAGED TO COLLECT herself before Simon and Emily came
from the music room. What could she say? She thought Simon had exor-
cised this place. Was it her own confusion and rage, her inability to trust
Simon, which had brought back this explosion of poltergeist activity?

Simon drove her to the police station, saying he would wait for her.

"I know what an ordeal this is for you, love. I remember how it used
to upset Alison; because when she saw violence, she had to some degree to
take it into herself. . . ."

"At least it isn't always tragedy. Sometimes it's farce," she said, and
told him about Peggy Terman, her cursed money and the gypsy switch.

"I thought I'd report the woman to the bunco squad, at least."

"Of course you must. But I can hardly believe it—that old trick had
whiskers when Alison was a girl. I remember her telling me about that,
and some other dodges that fake mediums do. And it's been written up

dozens of times—Gresham exposed it in his novel *Nightmare Alley.* I simply find it hard to imagine that anyone would still fall for it in 1983! What was it—was it P. T. Barnum said? There's a sucker born every minute—"

"My Dad used to say, A sucker born every minute and two to skin him," Leslie said.

Simon nodded. "I think it was H. L. Mencken who said nobody ever went broke underestimating human intelligence."

That struck her unpleasantly as something Joel might have said. "This shouldn't take long, but of course I don't know—" and let him escort her in.

At least, if she was now able to criticize, even if only in her mind, what she heard Simon say, then at least she was no longer bewitched or besotted. Or was she now moving to the other extreme, hypercritical of the man she professed to love? Either idea dismayed her.

Patricia Ballantine, the young officer to whom she had talked that afternoon, found her a comfortable chair and pulled out a file. Before putting it into her hands, she said, "If it will be easier to go over to his apartment—we can run you over there."

"Let's see what happens with the pictures first," Leslie suggested. She had never had to have close contact; with Phyllis Anne Chapman she had actually picked it up from the mother's voice on the telephone. Officer Ballantine held out a photograph, and Leslie passed her hands over it.

She turned the photograph in her hand, feeling confused, with no clear sense of anything wrong. She said, "I don't know what you mean. This man is home with his—his grandmother." She had not known what she was going to say till she heard herself saying it.

"What did I tell you, Pat?" It was the burly officer Schafardi. "I said she'd know. Pardon me, Dr. Barnes, just a little test, kind of like a lineup. That picture in your hand is one of our young plainclothes detectives. There's psychics and psychics, and I get a lot of grief from the guys in the squadroom for listening to any of them. So I figured, if you were on the level, you wouldn't mind a little test. Miss Margrave was on the level, and I figured you must be too."

"Thank you—I think," Leslie said dryly.

Patricia Ballantine landed her another folder. "This is the file we have on Gus Hansen—that's the missing kid."

Leslie had confused impressions: an apartment with plastered walls, a poster of some rock singer, a rumpled mattress, a young man's face, hiking boots, an orange backpack— She said, hesitating, "Did they find his backpack?"

"Pat, did anyone say anything about a backpack?" Schafardi asked, and Patricia Ballantine shook her head.

"I—don't get the feeling he's dead. He's somewhere wearing hiking boots, a backpack—he went somewhere with a girl. I think the girl is pregnant. Only about six weeks—"

"They did say he was worried over a girl," Pat Ballantine said.

"The girl's underage," Leslie heard herself say. "Not quite sixteen. So he hadn't told his family. They bought a map. Check a—a camping store. They wanted to talk alone, decide what they wanted to do. It's cold where they are. They're all right, but they can't get down. . . ."

"He lives about half a block from a big sporting goods store," Schafardi said.

Leslie handed back the file. She did not know she had been holding her breath till she heard it go.

"They're all right. They're going to get married," she said, and then it was gone, she had no idea what she had said, it was as distant from her as the hieroglyphs on the walls of the pyramids, and meant no more to her. Had she ever been involved, feeling the young man's fear and the girl's panic, their need to get out into the woods and be alone without anyone else to complicate their problem? The girl was younger than Emily, and pregnant. But at least they were alive, and trying to work out their trouble, and she did not realize how much she had feared seeing, feeling, *being* another corpse.

She said, "Do you have many missing persons?"

"A good number," said Patricia Ballantine, "but most of them are the kind nobody's looking for and if anybody noticed they were missing, it would only be to say 'Good riddance.' Small-time crooks. Street people. Prostitutes. People nobody really cares whether they're alive or dead because they're not any good to anybody, least of all themselves. If they turn up dead in an alley somewhere, at least they're not contributing to the crime rate any more."

A callous appraisal but, Leslie supposed, a necessary one. It did little help to become emotionally involved. She asked them to let her know if they found the young man and his pregnant girl friend. She could see the girl, freckled, untidy fair hair, sneakers and hiking shoes. She didn't want to see the girl. She didn't want to know anything about it. They would need to have a helicopter rescue them off the ledge, she thought, and determinedly cut it off. It wasn't her business, she simply would not get involved. How did you cut it off, anyway? If Simon could teach her that, she would bless him.

She was getting up to go when she remembered Peggy Terman and her cursed inheritance. "Is there a fraud squad, a bunco squad, whatever you call it here?"

"Sure," Schafardi said, "but they're only on duty on the eight-to-four; here on the four-to-midnight we never see them. Why? You being swindled?"

"Not me; not even any of my clients," she said. "This is just something I heard today." She told the story, and Pat Ballantine snickered, while Officer Schafardi looked angry.

"I remember old Miss Margrave telling us about that one, ten, fifteen years ago," he said. "That kind of racket gives psychics a bad name." He sat with his chin on his hands. "I'll check out Mama Jessie," he said. "She reads cards down by the wharf, but I heard she had some cute little sidelines, and this sort of smells like her work. Thanks for the tip, Dr. Barnes. If your client won't testify we can't do much, but maybe I'll pass the word around to keep an eye on her, and it might keep her out of mischief for a while."

It was a relief to get back to Simon in the waiting room, his slender well-dressed elegance in sharp contrast to the grubby surroundings of the room. He rose promptly as she came in.

"Ready? Let's go."

Even when working in the garden, she thought, he seemed the same, civilized, perfectly composed. She could not visualize him wearing overalls or Frodo's cotton rainbow-dyed pants and tunics. Yet that very image was what Frodo had rejected. Yet this was the tradition of the classical musician. What would make a young man of Frodo's talent and wit reject it so completely? And if he did reject that tradition, was he right for Emily's life? She had chosen her world, and Simon, not Frodo, was her mentor in it. Yet they had seemed so happy together.

"I'm still having some trouble with the glasses, Leslie. Will you drive?"

"Certainly, darling."

"Sure you're not too tired?"

"No, of course not." It was not physical but mental and emotional fatigue that wearied her; once she was away from the problems of her patients, and the bewilderment of Alison Margrave's complicated legacy, her mind was at rest. She took the wheel, sighing. For economy, and a little because of conscience, Leslie drove a subcompact car, but she was almost ashamed of the pleasure it gave her to drive Simon's big, unabashedly luxurious and, she suspected, energy-wasteful Mercedes.

The white wine she enjoyed had become a ritual with them before lovemaking, but tonight as they lingered over it. Simon reached over to clasp her hand in his scarred one. "Leslie, we should be living together, you know that. It's right for both of us."

She knew he was right. Yet there was something mad about it too. She had known this man so briefly. And in her practice she had been made more than usually aware of the dangers of a liaison based on overpowering sexual passion. Yet in her feelings for Simon there was something that went far beyond passion. She thought, *We have been together forever*, and did not know what she meant by it.

"I know. But I have to think of Emily. I can't leave her alone yet."

He drew her over against his shoulder and she was content to lie there. "Emily is part of my family too. You know that. If it should happen—" Lying against him she felt his whole body tighten and wondered at the calm in his voice, the courage that allowed him to say, "If it had been intended that I should never play again, I could perhaps have been content to think of her as my protégée, to make her career almost my own. There are times when that is so strong a temptation that I am almost unendurably tempted by it. To give up the fight, and the pain—" She felt the breath go out of him. "To surrender, Leslie. Just to let go."

Her voice was almost a whisper. "You can't do that, Simon?"

"I can't." His voice was faraway, almost desolate. "I have no choice. I—*will*—not. I will not be—conquered."

She wanted to cry, she wanted to beg him. The fight was destroying him, driving him to inhuman measures, the terrifying lengths of excess he had confessed to her. What whips of inner passion drove him relentlessly this way? How could she use her influence to try and make him a lesser man than his will made him?

His arms tightened around her. "I woke up this morning with all the themes for the finale of the concerto in my mind. And all day I had to—

to teach—to waste my time, when in all that class there is not one, not one even with half of Emily's gift. Yet I allowed myself to be committed to them, chained down to go and lecture when none of the young brutes will ever remember or profit from anything I said. . . . Alison did that, her gift wasted on cheap little people, like casting pearls before swine. And you, my precious, wearing yourself to the bone for people who will never know or appreciate your worth . . . I cannot stop you from doing what you must. But must I join you? I want to do what I am designed by nature to do, that is my place—"

He tore himself restlessly away from her and went to the piano. He began to play, a whisper of the theme he had played to Emily, his concerto. His hands strayed from the broad and spacious theme into another, a thread of despair and anguish twisting and tracing into the concerto. She felt him struggling with the theme, working it into a frenzy of loss and despair. He said through the chords, "The concerto. I must play it for my return concert. I must have it ready!"

The clock on the wall said it was nearly midnight. She said hesitating, "Simon—at this hour—the neighbors—"

"I spent a fortune soundproofing this place so that I could play at any hour of the day or night!" he told her impatiently. She sat listening, hearing him working and reworking the theme. She lost track of time as she listened. Once or twice he paused to take a sip or two of wine, but she suspected he did not know what he was doing. The rare vintage might, for all he could taste it, have been water or coffee or root beer. His face was furrowed and distant, and now it began to sound like a struggle. She was so closely attuned to him that she could hear and feel when the fingering faltered; his injured outer fingers were beginning to stumble, he was not up to the complexities of his own music. He heard it too, repeated the more difficult passage again and yet again, his face drawn and contorted with rage. Finally, in a frenzy, he swept his hand across the keyboard; the wineglass flew across the room and shattered there, and Simon slumped forward, his whole body in a tortured spasm of agony, motionless, only his shoulders shaking. Leslie could feel the silent sobs that racked him.

"Simon," she entreated, coming to him, encircling him in her arms. "Don't. Come now. Come to bed."

"I *will*, Leslie. I *will* play it." His voice was almost inaudible, "Nothing is impossible . . . to the . . . trained will. . . ."

The words were almost a whisper. Yet to Leslie they were a shriek, a primal scream of rage and determination. She held him against her, and after a long time he raised his head.

"Leslie," he said, as if he had not known she was there. "What a fool I am, playing at this hour and keeping the most beautiful and seductive woman in the world waiting!" He rose, encircled her with his arm and led her to the bedroom.

SHE WAS IN THE garage, and there was a circle of blue light she could not pass; she was trapped inside it, playing the harpsichord. Then she remembered that in this life she was not supposed to play, it was Emily's turn. She moved through nightmare dark and could somewhere see Simon hovering above them, trying to decide, for his hand was bleeding and she knew he needed yet another sacrifice. She could hear Colin saying, I would gladly give my hand for yours; but Colin's hands, she thought, are no use, he does not understand music in this life, it must be Emily or myself. I could have played as well as Emily, but it was her turn, this time I must support her and stand aside while all the applause goes to her. But Simon cannot bear to let anyone else have it. . . . The cat was bound on the altar and somewhere Susan Hamilton was looking for Chrissy, but Simon laughed; I have changed Chrissy into a cat, he said, pointing to the form of the bleeding cat lying broken and torn at the center of the circle of blue light, certainly she has not nearly as much value as one of Alison's cats.

And then she was holding Simon in her arms, while the paroxysms of agony tore at him, because the cat had clawed at his eye and blood was gushing from the socket. He said, Nothing is impossible to the trained will, and she asked him if he would need more blood sacrifice. And he held to her, and cried out in pain, I hope not, ah, God, I hope not. . . . But what I must I must do, because I will not be conquered. . . .

"Leslie?" She twisted away as she heard his voice, then knew it had been another nightmare. She sat up, seeing his eyes dark and troubled over hers.

"Only a nightmare," she whispered. "Thank God, only a nightmare. . . ."

"You must be picking up my nightmares. My hand is giving me hell. I'm going to go and take one of my sleeping pills—want one?"

She shook her head. She distrusted sleeping pills, knowing they inhibited REM sleep, so that what happened was not truly sleep at all, without dreams . . . *maybe that was what she needed, to free herself of the nightmares.* He padded naked to the bath, came back with a bottle in his hand.

"Sure?"

"I'm sure." She watched him shake out a pill. Who was she to demand he refuse the deadening of pain like this? He hesitated, looked at her, shrugged and put the pill back into the bottle.

"I would rather stay awake with you than sleep," he said, crawled back into bed and stretched out at her side.

"Tell me something about yourself," he said. "A gift like Emily's does not appear from nowhere. Were there musicians in your mother's family or your father's?"

She told him about their Swedish grandmother, about the harp which had come down to them, about Emily as a child of five crying because her fingers would not encompass the strings for the music she heard. He told her for the first time something of his own childhood, tormented and vulnerable in a military school, escaping alternatively into the infirmary (I was allergic to everything, he told her, because when I was sick nobody bothered me and I could lie in bed and read and listen to music on the radio) and then discovering that the piano freed him even more from the hated routine.

He had been a poltergeist for a time, he told her, and that was how he had met Alison; he had shattered his roommate's guitar strings while the guitar hung on the wall, and then his mother had taken him away from the school and consulted Alison. And then he had become her protégé and then her colleague. Leslie thought of Eileen, shattering violin strings at a school orchestra rehearsal.

"I hated that boy: funny, I can't even remember his name, but I remember that wretched guitar. All he ever played was hillbilly music. I wanted to break it over his head. Mother had me in a military school because she believed that a woman alone, if she tried to raise a son, would turn him into some kind of effeminate, perhaps a homosexual," he said scornfully. "I could have told her there was never any question of that, and if there had been, a boy's boarding school was hardly the place to prevent it. On the contrary."

"I assume your father was dead?"

266 | MARION ZIMMER BRADLEY

"I haven't the faintest idea," he said, shrugging offhandedly. "She encouraged me to think I arose from spontaneous generation. I think Alison knew, but would never tell me. I'm a bastard, of course."

Casual as he sounded, the voice was filled with old pain, and Leslie moved to another topic.

"You were a poltergeist? I have one among my patients—"

"A girl, I suppose; there are four girls for every boy among poltergeists. Perhaps because girls are encouraged to cry and tell people their troubles, but it's not ladylike to show real anger or rage. I've often wondered; how many other psychological troubles are linked to sex? I understand that mostly men get ulcers—"

"That was true until women started being executives and working in the rat race," Leslie said. "But there are eight autistic boys for every autistic girl." This was one of the reasons she had hesitated to accept the diagnosis of autism for Christina Hamilton. "It may be hereditary, or chromosomal damage, at that, because it is so linked to gender."

Simon's lip curled. "That may be why such children are still considered worth wasting a therapist's time on—boys, after all, carry the precious family heritage. Perhaps I was fortunate to escape that, having no father. I have known men who consider a gifted son almost as much a family disaster as a retarded or brain-damaged one; neither are likely to go into the family business. I am positive, for instance, that if hemophilia had appeared only among girls, sensible laws would have permitted, or even required, euthanasia for such children. But what father would sacrifice a son?" Then he laughed in the dark. "Mine did. I wonder if he ever knew?"

"I can't imagine a father who would not welcome or rejoice at a son like you, Simon."

"I don't have to imagine it," he said hardily, warning her off again. "I had one. I think we probably should try to get some sleep, darling."

The surprising thing was, she thought, lying sleepless in the dark beside him, that he had never attempted to remedy his fatherlessness by himself fathering a son; a common compensation, to give one's children what one has missed in one's own life. Yet Simon had another inheritance to give. His children would be gifted with his own talents. She thought, shyly, that she would like to have a child of Simon's. But she was not ready for children, and suspected Simon might never be ready for them. Well, he would leave the world his music, whether or not he ever fathered a child of his body; all the more if he continued to teach. Yet a teacher must make compromises and teach hundreds with little or no talent, casting the bread of his own skills lavishly on the waters for the smallest of returns, and how many teachers found even one genius in a lifetime of teaching?

Then she wondered, at the very edge of sleep, why she was thinking this way. Simon could justify his whole life on what he has already done for Emily, she thought, why was she thinking of him as if his career was truly over? Was she allowing enough for his tremendous will and determination? *Nothing was truly impossible to the trained will. . . .* Was that simply magical thinking, refusal to accept the inevitable, or was it the true key to the Universe? How could anyone ever know?

The master cass to which he had taken Emily was the last in the current series in San Francisco; he had still a commitment to a single class at a music school in Dallas. Leslie drove him to the airport on Sunday morning.

"When I come back, love, we really must take some thought to how we can manage living together. I don't want to be separated from you," he said. "Obviously, this is no time for a proposal of marriage, but we've got to do something about these separations!"

"I couldn't travel with you, Simon," she said, hating to say it; this was what had broken her away from Joel. "I have my work. I've made commitments too; I can't leave it."

"Of course you can't," he said, with a promptness and generosity that overwhelmed her. "And now it seems you will be doing Alison's work too. But anything can be worked out, even the conflicting demands of two careers—no, three, for we must take Emily's into account too—if we put enough time and thought to it. No, darling, don't try to park in the building, just drop me where it says 'Departing Flights'; I hate saying goodbye at airports. Keep the Mercedes for the week, why don't you? You drive it better than I do now."

"When will you be back? Tuesday, Wednesday—?"

"Probably not until Friday," he said. "I am flying to Chicago on Wednesday. I don't suppose you have met him personally, but surely you know who Lewis Heysermann is—"

"The conductor?"

"He's been invited to conduct in Chicago this year, and we've been friends since I was at Juilliard," he said. "He owes me some favors. I'm going to try and convince him to schedule the concerto next year, or the year after. At a return concert."

Thank God, Leslie thought. *In spite of that night, he thinks he's ready, and he must know.* She said, "I don't know whether to say *Good luck,* or *Break a leg!*"

"Just bid me Godspeed, darling, and hope the little brutes don't get me down," he said. "How I despise teaching! Yet I suppose there is a responsibility, too." She drew up before the Delta Airlines terminal, and he leaned over to kiss her. Then he gestured imperatively to a skycap, who came at a run to get Simon's slim suitcase out of the back seat of the Mercedes. Leslie, in her VW, would have had to wait fifteen minutes for that kind of service. "I'll call you from Dallas, darling. God bless." She was astonished. She had never heard him invoke the deity before this. She sat and watched his grey-clad form disappear within the terminal until a taxi driver yelled from behind, "Come on, lady, have a heart, move the damn car already," and she put it in gear and drove away.

C H A P T E R

Nineteen

SIMON CALLED BRIEFLY ON Wednesday evening; he said only that the master class had gone well and that he was flying to Chicago the next morning.

"How is Emily?"

"Judging by the sounds I heard this morning and afternoon from the piano and harpsichord, she's fine. She's cutting up lemons for marmalade."

"Can I speak to her?"

Leslie passed the phone across the table to her sister, who received it with a wry face at her lemon-dripping hands. She listened for a few moments with a smile, then asked, "Do you need to speak to Les again? Okay, g'night, then," and hung up.

"He says to give you a hug, but you'll have to take a raincheck, my hands are all lemon. Lemon juice is *good* for your hands, it fades out freckles and age spots."

"And I am sure your hands are positively covered with age spots," Leslie said dryly. "What did Simon say?"

"Simon says—sounds like that old game—you know, the one where you take giant steps and baby steps and you can't move unless you ask 'May I'? Simon says nobody at the master class played Rachmaninoff as well as I do, and don't put too much pectin in the marmalade. And he loves us, and he'll call again Friday night for sure and tell us how it went with—Heggerman?"

"Heysermann." Were they all playing a game called *Simon Says?*

Thursday she went over to the Haight to buy shampoo, and passed the bookstore without stepping inside, even though she would have liked to ask Claire about the fraud attempted on the woman who had called her. Monsignor and Poltergeist were in the window and she could see Colin reading behind the central desk, and the atmosphere was so inviting that Leslie had to fight against going in, but she told herself that she had no time today, and anyhow Friday was the day Claire was there. Asking herself why she feared to face Colin, she told herself it was because of his negative attitude toward Simon; she did not want to be drawn into an argument. What a shame they could not compromise or agree to differ on their varying definitions of magic; they were both men of good will. Then, with a terrible sinking, she remembered what Simon had confided to her.

Could Colin compromise with that and would she want him to? she wondered, and then was angry and amazed at herself. What was Colin to her? Was she trying to make him into some kind of father figure? She moved along the street, tempted to stop in one of the delectable little bakeries and treat herself to a cappuccino and a croissant, perhaps even a pastry. She could skip lunch if she felt it overpowered her diet too much with chocolate or sugar. Certainly it was wicked, but she had very few chances these days to try out even this harmless naughtiness. She stepped inside the place, sniffing appreciatively at the delicious buttery, chocolaty smells that filled the air, the cinnamon/coffee/cocoa scents all round her. She was approaching the counter and trying to decide between strawberry tarts with whipped cream, or a rum pastry, layered with fudge and cherries, when she saw a familiar tie-dyed green shirt and long fair hair swept into an elfin ponytail. Frodo did not see her; he was leaning across the table, his forehead almost touching Emily's, while neglected cups of something foamy steamed in front of them. They were holding hands, and Leslie, troubled, turned before the counterman could approach her and went quickly out.

Oh, my darling, I was afraid you were playing "Simon Says" to such an extent you couldn't even take a baby step. On the other hand, Simon had been so good to Emily . . . but it was not and could not be a love affair. She went home, hardly remembering to congratulate herself on not breaking her diet. She hadn't wanted the pastry anyhow. Simon might be cross with Emily if he saw her with Frodo, but he would simply have to learn he could not control every facet of the girl's personal life. He felt, he said, as if she were his daughter. Daughters grow up; Simon, like any father, would have to learn it. But she said nothing to Emily. When Simon called tonight she would say nothing, either.

Emily would be eighteen in August. Perhaps for her birthday they could give a delayed housewarming party; the studio/garage would make a pleasant place to hold it, and it could spread out into the garden. Perhaps, if Simon actually saw her with young friends, he would feel more resigned. The friendship with Frodo, after all, was still a childish thing: Emily had never had ordinary dates, and this was her first tentative-stage-of-interest-in-a-boy affair, simple and childlike. Perhaps Leslie could invite the neighbors on either side, and the people she knew from the bookstore, at least Claire and Colin, and perhaps Rainbow, but it would be Emily's party really. She must have friends at the Conservatory. And Frodo, of course.

All during dinner—she had cooked herself a chop, while Emily baked a potato and smothered it in grated cheese—she was waiting, keyed up for the sound of the telephone. She went in the study to write up notes from her day's clients. She found she missed the cuckoo clock badly; if it could not be fixed, she would have to get another one. The telephone rang; she rushed for it, but it was a girl from the Conservatory, wanting to ask Emily for an address for sheet music. The next time it was someone offering her a two-months-for-one deal on the *San Francisco Examiner*. No, she did not want a newspaper. By ten-thirty Simon had still not called, and when she went up to bed, she was beginning to be troubled. Oh, well, he and his conductor friend could have spent the day together; there was a time difference and he could have forgotten, as she often did, which way it went, and think it was later rather than earlier in California, thus fearing to disturb her too late. He would call in the morning. She drifted off to sleep, wishing she could somehow reach out to him, to tell him how much she loved him. Even if he was on top of the world with good news from Heysermann about a return concert and his concerto, she would have liked to hold him, reassure him. Even when she slept she was still braced for the telephone, hoping he would realize that she would not mind being wakened by his voice.

AT FIRST SHE THOUGHT it was the telephone that had awakened her. She listened for Emily's voice across the hall; another nightmare. Then she heard the sound again; a frightful smashing, slamming sound as if someone had dropped thirty trunks full of old ironware and rolled them down the stairs. Emily, in a shorty nightgown, her hair hanging almost to her waist, appeared in her door.

"What *is* it? I thought it was you, Em."

"God, no! How could I make that noise? Sounds like somebody breaking up old cars. I'm so glad you heard it too," Emily quavered, then grabbed Leslie as she was about to go down the stairs. "No, don't, don't, let me call the police—"

Grimly, Leslie wanted to be sure that the poltergeist was not breaking things again before she called in the police on such an alarm. But of course she could not delay. "Dial nine-one-one and report a prowler," she gasped as the terrible crunching noise came again. Emily dialed, babbling terror into the mouthpiece. "Whoever it is, they're breaking up furniture all over downstairs—"

She put down the handset. "They'll send the nearest squad car right away. I'm going to get into some clothes," she added, staring at her long bare legs, and started to vanish into her room when the dreadful metallic sound came once more, and this time Emily, holding up a hand for silence, heard the sound of resonant strings as if someone had tipped over the harp.

"Les, that was in the music room! If they've hurt Grandma's harp, I'll *murder* them," she gasped, and ran barefoot down the stairs.

"Emmie, no! They could hurt you—" Leslie fled down after her sister. She saw Emily fling open the music room door; then she heard Emily's scream, and she almost stumbled as she broke into the music room. Emily had flipped on the light and stood there. Her mouth was still opened in a silent scream, and the scene before her was one of chaos.

It looked—it was as if someone had swung a sledgehammer into the curve of the gleaming, polished black Knabe: the raised top was broken, the black wood shattered. Some heavy blow had been brought down again across the keys and shards of ivory were splintered across the floor. The harp had been kicked over; someone had put his foot through the strings, although she thought the frame was unbroken. The vandal had done his worst on Simon's harpsichord; from where she stood it looked as if the sledgehammer, or whatever it was, had been swung again and again with almost unbelievable violence. The polished wood was in splinters, with fragments of wire and quills and metal scattered from one end of the room to the other, as if after pulverizing the instrument the vandal had jumped on them and kicked the bits into the four corners of the room.

She said almost inaudibly, "Oh, my God!" It was almost a prayer. Behind her Emily burst into hysterical screams.

"No! No! Oh, God, no, no—"

And then there was the revving of an engine and the sound of a siren and through the bay window she saw a police car with the blue-red-yellow flash of its lights swing around the corner and pull up inside and two policemen run toward the house. Emily was still screaming, staccato wordless shrieks now; Leslie ran into the hall, frantically twisting at the deadbolt to let them in, and a man and a woman pushed past her and ran into the music room where Emily screamed on.

"Jesus Christ! Which way did the bastard go? How'd he get out?" In a flash she recognized Schafardi's face and bulk, while Pat Ballantine went to Emily and put an arm around her.

"Try to stop screaming and talk to us, honey. It's all right now. He's gone." Emily collapsed, sobbing, and while Pat Ballantine stood with an arm round her she asked over Emily's shoulder, "Was she raped? Was she attacked?"

"No," Leslie said, "she was upstairs with me, we heard this awful noise—"

"And you came down to find this mess." Schafardi looked warily around. "Which way did he go? Out the back window? It doesn't look as if it was broken—" He went back into the hall and into the kitchen. Pat Ballantine pushed Emily down on a cushion and ran after her partner, her hand on the holster at her waist. "Watch out, Joe, the guy might be out there—"

"No," Schafardi said in a puzzled voice, "the deadbolt lock's still on back there. Somehow he must have gone out the window and got it down again." He came slowly back into the music room. "Pat, I'm going out and check the nearby yards. You get their story."

Pat Ballantine stood twisting the dials on her walkie-talkie. "Ballantine here, breaking and entering, substantial property damage; some guy got in by the window and broke up a couple of pianos. . . . No, not a store, a private dwelling . . ."

Leslie dropped to the cushion beside Emily and took her sister in her arms. Emily was still sobbing hysterically, her frail body shaken by the violence of her weeping. Officer Ballantine came and said gently, "Do you want to call your family doctor, Dr. Barnes, or take her to the Emergency Room? If she's been attacked, I can run you both over to the hospital, and take your story there."

Leslie said, "Emmie, Emmie love, can't you stop crying for a minute? Was there anyone in here when you came in? Did you see who did this?"

"No. No, there was nobody here at all," Emily gasped, "but oh, the piano—the harpsichord—oh, God, just *look*—"

"Somebody certainly did a job on them, all right," agreed the young woman officer, taking out her notebook.

"I ought to get this down. Did you hear the intruder getting in?"

"I was asleep," Leslie said. "I don't know what woke me; then Emily came out and said she heard it too. I called the police. I wanted her to wait until you got here, but she ran downstairs—"

"Was the light on or off in the music room—Emily, is it?" Pat Ballantine spoke to Emily as if the girl were much younger; with her hair down her back, in her childish nightie, she looked about ten.

"It was off. I turned it on."

"And did you see the intruder? You're sure he didn't strike you, brush against you—?"

"I didn't see him at all. I heard him tip over the harp, so I ran in, and I saw the piano—and the harpsichord, the harpsichord—" Her sobbing had subsided to gasps and snuffles, but it threatened to break out in screams again as her voice rose in hysteria. Pat Ballantine's first question had been whether she was raped. Leslie realized that in a very real sense her sister had been violated by this intrusion, this violence against what was most precious to her.

"And everything in here was just as you see it? You didn't touch anything?"

"I couldn't," Emily said. "I couldn't move."

The young officer put her notebook back in her pocket. "I'd better search the house, at least make sure he's not hiding somewhere inside here, see how he got out." She went through the kitchen; her hand on her gun, she opened closet doors, kicked open the bathroom and laundry room, but there was no sign of the vandal or of his passage. Upstairs, the guest room and bathroom were empty, Leslie's bed still warm, but even so, Pat Ballantine searched the closet, the private bath, the dressing room. She stepped into Emily's room.

"Your window was open like that, Emily?"

"I thought it was latched when I went to bed," Emily protested. She was still hiccuping. Leslie grabbed a warm robe from Emily's closet, wrapped it around the young girl, shoved her sister's feet into slippers. Things were bad enough without Emily catching cold, and if she was half as shocked as she looked, she should be kept warm. She could hardly tell Officer Ballantine that the lock would not stay shut, even with the chain bolt fastened.

"He must have got out a window somewhere," the officer concluded, coming down the stairs again. She stepped into the office, where the pieces of the broken cuckoo clock lay piled on the desk.

"Some more of the guy's work? Did he start up in here, or come in and finish?"

"No, I broke that myself the other day," Leslie said. "I just hadn't gotten round to taking it to the repair place."

Pat Ballantine went on into the kitchen. "Why don't you make your sister something hot to drink? She's still pretty shocked. There's Joe, coming back." Officer Schafardi was standing by the police cruiser; he started up the walk and Pat Ballantine went to let him in.

"Any luck?"

"No sign of the guy anywhere in the neighborhood," he said. "God, this is one for the books!" He came through into the kitchen. "Funny thing is, I was going to call you, just last night, Dr. Barnes, and then something came up and I put it off. Remember that missing-persons deal? The kid? We checked it out and found he bought a map of the Cascades, and the Rangers found him and the girl stuck on a ledge— They had food and they were okay, but the boy frostbit three toes and they had to get a helicopter to lift them down. The girl's parents had never even bothered to report her missing, for Godsake,

276 MARION ZIMMER BRADLEY

some parents! If we'd known— Well, anyhow, they're all okay, and I was going to tell you."

The teakettle began to whistle shrilly. Leslie poured hot water over a teabag for camomile tea and set it in front of Emily, shoving her into a seat at the table. "Anyone else want tea? Coffee?"

Both policemen accepted instant coffee, and she brought milk from the refrigerator for Schafardi's mug of coffee.

"Good, thanks," Schafardi said. "We'll put out a bulletin for some big bastard carrying a sledgehammer—" He shook his head in dismay. "What a mess! I don't think *I* could do that kind of rough stuff, and I weigh two-fifty and I'm five ten, which means we're looking for one hell of a big guy."

Emily said in a shaky little voice, "Maybe it's the same guy who broke the instruments up at the Conservatory. Someone busted into the orchestra room and smashed up a cello—"

"That's the big thing that looks like a violin only about five times as big?"

"That's right. And it looked like he put his foot—or a sledgehammer, you said?—right through the tympani—that's the kettledrum."

Pat Ballantine drained her black coffee. "Looks as if we've got a real nutcase on our hands. What kind of crazy bastard would run around smashing up musical instruments? Steal them, maybe, and fence them for cash. But smash them up? Like that?" She made a move of her shoulder toward the music room. "He practically pulverized the little thing—what was it, a clavier?"

"Harpsichord," Emily said dully, and began to cry again. "Oh, Leslie, oh, Leslie, what will Simon say? Miss Margrave's harpsichord! It wasn't really mine," she explained, sobbing, to the police officers. "It belongs to my teacher; he loaned it to me— Oh, Les, what can I tell Simon?"

"He made a point of telling us it was insured, so I suppose what we have to do is to get in touch with him, and have him notify the insurance company," Leslie said. "I have to call our insurance people tomorrow about the piano. I'm not sure just how much coverage we have, or whether it covers deliberate vandalism—Emmie, drink your tea, darling, I know it's an awful shock, but crying won't help now."

"What I can't figure is how the bastard got in," Schafardi said. "The back door still was locked and deadbolted. That upstairs window was open, you say, Pat?"

"Yes, but he'd have had to climb right over Emily—Miss Barnes," Pat said. "He didn't get in there, though I suppose he could have gone out that way when we were all down here looking at the damage and searching the downstairs."

"And he didn't get in the front," Schafardi said, "because Dr. Barnes had to stop and unlock the door for us."

Leslie mentally replayed it, feeling the deadbolt under her hands as she twisted it to let the police in. "It was locked," she confirmed.

"Too bad you can't use your psychism and find out who did this," Schafardi said. "Pat, are you sure there weren't any windows open downstairs? Did you check behind the draperies in the office and in the music room?"

"I thought I had, but I'll check again."

"Because if he didn't get in the front, and he didn't get in the back—" Schafardi, coffee cup in hand, got up, set the coffee on the table and went back to check the windows. From the study he called, "Here's where the bastard got in."

Shocked, Leslie went into the study. Behind the window curtain a pane of glass was missing. Not broken, not shattered, simply missing.

"I can't figure it," Pat Ballantine said. "He takes the windowpane out over in *this* side of the house, jumps in here without leaving any marks or breaking anything here in the office. Then he runs across the hall—did you hear any breaking glass, or any sounds downstairs, Dr. Barnes?"

"Nothing. I suppose what woke me might have been the glass—then the noises."

"So he runs across the hall, swings his sledgehammer three or four times and crushes three musical instruments, hides behind the curtains in here while you discover the damage and we come in, then somehow gets past all four of us and runs upstairs and jumps out the second-story window." Schafardi shook his head. "All the time dragging this thirty-pound sledgehammer because that's what it would take to do that much damage. Yeah. Some nutcase. Maybe we ought to call up the hospital—the psycho ward—and find out if they have any loonies missing, and if they're missing any sledgehammers someplace."

He stared gloomily out into the garden.

"Why couldn't we get lucky for once and have the creep break his ankle when he jumps out the window with the goddam sledgehammer in his hand?"

Leslie looked out behind him. The garden was empty, except for the white cat, who slithered along the wall behind the lemon tree and sat in the moonlight washing its face.

"Kitty cat," Schafardi said, "I sure to God wish I could call you into court as a witness, because it looks like you're the only eyewitness there is to this crazy stuff tonight. Hey, Dr. Barnes, you okay? You ought to have some of that coffee yourself, you look like you're going to faint. Pat, get some of that coffee over here for the doctor."

CHAPTER

Twenty

"AND YOU ALREADY REPORTED this to the police? Okay." The insurance investigator walked to the missing window. "I wonder what he did with the broken pane? If he simply lifted it out intact, it ought to be somewhere in the garden. But no glass fragments anywhere. I'll talk to the police. Meanwhile, go ahead and rent a piano until our people decide whether they want to fix this one or replace it. The harpsichord—you say that belongs to someone else? What lousy luck! Our insurance will do something, but—"

"It's covered. But I have to wait till he gets back before I can ask him who insured it." He was looking at the clock in fragments on the desk.

"More of this guy's work?"

"Oh, no. That one—fell off the wall a couple of days ago. I just hadn't got around to having it fixed."

The insurance man grinned. He said, "You know, Dr. Barnes, about three-quarters of the time when I go to investigate vandalism, they throw in everything that's been broken in their house, or missing, for the last year! You're an honest woman. Just for that I ought to write it up for you for replacement!"

When he had gone, Leslie sat down wearily at her desk and tried to compose herself. Emily had cried herself to sleep last night and still looked dreadful, her eyes red and swollen, dark circles underneath making her look as if she had been ill for a month. When Leslie had asked tentatively, earlier, "Do you want to talk about it, Em?" she had snarled, "Don't use your fucking *psychology* on me, huh?" She had made "psychology" sound like a dirty word.

She herself felt violated, intruded upon, bruised, somehow dirtied by the brutality of the vandalism. Ordinary theft she could have understood. Not forgiven, but understood. Not this mindless, reasonless violence. She wished Simon would call. She picked up the telephone, wondering if the Conservatory would have Lewis Heysermann's address, then put it down. He would call her, certainly. Anyway it sounded as if Emily was using the kitchen extension.

At least, she thought drearily, she was getting some first-hand insight into the psychology of the victim. She went into the kitchen; Emily might not want to talk formally, but she should be close at hand in case her sister needed her. Neither of them had been able to eat; perhaps she should simply fix something tempting and set it in front of Emily. Anyhow it gave her something to do. She went out to the kitchen and began mixing brown sugar and flour and butter for their grandmother's special coffee cake. Emily was sitting at the kitchen table, her chin in her hands. She did not look up as Leslie came in nor while she creamed butter and sugar and sifted flour.

"I didn't hear the phone ring, Em. Were you calling the piano rental place? They'd be open by now, and maybe they could even have one over here by tonight."

Emily started to cry again.

"I want *my* piano. I don't want some damn piano from a rental place. . . ."

Leslie finished mixing the coffee cake and slid it into the oven. She sympathized with Emily, but what could she say? How could she even pretend she knew what Emily was feeling? To her, the big old Knabe was just a piano, and one piano very much like another. Anything she said might sound as if she were trying to make light of her sister's grief.

The back door opened and Frodo came in.

"Emily? I came as soon as I could, honey. Poor baby," he said, going to her chair and kneeling beside her. "Your eyes are all red. Here, blow your nose." He lifted her up bodily and sat down again with Emily on his lap. "There, there, baby, don't cry, it must have been perfectly awful."

Emily threw her arms around him and began crying again, while he rocked and patted and crooned to her like a baby. Leslie would never have thought of calling Frodo, but she was glad Emily had thought to do so. She went quietly out of the kitchen; when she came back to take out her coffee cake, Frodo had made Emily a cup of tea and some toast and was feeding it to her like a child.

"Come on, baby, you've got to eat, and then I'll take you over to the piano rental place and help you pick out a good one. I know pianos; my uncle's in the business, and he showed me how to tell a good one from a piece of junk. I'll make sure you don't get stung. And if the insurance people can't get yours fixed, I'll make sure you get a good one. I won't let them palm off some old clunker on you."

"Oh, Frodo, it was so horrible, so awful. Why would anybody hate us that much? Grandma's harp. And my piano, and Simon's—" she threatened to break down again, "Simon's beautiful harpsichord—"

"Show me." He went back with her to the music room. The fragments had been left in place for Simon's insurance people. He whistled. "God, what a mess! Listen, Emily, I know some people up in Guerneville who really know harps, they build them. Instead of leaving this one just to anybody, you ought to take it up there. I'm sure the insurance people would approve of them, because this guy is the real expert on harps in the whole Bay Area. If there's a hassle getting it up there, I'll borrow the truck again and take you."

She smiled, a watery smile, at last. "Do you know *everybody* in the music business in the whole Bay Area?"

"Just about, I guess. For a while after I quit playing I thought I'd try my hand at building instruments. I worked with a guy who makes medieval instruments. I made a krumhorn, and a racket, and even tried my hand at building a viol. About the closest I got to it was making a pretty good hammer dulcimer. And I put together a little harpsichord out of a kit. It's a nice little thing, though I don't play it much. You can use it if you want to. Hey, listen," he interrupted himself, "I ought to ask your sister something. Dr. Barnes?" He popped his head into the kitchen. Leslie was slicing the cake; he took a chunk and sniffed the cinnamon and clove flavors appreciatively.

He took a huge bite. When he had swallowed it, he asked, "I guess the insurance people asked if you had any enemies?"

"Yes, but I couldn't think of any." Twenty years ago, she thought, this might have been a valid question; nowadays random or reasonless violence was the rule, not the exception.

"Listen, did it ever occur to you, maybe whoever did this wasn't trying to get at you at all, whoever it was, maybe he was trying to get to Simon? There's a lot of people who don't like him, and he knows an awful lot of— of crazies and crackpots. And whoever the creep was, he just took a swing at the piano and knocked over the harp, but he really made a good job of Anstey's harpsichord."

She had thought that was simply because the harpsichord was more fragile than a piano, easier to break into pieces. The idea made her pause and think it over.

"But if they were going to look for Simon's enemies," she said reasonably, "the insurance people might even come looking for you. Or Claire. Or Colin."

"Do I strike you as being that crazy?" he retorted. "Anyway, I couldn't even *lift* the kind of hammer, or maul, or whatever it would take to do that kind of damage. And Claire's not young, and Colin's an old guy and he has a bad heart. Forget it, Dr. Barnes. I can't say I have any use for Anstey, but if I went after him, I'd take a poke at him personally, not sneak around in the dark busting up musical instruments. I'm no weakling, but I couldn't *begin* to do that kind of damage. I mean, me and what army?"

And she knew he was right. Even Joe Schafardi had said much the same. At one point he had actually wondered if they were looking for some circus strong man or karate expert. Not in the wildest stretch of her imagination, could she conceive of the gentle, elflike Frodo attacking musical instruments in such a frenzy. She had seen the tender way he caressed his guitar.

Emily came and sniffed the coffee cake. "Oh, good. Cut me a piece, will you, Frodo?" Her eyes were still red and dark-circled, but she looked alive again, and Leslie was grateful. She sat at the table, eating coffee cake and drinking more tea.

The telephone rang; Emily reached for it, but Leslie got there first.

"Dr. Barnes's residence—Simon!"

"Hello, darling," his voice came, warm and living, across the miles, and suddenly Leslie wished she could do as Emily had done with Frodo, collapse in his arms and cry.

"Oh, Simon, if you'd only been here!"

"Simon? Let me talk to him," Emily insisted, but Leslie shook her head. "Wait, Emily." He was saying, at the far end of the wire. "Darling, what is it? Is something wrong?"

She drew a long breath, trying to hold on to her self-control. "Remember, maybe Emily told you about some—some psychopath who broke into the Conservatory orchestra room and destroyed some musical instruments? He—he broke in here last night. With a sledgehammer or something. He smashed Emily's piano and the harp, and oh, Simon, he wrecked your beautiful harpsichord!"

"How terrible for you both!" His voice was shocked, warm, full of concern. "If I could only have been there! Are you all right? He didn't hurt either of you?"

"No, neither of us was touched. Not hurt physically at all; he was gone by the time we could get downstairs," she said. "But of course we were both very upset, and Emily was in a dreadful state." She wondered suddenly what Simon would say if he knew Emily's first thought had been to call Frodo. She did not think he would be pleased.

"The police have been notified," she went on, "and my insurance people. But I need to know who carries insurance on your harpsichord."

He told her, and she wrote it down.

"It's irreplaceable, of course; it was one of Alison's, but of course, as I told you, love, it wasn't particularly valuable as harpsichords go. The important thing is that neither of you were hurt. To think that one of you might have caught that creature in the act, and been hurt by him! I hope the police catch him, and that they skin him alive—and that would be too good for him! And I can't even be there! You know that if it was possible, I'd be on the first plane home. But Heysermann is being an uncooperative jackass. I have to fly to Montreal tomorrow, and although I hope to be back Monday, I can't be sure. I'd feel safer, love, if you and Emily would go and stay at my place. I'll call the building supervisor, and you can stay there safely—the building has its own security force—until I'm back. And of course Emily could use my piano, and any of my harpsichords. And my mind would be at ease about you until they have that—that miserable wretch behind bars where he belongs. Preferably in a

284 MARION ZIMMER BRADLEY

strait-jacket. I can't imagine anyone who would do that could possibly be sane."

Nor could Leslie.

"Simon, it's wonderful of you, and perhaps I should send Emily there, but I really can't leave the house alone. It's my home, after all, and leaving it would be just inviting more vandalism. He's done his work—why would he come back? And the police are friends, and they'll be checking up on us."

"Well, I suppose, if you feel that way," he said doubtfully. "Love, if you really need me, I *will* come back. But Maestro Wayland is in Montreal, and I really should try and see him before he flies to Buenos Aires next week. I swear, I will never forgive Heysermann for putting me through this, or for making it impossible for me to come back when you need me," he said vehemently. "Be sure you call a good locksmith and have all your locks and bolts replaced, and the grilles on the window checked."

"Simon, Emily's going to throw a fit unless I let her talk to you," she said.

"Tell Emily I'll talk to her when I come home, love. I really have to get on the telephone with a travel agent and get a flight to Montreal. Are you sure you don't really need me?"

"I'm sure, love. Do what you must," she said, wondering what had gone wrong with Heysermann.

"I'll call as soon as I know when I can get back. Love you," he said softly, and replaced the receiver. As Leslie hung up, Emily protested, "I wanted to talk to Simon!"

"Em, he was in a hurry, between planes," she said. But why had he not been willing to comfort Emily?

"I wanted to ask him how it went with Heysermann," her sister said. "Of course, he's not ready to play himself yet, but he should get the concerto into Heysermann's calendar right away for next winter, and sew up somebody like—oh, Clayborne, or Di Arcangeli, or Madeleine Lucas, to perform in it."

"He wanted to play it himself, so I understood," Leslie said.

"You must have understood him wrong, Leslie. He's never going to be able to play that, not for years, and after that much time—no, Simon's more realistic than that," Emily said, very positively.

"Well, of course, you know better than I do—"

"I have *ears,*" Emily said. "Simon has more sense than to think he could play *that* concerto. He might be able to manage the Grieg, even the way his hands are now," she added, with an arrogance Leslie knew was completely unconscious, "but nothing *serious, of* course."

No wonder Simon was at his wit's end, if an informed ear could tell this so quickly. Yet he had seemed so sure. She told herself that Emily was always being positive, never imagined that she might be wrong, and that her opinion was like her opinion about herb teas and eating meat, the result of a prejudice, only an opinion. Not a judgment. Would a student know more than he knew himself? Of course not; how furious Simon would be if he heard Emily say that. Emily was entirely too sure of herself about everything. And of course now she was in a state of agitation, and striking out.

"Dr. Barnes, can I use your phone?" Frodo asked, and Leslie said, "Certainly," cutting herself a belated piece of her coffee cake. But she found she did not want it. Frodo disappeared into the hall to make his call, came back and thanked her.

"Come on, Em, shall we head for the rental piano place? You have to have something right away to practice on. Dr. Barnes, I don't have my Dad's truck today, do you suppose I could borrow your car?"

She took her keys out and handed them to him. She wasn't going anyplace until the locksmith came, and if she really needed a car she had Simon's. She had to telephone Simon's insurance agent, and it was not a task she welcomed.

"Leslie, is it okay to write a check for a month's rental if I see something I really like?"

"Sure, honey, and arrange to have it delivered Monday if you can."

"To hell with Monday," Emily said, "if they can't deliver it this afternoon, I'll go somewhere else." Frodo helped her into her coat as if he was handling a rare and precious jewel, and they went out.

Between the insurance man and the locksmith, she spent the rest of the day. Sometime after four, the police cruiser drew up at her gate again, with Schafardi and Ballantine.

"Just thought we'd stop by and make sure you were all right," Joe Schafardi said, "and the little girl. I see you had the windows replaced, and the locks. Good deal. It's probably locking the stable after the horse is gone, but the way things are, you can't be too careful."

"Coffee?"

"Sure, we're off duty," Schafardi said. "Only we wanted to drop around. How's the kid?"

"Very shocked, of course. But she went with her boyfriend—" how natural it seemed to say that, "to arrange for a rental piano so she could go on practicing."

"That was a good idea," Pat Ballantine said. "The less her routine is disturbed, the better off she'll be." She smiled at the coffee cake Leslie set before her. "This looks delicious. There goes my diet again!"

"Ah, come on, Pat," Schafardi said. "You're skinny as a fence rail. You need to put a little meat on your bones! This cake is great; where'd you buy it? I want to tell my wife where your bakery is."

She told him she made it herself, and he said, "Wow! Then I want the recipe!"

Kindness. But in a way she was one of them. She was Sergeant Beckenham's friend, and she had helped them in law enforcement, as Alison had done before her. She was proud to have made them her friends. As there was nothing worse than a corrupt policeman, so Leslie believed there was nothing better than a good and honorable one, doing an undervalued and despised job to protect the weak and vulnerable. Leslie was glad to have added Schafardi and Ballantine to her list of friends. By the time the coffee cake had disappeared they were calling one another Joe and Leslie and Pat, and the two officers went over the house with her, checking the work of the locksmith.

"Yeah, up at Key Korner they're good people," Schafardi agreed, approving it. "He's the guy I went to for my own deadbolts when they passed the law you had to have them. You ever figure out how the guy got in?"

Leslie shook her head. It was still a riddle to her.

"I stuck out my neck for you a little bit," Schafardi said. "The insurance guy—not the one from Federal, the one from the other place, what was it, the one who had coverage on the harpsichord. He came down to the station and asked if I thought it could have been an inside job. He couldn't figure out how anybody got in or out. I told him, What did he think you were, a strong lady in the circus, or something?"

Leslie felt a sickness in the pit of her stomach. She had wondered why Simon's insurance adjustor had sounded so unfriendly.

Patricia Ballantine sounded apologetic. "He did say he wanted the pieces analyzed by somebody who knows musical instruments. He said it was insured as a valuable antique—you might not have been involved, of course, but someone could have been hired to break in here, smash up a cheaper instrument, a ringer, and then claim the insurance while the valuable antique is in storage somewhere. They have to ask things like that, it's their business."

So that was why the adjustor had been so insistent the fragments must be left in place, not moved or cleaned up. She supposed, after hearing about Peggy Terman and the gypsy switch, that she should not have been surprised. She was feeling very cynical about the human race just now. If it had been anyone but Simon, she might indeed have wondered if he had made her party to a clever insurance fraud. But what could his motive possibly have been? Surely he didn't need the money.

She was glad to have Schafardi's good will. With a cop for a character witness, you had to be on fairly solid ground. "Thanks, Joe. Let me get that coffee cake recipe for your wife."

THE DAYS WERE DEFINITELY shortening again. Two weeks ago at this time it had still been full light outside; now long shadows darkened the garden and the white cat slipped noiselessly through the herbs that she and Simon had planted last weekend. She no longer tried to know, nor cared, whether this was the ghost of Alison's cat, dead on Simon's altar, or one of the neighborhood prowlers. She kept her mind away from the whole subject. It was simpler that way. All afternoon she had been expecting the piano movers to pull up; now she definitely abandoned the notion. Emily must have failed to find any place that would deliver a rented piano on Saturday, which meant they had all of Sunday to get through, she would miss two days practice, and would in consequence be hell to live with.

When the bell rang she wondered if Emily had forgotten her keys—she had been in no condition to remember such things when she went—or if the insurance man had already arranged to have the smashed harpsichord inspected *in situ* by an expert. Instead, when she hurried to the front door, she found Claire Moffatt on the porch.

"Frodo called," she said. "He thought you might be worried, alone after dark. He took Emily over to Sausalito for supper. Leslie, what a terrible thing to happen! I could have come sooner, if you'd called me."

"I'm not really afraid," Leslie said. "I think he's done his worst. And we have new locks, anyhow. But it's good of you to come, Claire."

"What are friends for? I'm glad Emily has Frodo to look after her; she's a darling girl and she seems to have a lot of guts, but something like this—I'm sure she would rather be attacked herself than have anyone strike at her musical instruments. But Frodo will be good for her; somebody to hug and hang on to. Isn't he a delightful teddy-bear?"

Leslie smiled. "I always see him as some kind of wood-elf, myself. A sprite."

"Frodo's a lot solider than that," Claire said. "Aren't you going to offer me a cup of tea, Leslie?"

Leslie laughed, leading the way back to the kitchen. "After a day like this, I was just beginning to think that what I needed was a good stiff drink!"

"I can perfectly well sympathize with that," Claire said, "and Colin would tell me I shouldn't give you unasked advice, but really, Leslie, I wouldn't. Whenever there are bad vibrations like this in a house—and a madman like that couldn't possibly give off anything but the very worst—anything with alcohol is likely to make you more sensitive and vulnerable to it. Quite apart from being a depressant."

Simon had said something like that as a reason for not drinking. Independent confirmation, she thought. "Tea it is, then. Emily has fourteen or fifteen kinds of herb tea."

"Whatever you're having." She sat down at the table across from Leslie. "What a pity you are having such dreadful luck in this charming house!"

Leslie stared at the tabletop, stirring her tea. She said in a low voice, "Sometimes I feel this house isn't mine at all. It's still Alison's and she's trying to run my life."

And now, she thought, Claire would jeer or laugh or suggest that she needed a rest or perhaps tranquilizers. Maybe Emily's herbal tranquilizers. But Claire said nothing of the sort, taking a sip of tea and setting down the cup.

At last she said, "That would have been the last thing Alison would want. It's true that in her last days, she felt very unhappy because she had not trained a successor, and I do feel that you were led to this house because Alison felt you the right person to take over the work she left undone. But if that had *not* been your appointed task, and if you had not chosen it somehow, she could never have brought you this far, or reached you if she did."

Leslie said, hesitating, "Simon helped me to clear this place, at the solstice. I can't imagine why there should still be trouble of that kind." And when she had said it, she regretted the weakness that had led her to that confession. Claire was Simon's enemy, at least on a philosophical level, and would be quick to condemn his magical work.

"I can tell that the house has been cleared," Claire said, "and wondered if you had known how to do it. But I don't know how sensitive Simon is to certain types of atmospheres. One of the reasons Colin sent me instead of coming himself is that I am what he calls a sensitive. I suspect if you were trained you would be one yourself, but you're *not* trained. Any magician really should work with one: by himself Simon might not have known how to detect certain kinds of vibrations. That studio—the old garage—" Abruptly, sitting at the cheerful kitchen table, she shivered. "I don't know what happened between Alison's death and the time you came here, but something drove out Betty Carmody, something caused a suicide in this place. Whatever remains in that studio could attract evil vibrations. Hence your piano-smashing psychopath. He could only have come into a place where he found some echo for his own evil and violence."

"Then why did he come into the music room? You can't tell me that the vibrations in *there* were all that evil," Leslie said, inclined to be angry. "I could understand it if he had gotten into the studio. I could believe that the vibrations in there are just about as bad as they could possibly be! But it happened in the music room!"

"We don't know all the laws by which these things operate," Claire said. "As for your music room, the proximity to that garage would carry the— How can I say this? Psychic contagion, is the best way to put it. No matter how well the music room was sealed, something could get in through the garage. As I said, I don't know how sensitive Simon is to that kind of thing; he might not have been aware of the level of evil in that garage, or know that it needed anything more than the ordinary routine banishing."

Leslie was trying to remember if, during the solstice banishing, she and Simon had ever gotten as far as the garage. No; they had been interrupted soon after they had finished with the house proper. "Now you are making me feel guilty," Leslie said, "for not knowing how to protect my house against—against violence!"

"Oh, my dear, that wasn't what I intended at all; you're not trained. The important thing is to protect you from any more violence. If the place has already attracted one psychopath, we really must take steps to make sure it doesn't welcome every incipient Charles Manson in California. Quite apart from the fact that you really shouldn't be alone in the house, any place where there has been murderous violence is unfit for human habitation until it has been cleared."

Murderous violence. True, it had been directed only at inanimate objects; it was terrifying to think that something actually within her house might have drawn the lunatic to it, rather than another site for his violence.

Claire finished her tea and set down the cup. She said, "I really came to offer you what Colin calls 'psychic first aid.' Eventually, perhaps, this house, or at least the studio, must have a full-scale clearing and banishing, but something can be done to protect you until you are able to do it yourself. The solstice clearing would only take care of ordinary residues from the past season; it wouldn't deal with anything as powerful and dreadful as whatever got into that garage. I can't imagine how, in Alison's own house—" Claire broke off and sighed. "I suppose, after Alison's death, the very strength of her good could have attracted its opposite. Colin would tell me not to waste time speculating without data. Let me see the scene of the crime, as I'm sure the police called it."

Leslie rose and led the way into the office. She said, "You yourself put up the pentagrams; I can't imagine how it happened, but this is where he seems to have come in." She showed the window where the pane of glass had been removed. The glazier had restored it. "The odd thing is that he seems to have taken away the glass, unbroken; we didn't find any smashed glass."

Claire frowned, put her fingertips on the glass, shook her head.

"I don't feel anything here. I suppose it's possible—" She broke off and shook her head.

"What, Claire?"

"Nothing. I don't know. Did he break the clock, too?"

Leslie shook her head. How could she confess that she was the uncontrolled poltergeist who had done so? "I think there may have been a small earthquake; it fell off the wall," she said, and Claire touched it lightly.

"Nothing very inimical *there,*" she said. "This room seems quiet enough. Let's see the music room."

She stood looking at the smashed instruments. Emily and Frodo had set the harp up again on its base, so only the smashed strings and a few chips from the gilt post showed the damage; but the piano looked as if some huge troll had taken an ugly bite out of its curved side, and the shattered harpsichord was lying untouched in its fragments on the floor.

"How terrible for Emily! For you too, of course, but especially for her!" She went and stood near the piano, her face contorting in distress; she spread out her palms over the broken keyboard, moved to the curved side, where the vandal had swung his sledgehammer. She ran her fingertips over the post of the harp, where strings hung broken or trailed on the floor. Finally she went and stood, her eyes squeezed shut as if reluctant to face it, over the shattered fragments of the harpsichord.

"Complete, unreasoning violence," she said in a whisper. "I cannot imagine anything human showing such savagery."

"It was human enough. At least it was solid enough to break windows and swing hammers."

Claire shook her head. "I suppose so. Yet it still does not seem quite human to me. Not—how shall I say this? Not *personal* enough for rage at any specific human being. Alison had no enemies. I'm not sure that whatever came in here was material at all."

"Are you trying to say it was a poltergeist?"

"No. Poltergeists are usually harmless. Something much, much worse. Something—" At last she said, "Something demoniacal."

"Are you talking about black magic? Satan? The devil?"

"I don't believe in Satan," Claire said, "and the only devils I know are the ones that can be raised in the human psyche. And you, as a psychologist, know as much about those as I do."

"I thought black magic and the devil were all another way for talking about Satanists. Evil forces. You said 'demoniacal.' "

Claire sighed. "Your old stereotype devil is no more than horns and hoofs and a goat—the medieval Christian version of the Great God Pan. Pan was harmless—even benevolent. And that's one of the archetypes from the collective unconscious that keeps turning up in the human race's psyche. But the church fathers in the Middle Ages were so inhibited and sexphobic that whenever they got a glimpse of that particular archetype they had to believe it was the devil."

"Why would they mix up Pan with the devil?"

"Because the human is the only animal, except the goat, which has full-time sexuality. Other mammals turn it off unless they're breeding. And the goat has always been the archetypal image of unbridled sexuality.

Which scared hell out of your church fathers, who preferred dividing sheep from goats. Pan *would* be a devil to people whose prime objective was repressing their own sexuality."

"You sound like Jung, with all that stuff about the collective unconscious and archetypes. But when you start in on sex and repression, it sounds like pure Freud."

"Guilty as charged," replied Claire promptly. "I got enough Freud in my training to know the language; and sex is true and repression is true, whether you happen to believe in all of Freud's theories or not—which I don't. It's a handy way of putting it. Then when I began training on the Path, I discovered Jungian psychology and the theory of archetypes and it made sense to me. But I'm afraid that whatever came in here and smashed these instruments was nothing so simple as the good old healthy-minded goat of sexual freedom. I don't think it had anything to do with sex at all—which ought to convince you that I'm not a Freudian—a pure Freudian psychologist would tell you that *everything* had to do with sex!"

"What could it be, then, Claire?"

"I wish to God that I knew, Leslie. If it was human at all, it could only be someone gone berserk with pain or rage; someone giving way, some dreadful monster of the *id*—now I am talking like a Freudian again, but it's a useful concept; the buried part of the mind, the part that knows only pure insensate emotion, the part of the brain which is buried below rational thought and responds only to instinct. And *that* is more terrifying to me than any classical Satan from any medieval grimoires!"

She stood for another moment by the fragments of the harpsichord. "Alison?" she whispered, turning from side to side, listening, and Leslie felt gooseflesh rising on her arms, as a whisper of wind, a sigh from nowhere, a ghost of sound, rose in the closed room and was gone.

Claire whispered, "Alison is not happy with what has happened here."

Mediums, Leslie thought in disgust. Why did they never have anything to say except the obvious? Quoting from the world's most famous ghost story, she said aloud, dryly, *"There needs no ghost, my lord, come from the grave/ To tell us this."*

Claire chuckled. "Shakespeare knew about it, didn't he? Colin says he is sure Shakespeare was a trained occultist. Remember what else he said: *'I can call spirits from the vasty deep,'* and someone answering, *'Why, so can I, and so can any man, /But will they come when you call 'em?'* " She looked relieved, perhaps at the touch of humor, and managed somehow to move away from the ruined harpsichord. Once again she appeared to be listening, and a frown came over her kindly face. But she said, "Very well, I will tell him. When I can."

She looked at Leslie and said, almost curtly, "Nothing further to be done in here."

As she moved outside Leslie said, "Did Alison have anything else to say?" She was sure her hostility and skepticism must have been clear, and Claire smiled. She said, "I don't understand it at all. You must have had some experience, even with the police, in getting messages which have no meaning for you."

"Some message for Colin?"

"No, for Simon, and I'm damned if I understand it," Claire said frankly. "What I got was simple: *Tell Simon I forgive him.* And knowing Simon, he's not going to be happy with that message at all."

"No," Leslie said, "I don't think he is."

Before tackling the garage, Claire asked to go upstairs. She frowned a little to see Emily's window standing open again, but after she had walked through the rooms, sighed and came out on the landing.

"Nothing up here," she said. "I'm not familiar with Simon's style of working, but I can tell the place is properly shielded and he was eager to protect you."

"You seemed to think," Leslie said dryly, "that Simon was a black magician. No black magic here?"

"Oh, my dear—it's a matter of emphasis. Colin trained Simon on the Path, as, much later, he trained me. Tools are tools. A carpenter's tools, an architect's skill at blueprints, can be used to design and build a children's hospital or a concentration camp. The same nuclear technology can build a desalinization plant to make the desert bloom like a rose, or a first-strike missile to destroy civilization. The tools are the same. Simon was trained with the same tools. But he favored using them for things we considered—unethical."

You don't know the half of it, Leslie thought, almost in despair, but she could not betray Simon's confidence.

"And that's all I am going to say about it. There's nothing dangerous or inimical in here. And no matter what Simon's beliefs may be, Alison loved him, so I'll say nothing about *him.* Who am I to judge? Let's have a look at the garage."

They went downstairs and out to the remodelled studio. Claire looked distressed as she crossed the threshold.

"Strange," she said. "In the music room, even after all that murderous violence, I felt nothing—nothing human, nothing malevolent. The striking force was—almost impersonal. But here—" She moved, slowly and deliberately, around the room, her face drawn in lines of distaste.

"Not a place any sensitive person could inhabit, and I can see why it—attracted something evil. I don't mind telling you," she burst out, "if it were mine I'd have it torn down! Alison could never have lived with it; it must have happened *after* she was dead or disabled." She moved to the very center of the room.

"Whatever happened, is focused here," she said slowly. She cocked her head on one side with that *listening* attitude. "I sense—pain. Terror. I don't know what it is—" Abruptly her face changed and she rushed outside, and Leslie heard the sound of retching.

Well, she's consistent anyhow. That's exactly where Emily said she'd seen the dead cat. She could imagine that the ritual sacrifice of a harmless animal might be distasteful to anyone of Claire's sensitivity. Simon had admitted that he had not found it pleasant. *But it worked. Purely from a pragmatic point of view, it had worked.* What was the life of a cat compared to Simon's eyesight, the use of his gifted hands? What was the difference whether the cat was sacrificed in legitimate medical research, or for magic of whatever color? She did not believe the death of the cat had had anything to do with it; it was the same mechanism which focused the will to self-healing. It was regrettable that Simon should have felt this method and no other would focus his will, but surely if Claire knew all she too would refuse to judge him.

"I'm sorry," Claire said, wiping her face, "it just overwhelmed me. I wasn't expecting anything nearly that strong. I'll be all right now."

"Can you tell what happened?" Leslie was almost afraid to ask.

"I don't see particulars. It's why I can't do what Alison did, what you do; find missing persons or see murderers. I only pick up raw emotion. All I know is that someone went through absolute *hell* in that place. I've never felt such despair. I can believe that someone committed suicide in there; if I stayed there long enough, I think I would. The sense that everything was over, it was the end, total destruction of everything that made life worth living. A sense of total damnation and despair."

She and Emily had both picked it up in their own way; that despair, the sense of being at a dead end, with nowhere left to turn. They were both basically healthy; it had not lasted long. But now she knew what she had picked up; Simon, in the despairing aftermath of his mutilation. If this was how he felt, how could anyone blame him for whatever mad ritual he had done?

That very day, he had said, he had begun to heal. If the sacrifice of a cat could cast off that burden of despair, she would have handed him her own cat—*her own hands, her own sight*—to free him. And he had been freed. The despair remained behind, leftover force, here in the studio.

"Can we get rid of it?"

Claire drew a deep breath. She said, "We can certainly try. Do you have any water in the house which is pure—spring water, distilled water for your steam iron, anything like that?"

There was half a gallon left after the banishing they had done at the solstice. No wonder Simon had not wanted to go into the studio, associated as it was with what must surely have been the darkest night of his soul!

"And I should have salt. Preferably sea salt or rock salt."

She blessed Emily's health-food kick. She found Emily's carton of sea salt, the bottled water, and gave them to Claire.

"I don't suppose you have your own ritual elements—"

"You didn't see the altar in my bedroom? Is that what you mean?"

"That will help, then," Claire said. "Bring your own chalice; I have one I use, but the house belongs to you and you should cleanse it."

"I don't know enough, Claire!"

The older woman sighed. "Very well; though it would be more effective if you did it." She took Leslie's chalice, filled it with the purified water, murmured some formulas over it; consecrated the salt almost exactly, Leslie thought, as Simon had done.

"Creature of earth, I cast out from you all impurities; lend us your force in this operation. . . ." Leslie did not hear all the words. A tool was a tool, only purpose separated them. The words did not matter. Simon had said that there was no difference whether the banishing was subjective or objective. But the force in the studio was certainly objective enough in its effect on the unguarded mind.

"This is only psychic first aid," Claire cautioned. "When you are able you must do a full-scale cleansing and banishing. But I think we can keep it from harming anyone else, at least for a single moon cycle; before the Equinox, certainly, you should know enough to cleanse it properly."

"What must I do?"

"Wash your hands, saying whatever prayers you believe will be effective, to cleanse you of mundane fears and worries, and hold you in perfect peace and love," Claire said, "and if you can't stand that kind of jargon, make up your own words. The *intention* is what matters; to cleanse and make you ready."

Magic, Leslie wondered as she went to obey, or countersuggestion, and did it matter? When she felt cleansed, she followed Claire to the garage, holding the candle. Claire bore the chalice. As she stepped over the doorsill Claire signed herself with some sign—Leslie could not see what it was—and murmured as if to herself, "Into Thy hands, O Lord, I commit my spirit."

Leslie felt a cold wind sweep across her face, the chill down the spine. Claire took the candle, handed her the chalice, and went to the very center of the room. She raised the candle high over her head, turning clockwise, and Leslie thought she looked very pale. She also thought, irreverently, that she looked as if she was playing charades and acting out the Statue of Liberty. She kept herself from a giggle by main force.

"Where there is darkness," Claire said, her voice low but clear, "let there be light. Where there is hatred, let there be love. Where there is despair, let there be trust and confidence. Bring light to all our darknesses, O Holy Fire, as I bring light, knowing that the symbol is nothing and the reality is all."

She finished a complete turn around the circle; she carried the candle into each corner of the room, repeating softly, "Where there is darkness, let there be light." She stood again at the center of the room, letting the candle light her face; then handed it to Leslie and took the chalice in her hand.

"Be far from this place, all that is profane or evil. Remain ye afar from us, darkness and despair; as the light of truth and hope has been brought into the darkness, so I cast out, I cast out, by Water and Earth I cast out all evil from this place, and I say to you, begone, begone, *be ye gone!*" She turned slowly clockwise (*sunwise,* Leslie thought suddenly) in place; then cast a few drops of the water and salt to each of the four corners of the room, crying out again, "Begone, begone, *be ye gone!*" at each corner.

She returned to the center of the circle and again turned in place, murmuring, "O Water of purity and Earth of reality, cleanse this place of all that is evil and false, knowing that the symbol is nothing and the reality is all."

Only a few drops remained in the chalice; she handed it to Leslie and thrust a taper toward the candle; fire kindled it, and Claire returned to the center of the room. She laid a small clay dish at the very center, and thrust the taper into the dish. Smoke swept upward, sweetish and fresh, spiraling blue, and Claire rose with the dish in her hands, thrusting the taper at Leslie, who took it without thinking. Again Claire turned clockwise in her place.

"Air of Earth and Fire!" she cried out. "We have cleansed this place; now come into the place we have swept and garnished, lest seven demons enter where one was banished! We invoke here the spirit of truth and the reality of love, banishing all falsity and evil, as it is now, as it was in the beginning and as it forevermore shall be, for all time is one. O Thou which art four elements in one, O Thou which art all created things, we know that what we do here is no more than a sketch of thy truth and our symbols only gestures toward the inner reality; grant, O thou eternal spirit of truth, that what we have said with our mouths we may believe in our hearts and practice in our lives. Fill this space and our hearts with that Light in which there shall be no darkness, and thus—" she moved in turn toward each of the four corners, drawing the symbol of the pentagram with the lighted incense—"I call upon the forces we have invoked to say, Amen, Amen, Amen."

Leslie whispered, "Amen." She had not said it since she had last been in church when she was fifteen, and then she had not given it meaning. She did now. There was gooseflesh on her arms and she could feel again the cold wind sweeping past her.

Claire led the way outside. She crushed the incense on the threshold, whispering, "Return to the elements of air and earth and fire," snuffed out the candle, and poured the final drops of water from the chalice on a rosebush.

When the dishes had been returned to the altar, Leslie asked, "What now?"

"Now," said Claire prosaically, "we scramble some eggs or something. We both need food, to close down the psychic centers." And when Leslie would have asked questions, Claire shook her head. "Don't talk about it," she said, "it dissipates the power. Later."

"Sit down," Leslie said. "I'll fix us something to eat." Claire sank into a chair with a sigh. She looked exhausted.

"I'm not as young as I used to be," she said, but when Leslie brought an omelet to the table, she sat up and began telling funny stories about the bookselling business.

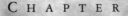

CHAPTER

Twenty-one

THE RENTED PIANO WAS in place. Emily's Knabe had been hauled away for repairs. The harpsichord fragments had been picked up, meticulously numbered, and carried away for analysis by the insurance agency's chosen authenticator. Emily and Frodo, working together, had re-strung the harp. Frodo had even brought gilt paint and tiny brushes and meticulously touched up the chips in the upright post. Leslie had found a clock shop which promised to repair the cuckoo mechanism and restore the shell. Outwardly all was at peace.

The damage to Leslie's nerves was more abiding. She still slept badly, starting awake at every tiny sound. She managed to pull herself together when her clients were present, but she discovered she had an aversion to being alone in the house after dark.

Simon had been away nearly a week when he called and told Leslie the number of his return flight. Near sunset she drove to the airport to pick him up, waiting in the arriving lounge for his flight to be called and crowding with the mothers, wives, husbands, children awaiting the touch-down of the plane, near the very entrance of the gate.

Simon was immediately recognizable in the tunnel, slender and ele-gant, apart from all the pushing throng. She had not realized how tall he was; he stood out almost a full head above the crowd. He saw her and waved, and without being fully aware she was doing it she pushed forward toward him and he leaned to her, kissing her lightly on the cheek.

"Leslie, darling! You shouldn't have come down into this crowd," he said, as the floods of people shoved around them. "Let's get out of the traffic." He hurried toward the parking area. He looked tired and he was carrying his hand in a sling again.

"How was the trip?"

Simon shrugged impatiently, and gestured to Leslie to climb behind the wheel of the Mercedes. As they edged into the line of cars toward the exit gate, shoved money at the parking attendant and swung into the freeway traffic north, he sat with his hands covering his eyes as if the light bothered him. Finally he said, "I thought Heysermann was an intelligent musician with a conscience. I also thought he was my friend. I was wrong on both counts."

Heysermann turned him down, Leslie thought. She had some idea of what it must have meant to Simon to go begging for a chance at a comeback; rejection must have scorched his very soul. How could the man so casually destroy the fresh new buds of a hurt man's self-confidence? Had he enjoyed the sense of power it gave him, to sit in judgment over a former colleague and classmate?

"But what about the other man, I don't remember his name, the one in Montreal?"

Simon's face tightened and she wished she had not asked. "The whole trip was a waste of time, a total waste, I should have stayed home, saved my—my time and energy, saved face, been with you and Emily when you needed me." He fell silent again. Despair seemed to flood outward from his slumped, defeated body.

Leslie said, trying to break the mood, "The insurance men seemed to think I was perpetrating a fraud, darling, or that I'd conspired with you to spirit your valuable antique away and hired someone to break up some-thing like the cheap one Frodo built from a kit. I never knew they had such vivid imagination; I never suspected insurance men of having any imagination at all. Emily told them when they took it away that they ought to be writing whodunits, that even on television nobody would buy a plot like that."

"I'm sorry they badgered you about it," Simon said. "I would much rather have taken the loss than have had you troubled or worried. The museums have the really valuable pieces. I'm sorry it happened, of course; it had a lovely tone, and was one of Alison's favorites. But apart from the purely sentimental value—" He shrugged. "The place is quiet now? Have they caught the psychopath who did it?"

"No sign of him." Leslie started to take the turnoff which would lead to his condominium, but he said, "I'd rather go to the house, Leslie, do you mind?"

"Of course not; I thought you might want to leave your luggage, but I'll take you straight home," she said.

"It's insane living in two houses like this. We'll have to find a way," he said. "Perhaps next year we can arrange for Emily to go to Juilliard or to study in France with Reszke or Goldblatt. I would work with her myself, but by that time, God willing, I will be back on tour again, and she needs someone who can devote himself to teaching. All conductors are not like Heysermann."

But Emily had said it, that he was not ready. And now Heysermann and the conductor in Montreal. Could they all be wrong? Leslie's heart sank. It was, she thought, one thing to have self-confidence and to keep a hopeful spirit. But was Simon refusing to accept realistic limitations? Was it so terrible a fate to accept a career as conductor, composer, teacher?

Nothing is impossible to the trained will. Was she cruel and disloyal to doubt him, and could her doubt contribute to failure? Where did reality begin and end? But looking across at his slumped body, she remembered something else he had said.

Only the audience counts; the rest of the time is death. We only come to life on the stage. He would not be himself if he accepted anything less than complete recovery and perfection, at whatever cost. She guided the car up Haight Street, inching along behind a trolley car with PARNASSUS in the window, a bus, loaded trucks; finally, with relief, swung off the crowded street and up the hill past Buena Vista park. As she pulled up in front of the house, she saw with her heart sinking that Frodo's truck was in front. Really, this was tactless of Emily, knowing how Simon felt about the young man.

Inside the hall he sighed and turned to her, holding her close. He was not the kind to be demonstrative in public; his kiss in the airport lounge had been the kind he would have given to a sister or grandmother, but here he made up for lost time. When Leslie finally surfaced, she realized that Emily was standing in the door of the music room. smiling and silently applauding.

"Bravo! Welcome back, Simon," she said, then flung herself on him with an enthusiastic hug. He patted her back, laughing.

"You seem in good spirits enough," he said, and her face clouded.

"Oh, Simon, your beautiful harpsichord—"

"Never mind," he said, his arm about her shoulders, following her into the music room. "Did you find a decent piano to rent till yours is back? A Steinway; yes, that's a good instrument. So many rental places try to push these new Japanese pianos on you. I wouldn't have one as a gift. There is no current American piano that is worth giving house room—"

He broke off as he noticed Frodo in the corner of the room, kneeling beside a small harpsichord. The wood was pale and new, but looked polished and well-cared-for.

"What is this miserable piece of junk doing there?"

Frodo straightened. "I built it, and I loaned it to Emily. I'm sorry yours got smashed, but I thought Emmie ought to have one to practice on. I can't play it well enough to be worth keeping it at home, so why shouldn't she have it here?"

"Don't you dare be horrible to Frodo, Simon," Emily cried. "He put my harp back together good as new! Just look at it! You should have *seen* it, with all the strings broken—"

With an effort, Simon controlled his face.

"I'm sure it was very kind of you, Paul." Making what Leslie recognized as an extraordinary effort to be civil, he walked over and bent to inspect the instrument. "A Zuckermann? Or—no, you built it from a kit, right? I must compliment you on your craftsmanship."

Emily said, "I'm sure someday people will talk about a Frederick harpsichord!" She sat down and ran her fingers lightly over the keys, and Simon smiled, stiffly.

"I know it can't compare with Miss Margrave's wonderful antiques," Frodo said, "but for what it is, it's not a bad job at all. You can try its sound, if you like."

Simon shook his head. His eyes were half closed as if they hurt him, his gloved hand cradled in the other one. "I'll leave that to Emily," he said, sitting on the piano bench. Emily began to play some Bach. She had not, Leslie noted, asked him anything about his trip. She had, after all, been prepared for the news of his failure. She had known he was not ready. And Simon was not surprised at the omission, and somehow that was worst of all.

"Simon, you look dreadfully tired," she said, when Emily stopped playing. "Can I fix you something? Did you have dinner on the plane?"

Frodo rose and said, "Hey, Emmie and I ought to be running along. We're having dinner with my family in Sausalito."

"Oh, Simon, I didn't know you were going to be back—" Emily said mournfully, expecting an outburst, but he patted her cheek.

"Run along and have fun, sweetheart. Paul, drive very carefully."

"You'd better believe I'll take good care of her, Dr. Anstey!"

When the old truck had driven away he put his arms round her, and said, making a burlesque of it, "Alone at last. I suppose this is how a parent feels when he has a chance to get the children out of the house. I'm not hungry—they fed us on the plane—but it's nice to be home with you. What I really want—" He leaned forward to kiss her eyelids, her lips, then turned toward the stairs.

It would be the first time they had been together under this roof.

IT WAS VERY DARK and still; one of the rare nights when the fog-bank remained at sea. The moon, brilliant and almost at full, turned the sky to an opalescent indigo pallor reminiscent of a Maxfield Parrish painting. Simon paused for a moment near the single red eye of Leslie's altar—she had not known that he had paid any attention when he came into the room—then threw the window open, looking down on the panorama of city lights far below them.

"Alison never was impressed by the Freudians," he said, trying to take it lightly, "but I suppose a proper Freudian would say that Alison is a mother figure to me, and this having been her bedroom, I was naturally unable—" He broke off, and Leslie came swiftly to the window at his side. She could not bear the defeated sound in his voice.

"Darling, you're tired after that long trip, and discouraged. Don't worry about it."

"I'm only sorry for having disappointed you."

"Beloved—" She circled him with her arms. "Do you think that's how

I judge you?" She could not believe she was saying these old worn things, yet what was there to say?

"I'm too old for you," Simon said, "too old for a woman as young and—and vital as you are—"

She could not endure it, that he should flay himself this way for her sake.

"You're the one I want, and I won't have you talking as if you were Methuselah. You're tired, Simon, and naturally depressed. Come and sleep."

He turned impatiently away from the window. "I'm not sleepy. Let's go down and raid the refrigerator. Maybe I should have had supper after all."

But while she was making grilled cheese sandwiches, he wandered restlessly out into the garden. Leslie put the sandwiches on a plate in the warming oven and went out in search of him. The moon was very full and bright and the studio door open. She came in and found him there, silent. "Who has been in here?" he asked.

She might have known that he would notice the changed atmosphere. She had been out there the day before sewing cushions, with no hint of the depression which had seized her on the last occasion she had tried to work out there. "Claire and I did a banishing; the place was really unin-habitable, Simon."

"I should have known. I haven't been inside the place for more than a year, and who knows what that insufferable jenny ass Betty Carmody might have brought here? Never mind, I can soon build up the kind of atmo-sphere I want," he said. He was standing at the very center of the room, where Claire had stood to make her benedictions. Then he glanced at her, hesitantly. He had not turned on the electric light and the only light was from the open door on the moon-flooded garden.

"I am taking it for granted—that you will not object to my using it again as a Temple."

What could he possibly be expecting her to say? Her breath caught in her throat.

"I thought I had gone far enough," he mused, half aloud. "This trip must have been intended as a test of my will and resolution. Nothing is impossible to the trained will," he added, and now his voice was barely more than a whisper. Something in the note turned Leslie's blood to ice, but she dismissed the notion. This was the twentieth century, not the fourteenth, and the man at her side was a sophisticated cosmopolitan, not an ignorant primitive. She was silent at his side so long that he turned to her, questioning, then smiled and hugged her tight in his arms.

"Those grilled cheese sandwiches must be tough as old rubber tires; let's go in and have our midnight snack and get up to bed before Emily and the youngster—what is that absurd thing he calls himself, something out of Tolkien—Bilbo Baggins?—before they get home and catch us smooching like teenagers in the kitchen!"

SHE HEARD THE CLOCK strike twelve and then one, before Frodo's truck drove up outside. Simon was asleep, exhausted after another of the disabling attacks of pain, but Leslie lay awake, deeply troubled.

I thought I had gone far enough. Perhaps this was a test of my will and resolution, Simon had said, and she wondered if he had again the mad notion of ritual sacrifice. After all he had been through, what wonder if he would grasp at any straw? The only question was, How far was he prepared to go? And could she stand aside, in the hope that it would provide a focus for his will to healing? If not, how could she interfere?

I would give him my own hands, my own sight if I could, she thought in despair. Before this when she had heard people make extravagant statements in the name of love, she had felt it was romantic exaggeration. Yet she knew it true. Her own work did not depend on hands or eyesight, and she knew that while she would suffer terribly with deprivation, it would not destroy everything for her in life.

Would I give my life?

No. No, not that. That was not love, that was insanity. But anything short of that, anything which left her, however outwardly damaged, a whole person within—yes, that she would sacrifice for Simon without counting the cost; her mind drifting over the edge of sleep, she thought, *Perhaps there could be a ritual which would restore his hands at the cost of making mine useless, and I would gladly give that. . . .*

Frodo's old truck rattled up before the gate; there was such a long silence that Leslie crept to the window and saw them standing enlaced. Well, Emily was certainly entitled to a puppy love affair, and Frodo was a dear boy. Even Simon had finally capitulated to that.

• • •

BACON WAS SENDING ITS delicious sizzling smell through the house when Emily came down. Seeing Simon in his robe at the breakfast table, she dropped her eyes and turned her face away.

"Yuck, bacon! Don't you know that stuff is all full of nitrites and salt and it will *poison* you?"

"Well, you don't have to eat it, love," Leslie said. "Do you want some toast?" She put a slice into the toaster.

Emily was making herself some of the mouthwash-colored tea. She cut a lemon from a bowl on the counter, left over from the marmalade. "I made eighteen jars of marmalade, Simon. I put a couple of jars aside just for you." She squeezed lemon into her tea. "It's wonderful to have fresh lemons."

"I'll try some on my toast. No, I mean that marmalade, child," Simon chuckled, waving away the fresh lemon half Emily offered him. "Mmmm, this is delightful. I'll make a gourmet cook of you yet," he said, sampling the marmalade. "What are your plans for today, darling?"

"I have Susan Hamilton coming in at eleven-thirty."

"That's the woman with the idiot child?"

"Christina is not an idiot," she reminded him, but Simon shrugged. "She is no more use to anyone than if she were. I will reserve my sympathy and attention for children like Emily, who deserve it. In all honesty, Leslie, anyone who struck and killed that child in a street accident, sentiment aside, would be doing the mother a favor, the child herself a favor, and all of society a favor."

"I think we'll have to agree to differ on that," Leslie said, but Emily chimed in, "You know it as well as I do, Leslie. I know you can't say it to your patient, but honestly, wouldn't it be a relief to all concerned, even to the kid's mother?"

Leslie sighed. "We've had this argument before, and I'll have to reserve judgment just as I did then. I'm not interested in playing God, and thank God it isn't up to me." She piled Emily's marmalade on her toast. "This is lovely, Em. What are you going to do today?"

"I should talk with the insurance people about the harpsichord," Simon said, "and I must go back to my apartment to make some telephone calls. And Emily, it has been more than a week since we had a lesson; can you spare me an hour, if your young friend has left you time?"

"I always have time for you, Simon. And anyway Frodo's working," she said. "I wanted to talk to you about that. Last night we were over in Sausalito talking to Frodo's parents, and he's going to quit work at the bookstore and go into business for himself. They're going to lend him the money and he's going to open an instrument shop and build lutes and mend violins and guitars, and since he'll have a lot of time between customers, he can build and sell harpsichords."

Leslie said, "Congratulations!" but Simon raised a critical eyebrow. "I trust this does not mean he is thinking of settling down and raising a family," he said. "I warn you, my dear, if you elope, I shall be most seriously displeased with you."

"Oh, no," Emily cried, blushing. "I wouldn't even think of getting married, not for years and years and *years!* Maybe when I'm thirty or forty!"

He cocked his head on one side. "You may not believe it at seventeen," he said, "but old people of thirty or even forty still have ambition and energy and they still enjoy life. If it is your idea that by forty you will be too old to care any more about love and careers and independence, perish the thought!"

"That wasn't what I meant," Emily insisted, but she colored and Leslie suspected that was *exactly* what she had meant.

After breakfast Simon and Emily disappeared into the music room and Leslie went to tidy her office, check her answering service and go through her files. Susan had had to bring Christina again, but the little girl went obediently into the garden and when her mother put her into an aluminum lawn chair she stayed there without trying to move.

"How is Chrissy this week?"

Susan shook her head. "I'm losing hope again. She seemed to be making progress, but this week she won't even look at me again. My sister Margaret says I should start dating again, but how would a man react to me when he knew I had a brain-damaged child? I should have started right away when I could still have had more children of my own. . . ."

Leslie settled back, shoving a box of Kleenex at Susan, and thinking of what Simon had said. Would it not be doing this woman a favor to remove her hopeless and helpless child from her mother so that the woman could build a new life before too late?

Later, when Susan had gone, she left Emily practicing Bach and went with Simon to his apartment, where she helped him unpack and listened as he called the insurance company.

"Our honesty is exonerated," he said dryly, as he hung up. "I know the man who did the authentication; he verified the date of the fragments and the technique of wiring the jacks. Did they really believe me capable of such a petty fraud as that, a mere fifteen thousand or so?"

"Insurance frauds have been done for a couple of hundred dollars, Simon."

He shrugged that off. "If I were ever to commit a crime, it would not be a sordid one for money," he said, while she remembered, ice chilling her spine, what he had told her one night here. Had she fully faced it— that the man she loved had committed at least one premeditated murder?

He sat down at the piano, pulled his glove slowly off his damaged hand. "I should practice more," he said, flexing the fingers with the fingers of the other hand, slowly. "I should not let setbacks discourage me like this." But he got up and moved restlessly to the harpsichord.

"I offered this one to Emily, or said she could take her choice of the ones in storage, and she refused me. She refused! Do you think she is as serious as *that* about the Fredericks boy, Leslie?"

"I can't imagine Emily not being perfectly forthright; if that was her reason she'd have said so," Leslie said. "Was that the reason she gave? That she was attached to Frodo's harpsichord?"

He shook his head. "No, what she said was that she didn't want to move a valuable one in there until they had the psychopath behind bars and knew it was safe. I thought she was being tactful—"

"Frodo's, presumably, being expendable," Leslie commented. "Simon, you should know by now that Emily doesn't know the meaning of the word 'tact'!"

"I hadn't thought of that," he said, and looked relieved. "If I thought she had given an instant's thought to giving up her career for that wretched boy, I swear, I would murder—" He stopped, midsentence, sheepishly. "Well, I would really find it almost impossible to forgive either of them." He picked up his glove from the piano keyboard, closing the cover. It had a curious finality.

She watched him tend his altar in the bedroom, impressed, now that she knew what the words meant and implied, by his power with ritual. He and Claire had been trained in the same school, by the same man. Could their ethics really be so far apart? He paused for a moment, arms outspread as if in supplication; then cast incense on the smoking charcoal; not the usual bitter-clean fragrance, but something new and unusual.

"What is that, Simon?"

"Juniper," he said. "And . . . other things associated with Pan the Satyr. Whether Alison's influence or another—I will not allow it to rob me of potency . . . or of you."

"You can't believe that, Simon!" But the protest was automatic, no more. After the last few weeks, she knew she did believe, and Simon smiled, pulling her close and kissing her fiercely.

"Come and see for yourself," he urged. His hands were already loosening her clothes. And whatever the effect, ritual or psychological, the results seemed to be most satisfactory.

Lying at ease later in his arms, a languid half-eye on the clock—she had a client at five, but nothing before then—she was surprised when he suddenly seized her and demanded, "Leslie, let's go away!"

"What? Where, Simon? You mean for the day? The weekend?"

"Let's not plan, let's just go. Hawaii. Europe. Rome. Egypt. Let's call up a travel agent and go! If you have scruples about travelling with a man not your husband, we can be married day after tomorrow—there's a forty-eight-hour waiting period for a license and blood test, I understand. Just think, we could have breakfast in Paris Saturday—or Honolulu the day after tomorrow!"

She was breathless at the suddenness of this. "Simon, you're joking! How could I leave Emily?"

"If Emily's afraid to be in the house alone, she can come and stay here while we're gone. There's excellent security here, and she has friends who can help keep an eye on her."

"My patients—"

"I should have known you would have felt compelled to make practical difficulties," he said mournfully. "I don't suppose you would consider trying to find another doctor or counselor to take over your practice? Just while you were on your honeymoon? Can't you imagine that I could need you more than they do? I know a man in the passport division, he can rush it through."

"Oh, Simon, it would be wonderful, but how can I do a thing like that at a moment's notice? I'm always telling people how important it is to act on rational grounds, not to do irrational things on the spur of the moment! I'm not refusing you. I—" she paused and took a deep breath at the enormity of what she was saying, "I do want to marry you. But does it have to be immediately? Won't you love me if I stop to think it over?"

He put his arms around her. "I will love you for the rest of my life, and as long thereafter as God wills," he said seriously, pulling her down for a lingering kiss. "But Leslie, I think it could be terribly important to us both, just to get away. . . ."

"Let's plan it," she said gently. "Let's do it with time enough to think about it and do it right. Even—" she swallowed again, unable to believe how her own feelings on that matter had changed, "even about getting married. Not overnight. But soon. As soon as we can arrange it."

He sighed, letting her go.

"Whatever you wish, my beloved. But however soon we can make plans to go, I am afraid it may be too late."

"Darling, what do you mean by that? Are you—" her throat caught, "are you having some kind of premonition?"

He kissed her again.

"No, darling. I was just—just suddenly overwhelmed with the desperate desire to get away. I know it isn't rational. I know it doesn't make sense. We'll do it your way. Slowly, reasonably, sensibly. I'm sure you're right, Leslie."

Only later, when the hand of tragedy had fallen, did she realize why Simon had been begging her to take him away.

CHAPTER

Twenty-two

"YOU KNOW, DR. BARNES, I really think Pete's getting tired of bugging me," Evelyn Sadler said. "I haven't heard anything in the last two weeks except a couple of knocks and bangs, and I just say, 'Oh, go on, Pete, let me alone,' and they go away. Of course I'm not there to hear it a lot," she added. "I'm really enjoying that art class. Who'd have thought anybody my age could start painting? My teacher suggested I take up art therapy—helping disturbed children and sick people in chronic-care places paint pictures. I think I'd love that, and she says I can get a certificate to do it."

Leslie thought that the intrusive ghost would hardly have recognized his cowed little wife; this new woman, smartly and tidily dressed, her hair professionally styled and well combed, her art materials in a portfolio and her eyes bubbling with enthusiasm, would have been a difficult problem for a ghost. She gave Evelyn a copy of the banishing ritual she had done with Claire on the studio and said, "You might try this against the knocks and bangs."

Evelyn Sadler glanced over the ritual. She demurred. "Oh, I don't know, Dr. Barnes. I'd feel awful foolish doing this kind of stuff. Specially since Pete's not bothering me now."

"Suit yourself," Leslie said, smiling, and extended her hand. "Do you want to make another appointment?"

"Well, that was what I wanted to talk about. I'm at the art school three days a week now and down at the hospital one day, and I don't have time any more. . . ."

Letting her out the door, Leslie reflected that here, at least, was one success she could chalk up to her new methods. Simon's car drew up at the gate, and he came to kiss her.

"I didn't know we were going anywhere, darling."

"We're not," he said. "Tonight I'm deserting you to take Emily out. You don't mind, do you, beloved?"

"Of course not. Enjoy yourselves," she said, as Emily came running down the stairs, fresh and bright in a sapphire blue leotard and a matching skirt. Her hair was coiled low on her back and she wore sandals. "Will you be very late?"

"No, not very; I'll probably have her back by ten," Simon said, kissed her again, and handed Emily gently into the car.

Leslie went in and turned on a concert broadcast from one of the two classical music stations, a rebroadcast of a live performance from Munich several years ago. The announcer named the orchestra; the conductor was Lewis Heysermann, and she heard, with a sense of inevitability, the name of the guest soloist: Simon Anstey. She listened as the quiet neutral voice, a faint British accent, translated the announcer's voice, recapitulating the prizes Simon had won, the world-famous orchestras with which he had played. Then she heard applause, even before the conductor had begun the music, and knew it was the applause which had greeted her lover; then the eight chords, beginning *pianissimo* and moving swiftly to crashing *fortissimo*, marking the opening of the Rachmaninoff concerto.

He spoke often of what they would do when they were married, but had not again pressured her to set an immediate date. She for her part had ceased to accept any new patients and was beginning to speak to one or two of her present ones about terminating therapy. Unlike the Freudians, she tended to feel that if she could not make significant changes in her clients' lives or guide them to such changes within a few months, years of therapy were not likely to do much more, except add dependency on the therapist. She would take up her practice again after they were married; if Simon was to be travelling a great deal, she would need to keep busy, unless she was to sit home waiting all the time. But the first months of their marriage should belong to Simon and only to him.

When the concerto was over, she listened to the encore; a pair of Chopin preludes. One of them she had heard him play only a day or two ago. She was aware that she did not have the experience to judge between the way he played now and the way he had played then. But he knew, and it was crushing him.

At ten-thirty she heard Emily's step in the hall and hurried to the door. Emily, her eyes dreamy, stood there with a long-stemmed crimson rose in her hand; she sniffed at it as Leslie asked, "Where is Simon?"

"He decided not to come in," Emily said sleepily, smelling at her rose. "He'll call you tomorrow."

"Did you have a nice time? Where did you go?"

"Simon took me to a Lodge meeting," Emily said.

"What? For goodness' sake, what do you know about such things?"

"Well, Frodo's told me a little about the Path," Emily said, "but mostly I was curious because someone told me he was a black magician, so he said he'd take me and I could see for myself."

Out of this tangle of "he" Leslie deduced that Frodo had told her, that she had asked Simon, and he had taken her to a Lodge meeting.

"What was it like?"

Emily yawned. "Boring," she said. "Awfully boring; I went to sleep toward the end."

"Are outsiders allowed in, then?" This sounded quite different from anything she had ever heard.

"Well, I wasn't exactly an outsider," Emily said. "There's a place in every Lodge for a girl who isn't exactly a member. I forget the name they call her, but I had a pretty white robe and a rose in my hand." She giggled. "Simon asked me if I was a virgin. I think he was more embarrassed than I was, but he was very insistent on it. I mean, he made it obvious that nobody would *touch* me—I read some gruesome story about a girl who was taken to one of these things and she had to be a virgin and they ended up the party by gang-raping her, so I wanted to be sure that wasn't the idea here. But I guess it's just sort of a symbolic thing."

Leslie was glad that she had escaped that particular piece of horror fiction. She had had enough nightmares already.

"So no one touched you?"

"God, no. They left me in this weird little cubbyhole to dress up in the robe and hood, and then they gave me a rose and told me to sit at a chair at the end and keep silence. So I sat there and listened till I got bored, and then I went to sleep."

"But, but, but . . ." Leslie was dismayed with curiosity. "What did they talk about?"

Emily shrugged. "I couldn't make head or tail of most of it. They were discussing folklore, I think, and somebody read a paper about the witch cult in—I think it was Ireland, but maybe it was Finland. Oh, yes, and they put Simon in the middle of a circle and everybody prayed for him to be healed. And they all gave each other what they called the kiss of peace— they all kissed each other, old men with beards and all. And then I fell asleep. Weird. Somebody challenged me, said I looked too old. I gather they expect virgins to be under twelve. They asked me if I would swear on my honor that I was a virgin, and I said yes. I suppose it is kind of kinky, a girl my age still being a virgin." She yawned again. "Leslie, do you think there's something *wrong* with me? Nuts, you wouldn't say so if you did, you'd only ask me who told me it was wrong! I'm going up to bed," she concluded, and went upstairs, still holding the rose in her hand.

It certainly did not sound like any black magic Lodge she had ever heard of, or for that matter any white one either, but it sounded harmless. Of course, if Emily had been drugged or hypnotized to account for her abnormal sleepiness . . . But the truth was probably just what Emily said, she had found the proceedings so boring she could not (and didn't want to) tell Finland from Ireland. She was still troubled as she went up to bed and finally identified her own emotion: she was jealous of Emily.

It was obvious that Simon would always share with Emily that world she could enter only as an outsider, the world of the professional musician. But this, which touched on her own world, the world of psychology, parapsychology, magic? She was jealous, and ashamed of herself for being jealous.

Yet when next she was with Simon in his apartment, it seemed too small and petty to bring up. And she had a more overriding worry. The crippling spasms of pain in his eye were less now, but they came on with the same disabling and unpredictable violence, which was why he had almost completely ceased to drive his car, asking Leslie to drive him when she was free, taking taxis when she was not. Once she asked him, gently, "Simon, can't the doctors do anything about these?"

"It is nerve damage; it may subside in time, but nerves heal in their own way or not at all," he said. "Their only answer would be to drug me into insensibility. I would rather suffer and be myself the rest of the time than go through the rest of my life in a—a drug-induced fog."

She could only respect him for that, but it tore her own heart asunder to watch him like this. He had learned certain self-hypnosis techniques which, he said, gave him a little relief from the more acute stages of the attacks. But it was a wonder, she thought, that all this had not reduced him to madness anyhow. When he slept, she lay awake watching him, deeply disturbed. If, she thought, he asked her again to marry him and come away at a moment's notice, she would do so. Her patients would survive; they would find other counselors, or somehow manage their problems without one. Simon needed her, and she could do so little for him.

She was half asleep herself when he cried out and sat upright in bed, staring about him wildly. She was prepared to soothe him through another nightmare, but he cried out, "Alison!" and was abruptly wide awake.

"Did you want to tell me about it, Simon?"

He was covered in cold sweat; she thought for a moment that he was in pain again, but he shook his head when she asked.

"Nightmare?"

"No," he said, his teeth gritted. "I would swear I saw—Alison. Yet how could that be? She was never here in life, and there must be some— bond with the living."

"Why shouldn't she come to you, Simon? She loved you."

"We quarrelled, over—what I told you before. She wanted me for her successor. She wanted me to be an—an ineffectual idiot of Colin's kind, content to study and never to use what I learned— After her stroke, she discovered—the cat—"

"I thought that was after she died, Simon."

"No." He stared into space, bleakly. It was, she thought, the right time to tell him this.

"Simon, after the—the vandalism. When Claire was there, she—in the music room. She said Alison had come to her—" Leslie stopped. She felt foolish using the language of spiritualism; no matter how much she liked Claire or how much she might personally entertain faith in survival after death, she was not comfortable with the language. Was it, she wondered, because such things were essentially non-verbal experiences, and trying to put them into words diminished them?

"She told me Alison said; *tell Simon I forgive him.*"

But Simon only stared bleakly at the wall and said, "That is the sort of message Claire would expect, and therefore I am sure she believes that is the message she got," in a tone that closed the subject.

Does Simon truly believe that Alison Margrave went to her death unforgiving? Living in Alison's house all these troubled weeks had at least given her an idea of the woman, and while Alison might disagree strongly with whatever Simon believed or did, if anything survived after death Leslie could not believe it was a grudge of this sort. But did Simon believe that Alison was hounding him from the other side of death, badgering him to give up his evil practices? He had become impotent in Alison's bedroom. Alison was a mother figure to him; the guilt he could not acknowledge in himself for whatever he had done (murder? However he rationalized it, murder) he could easily displace and say that it was Alison who blamed him for it. Even someone untrained in psychology could have little trouble in guessing that.

He said after a long time, "The house, you know, was to be mine. She knew my interest in thaumaturgy—what Colin called 'black magic'—but believed it was youthful curiosity for which she had forgiven me. When I was—injured—" his jaw tightened; he always had trouble speaking of the accident—"and she discovered that after her stroke, I had not asked her leave, but took this measure to raise power for healing, she disinherited me. She left me the harpsichords because she knew no one else to whom she could leave them; but she no longer trusted me to give the prizes of the collection to museums; she altered her will so they went there directly. And now—Leslie, tell me again about the vandalism. I have a reason for asking."

Leslie had no desire to relive the nightmarish events of that night, but nevertheless she rehearsed how she and Emily had been wakened by dreadful noises from the music room, how they had run down to find the intruder gone with no sign of his passing, and summoned the police.

"And they found no sign—"

"None. Nothing whatever. They couldn't imagine how he had gotten in, but even more, they found no way he could have gotten out!"

There was a long silence. Finally Simon said, "My love, have you ever seen a poltergeist?"

"Yes." She did not elaborate.

"Did it occur to you that the destruction in the music room—was more dreadful than any human vandal could compass?"

Claire had suggested this.

She had called it *inhuman.* There had even been a terrible moment when Leslie had wondered if somehow the monstrous thing that plagued her, that had thrown a glass of wine into Joel's face and jangled unwired doorbells, had raged there that night. But why? Why would she have done this to Emily, of all people in the world? *Are the Freudians right and all my love for Emily only a rationalization for hatred and jealousy?* She felt that her breath was trapped in her throat.

"Simon, do you think that I—I—"

"You?" He looked at her blankly. "What are you talking about? But Alison died hating me. And what do you think, if she tried so hard to find a successor to her house, what do you think it might mean to her to know that you and I had come together, as it was meant; that I had come into the house again, that I was your lover, that I was entrenched in the house once more and accepted there as a friend. The violence to the piano and harp was almost random, Leslie. But my harpsichord, the harpsichord which had been *hers* and was now *mine,* was smashed to splinters. The insurance authenticator told me. I tell you, it was Alison's rage against *me,* Leslie. Her way of telling me to get out, that she would not have me in *her* house, in *your* life. She wants you, Leslie, for a successor; but she is trying to save you from my wickedness."

She looked at him in dismay. This was completely alien to everything she knew about Alison. And yet—

Claire had said it; Alison was no saint. She could be unforgiving. The house had become uninhabitable after her death. From beyond death, she had ruthlessly taken her own path. What, then, would be her fury when she found that the man who had been like a son to her, who had—in her mind—betrayed her and in return been disinherited, had come into the life of her carefully chosen successor?

And if a poltergeist on this plane could be terrifying—and Leslie had known that terror—what would it be for a woman no longer bound by the confines of space and time?

"There are other reasons for Alison to hate me. I would rather not go into them all," he said, "but I think you brought this upon yourself, Leslie, by accepting my friendship. And my love. Alison—" his voice all but strangled in his throat, "Alison, I think, will stop at nothing to prevent that. If we marry and I come to live in her house—we might be in terrible danger, Leslie. She might drive us out—or worse."

She remembered the phrase from the book Simon and Alison had written together: the old rules of life had been shattered, and the new parameters of existence were not yet made clear. This was turning all her old beliefs on their head; she had believed that malevolence could not survive the grave, yet this made many things eerily clear. If, rather than a benevolent guide from beyond, helping Leslie to carry on her work for the benefit of mankind, Alison Margrave was searching for revenge against Simon, who had betrayed her; if she was not content with disinheriting him, but must continue to make certain that Simon did not inhabit her house even after she had ceased to have any use for it—

Leslie felt bereft. She had truly come to think of Alison as a guide, a benefactor, a friend who was leading her to a new kind of practice. Yet, examining what Simon had said, she found in it no immediately identifiable flaw.

"Is there any reason you must live in the house, Simon? After we are married we will have this place—and we can live anywhere. Let her have her triumph; why should we carry on the fight?"

"Is that what you want to do, Leslie? Just withdraw and go away? I'm disappointed. The house is yours now; I will not have her drive you out! Nor will I let her put limits upon me, as if I were a small boy still under her guardianship!"

"But what can we do?"

"There are ways," he said quietly. "She can be driven off this plane. I do not deny that there is danger. But I am not afraid of her." His good eye gleamed with anger. "I would not harm her, but I would send her on her way to whatever afterlife she wishes and deserves. By her own principles, she would be glad of that. She has always said that the dead have no right to remain and disturb the living. Among other things, I suppose, she would stop at nothing to prevent—what I now know I must do," he finished, looking away from her, and Leslie's heart sank.

This conversation, any part of it, was enough to convince any outsider that they should be locked up in adjoining cells in Napa Mental Hospital! And now Simon was returning to his mad belief that by sacrifice he could raise power to heal his hand and his eye. Was it any madder than the belief that Alison, from beyond the grave, had smashed Simon's harpsichord, and would attempt to prevent Leslie and Simon from loving and working together?

"I can fight her," he said, "but first I must be strong. There is only one way—" He broke off, bending over her, kissing her, touching her face. "My poor love, this frightens you. You don't need to know anything about it unless you want to. In any case there is no time to train you to work at that level. Leslie, I have something to ask you. Are you intending to use the studio for a week or more—a month, perhaps?"

"Why, no," she said, bewildered by the sudden shift. "There's nothing in there but a sewing machine and an old dress-form. If you want to use it—" And her heart almost failed her. What did he want to use it *for?* And would she cooperate in this monstrous business?

"Then—Leslie, may I have it for a month? No more; I solemnly swear, by that time I will have accomplished what I set out to accomplish, or I will abandon it as hopeless."

She said, clinging to his hand. "You know that anything I have is yours, Simon." He had been so generous with her and with Emily, and she could make so little return to him. She even had the house, which should have been his.

"Will you let me have a new lock put on? I will give you a key for emergencies, if you do not trust me—"

How could I possibly admit that I did not trust him? In all but this, this obsession, I do trust him. She had never asked herself before: if he should come to her and ask for help in one of these sacrifices, what would she do?

But surely all he means is that he means, again, to attempt an animal sacrifice. And while cruelty to animals is a technical misdemeanor, it is, after all, a matter of conscience. Huge numbers of dogs and cats are sacrificed in medical research, and certain kinds of monkeys are bred for no other purpose. When it is done by big business, it is perfectly legal. The hypocrisy of the law says it is illegal for a man to sacrifice a dog or cat, yet allows wholesale slaughter for food, for business or for medical research. Why should she object to that?

And if he intended anything stronger than that, he would not have told me exactly how and where. Simon would not make me accessory to murder; he knows I assist the police in these things; he would never believe I would be silent about a human life.

"Do as you wish, Simon," she said. "I trust you."

CHAPTER

*Twenty-
three*

SHE WAS GETTING READY for Susan Hamilton when she saw the locksmith's truck. Emily was practicing; Leslie knocked and went in.

"Do you need anything out of the studio for a few weeks, Emily?"

"I don't think so; why?"

"Because the locks are going to be changed and I won't have a key; if you want anything—the sewing machine, for instance—"

"When would I have time to sew?" It was so absolutely a rhetorical question that Emily did not wait for an answer. "I've got to get ready to audition for keyboard placement this year, and I'm taking a course in literature for the harpsichord. I need some new clothes—was this just a polite way of telling me I'm going to have to sew them myself?"

"No, no, I think we could afford a few things, provided you're willing to be reasonable. But the place will be locked, so in case you wanted the dress form or something—"

"If I do," Emily said, "Simon will get it for me, I'm sure. He told me he was going to be coming and going in the place for the next few weeks." She bent again over the score on the piano and Leslie felt again that small ignoble seed of jealousy. He had told Emily, then, and never mentioned it to her.

The locksmith was working on the door, and Leslie went in to check for anything she might need during the next weeks. She took the small box which contained needles, pincushion and colored thread, scissors and mending tapes; she would not need the sewing machine, but she knew that as surely as she locked all her sewing things away, something would need mending.

"It's all right, come in, little girl," said the locksmith, smiling up genially, and Leslie saw Christina Hamilton standing in the door.

"Chrissy!" Susan called.

"She's back here, Susan." Leslie took the child's hand in hers. Chrissy's hand felt smooth and dry, like a small animal's paw; but when Leslie would have led her out of the room she resisted silently, going directly to the center of the studio and turning slowly around, clockwise. Exactly, Leslie thought, where Claire had stood. She had once heard a theory that retarded or non-verbal children were psychic to such an extent that they could not shut out the assault on their extra senses, and therefore closed off access to the outer world. She did not know if she believed it, but Chrissy was certainly recapitulating Claire's movements, raising her hands as Claire had done in ritual.

Then she said clearly, aloud, "Kitty."

"I don't see any kitty, darling," Susan said from the door. "Come on, Chrissy, let's play in the garden, not in here. Come out in the sunshine, sweetheart." She came and lifted her passively resisting daughter, carrying her outside. Christina did not struggle, but the moment Susan put her down she rushed inside again and Susan had once again to carry her out.

"It's all right," Leslie said, "the door will be locked."

"Play here under the trees, Chrissy. Mommy will be out in an hour," Susan said, but Chrissy had retreated into her inner world again.

"Did you hear her, Leslie? Oh, God, I thought I imagined it, but she said "Kitty." She *can* speak. But why doesn't she?" Susan was almost in tears.

Language is never acquired, or if acquired is lost. That was the definition of an autistic child. But Christina was not autistic, not at least in the typical way. But why did she never speak? Leslie could not imagine.

She went to speak to the locksmith, but he said he had had his instructions. "The gentleman is going to meet me here, he said. I think that must be him now." Leslie raised her head and saw Simon coming across the walk. She smiled at him and said, "Your locksmith is here, love. I have a client, but I'll be with you in an hour."

Simon smiled affectionately, and since Chrissy was in the very center of the brick walk, turned slightly aside so as not to step on her. Chrissy raised her face and screamed. She stumbled back, screaming again, and fled to the farthest corner of the garden.

Susan went quickly to see if something had happened.

"Maybe a bee stung her! I didn't see anything, but maybe— Chrissy, Chrissy, what's the matter? Show Mommy." Chrissy stood screaming under the castor beans; Susan bent over her, examining her hands and arms, her bare scabbed knees, her face contorted with shrieks. As her mother touched her she quieted.

"No, no stings," Susan said, and came back to them.

Simon said, "I don't think your daughter likes me, Mrs. Hamilton. Truly, I'm not an ogre." He reached in his pocket. "Here, maybe this will quiet her." He brought out a chocolate wrapped in gold foil, and handed it to Susan.

"Dr. Anstey, Susan. My fiancé."

Susan looked up at him helplessly. "She doesn't mean any harm by it, Dr. Anstey. She—she doesn't talk. We don't know how much she understands."

Simon shrugged. "I gathered that. I'm sorry if I was the occasion of frightening her; I hope the chocolate will make my apologies." He nodded with distant courtesy and went to talk to the locksmith.

"Candy, Chrissy. Want some candy?" Susan unwrapped the chocolate and held it out to Chrissy. Chrissy let Susan put it into her hand, then deliberately dropped it to the ground and stepped on it, walked away, knelt down and began playing with a stone.

Maybe she is psychic. Maybe she knows that Simon has said, a couple of times, that she would be much better off dead. Leslie had never before observed any truly purposeful action on Christina's part, but now she understood why Susan felt there must be some intelligence, however hidden, in the child.

"If she'll be all right there, Susan, why don't we come in and get started?"

"Yes, she'll be all right." Susan looked back at her child with uncontrollable anguish as she went inside, but when they were inside the office she was resigned again.

"It could be worse," she said with hard flippancy. "One of the mothers in Chrissy's school has a retarded daughter; she looks seventeen or eighteen, but inside she's about five years old, and she'll go anywhere with anybody. Helen is afraid to let Jenny out of her sight. At least I don't have to worry about Chrissy taking candy from strangers."

WHEN SUSAN WAS GONE she found Emily in the kitchen, packing sandwiches. Shells of hard-boiled eggs, strings peeled from celery, an empty mayonnaise jar lay on the counter. Simon strolled in from the studio.

"That smells good, Emily. Devilled eggs for supper?"

"There are a couple for you and Leslie on a plate in the fridge," Emily said, her hands busy with plastic wrap. "Frodo and I are going to have a picnic supper out in Muir Woods. A friend of his who makes medieval instruments is coming along, they're going to talk about the shop. He thinks he may be able to lease a place in Berkeley."

"It sounds like an interesting business," Simon said genially. "If Paul—what is it you call him? *Frodo?*—if he would like a look at some of the harpsichords in storage, tell him to call me. If he is going to be building them, he should have good models."

Emily flung her arms around him. "Oh, Simon, I can't tell you what it means to me, to have you and Frodo being friendly! The two people I love most in the whole world—"

"I really can't imagine what you see in that young gentleman," Simon said, and Emily giggled as she polished a pair of apples with a clean dishtowel.

"Well, I think he's cute, and sexy, and handsome—"

"I fear I have the wrong hormones to appreciate that," Simon said, laughing, "and I doubt if it would please you if I thought him sexy! Personally, I think he has about as much sex appeal as Kermit the Frog."

"Well, *I* think Kermit is sexy," Emily said. "That cute grin and that shy little voice."

Simon spread his hands, teasingly appealing to Leslie.

"You are better qualified to judge than I, love. Is Kermit the Frog sexy?"

Leslie laughed with him. "I must admit that when it comes to charm in men, my tastes are hardly typical. Frodo is charming, but he doesn't turn me on. Maybe I'm just in the wrong age group." She sketched a kissing gesture at him behind Emily's back and whispered, "You know the kind of man I think is sexy."

Emily finished packing her picnic into a basket. "Can I take a couple of spoons, Leslie? I hate eating out of plastic."

"Just bring them back when you're finished." They stood together and watched the young people drive away.

"Was I ever that young?" Simon asked.

She could not imagine him being callow, unsure, without a sense of driving purpose. In that sense perhaps he had never been young, any more than she had herself.

"Do you want to go out to dinner, Leslie?"

"Not really. There are Emily's devilled eggs in the refrigerator, and I could make an avocado salad, or some sandwiches."

"Or there is leftover bacon; what about a bacon and avocado omelet," he suggested, "and leave the devilled eggs for another day. Why devilled, I wonder? I have never understood what eggs have to do with necromancy, anyhow."

"Maybe the hot taste was like the fires of hell?" Leslie suggested.

"The only eggs I ever wished at the devil were some *huevos rancheros* I got down on the Mexican border," Simon said lightly, taking out an avocado to peel. She loved him in this domestic mood; anyone could be glamoured by a concert or movie idol, but when he sat peeling fruit in her kitchen, he was most truly the Simon she loved, gentle and smiling, not torn by ambition or tortured by memory. "I took one bite and howled for the cracked ice; I think they must have used a whole red chili pepper in the sauce!"

"I can imagine why *they* would be called devilled eggs," Leslie folded napkins and laid silver on the table while Simon put a bit of butter in the omelet pan and moved it skillfully over the flame. He tilted the pan and poured in the beaten egg, as Leslie put plates to warm. He was getting very good at doing things one-handed. Would he, in the end, resolve himself to accepting what he had, being glad of the medical miracle which had saved him some normal function in the fingers?

"There's some of the wine you brought over a few days ago, chilled in the refrigerator," she said. "I'll pour some, shall I?"

"Please." He was sprinkling the bacon crumbs and avocado slices over the surface of the omelet, preparatory to folding it. Leslie put the glasses on the table as Simon deftly divided the omelet on two plates and set them on the table.

"There we are. Bon appétit," he said with a flamboyant gesture, seated himself and unfolded his napkin.

"Lovely," Leslie said, tasting appreciatively, bit down and coughed, spluttered and choked. Something crunched sharply between her teeth. "Good God, Simon, what did you put in this?"

He stared, frowned, took a careful bite, then spat.

"Eggshells! But I was very careful, and when I beat the eggs I put them into the garbage—" He leaped up and checked the plastic-lined garbage can. "See, four eggshells which I put in here—and he stopped, staring. The eggshells Emily had used for her devilled eggs were lying smashed in fragments on the counter. Simon caught up the omelet again, bit, spat.

"It's *full* of eggshells! How in the name of—" he broke off. "I swear to you, Leslie, I did not—here, give it to me." He scraped the omelet into the garbage, regretfully. "Shall I make another? Some kind of idiotic accident, I suppose."

Yet the eggshells had been lying, neatly divided in two, and Simon had not been working on that end of the counter. How could he have managed to get the eggshells into the omelet? She had been watching him work, admiring the skill with which he did it.

Poltergeist activity? But there had been none since the cuckoo clock had broken, and she had believed that Claire's banishing would have rid the house of that.

"Let's eat Emily's deviled eggs," she suggested, taking them from the icebox. There was, after all, a funny side to this. This kind of childish mischief. It hardly seemed worthy of a grown person. There was a childish tinge to most poltergeist activity, Alison had said. And yet when it happened to a well-adjusted adult . . .

Simon looked a little troubled, but he raised his wineglass to his lips. A moment later he coughed and choked, frantically rushing to the sink, rinsing his mouth and spluttering hard.

"This isn't funny!" he roared, and shouted, "Alison! Damn you!" He flung the glass across the room, where it shattered.

"Simon! Darling, what—"

"Can you honestly believe Emily, or I myself, would put *red pepper* in my favorite white wine?" he yelled, and Leslie raised the glass cautiously to her lips. She sniffed, took a careful sip. *Red pepper. No, but really, this was outrageous. Why should anyone play such a trick?*

Emily wouldn't. Simon couldn't. I didn't. Who does that leave? Why this petty malice from Alison? Did she truly resent Simon's presence in her house? She had lost the impulse to share the charming supper they had planned together, but she unwrapped Emily's eggs, which did look nice, the whites neatly divided in halves, the mounded yolks sprinkled lightly with paprika, and set them on a plate. She buttered crispbread and cut cubes of Camembert.

At least the eggs seemed all right. The yolks were delicately spiced, smooth as cream. Simon took a bite and coughed again, swore as she had never heard him, dabbing frantically at his lips with a napkin. The napkin came away bloodstained. He held up in his fingers a long splinter of broken glass; the glass from the shattered wineglass, which lay on the floor at the opposite end of the kitchen. Yet somehow it was in Simon's devilled egg and had cut his mouth.

THERE WAS NOTHING FUNNY about it. Leslie was terrified.

Neither of them had tried to eat; Simon had flatly refused to set foot in her bedroom, where she had wanted to take refuge. She could not blame him. The last night he had spent there had been a disaster, and she knew now that they were lucky it had been nothing worse.

"It's my own fault. When I did the banishing in the house I specifically did nothing to banish Alison," he said, slumped, his hands hanging loosely between his knees. "Leslie, let's get out of here. It may be safe enough for you, but I don't think Alison's going to let up this time until I go away."

She hesitated. At last she said, "I feel a certain hesitation in leaving the house alone. Poltergeists have been known to set fires—"

"But they draw their energy from the living," Simon said. "Nothing will happen if we're not here, if the house is empty. Actually," he added with a grimace, "it ought to be enough for me to go away. Is that what you want?"

She caught at him. "Oh, no, no, Simon, never— What shall we do? Go to the apartment?"

"I think we'll be safe there," he said wryly. "Of course, it's not impossible she'd follow me."

But when they arrived in Simon's apartment she returned to the topic.

"What can we do, Simon? Simply let her drive us out?" And then she exploded in rage. "*Damn* her! She's *dead!* What does she want with me? What does she mean, hanging on to *my* house, trying to dictate who *I* may or may not have there?"

"I can stop it," Simon said, "if I can build enough power between now and the equinox. I don't want to do that to Alison, but then I never thought she, of all people, would let herself be trapped into staying earthbound! And to do this, out of malice toward me!"

She supposed he meant he could stop it by ritual, a banishing such as he had done at the solstice. She realized, in shock, that she was afraid to ask. When had she begun to be afraid of Simon's magical powers? She knew the answer to that and did not want to think of it.

But before she left him the next morning, he gave her, unasked, a key.

"I have said before; if I have to go away again, I want you to have this. I have already told the superintendent that you can come here and use this place as your own, or Emily, either." His face was pale and grim. "If Alison makes the place unlivable for you—you might need to take refuge here."

"I hope I'll never have to use it, Simon."

If she married Simon—*when* she married Simon—the house would be theirs. Somehow it must be habitable for them both.

During the next week she walked warily, but there was no sign of presence in office or music room. Once, late at night, when she had come home alone, Simon having pleaded an engagement about which he volunteered nothing, she saw lights in the studio. The sight made her shiver. But she had promised to trust him, and she would do so. She turned over and went back to sleep.

Where had the summer gone? The heat of August was beginning; for several nights in a row the fogbank stayed out at sea, and Emily, drooping in the heat, accepted Frodo's invitation to stay nights with his parents in Sausalito; she came into town every day and spent hours practicing, but nights were cooler in the little beach town, and she rode back and forth with Frodo.

Three of Leslie's clients terminated therapy, and she made no effort to find new ones. Simon now spoke as if it were a settled thing that they would marry soon after the Equinox; they would close this house for the fall, at least, and Emily would live in Simon's apartment, where she would be safer alone than here. She knew she was marking time. She was broaching the subject of finding alternative therapists with her remaining clients, but one afternoon in the third week in August Leonard Hay marched into her office looking pale and solemn.

"I have something important to say to you, Leslie."

"I'm listening," she said, thinking that he looked more decisive than she had ever seen him.

"I'm—I mean I've been thinking about—" he was nervous, almost stuttering, "I'm going to find another therapist!" He said it with a bounce and a nervous gesture, as if he had silently added, *So there!*

"Excellent," she said. "I'm glad you took this step on your own; I am going to be out of town beginning in September, and I was waiting for a good time to suggest it. Have you chosen one?"

"N-n-no, I haven't, but I'm going to find a male therapist. A gay male therapist who can really understand my homosexual side. And my mind is really made up. I was going to write you about it, because I thought—" he swallowed, "I thought you were going to be mad about it."

"Why would I be angry with you?"

"Well, I was your client and I didn't think you'd want me going behind your back," he said, scowling at the floor. "But if you were going to get rid of me anyhow—"

Most patients, however ambivalent they are toward the therapist, have a certain dislike for terminating therapy. It's scary to be on their own. And certainly he would feel now that she had rejected him again. So in spite of the fact that it was not usually considered suitable to involve the patient even slightly in the therapist's life, she said, "It's not so much that I am getting rid of clients; only I am going to be married and we are going to travel for several months. So I think you have made a good choice. Do I know the therapist?"

He told her the name and she nodded. "I don't know him personally, but I know some of his friends. I understand he's a good man," she said, shook Leonard's hand and wished him well. He seemed surprised; evidently he still believed she had wanted to dominate him. Possibly no woman therapist could have overcome his underlying suspicion that her sympathies would be entirely on his wife's side.

She had hardly let Leonard out when the telephone rang and Susan Hamilton's frightened voice said, "Leslie! I probably shouldn't call you, but it's a chance—"

"What's the trouble, Susan?"

"Chrissy's gone!"

"Gone? You mean she's lost, she's run away?"

"Lost, or run away, or been kidnapped," Susan said, her voice shaking, "and the horrible thing is, she can't talk, she can't tell anybody her name, or where she lives— She wouldn't just go off with a stranger. I don't *think.* But she's so little, anybody could—could just pick her up and carry her—"

Susan was sobbing aloud now.

"Calm down, that's the first thing," Leslie said, "and tell me what happened."

"She wasn't on the school bus. I always wait outside to take her in, but she wasn't on it. I called the school. Her teacher said he put her on the bus himself. But it was a new driver and he didn't know all the children, and he didn't remember which stop she got off. I called the police right away, but I keep remembering the time she ran away before. All the way up to Tilden Park alone. *Alone,* which meant she must somehow have gotten a city bus. Leslie, she could never have walked it, it's *miles and miles!* And if she could get on a bus, Leslie, she could be *anywhere!*"

"That's probably the answer," Leslie said calmly. "She's gone somewhere on her own; after all, she can't tell you when she wants to go somewhere. The zoo. A park. Even here in the garden—"

"She's been there three times. I remember she didn't want to come out of that garage of yours, we had to carry her out. She said *kitty,* remember? Maybe she was playing some imaginary game. Would you go and look, Leslie?"

"We've been—been keeping the place locked," Leslie said. "But I'll look in the garden."

"Oh, God, Leslie, what shall I do, what can I do—"

"She's probably all right, but whether she is or not, she'll need you when she's found. I'll look in the garden and call you back."

She went out and looked, but she knew it was a hopeless gesture. To get here on her own, Christina would have had to change buses twice, and anyhow she had only come here in a car. She called Susan back.

"I'm sorry, she's not anywhere in the garden. If she should turn up, of course, I'll call you immediately, and bring her home in my car. I wish there was something else I could do—"

"There is," Susan admitted, "but I don't know if you'd be willing to do it."

"Why, Susan, I'd do anything I could—"

"I read the piece about you in the *Enquirer*," Susan Hamilton said. "I never mentioned it because I figured you wouldn't want to talk about it. But—" her voice cracked, "Chrissy's so little—and you found that girl dead—and if you could just—just tell me if she's alive—"

Her voice trailed into silence, and Leslie stood, silent and stricken by the phone. She should have known this would happen. She said at last, "Susan. I would even try that. But I'm not sure it will work. I can't always see anything, and especially something where I'm personally concerned. I know Chrissy and I know you. I'll try," she promised, "but I can't promise anything—"

"Oh, yes, I know that. I feel crazy even asking you," Susan said, shakily, "but I keep seeing her floating in the reservoir. Or lying dead somewhere on the freeway. Or in the hands of some—some psychopath—"

The particular hell reserved for mothers of daughters. She would not wait to see if Christina Hamilton was dead, she would look now. Tentatively she tried to look within—she had done this over the telephone more than once—but nothing came.

"Susan, I'm going to try, and I'll call you back," she said, "but you should keep your phone line open in case the police are trying to call you, in case they've found her. I'm going to hang up now."

She did not know that Susan, all this time, had known of her psychic abilities. She was still hopelessly reluctant to use them, but after months in this house she was resigned. It was her calling, and Alison's example and encouragement had helped her to accept it.

But she found it hard to reconcile the Alison who had brought her to this house and, she now knew, subtly guided her, with the Alison who had played malicious tricks on Simon.

She could not use any psychic faculty when she was this troubled. After a time she went quietly to the altar in her bedroom. She did not pray. She had outgrown the prayers of her childhood and had not yet discovered any new ones. But she sat there quietly until she was calm; then, as she had done for Phyllis Anne Chapman, as she had done for Chloe Demarest's son, she reached out, trying to see Christina Hamilton.

Christina was alive. That was the first thing she saw, Christina's face, vacant, staring in front of her, the limp brown hair, the slack mouth. Christina was lying on a couch upholstered in white plush. Her hands were tied.

And seated in a chair not far from her, looking down at her with implacable sternness, was Simon Anstey.

THE SHOCK BROUGHT HER physically to her feet, in outraged rejection.

She cried out, not knowing what she was going to say until she heard her own voice. "No, Alison! I won't let you make me believe that! I won't!"

Behind her eyes, as if etched there, the picture remained; Simon, looking at Christina.

Why? Why this?

He had said it more than once; Chrissy's life was of no use to anyone; she was less valuable than Alison's white cat. And she had known; she must have known that he was building again to the idea of a further sacrifice, believing it would restore his hand to full use. Even Emily agreed with him, and he had now chosen Emily to work magic, had hypnotized her, and taken her to a Lodge meeting. . . . Emily had fallen asleep. Or had she been hypnotized so that she remembered nothing?

He had chosen the child, as he had chosen the junkie prostitute, because he believed her valueless to society. Leslie found herself on the way down the stairs, her hand already on the doorknob of the studio before she remembered that Simon had the only key. She sought to look with the *other* sight inside the place; but nothing came, only a split-second picture of the vision she had had once before inside this place, Simon, standing with his hands raised in supplication—and then, swiftly wiping out that picture, a surge of despair, suffocating her.

What had they done, to defile her beautiful house, this lovely, dedicated place . . . She had felt this, too, once before. Was this what Alison had felt, was this the knowledge which had caused her to disinherit her protégé and pupil who should have been her successor, the inheritor of her powers?

She could not, she dared not call Susan and tell her this. If she had seen Chrissy in the hands of any other person alive, she would instantly have called the police. Even now she was sure there had been some mad mistake. Simon had been investigated in Alison Margrave's death; he had actually been in the hospital operating room at that time.

Yet he was a murderer; at least once he had committed a premeditated murder. She realized she had never fully believed it till now. With her hand on the doorsill she tried desperately again to project her sight inside the room.

Chrissy had screamed at the sight of Simon. She had thrown his candy into the dirt and stepped on it, the only purposeful act Leslie had seen her do.

Alison . . . had Alison indeed been trying to warn her against Simon? She thought back over the episodes in this house. Alison had certainly been trying to attract her attention. *The Unseen coming in search* . . . yes, that described it, and the nasty tricks played on Simon, the smashing of Simon's harpsichord. Malice, revenge on her faithless pupil? Or a warning to Leslie?

She went heavily into the house. After a moment she lifted the phone and called the number of Simon's apartment, but hung up before he answered. What could she possibly say?

Simon, do you by any chance have Christina Hamilton there? You know, the brain-damaged child you said would be better off dead, and are you perhaps trying to remedy that defect in God's judgment? The very thought was unspeakable. This was not the kind of question you asked of someone you loved.

Simon. The gentle man, the tender, passionate lover. The tormented man, tortured in body and mind, his career smashed. Which Simon? The ruthless man who confessed that he had worked black magic and known it to work healing on his smashed hand and damaged eye? The kindly man who teased Emily, lavished her with gifts? There were a dozen Simons. One of them might have, in a moment of despair or madness, taken Chrissy . . . and the frightening thing was that, knowing this, she loved him no less.

But she would not let this go on. She would try her best to find him, to find Chrissy, before he put himself knowingly outside the limits of humanity. The previous murder—if it was, indeed, a murder and not a figment of a tortured man's imagination—must have been done in the insanity following the shock of mutilation. Now he was sane, and if he went through with this madness, he would pay the full penalty, unless she could stop him in time.

Where had he taken Chrissy? There were so many possibilities. The Lodge where he had taken Emily? His apartment? Some more secret hiding place kept only for this purpose? She must at least, exhaust the possibilities known to her.

She climbed into her car, twisting the key frantically, inched along the Haight behind a Parnassus bus and turned onto the upward streets that led up to Twin Peaks. She had to shift into second, then down into first gear; by now she was used to Simon's Mercedes, whose powerful motor could take the entire hill in high gear. She left it on the street; the doorman knew her by now and would insist on announcing her, and if Simon actually had Chrissy there she wanted to surprise him.

But even as she twisted the key in the lock she felt the emptiness of the place. She stepped in, closed the door behind her and called, "Simon?" But she knew there would be no answer; she waited, hearing her own voice echo, and called again.

Then she searched the apartment; closets, bathrooms, the quiet echoing room where the Baldwin piano and the harpsichord stood closed and mute, the kitchen, the big living room. The scent of incense, sharp and bitter, unfamiliar, clung around his altar. *Some special incense intended for sacrifice?* She cut off her angry despair; there was no time for that, or for any emotion.

Had he truly had Chrissy here? She prowled through the living room. The white upholstery was confirmation—or was it? She knew the apartment now nearly as well as her own. She had seen Chrissy sprawled on that sofa. . . .

There were mud stains there, mud stains such as might have come from a careless or unknowing child's shoes. Mud stains Simon would not for a moment have tolerated, and which his cleaning service would have gotten rid of, had they been there for as much as three days. Not proof, not yet. There was a wrapped chocolate in gold foil, unopened. She clenched her fists, praying without knowing it, *Let there be proof, let him have made some mistake. Or else let there be proof that she was never here, that I am wronging him, that he is innocent. . . .*

A faded red caught her eye. Dull, worn, faded, not a color Simon himself could ever have worn. Slowly Leslie bent and picked it up. A child's jacket, old and worn. She turned the jacket in her hands, feeling the soft worn corduroy. The elbows were patched.

Be careful what you pray for. You might get it. Here it was in her hands, proof, a name-tape crudely marked with a laundry pen: *Christina Hamilton.* She heard herself cry aloud, a moan, a wail of despair. Christina had been here. Surely she could have persuaded him, begged him . . . *Simon, don't do this, you will destroy yourself, Simon, if you love me . . .*

And now it was too late. What could she do? Go home to her haunted house where Alison tried in vain to attract attention to the blindness of her love for Simon? Wait for the news, the despair, the scandal? Try to find Simon wherever he might be in this big city? Would he feel it necessary to bring her to his own place of working, the place to which she had, mad and trusting, given him a key? She thought, *If he involves Emily in this I will destroy him,* and cut it off. She must prevent him from destroying himself; that was what mattered.

Emily. He had her brainwashed, hypnotized. And then it was as if the familiar presence of Alison supplied the answer Alison would have made:

He cannot destroy Emily unless she consents to be destroyed. Shivering, she remembered Emily saying that children like Christina had no right to live. Was Emily already destroyed, consenting?

I can judge no one but myself. When I accepted what Simon had done, I made myself no better than he is. Now I can only try to make amends.

She went to the telephone. There was only one thing to do, now that she had proof, Christina's jacket, the things she had heard him say. She should call the police, ask to speak to Joe Schafardi or to Pat Ballantine; they would listen without prejudice, they were aware of her psychic gifts; they would look for Simon without scandal until it absolutely could not be avoided. Better that they find him with Christina in his hands, still unharmed, and that he suffer some charge of kidnapping, child molesting; if she was still unhurt he might even claim he had found her, and knowing she should not be out, had been trying to return her to her mother. Better, a hundred times better that, than that Christina be found dead and all of them destroyed forever. She dialled the police precinct number, bracing herself to ask if Joe Schafardi or Patricia Ballantine was on duty. She heard the ringing once, twice, three times.

"Ancient Mysteries Bookstore," said a clear familiar voice on the other end of the line.

There are no wrong numbers. A wrong number is a cry for help. "Claire," she almost gasped. "Claire, it's Leslie. May I speak to Colin, please?"

"Why, he's not in today, Leslie," Claire said. "What's the matter. Is something wrong? Can I do something to help?"

No, the voice driving her said loud and clear in her brain. *Claire cannot handle this. Go directly to the one you can trust most. Colin is an adept; Claire, friendly as she is, is still a novice. Even if you told Claire, she would only have to pass it along to Colin.*

"Claire, can you help me get in touch with him?" She wished with all her heart, now, that she had some of the training they had, that she knew some of the passwords which must exist somehow. "Claire," she said, knowing it sounded impossibly melodramatic, "It's a matter of life and death."

She heard Claire's indrawn breath on the far end of the line; but Claire wasted no time in questions. She said promptly, "I'll give you his home number. Got something to write it down with?"

Leslie scribbled frantically on a piece of paper. A moment later she heard Colin's calm temperate voice.

"MacLaren here."

"Colin, it's Leslie Barnes. Something terrible has happened—"

"I think you'd better come right over, Leslie," Colin said quietly. "I'd rather not talk about this kind of thing over the phone. Where are you now?"

"Up on Twin Peaks—"

"Simon's place? All right, I can give you directions from there," he said, unsurprised. "I'll be here to let you in."

COLIN'S APARTMENT WAS OFF a grubby hall and stairwell, but inside, surprisingly light and meticulously clean. Books and manuscripts were piled everywhere. She supposed the business of selling occult books could not be all that profitable. It was surprising and uncomfortable to think of herself as well off. Colin let her in and fussed around kindly making tea; put her into a chair, first scooping a stack of books off the seat.

Then she saw something which put her at her ease at once; in a corner of the room a small low table made from a redwood boll, polished and clean, with a candle burning at the center, assorted oddments—one looked like a Malayan *kris,* the long wavy-edged knife—but the familiar earth, water, air and fire elements among the others. Nothing essentially distinguished it from Simon's or from her own; the symbols were the same. *The symbol is nothing; the reality is everything.* Was Colin's reality and Simon's basically the same, and the difference only one of emphasis?

"Now tell me about it, Leslie."

She had a final swift thought that this would all seem insane; the old bookseller would surely think that she should be under the care of one of her own colleagues. Then she turned again to look at the altar. He would understand.

"I don't know how much Claire has told you—"

"There are ethics in our profession just as there are in yours, Leslie. She's told me nothing. But I've known Simon since he was a boy. Dorothea—his mother—was a cousin of mine, and the boy was my godson. Anyone who believes—what we believe—takes that much more seriously than the gift of a silver christening cup. Dorothea was—seriously unstable for part of her life, but I thought Simon was solid stuff, and if it had not been for his accident, perhaps everything would have been all right. I have been very troubled about him. Leslie, tell me."

She buried her face in her hands. Simon had told her this in confidence. Yet, raising her head to look into the old man's calmly levelled eyes, she felt as if she were speaking to a priest.

I am speaking to a priest. No, that's not in this life, but it's all the same.

"He told me that when he was only a boy, he had experimented with the sacrifice of animals," she began, "as a means to power—"

"I know all that, yes. What else?"

He listened quietly as she told him, but when she spoke of the nightmare, of what Simon had said—*the woman had repeatedly attempted suicide*—he raised his eyes and met hers in a kind of levelled glare of outrage; and Leslie felt as if she had been trying to excuse the inexcusable. Colin always did see through me, she thought, and wondered what she had meant by it. Stumbling, she told him about Chrissy, and finally showed him the jacket. Then she fell silent, feeling as if she stood in the dock.

"And you think that he has taken Chrissy for sacrifice."

Leslie struggled to control tears. She couldn't speak; she only nodded.

"But Simon knows better than that," Colin said. "It would be of no use to him to sacrifice Chrissy. She is nothing to him; he despises her, in fact. You cannot sacrifice garbage. You can sacrifice only what is dear to you personally. Why would Simon try to sacrifice this child?"

"You call Chrissy garbage too?" She was shocked at the word.

Colin shook his head. "Of course not. My attitude toward children like Christina Hamilton is very different; someday I will try and make it clear to you why I think they choose this difficult and tragic path of atonement. But that is what *Simon* thinks. Why would he even attempt such a thing?"

"I think he has gone mad!" she cried.

"I am surprised to hear a psychotherapist use such language," Colin said.

"I mean—he is no longer capable of thinking rationally, he is in the grip of delusion—"

"You are still not understanding me," Colin said. "*Think,* Leslie! If you believe that Simon's thought processes are the result of delusion, then you must admit the delusions would follow an orderly process based on his beliefs; and I know and you know what those are. The word 'sacrifice' in itself means to give up or destroy something dear to you. Therefore, by Simon's own beliefs—whether delusional or factual—the sacrifice of Chrissy would be of no value to him."

"The other woman—the prostitute, the junkie—"

"I do not know how much you know of these things," Colin said, "but Simon would have a means of creating a tie with her. Sex, no matter how casual or commercial, constitutes a strong psychic bonding; in our society, where sex is of necessity furtive unless it is of the most conventional kind, the psychic bonding of that sex which is called perverted and practiced in secret creates a bond far stronger. With a prostitute such a bond could easily be created. This is one of the reasons behind the occasional abhorrence of homosexuality at some times and places in history; a necessarily secret bond, causing a deeper level of betrayal when it is broken. This is why even those who tolerate homosexuality draw the line at sado-masochism, and why sadism is still taboo even among heterosexuals. There is some notion that the notorious Gilles do Rais explored the potential of working this—this monstrous exploitation of power—with young children. But Christina, as you say, is brain-damaged, non-verbal, he could not create enough of a bond with Christina to betray it. And therefore, I say again, Chrissy is not his objective. He would not waste the effort it would take to sacrifice her."

"Then why has he taken her?" Leslie cried, but even before Colin answered, she was struck with horror, and it was almost anticlimax when she heard him say;

"I think she is a decoy. A diversion. I think he knows it will bring you into his hands. You. Or—" he hesitated, and finally said, "or even more likely, what is dearest to him. Emily."

Leslie lay back in the chair. She thought that she would faint. She whispered, "But he loves Emily—"

"All the more reason." Colin's voice was implacable.

"And he thinks that I—that I would—" Literally she could not speak. She had always thought that the phrase *horror had her by the throat* was a poetic figure of speech. Now she knew it was a literal description.

At last she managed to whisper, "What can we do? How can we stop him?"

"Maybe we cannot," Colin said. "First we must find what place he has chosen for working . . . and you may be sure he has hidden it well. Claire is a sensitive; perhaps she can find it—"

"But I know it," she said, sitting bolt upright. "I gave him a key to the garage, the studio—"

"He used it once before," Colin confirmed, "when Alison was first abed after her original stroke. He would think it a place of power. She disinherited him for that; he had defiled a place sacred to her. Would he use it again though, when you know where it is and what he may be doing?" He stopped to consider. "It depends on how far his paranoia—no, by now I would have to call it megalomania—has taken him. If he thinks you are so enamored of him that you would keep quiet even in a case of murder—"

But Simon was not thinking. She understood this now. In some part of himself, maddened with despair, he was not aware that one part of his mind had contrived a scheme that would alienate him forever from the other part. One part of him wanted, sincerely and with desperation, to marry her and live with her and to make Emily his cherished protégée; the other part, dark and now out of control, wanted only, blindly, to stop the pain, to restore the applause, the center of the stage. Now, crazed with pain and despair, he was no longer aware that he could not have both; with one part of his mind, she now knew, he could sacrifice Emily and with the other still expect her and even Emily to share his restored success.

And he has been hypnotizing Emily, until perhaps she believes this too . . . that it is her duty and desire to sacrifice herself for Simon. . . .

Colin was already on his feet.

"Let's go and try to stop him," he said. "Let's keep on believing that there is at least a part of him that wants to be stopped."

All the way down to her car, numbly, Leslie thought of that. In every— criminal, or madman—there is a part of him that wants to be stopped. William Hierens, scrawling on the wall in lipstick, *Stop me before I kill more.* Simon begging me to come away with him. *Let's not think about it, let's just do it.*

In her haste and dismay she had parked the car in a no parking zone. Now an orange and white envelope fluttered under the windshield wiper, like some trapped thing bound for sacrifice. She thrust it uncaring into her pocket, only grateful that they had not towed her car away.

"You must remember," Colin's quiet voice went on as she started the car. "He thinks himself already damned as a murderer. He knows he killed Alison."

"But he couldn't! The police investigated, he was in the hospital—or are you saying she died because of what he had done—?"

"I am saying I have seen what you saw in that house," Colin said sternly. "What Alison saw. Yes, Simon was in the hospital, yes, he was drugged so that he could not control himself—"

I think it is I who am haunting your house. Suddenly it fell into place, what Alison had seen in the music room, the apparition that had killed the frail old woman as surely as if he had wielded the psychic sledgehammer which had broken her harpsichord. *Simon, naked and bleeding, his eye streaming blood, his hand crushed to a bloody lump.* A woman already old, already weakened by a stroke, her bones thinned with age; such an apparition would fell her like a hammerblow, even without the skull crushed by the fall against the piano bench. *Simon would not knowingly have done this. . . .*

But he had not known! He was drugged, half mad with pain . . . and raging against the fate that had smashed hand and eye and career.

Simon, frantic, projecting himself as a poltergeist into Alison's music room, showing himself to her in his naked despair—she twisted the wheel of the car into her driveway. Chrissy. I must call Susan about Chrissy. Had he known that the search for Chrissy would keep me occupied? Had he counted on the blindness of the psychic for matters in which she was personally concerned, so that she would run around in circles, searching for Chrissy, until Simon had finished his work?

Colin laid a hand on her wrist as they got out of the car. He said quietly, "Don't assume the child is safe. He would know that her sacrifice would do nothing to restore and heal him, because she is nothing to him. But the power of her blood spilt might raise the surrounding force so that the real sacrifice would—would penetrate further into the realm of the unseen. There is no hurry. He will not strike until—" leisurely, he consulted a pocket watch, "until five-fourteen. And it is still a little before five."

"Why do you say that?"

"Because I know the forces and currents on which he is working," Colin replied quietly. "He will strike at the moment when Mars, conjunct the Moon in Scorpio, enters the conjunction with Saturn, the lord of death."

The very calm, the certainty with which he spoke, made Leslie's blood turn cold in her veins. It was not the madness of this which terrified her; it was its rational, impersonal logic.

"Do you think I have not been tempted in this direction, Leslie? It is part of the training on the Path—the temptation to misuse what you know. This—" he moved his head, just faintly, toward the garage, "is your tempting; keep that fast in your mind as we go through this, my child."

Somehow the tone of the words were like a blessing, quieting the racing hysteria of her mind, as they went up the drive.

Suddenly Colin stopped in dismay; put a hand to his heart and swayed on his feet. Leslie felt it too, a sticky feel in the air as if she were wading through tar, and felt too the sharp pain at Colin's heart. He was old too; as old as Alison, she thought.

Colin gasped, "He has warded the place with—with what I find hard to pass. It will take all my strength to—to fight him—" and raised his hand, struggling. His lips moved. Leslie could not hear all the words, but caught a whisper: "I will . . . put on the armor of Light . . . into thy hands, O Lord . . ."

Leslie could almost see it before her eyes, a thickening and curling in the air. Her mind never retained afterward the images of the *Thing* that barred them away, only stray reflections which brought to mind snakes or scorpions, no, nothing so healthy, things with scales and fangs and stings, never really there, but battling to hold her back less with physical force than with revulsion.

Frantically she sought to call to her mind fragments of Claire's ritual, visualizing a candle's flame in her hand. Thought-forms, banished by thought-forms; she thrust the candle at them, forming in her mind the words, *Where there is darkness let there be Light,* then with growing confidence knew what she must do; visualizing the drops of water that Claire had cast to the corners, crying out aloud, "Begone, begone, *be ye gone!*"

Before her eyes the water drops struck the Things and she smelled something foul, a stench of sewage as they shriveled and were gone. The garden was filled again only with jasmine and honeysuckle scent. She put her hand under Colin's elbow and he leaned on her. Objective or subjective? It had worked.

She laid her hand on the doorknob of the garage, and fell back in shock; she did not have a key. How carefully he had insured that, *I will even give you a key, if you do not trust me,* and after that how could she confess mistrust?

Yet as she stood with her hand against the door, terror seemed to beat from inside the room, in great waves that made her sick. She had known that terror before this, in nightmares. For a moment, hopelessly, she wished that she could wake and find that this was another nightmare, that she was lying beside Simon and that he would wake her from this bad dream.

And then Colin's hand was on the lock.

Later she told herself that he must have worked some trick unseen with a celluloid card, with a hairpin, with some hidden gadget in his hand. Yet Leslie had been trained to intellectual honesty and she knew perfectly well what she saw. Colin laid his fingertip on the lock and whispered something that she did not hear. She was never sure but she thought she had seen the tiniest flash of blue lightning. Then Colin simply turned the doorknob and they walked in.

Emily was there. That was the first thing she saw, even before altar or candles, even before Simon; Emily was there, in a white robe cut low between her breasts and in a shocked moment the crimson stain between her breasts looked like blood. Then Leslie saw that it was a crimson rose. Her hair hung unbound around her face. At the center of the room, inside a chalked arrangement of lines (a pentagram, Leslie thought at first, but somehow it seemed subtly different), lay Chrissy, and it added to the horror of this that she was still wearing the grubby blue jeans and a faded knit shirt with red and white stripes. She lay very still, so still that Leslie thought for an awful moment that the silence was of death. And as she lay motionless, Leslie felt that she could see, coming and going through the sight of Chrissy, silent and unharmed, the shifting shadow shape of the white cat, smeared horribly with blood.

All this—Emily staring, her breasts naked, Chrissy motionless, the shifting shadow of the bloody cat—Leslie took in in seconds. Then she saw Simon and everything else paled.

He was wearing a great, voluminous crimson cloak, and around his waist a leather belt in which there was a leather sheath or scabbard, and not a stitch else. He stood half crouched over an altar on which burned fire and strange dark-scented pungent incense, and somehow the sight of the familiar things put to this blasphemous use made her pulse quicken and her heart pound with rage. A few minutes ago she had been sick with fear for Simon, pity for his madness. Now she knew that it if she had had a weapon in her hand she too might have been capable of murder. She did not realize, not then, why these emotions were so near to surfacing. In a swift glance she saw, too, something else on the altar; it was a knife, polished and gleaming, the candlelight striking a razor edge.

And the worst horror of all was that, while she and Colin had made an ordinary amount of noise as they entered the studio, not one of the three had heard them or moved so much as the flicker of an eyelash. Not Chrissy, mute and staring vacantly at the ceiling. Not Emily, lolling as if drugged with the rose between her breasts. And worst of all, not Simon, crouched naked before that dreadful altar, his mutilated hand just reaching to grasp the hilt of the knife.

And then Colin cried out, "In the name of almighty God and the Light into whose presence I first brought you, Simon, Pilgrim, Magister, servant of God, I say, *no!*"

Simon sprang up. His face was drawn, his bad eye twitching with spasms of pain, his hand curled into spasm. His lips were drawn back over his teeth like a wild animal's. He made some incoherent feral sound. His good hand clenched on the knife and its razor blade gleamed in the candle light.

Colin made a ritual gesture. Again there was the little flash of light—

or lightning?—and somewhere thunder crackled in the room. Simon stood as if he had been struck with paralysis; even his eye was not twitching now; from between his lips came a small and horrible snarl. Colin made a great stride into the room and kicked the altar over; his booted foot scattered the incense and trod out the flame.

"No," Colin roared again, whirled, and slapped Emily hard across the face. She sprang up, gasping, but her eyes still held that staring gaze, sought out Simon. Leslie could hear her own breathing, but there was still the terrible silence in the room. Then Simon snarled again and dropped to a crouch. He shifted his grip on the knife and came at Colin, braced for a slash. He was not even remotely sane now, and in his face Leslie could see nothing of the man she loved.

"Simon," Colin said again, standing unmoved in the path of the blade. "Take me instead. I am old. My hands and my sight are nothing to me, and the years remaining for me are few. But such as they are I freely bestow them on you, for love of the one who led us both into the Light. Simon, listen to me! Wherever your soul is hiding, I call it forth! Take a freely given gift of love, if you cannot resign yourself to the will of the Lords of Karma. Strike at me, not at these harmless children who cannot resist you!"

The knife came down. It caught Colin in the breast; the terror held Leslie even when she saw that he did not flinch from the knife. But as it struck, Simon staggered back as if he had been struck by the lightning. He fell to his knees. Colin was bleeding; but the knife had gone in only a fraction of an inch and fell from the wound, making a harsh metallic sound on the floor.

Colin scraped his foot over the chalk lines on the floor, but then Emily cried out, and Leslie's eyes, jerked back to Simon, saw that a curious glow surrounded him, and in it, *through* it, she saw Simon, but not the Simon she had ever known; but Emily cried out, still wordless, in a note Leslie had heard before. Then Simon stood before them, over and *through* the real Simon who still crouched naked on the floor.

His eye streamed blood; his other eye gleamed with cobalt blue lightning. His hand was a crushed bloody lump, and a wordless howl of terror and agony rang in the silent air. Leslie heard herself draw breath. And then Chrissy sat up.

It was a purposeful movement. The slack mouth settled into firm lines. And then she spoke.

But it was not the vacant child's voice that had cried out before. The head turned slowly to Simon; not the real Simon but the wavering astral form, the mutilated man, convulsed in his blood.

"Simon," she said, and the voice was no child's voice, but a woman's voice, gentle and stern. "Simon. My darling boy, I had no chance, I could not reach you before. I thought you were dying too, and I wanted to be there to greet you on the other side, or I would have somehow held on to life."

"Alison." It was the huskiest of whispers, but from the real Simon, not the wraith. He stared at Chrissy's body, from which the voice was issuing.

"I know you did not mean it. You would never have hurt me. Simon— Simon, my darling boy, I forgive you."

"Alison!" he cried again, in a voice full of anguish and dread, and he rushed to Chrissy's side. But the child's face was slack and vacant again, and she slumped back on the floor. Simon looked at the knife on the ground; at Colin, bleeding in a thick trickle down the chest; at Emily, tears streaming noiselessly down her face. Finally he looked at Leslie. The apparition of Simon, covered in blood, was gone. He passed the fingers of his good hand silently over his face, and his eye twitched; he trembled and Leslie knew he was caught in disabling agony. She wanted to rush to him, to soothe him, but horror held her motionless.

Emily found her voice. She cried out, "Oh, Simon—Simon, you're hurt—" And it was she who ran to him. "Oh, Simon," she wept, "I would give you my own hands if I could, if I thought it would do the slightest good—" And she stood sobbing. "How could you think— how could you—"

"I killed her," said Simon in a dulled voice. "I killed her. And I would have smashed Emily as I smashed her harpsichord. I could have killed both of you. I did break the other instruments, didn't I, Colin? And Alison's harpsichord. I was so—so full of rage. I couldn't live with it. I killed Alison. I broke the instruments at the Conservatory, didn't I?"

Colin said softly, "I'm afraid you did, my boy."

"Only I wasn't there. I was—I was in the hospital, getting to know that I'd be—be blind and crippled. That I'd never play again. My body was there and knew it. Only I—I went out, raging, to strike— And again, when Heysermann turned me down." Again, numbly, he shook his head. "I was mad. Surely I was mad. And now—" He looked, dazed, at the altar overturned on the floor, at Chrissy stretched out numb and silent now.

"Alison has forgiven you," Emily said, throwing her arms around Simon. "I forgive you. Now you've got to forgive yourself!"

"But it is not that simple," Simon said in a daze, though he held Emily tight in one arm. "I would have done this. It seemed so rational, to use that power to heal—it had worked before. With the cat. And so I felt this would be justified, to get all that back again—and look what I have done. To Emily. To you, Colin." He looked across at Leslie, and there was bleak despair in his face. "And to you, my beloved," he whispered softly. "What have I done to you, to your love, your trust? You are—you are—I cannot say I would willingly renounce my career for you. I can only say that if I must renounce it, only you could make it bearable!"

"Simon! Oh, my love—" she cried out, but Colin held up his hand between them, and it seemed as if the old man had grown tall and imposing and his hand was like a flaming sword.

"Simon," he said, and his voice was like the tolling of a great bell. "You stand at the crossroads. You have averted a thousand years of payment for this. You could have killed me. Worse, you could have killed this innocent child, this pure soul who has sought purity in a body of penance. What will you sacrifice, and what will you do with the power which must be dispelled from this place?" And as he moved his hand Leslie saw the crackle of thunder in the room between them. The temple seemed to vibrate with soft tension, and it seemed that there was the sound somewhere of a very distant bell, and Leslie knew that somewhere, sometime, in another world or another galaxy or another life, she had stood like this and watched a man she loved damn himself from life to life, and that he had turned away from the offered redemption. She loved Simon, but she knew that both their lives hung again in the balance and that if he turned away again from Colin's judgment he would be lost forever, she would take Emily and move to another city and their paths would never cross again.

And then somehow it all seemed to melt and for a moment the room was only a remodelled garage and Emily's robe a charade and Colin only a silly officious old man who had interrupted a foolish game. Nothing, she could almost hear Simon saying, could be proved. The knife had slipped when Colin got some silly notion that he, Simon, was going to hurt somebody. He had been playing a game with Chrissy and Emily. The girls would have been brought safe home. Or he could even convince them he had been praying for Chrissy's health. She looked at Simon and it seemed that she could see a calculating grin, almost a sneer on his face, and she wondered how she had ever loved this man.

Again the tolling of Colin's voice.

"Quickly, Simon! Time is running out where we stand here, though I hold it back for a little while! Choose darkness or light, and be forever bound by your choice!"

Time seemed to have stopped, even her breath disappeared in the molten present in the room, as if she could mold time and it could have never happened.

Then she heard Simon's breath, loud and shuddering.

"I will not—be tempted—to interfere again with the destiny which the Lords of Karma have given," she heard him say, his voice agonized and rasping. "So near and so far, and because of that, the temptation—I praise and cherish the powers of Light that my sight was saved. I—" His voice choked and strangled, "I renounce it forever, and that power I give to Emily—"

He turned and set his two hands on her shoulder; leaned forward and for the first time and last time kissed the girl full on the lips. She stood dazed, her face streaming tears. Then he turned and bent silently over the motionless Chrissy. He raised his broken hand and for a stricken moment Leslie thought he would strike the child. Then he cried out in a loud voice, "Lest I be tempted again!" and brought his hand crashing down on the upturned side of the altar. Leslie could hear the bones crunching as it struck, and his face twisted as if it had broken with them; then he stood hunched over in agony, cradling the broken hand in the fingers of his good hand.

"Emily," he whispered, "you will—play my concerto—"

Then Leslie's arms closed around him and she could feel him trembling with agony; but she knew with a knowledge beyond the world that he was hers forever, and that she would spend her life softening the brutal choice he had made.

Colin stood motionless, white as paper, but his eyes blazed out in triumph.

And Chrissy stood up, blinking.

"Mommy," she whimpered, "I want my mommy!"